Venom
in the
Blood

Also by Tracy Buchanan

Venom
in the
Blood

Tracy Buchanan

embla
books

First published in Great Britain in 2024 by

Bonnier Books UK Limited
4th Floor, Victoria House, Bloomsbury Square, London, WC1B 4DA
Owned by Bonnier Books
Sveavägen 56, Stockholm, Sweden

A CIP catalogue record for this book is available from the British Library.

ISBN: 9781471416361

This book is typeset using Atomik ePublisher.

Embla Books is an imprint of Bonnier Books UK.
www.bonnierbooks.co.uk

To Slinger, my partner in crime

Prologue

There's a trick to handling spider silk, especially when placing it into the fresh wound of a living man. Spiders have the advantage of an entire organ dedicated to the challenge. The spinneret, a cluster of nodules protruding from the abdomen like fleshy petals. Instead, we humans must use our stubby fingers for the task. One must respect the silk's unique strength, understanding it can ensnare your fingers in mere seconds. I find performing a strange little dance with my fingers works.

This is a particular challenge right now, in the clogging heat of summer. Still so warm, even at night, as the moon casts a silvery glow over the long grass and tangled weeds before me. The chirrup of crickets seeks to distract me. The cloying stench of lavender blurs my mind.

I take a deep breath to calm myself. Then I lift the scalpel and slice, gently, gently into the skin. I can see from the glow of my flashlight that the slit I make is barely an inch long. I wiggle the scalpel so the flesh is loosened in a way that will eventually allow the silk to fold in with grace.

There is a moan from the host as I do this, a moan that sends a shiver through me. I refuse to allow it to distract me and focus instead on replacing the scalpel with forceps, carefully extracting the silk from the phial. I take a strand between my latex-covered thumb and forefinger. It dangles above the wound. Then I lower it towards the bloody gash, rotating my hand (the dance, remember?) so the silk disappears within the folds of flesh until all that is left is a whisper of exposed spider thread.

All done.

I stand and admire the three hosts before me, mere moments from taking their final breath. So glorious in their helpless beauty. I

Tracy Buchanan

allow myself a few seconds to enjoy my work and then I walk away. They are no longer mine. Instead, it is time for them to be returned to the people of Greensands, and to one person in particular: Dr Vanessa Marwood.

1

Dr Vanessa Marwood observed the lock of chestnut-brown hair before her. She liked the fact that the officers had preserved it for her. Though the fly and maggot specimens were appreciated, having something personal in her possession made the scene feel more alive in lieu of being present at the scene of the crime.

Alive seemed a strange way to describe a death scene. But death could be dynamic with all those maggots – or larvae as she preferred to call them – squirming and flies buzzing. Even this lock of hair was alive. Glossy after death. Filled with hints and clues of life. Clearly dyed, and recently too. There were no split ends either. This hair had been well cared for.

Vanessa smoothed her gloved finger over the lock. In response, the wings of a dead fly unfurled from its hiding place. Vanessa skilfully used her gold-plated forceps, a gift to celebrate her ten years at the university, to remove the decaying fly. She then placed it under the microscope. Pressing her eye against the lens, she needed a mere second to confirm it was a *Calliphoridae* adult or, as it is best known, a blowfly. Beneath the microscope, its metallic sheen unfolded into a network of intricate patterns, the dense complexity of its compound eyes sparkling like tiny polished gemstones.

Vanessa reached across the large aluminium table that dominated her lab for a small plastic container, and placed the specimen within on top of some lab paper to stop it growing mouldy. She then popped the lid back on and added it to the other container that had arrived from the crime scene, crammed with larvae at different stages of the life cycle, their pastel colours – white, cream and pink – giving the impression of a macabre assortment of sweets. She placed them to the side, the model of a scarab beetle her father gave her before he died watching over them like a disapproving mother. A little family of sorts, Vanessa thought.

There was a knock on the lab room door, but she ignored it, instead turning her attention to the photos she'd been sent from the crime scene. There were several of them, printed at her request to A3 size, all spread out beside her microscope.

She didn't look at the photo of the deceased first, as other observers might. She preferred to begin by imagining them as they had once lived. So she focused on a photo of the kitchen, noticing magnetic polaroid-style frames carefully arranged on a blue Smeg fridge, all smiles and landmarks. Each featured a wavy-haired brunette who looked to be around forty, like Vanessa. The lack of any photos of children or a partner also made the two women similar. Were her reasons for having neither the same as Vanessa's?

Unlikely.

Vanessa studied the woman's smiling face, a face that wouldn't seem out of place in a yoghurt advert. The laptop on the side and thick brown leather organiser hinted at a busy professional life. But from the photos on the fridge, it was clear that when the deceased wasn't working, she made the most of her free time.

Yes, they really were similar. Except Vanessa was alive . . . and this woman was dead.

Vanessa was now ready for the photo of this woman's last destination: her deathbed. She drew the photo towards her and sighed as she stared at the deceased woman. Her once-pretty, smiling face was in active decay stage, those rosy cheeks now blackened by putrefaction. It seemed such an insult. Death's way of scribbling out a face in a photo. She lay at an awkward angle on top of her bed, clothed in an elegant, expensive-looking navy suit. Two apparent gunshot wounds made morbid stars in her neck and shoulder.

Vanessa studied the photos of the kitchen. Its white-tiled walls and soft pine surfaces were a crime scene investigator's friend, making the pattern of blood on the door frames and ceiling lamp instantly stand out. There were more examples of blood matter in other photos too, spread across the walls and windows of the kitchen, hallway and bedroom of the two-bed Thameside apartment. Such a distribution of blood might suggest to less experienced eyes this was low- and medium-velocity blood spatter, implying a fight. Maybe a violent burglar was disturbed? And yet there were no other signs of a fight. No tables overturned. No broken vases. Everything was in its place.

So what happened? This was where Vanessa's unique skill set came in, called upon by the detective in charge of the case. Her thoughts were interrupted by another knock at the door.

She reluctantly dragged her eyes away. 'Yes?'

'Sorry to disturb you, Doctor Marwood,' called a soft voice. Olivia. One of the PhD students. 'I know you're not to be distracted when working on a case. It's just that he says it's urgent.'

'Who says it's urgent?' Vanessa called back through the door.

'DCI Paul Truss. He says he's your friend. He's called three times now.'

Vanessa frowned. Paul Truss was an old school friend. They'd stayed in touch during the twenty-two years since she'd moved away from their childhood village of Greensands, often having dinner when he was in London. But still, this was unexpected.

She pulled her mobile phone from the pocket of her lab coat. Ten missed calls. A WhatsApp message too. She read it.

Jesus, your staff are like the Maginot Line in France! Need your help with a case in Greensands. Serious one. CALL ME.

Serious and *Greensands*. Two words Vanessa didn't like to see together. She closed her eyes and saw thistles as tall as her waist. She smelt the scent of summer so very specific to her childhood home – that intoxicating mix of arable weed petals and the rotting carcasses of baby birds pushed from their nests by magpies. She could almost feel the long grass whisper against her shins and the stern buzz of dragonfly wings in her ears. She glimpsed her brother, too, running through the grass ahead of her. One minute there, the next . . . gone. Her heart clenched as it always did when she allowed her mind to drift back in time, guilt and sadness vying for attention.

'Doctor Marwood?' Olivia called through the door. 'Is everything OK?'

Vanessa snapped her eyes open, letting the memories drift away. 'Come in, Olivia,' she said.

The door opened and Olivia walked in, weaving between some moving boxes that were scattered around the room. She looked younger than her twenty-five years, like a juvenile deer, with her gangly legs and her soft auburn hair pulled back into a ponytail. There was a nervous look on her face as she approached the doctor. In response, Vanessa gave her a reassuring smile.

'Holding Paul Truss off three times is impressive,' Vanessa said. 'He's a persistent little bugger. I'll call him back in a moment. But first, look at this.'

Olivia's green eyes lit up with interest as she walked towards the table. Olivia had arrived at the university's Forensics department the September before to focus on the influence of insects in the decomposition of charred bodies. Vanessa admired her enthusiasm. Officially, it was out of term, but here she was.

'The context?' Olivia asked.

'A woman found dead with gunshot wounds in an apartment in Chelsea Harbour.' Vanessa gestured to the photo of the kitchen, the sleeve of her lab coat riding up to expose the tattoos that crawled up her right arm. 'What do you see?'

'Blood spatter? Possibly from a medium-velocity impact?'

'Look closer. Describe it to me.'

Olivia took the dome magnifier from the side and placed it over the middle of the spatter, leaning down to look through the glass. 'Tadpole-like structure with random directionality.' A satisfied smile crossed her face as it hit her. *Good*, Vanessa thought. *She really is learning.*

'It's not blood spatter, it's insect speck, possibly from blowflies,' Olivia said. 'The flies fed on the deceased then regurgitated the blood later around the apartment, giving the *impression* of blood spatter.'

Vanessa nodded, feeling her own sense of satisfaction at watching a junior research assistant learn so quickly. 'Got it in one.'

'So what does this mean?'

'It's not really our job to answer that question. But between you and me, I think it's more than likely that this woman's life was taken by an execution-style shooting rather than the surprise attack the blood distribution first suggested.'

Olivia raised an eyebrow. 'Execution. But that's usually associated with drug crimes.'

'Hmmm. It is, isn't it?' They both looked at the smiling photos of the pretty woman on the fridge again.

Vanessa sighed. 'As I said, luckily it's not our job to figure out the whys, which is just as well as I have an impatient friend to call back. You've had your lunch break already, right?'

Olivia nodded.

'I'll take my break now.'

'You must be starving,' Olivia remarked.

'Don't worry. I'll make up for it this evening with a wildly extravagant airport dinner. These curves don't come from nowhere.'

Olivia's face dropped. 'It's a shame you're leaving. I get why. The New York lab looks amazing. But—' She shrugged. 'We'll miss you.'

Vanessa looked around her at the tired lab and the hints of the past ten years: photos of her with students and other academics at various gatherings as her laptop's screensaver. Small gifts of thanks she'd received too: various lab notebooks, usually insect-themed. A cute stopwatch shaped like a ladybug. Yep, she would miss this place too. But the job offer to lead entomology at a brand-new forensics lab in New York was just too much to resist. As much as she loved academic life, it was time for a change. And she'd always loved the idea of living in New York. Her mother had gone to art school there, and Vanessa had always been fascinated by her stories and the old photos she had of her time there.

'I'll miss you all, too,' she said. 'At least you'll have a contact if ever you want a job in New York, right?' Vanessa shrugged her lab coat off and replaced it with the vintage cherry-patterned raincoat she'd found at a boutique online the week before. As she got to the door of the lab, she paused and turned back towards Olivia. 'In fact, why don't you have a go at writing a draft of the report yourself? Only if you have time, and want to.'

The young student's face lit up. 'Absolutely!'

Vanessa smiled. The girl's response brought back memories of how it felt when her own mentor, Professor Cornisen, had asked her to advise on a case while she was studying for her PhD fifteen years ago.

'Obviously, we'll go through it together after,' Vanessa said. 'It'll be a good learning exercise. You'll find all the details in the shared area entitled *Hafferty*. There are more photos in there. Print them out and track the movement of the flies from the deceased throughout the house so we get a more holistic view.'

Vanessa strode to the door, and down the corridor, the square heels of her black Mary Janes signalling to any other colleagues spending their summer months researching that she was passing by. Many looked up, some waving through their glass-fronted labs. Before leaving the floor, she ducked into the break room and grabbed the two fish cutlets she'd made, using her mother's old Sri Lankan recipes, from the fridge.

When she stepped out of the tall grey building that housed the university, she pulled her hood up and dashed across the drenched road towards a small garden square. Relieved to find the bench where she often sat was free, she spent a moment breathing in the rain-soaked air. Petrichor was the proper term. Caused by the impact of raindrops on porous surfaces like grass and plants, inviting that exquisitely scented aerosol to rise. She unwrapped one of the cutlets and took a quick bite before returning Paul's call.

'Vanessa!' His familiar voice exploded from the earpiece. 'You took your time.'

She was instantly wrenched from the grey of the city and back into the greens and yellows of Greensands as birdsong and breeze sounded out in the background of his call.

'Bugs? You there?'

Bugs. Not exactly original, but it was a nickname that had stuck since that day in primary school when she'd kicked him for killing a woodlouse in the playground.

'Yes, I'm here,' Vanessa responded as she went to take another bite of her cutlet. 'I had a job on, you impatient twit. What's going on?'

'We've found three bodies on the grounds of the old butterfly farm.'

Vanessa sucked in a breath and carefully placed the cutlet back in its container. She didn't have an appetite anymore. 'Who?'

'Remember Michael Regan?'

Michael's freckled face swarmed into Vanessa's mind. 'Of course I do. He's Sharon's son. He used to work in the butterfly farm's gift shop. My God, poor Sharon. Who else?'

'Simon Taylor. He worked in the café? And then Tim Holmes, he used to drive the truck.'

Vanessa remembered them all. A few years older than her, all young men at the time, working at the butterfly farm together.

'How did they die?' she asked.

'We don't know yet. No obvious signs except . . .' Paul sighed. 'There were small slits cut into the men's stomachs, just below their belly buttons. And we found something in the wounds. It's the reason I'm calling you.'

Vanessa's nerves tingled. 'Tell me.'

'I swear it's spider's silk.'

Vanessa found she couldn't speak for a moment.

'Vanessa?'

She snapped out of her reverie. 'Are you sure? Has it been tested?'

'Not yet. But I've been around you long enough to know spider silk when I see it. We need you here.'

'Paul, I'm flying to New York *tonight*.'

'Jesus. Has it come around that quick?' Paul hadn't been delighted when she'd told him the news. The offer of free New York accommodation for him, his wife and their twin girls whenever they wanted it wasn't enough to bring him around, either. The idea of them living in different countries, in different time zones, seemed to pain him. She understood. But she *had* to move on.

'If you need a spider expert, I can recommend one,' she said, trying not to dwell on that pain. 'I know another great forensic entomologist, too. He's on the NCA database, actually.'

'Come on, are you serious? It has to be you, Vanessa.'

'But this isn't the way it's done, Paul. You can't just make a phone call and I turn up. There are official channels.'

'Bollocks to the official channels!' Paul shouted.

Vanessa pressed her fingers into her temples as they throbbed.

'I know what this is about,' Paul said, voice softening. 'I know how hard it'll be to come back.'

'Come back to Greensands? Paul, I have a British Airways flight booked this evening, and I'm picking up the keys to my new apartment tomorrow afternoon.'

'When does your job start?'

'Next week, but—'

'That's plenty of time. Delay your flight by a couple of days. I'll even pay the bloody British Airways service charge if there is one.'

'Helen will *love* you for that,' Vanessa said, referring to his wife.

'I don't care. I *need* you, Vanessa. The families of these three men need you. Sharon needs you. It can't be anyone else. It *has* to be you.'

Vanessa closed her eyes. She knew he was right.

'Fine,' she blurted, before she could regret it. 'I'll be there in three hours. Do *not* move the bodies.'

After she hung up, Vanessa watched a bee sucking pollen up from a meadow cranesbill plant, trapping it in the small sac in its stomach. She hadn't thought Greensands had much more to take from her. But it looked like she'd been wrong.

2

Detective Chief Inspector Paul Truss put his phone away, feeling some semblance of calm now he'd managed to convince his old friend to delay her flight. He understood her reluctance. But the three men lying dead in the butterfly farm atrium deserved the best, and Dr Vanessa Marwood was the best. As Paul strolled back to the bodies, his phone rang. Chief Superintendent Fiona Wright or, as she was more commonly known, The Banger, was calling. The nickname didn't come from a love of sausages – she was a vegetarian or vegan, or maybe pescatarian. He couldn't remember which. It was down to her knack for getting under suspects' skin with a loud, table-thumping interrogation style.

'So we have a triple murder on our hands?' she asked as soon as Paul answered.

''Fraid so.'

'In your neck of the woods, too. Were you close to the deceased?'

'Had the odd drink in the local.' That was putting it lightly. But Paul didn't want Fiona thinking he was so close to the case that she'd have to assign another detective to it.

'I can have DCI Mitchell look after this one seeing as it's your home village,' Fiona said, referring to a detective better known for her career-ladder-climbing skills than her investigation skills.

'You know you don't want to do that,' Paul warned.

Fiona sighed. 'True. But let me know if it gets too much. This is going to be a big one for Shire Valley.'

Shire Valley Police was the largest non-metropolitan police force in England and Wales. Though it counted several busy cities under its remit, Paul couldn't recall a recent crime like this and certainly not in one of its smallest villages.

'Were the men together before they died?' Fiona asked.

'Yep, they were at the pub on Saturday night, were last seen leaving just before midnight. Bit of a panic when none of them had made it home by the next morning, and police were called in when they still hadn't put in an appearance last night.' He let out a weary sigh. 'Then a dog walker found them during their Monday morning walk through the grasslands. Apparently the dog always likes to have a peek in the atrium for foxes. God knows how they get in.'

'Any obvious cause of death?'

'Not yet. Just some slits in their stomachs – not enough to be fatal.'

'Strange. CSI lot there yet?'

'Got here twenty minutes ago,' Paul said, eyeing three investigators standing over the bodies nearby, all dressed in full PPE like him.

'I've got a forensic pathologist on the way.'

'Makes sense. I want to get a forensic entomologist in as well.'

'A bug expert? Can't our CSI team handle the maggot side of things?'

'Not when there's spider silk in the men's stomachs.'

Fiona paused. '*Spider* silk? You sure?'

'Not until we get it tested, but looks like it.'

'Bloody hell,' Fiona muttered. 'The media'll lap this up.'

'Yep, even more reason why we need an expert. The forensic entomologist I have in mind isn't just a maggot expert, either. She knows all there is to know about insects and spiders in general. Plus she used to live in the village. Left years ago.'

'I see. She any good?'

Paul nodded. 'The best.'

'Expensive too, I bet? You know we've been told to cut back on using consultants.'

'We have three bodies. *Three.*'

Fiona sighed. 'Fine. I trust you. Get her in.'

Paul walked through the landscaped tropical greenhouse, brushing away thistles snagging on the hood shrouding his curly brown hair as he did. At least it wasn't the spindly legs of butterflies on his skin. He'd always detested the things. Detested all creepy-crawlies really, which seemed ironic considering where he'd grown up. In particular, the way butterflies moved unnerved him, jerky and erratic, like they were plotting something sinister. But right now, he'd choose to be trapped in a room with a million butterflies if it meant his three friends were still alive.

'Just make sure all the i's are dotted and the t's are crossed,' Fiona said. 'All eyes are going to be on us. I'm heading over to the station now. Keep me posted.'

'Will do.' Paul hung up the phone, then took a moment to compose himself. He knew these men, the victims. Had shared ales with them in the local pub. Even gone to one of their kids' christenings. Just normal men like him. No, not like him. He *chose* to thrust himself in the line of danger as part of his job. These men hadn't. They'd chosen quiet lives with their families in the village they'd grown up in. Their lives weren't meant to end like this.

'You OK, Boss?' He turned to see the officer who was guarding the inner cordon, watching him. PC Selma Traynor. Although still young, she was as sharp as the spikes on her short peroxide hair. This case was personal to her, too. Like him, she'd been brought up in Greensands.

'Yeah,' he replied. 'You?'

She peered over at the bodies, brow furrowing. They lay posed in the middle of the atrium, right in the centre of a large circular area marked off from the winding path by stones dug into the ground, a sorry-looking palm tree at its heart. The three men lay motionless in front of the palm tree, their three heads touching and their bare forms evenly spread out like the spokes of a wheel, bark chippings and dried wildflowers sprouting between their arranged limbs.

'Will be when we catch the fucker who did this,' she replied.

'Same.' Paul headed over to the victims, the CSI supervisor – a balding giant of a man called Gordon Starrett – standing over them like a sentinel. The first time Paul had come across the veteran crime scene expert was eight years ago when he attended a brutal car crash as a PC. He still remembered the metallic smell of the blood that had splashed out onto his new shoes when he'd opened the passenger door. 'New addition to your shoe collection there, Officer,' Gordon had joked in his Scottish accent. 'A lovely pair of scarlet brogues.'

'Where'd you disappear off to, Detective?' Gordon asked now. 'Needed to expunge that delicate stomach of yours?'

'Not a chance,' Paul replied. 'Years of the wife's cooking's trained my stomach to be tough as nails. I was making a call to an old friend, actually.'

'Is this really the time to make personal calls?' Gordon joked. Or was he joking? Paul could never quite tell.

Paul crouched down in front of Simon's body, staring at the hint of silk that curled up from the neat, inch-long slit that had been knifed into his stomach. It glinted gold beneath the rays of sun that beamed through the broken glass above. 'Yep, especially when that old friend is Doctor Vanessa Marwood.'

If Gordon recognised Vanessa's name from any of the forensic journals he subscribed to, he didn't show it. But one of the other crime scene investigators looked up from examining Tim Holmes's body with interest. 'You mean the forensic entomologist?' she asked.

Paul nodded. 'She'll be here in a couple of hours.'

Gordon gave him a dubious look. 'Do we really need a bug expert trampling all over the crime scene? What next, a psychic?' he added with a laugh that didn't reach his dark eyes.

'Forensic entomology can actually be very useful in crimes like this,' the younger CSI said.

The tops of Gordon's cheeks flushed pink. 'I know what forensic entomology is, Heena! What I'm trying to figure out is why we need another forensics person here when the team can offer our own understanding of entomology. In fact, I've already collected insect samples,' he said, gesturing towards his kitbag.

'Doctor Marwood isn't just a forensic entomologist,' Paul replied. 'She's a spider and insect expert, too. Her dad used to be one of the country's leading bug experts; she learned everything she knows from him.'

'And? What's that got to do with anything?'

'That material in the men's stomachs? I think it's spider silk.'

Gordon raised a cynical eyebrow.

Paul ignored the old goat and stood up, wiping bark from the knees of his baggy trousers. 'Time to visit the men's families,' he said, a feeling of dread in his stomach. 'Call me when Doctor Marwood gets here.' Then he turned on his heel and walked away, wondering about the fresh hell that had befallen this quiet village.

3

Vanessa drove towards Greensands, The Cramps blasting from her truck's stereo, the air conditioning turned up high. In contrast to the grey of London, the skies over Greensands bloomed bright blue, the high temperatures showing themselves in wisps of heat haze that curled up from the roads. The village was made up of a patchwork of meadows filled with long grass, and sloping woodlands all set across the sandy soil of the Greensand Ridge. The ridge stretched from Norfolk to the Isle of Wight and was once a shallow seaway in the Early Cretaceous period. It was now home to heathland and acid grasslands, ideal conditions for wildlife and vegetation to thrive.

Vanessa had told herself many years ago that she would never return to Greensands. Too many terrible memories haunted the meadows of her childhood there. But now she had no choice. Three old friends were dead. Three old friends with *spider silk* possibly woven into their stomachs. Could it *really* be spider silk? She felt a small, guilt-ridden fissure of excitement at the thought of it, the whys and hows of her analytical mind taking over the horror of it all for a moment.

She passed the sign announcing entry into Greensands, so achingly familiar with its faded butterflies and beetles traversing the letters. Then she turned onto the main road that ran through the village, passing a line of terraced, dark-brick houses, a small church, a pub, some shops and then the primary school where she'd avenged that woodlouse's death all those years ago.

She slowed down as she passed one of the houses, her childhood home. A porch had been added, and there was a kid's bike on the front lawn. Did the new owners know what had befallen one of the children who'd lived there? Vanessa peered up at the window where her dad's bedroom had been. She imagined him watching her pass by. Would he be proud of her? He'd died before she'd finished her

PhD. How would he feel about her moving to New York? She knew how he'd approve of her delaying that move to help the village he so loved. She'd need to keep reminding herself of that over the next few hours.

Oberlin Manor then appeared in the distance, rising like an angry fist from a curve on the horizon. 'Pass Oberlin Manor on your right and the Greensands Butterfly Farm is on your left,' was what visitors to the attraction were always told on the website. Were Arthur Oberlin and his sons still living there? Her stomach did a slight tilt at the thought.

She dragged her eyes from the manor and followed the curve of the road past some grasslands towards the butterfly farm itself, noticing straight away the two police cars and a small crowd of onlookers standing on the expanse of grass just outside. As she drove past, many turned to regard her. Vanessa recognised some faces, despite the years that had passed. She wondered if they recognised the black-haired woman in the bright red Mitsubishi pickup. She had aged, like them. No longer the slim, long-legged, summer-dress-loving youth with a tumble of golden-brown hair. That had been dyed a blunt black, and her straight lines were now curved, those summer dresses replaced with black capri pants and heart-neckline tops.

She approached the gates, and sighed when she saw how ancient and frail they looked now. The two large wooden gates had once been beautiful, carved with insect shapes: spiders, butterflies, beetles and more. Now the wood was rotting, one gate tied at the top with rope to stop it from falling away. They had been specially commissioned by Arthur Oberlin in 1990 to commemorate the attraction's thirty-year anniversary. He'd also commissioned Vanessa's mother to make one of her distinctive installations too: a twisted sculpture of iron and wood that looked like a massive insect in flight. It used to dominate the middle of the car park but was now gone. That was a relief to Vanessa. She didn't need her mother's work looming over her.

Two police officers stood guarding the gates. Vanessa flashed her ID card to one of them. He hesitated a moment. She looked darker in the photo. It had been taken several years ago after a research trip to Costa Rica, the Sri Lankan heritage her mother had passed to her always showing itself more when she had a tan. When the police officer was sure it was her, he nodded and pushed the gates open. As she drove in, it was hard to believe Greensands Butterfly Farm had once been the treasure of the local area's tourism industry. It had been closed for twenty years now, and it showed in the weeds that grew through the cracks of the large car park and the rubbish that was strewn across the bays.

Several police cars, an ambulance and three forensics vans were parked in the main section of the car park. Vanessa pulled up next to the ambulance and stepped out of her truck into the cloying heat. Oh, it still smelt so familiar. Grass and mud and intoxicating floral scents. Yes, the bones of the place were broken. But its heart still beat hard and true in her ears, as though heralding her return. She retrieved her kitbag then headed towards the rusting turnstiles, pushing the closest one until it creaked open. She squeezed through the gap and followed a small path into what remained of the gift shop. Peeling posters adorned the walls, advertising events long since past. The shelves were bare and dusty, and the till drawers hung open. How sad it was to see it so empty.

She wondered how Emi Craviso, the woman who'd managed the gift shop for so many years, felt to see it like this. Even sadder to imagine the cheeky smile of nineteen-year-old Michael Regan beaming out at her from the counter all those years ago, too. A smile now wiped away by death. She thought of his mother, Sharon. Sharon, who had been there for Vanessa and her brother Vincent when their mum walked out when they were kids, regularly giving them meals on the house at The Monarch and the Grasshopper, the pub where she was the landlady.

Vanessa walked through the gift shop and emerged into the main part of Greensands Butterfly Farm. A wooden pole sprouting several signs detailed the attractions that had once fascinated visitors: Ant Kingdom, Scorpion Valley, Spider Sanctuary, Insect Lift-Off and more. But it was the main Butterfly Atrium she needed to head to, so she followed the small path to her right until she reached the long, filthy plastic strips – once kept pristine and clear – which divided the butterfly area from the rest of the park. A police officer was standing guard outside.

'Doctor Marwood?' he asked.

Vanessa nodded and he handed over her PPE kit, getting her to sign in before gesturing to a secured space nearby for her to change. She quickly pulled the coveralls on over her capri pants and top, blowing her blunt fringe from her eyes as she placed a hood over her hair and slipped a mask on. Then she stepped into plastic overshoes and pulled on her latex gloves. The heat was even more unbearable now with all the gear on. She sighed and walked through the plastic strips, the vinyl of her trousers making that familiar *shush-shush* sound as they rubbed together.

It all looked so different through the lens of time, the glass ceiling cracked and bursting with ivy – some of the panes missing entirely, exposing the inside to the elements. Vanessa headed towards the middle of the atrium where a palm tree stood, clearly the focal point of the police and crime investigations team. Once a vibrant emblem of tropical grace, it now stood weary and forlorn. It had lost its companions too, the beautiful, exotic plants and flowers that had once surrounded it, hemmed in by stone bricks sunk into the ground.

'Bugs!'

A short man in PPE waved at her from the inner cordon in the distance. Even with his face covered, she knew it was Paul from his five foot six height and big brown eyes. She walked towards him down the atrium path past raised beds clogged with weeds and rubbish swept in from the surrounding grasslands, and ducked under the police tape. How long had it been since she saw him last? One, maybe two years? All she could see were his cherub cheeks and saucer-like eyes. Those eyes were haunted now, his skin ashen.

He placed a firm hand on Vanessa's shoulder, squeezing it. 'You came.'

'I said I would. I've emailed you the invoice from the British Airways service charge,' she said. 'Oh, I also had to pay extra for the pet relocation service to look after Nancy over the next couple of days,' she added, referring to her pet cobalt-blue tarantula.

Paul looked momentarily worried then he pulled himself together and nodded. 'Not a problem.'

She jogged her shoulder into his. 'You know I'm kidding, right? It wasn't much – I've covered it. You OK?'

He sighed. 'Just spent the past two hours informing the families.'

'Shit. That must have been tough.' She didn't have to ask how they'd reacted. 'So where are they?'

Paul stepped out of the way to reveal three bodies lying in the middle of the circular area. No matter how many crime scenes she'd attended, *nothing* could have prepared her for this. The way the three pale bodies were carefully arranged. The perfect slits in their stomachs. And yes, that hint of silk protruding from those slits.

More memories accosted her. Simon, sneaking her extra chips at the café all those years ago, and Tim giving her a lift to an exam in the farm's truck one morning. Michael, too, sliding into the seat next to her as she ate dinner at his parents' pub. All three had grown up to be ordinary men with ordinary lives, according to what Paul had told her over the years. Now they lay there dead.

She forced herself to go into professional mode. Memories wouldn't help these men. Facts would.

She could tell from the putrid smell that had some officers covering their noses that the heat had sped up decomposition. Even with some of the ceiling missing, there would still be a greenhouse effect in the atrium, pushing up the temperature on these hot summer days. Already, it would have caused the bodies' digestive enzymes to spread rapidly throughout, that stench of rotting bodily fluids and gases attracting insects seeking homes for their eggs. Usually the first on the scene were blowflies, evidenced now by several of the metallic-coloured creatures buzzing around the men's mouths and ears. It may have given the impression to the untrained eye that the bodies had laid there a number of days. But in this heat, it was most likely just a day or two, which would match what Paul had said about the men having gone missing Saturday night.

She wouldn't know that for a while though, not until temperature data was collected with the loggers she'd brought with her; and insect samples – dead *and* alive – were examined by her PhD assistant

Olivia back at the lab. She'd usually do all that herself, but she had a flight to catch. She just hoped the CSI team had done a good job collecting any insect samples.

She could see the team now, gathered around the bodies, all looking as sweltering as she felt in PPE. Another stood to the side, talking on her phone. Vanessa took in the woman's distinctive large brown eyes and recognised her. It was her old university friend, Mio Chan. She'd met Mio at a rowdy party in the dorms of Gonville and Caius College at Cambridge, and had kept in touch ever since, with London drinks in underground bars. She was now a leading forensic pathologist. *Only the best for a triple murder.*

Vanessa walked towards the group, everyone regarding her with interest, this new addition with her raven-black winged eyeliner. One of them glared at her, though. He was a tall and imposing man in his fifties. The CSI lead, Vanessa guessed.

A young, dark-skinned woman in PPE walked over and extended her gloved hand to Vanessa. 'I read the profile *New Scientist* did on you. I'm Heena Fountain, one of the CSIs. It's a real honour to meet you, Doctor Marwood. I find the field of forensic entomology *fascinating.*'

'Good to meet you too, Heena,' Vanessa replied, shaking the woman's slim hand. 'Shame it's not in better circumstances.'

The big, disapproving guy standing nearby didn't greet her, though. Instead, he walked over to the deceased men and stood protectively in front of them, crossing his bulging arms as he looked Vanessa up and down. 'So you're the one keeping these poor men here longer than they need to be,' he said. 'We could have had them in the mortuary by now. We're perfectly capable of taking insect samples ourselves, you know. I've already collected some eggs from the men's orifices.'

Well, this is going to be fun, Vanessa thought. 'How are you preserving the specimens?'

'The live eggs are in aerated sample tubes, of course,' he snapped back.

Good start, Vanessa thought to herself. She'd known of cases where eggs had arrived at the lab in sealed containers with no air, dying en route.

'We found some dead ones, too,' the man added. 'I've put them in a phial.' He was puffing his chest out now, clearly proud that he knew how to collect dead samples. But Vanessa was about to put a pin in his balloon of triumph.

'A phial of what?' she asked.

'Air,' he shot back sarcastically. 'What else?'

She resisted the urge to roll her eyes.

'They need to be preserved in ethanol otherwise they will decompose. Here,' she said, shoving a bottle of ethanol into his hand. 'Add it now, before it's too late.'

He didn't make a move to take the bottle, so Heena took it from Vanessa instead. 'I'll do it,' she said, giving Vanessa an embarrassed smile.

'Thanks,' Vanessa said, eyes not leaving the senior CSI. 'So, you found the eggs dead at the scene?'

He nodded. 'By the bodies.'

'Have you killed any of the live ones too?' Vanessa asked.

'Kill them *here*? Why on earth would I need to do that?'

Vanessa closed her eyes, pinching the bridge of her nose. 'Killing some of the live eggs here allows us to get an *accurate* reading about what developmental stage they're at and, therefore, when the flies that laid them may have first colonised the body. This could all help the pathologist determine time of death.' She opened her eyes again to see the man looked flustered. 'Don't worry, all is not lost. I can take some samples for you now. I won't be able to examine them myself at my lab as I'm due to fly to New York on Wednesday. But if you guys can deliver them by secure courier to my lab, my PhD student Olivia can examine and rear any live samples there. Sound good?' There was no answer. 'Sooo . . . if you can just let me through?'

He still didn't answer, instead glaring down at her. Vanessa was tempted to use a little move she'd learned in her Japanese Aikido classes to shove him out of the way. But she wasn't sure how that would go down in the middle of a crime scene.

'Jesus, just let her through, Gordon,' Paul said in a tired voice. 'She knows what she's doing – that's why she's here.'

'I second that,' Mio said, off her phone now and striding over, somehow imposing despite her petite frame. 'She's a fucking legend; she'll show us all how it's done.' She gave Vanessa a wink above her mask as Heena joined Vanessa. 'Good to see you, Vanessa.'

'You too.'

'We haven't got all day,' Gordon said, looking at his watch.

'Ignore him,' Mio said. 'Bark's worse than his bite. Go do your work. And you,' she added, jabbing her finger at Gordon, 'you let her through.'

Gordon reluctantly let Vanessa pass. 'Be careful,' he huffed.

Be careful. Vanessa resisted the urge to list the scores of crime scenes she'd attended over the years . . . and the zero times she'd contaminated them. She stepped onto one of the tread plates that had been placed at the scene, brushing a fly from her cheek as she crouched down beside the closest body: Sharon's son, Michael. He'd be in his mid-forties now. She could see he'd put on weight and was balding slightly, but he still had his freckles and hints of that vivid red hair, just like his mother's.

'Hello, Michael,' Vanessa murmured. 'Sorry we're meeting again under these circumstances.'

Her eyes travelled over his face, resting on his closed eyes where two greenbottle blowflies were gathered. She quickly placed a medium-sized jar over them.

'Why are you capturing them?' Heena asked, who had rejoined her and was watching with interest.

'It will help determine what species they are,' Vanessa replied. 'The life cycles of each species of fly has a different rate of development. If we know the species, it will help us be even more accurate about how old the eggs are, and therefore when the flies may have first colonised the body.'

'Oh, I see. Why *do* flies lay their eggs on bodies?'

'They want to give their young a hearty first meal, and decomposing organic matter is the ideal breakfast buffet for larvae. Plus places like eye sockets are usually secure from predators.'

'Delicious,' Heena said as she shook her head in amazement.

Vanessa smiled as she quickly placed a lid on the jar, holding it up to the light. 'Yep, both female,' she confirmed.

'How can you tell?' Heena asked.

'Do you have good eyesight?'

'Twenty-twenty,' Heena replied proudly.

'Good, take a look.' Heena did as Vanessa requested and leaned down to look at the flies. 'See how their eyes are spaced apart with a gap in the middle?' Vanessa asked. 'That means they're female, whereas the male eyes are closer together with no gap.'

Heena smiled. 'Oh yes. I can see. How fascinating.'

'I bet there will be some males hanging around the vegetation,' Vanessa said, eyeing their surroundings. 'They like to gather round bodies in the hope of mating with any of these flying beauties.' Vanessa handed the jar to Heena, who placed it in her evidence bag. 'I have data loggers, too,' she said as she pulled them from her bag. 'I'll leave one here at the scene to collect the ambient temperatures. Then another with the live samples to record the temperature in transit, plus during storage and rearing.'

As Heena stored the samples, Vanessa turned her attention to what the female flies had left behind in Michael's eyes: a cluster of tiny eggs in the corners and the crease of the lids. She extracted a small plastic spoon from her kitbag and scooped them up.

'Spoon,' Heena said. 'Never thought of that.'

'It's an airline spoon,' Vanessa explained. 'Ideal for this kind of thing.'

'Lovely. Makes airline food even less appealing.'

Vanessa gestured for the photographer to take photos of the eggs before placing them in a storage tube of ethanol and labelling them.

'What about the eggs you're keeping alive instead of killing?'

'Olivia will rear them to adult stage at the lab – another way to help us confirm the species. As I said, it all helps to estimate when the men's bodies were first colonised.'

'Which will help me and my colleagues estimate time of death,' Mio called over from her position crouching over one of the other victims.

Vanessa nodded. 'Got it in one.' She examined the other orifices, finding more eggs but no larvae, which meant the bodies had not lain there long enough for eggs to hatch yet. When she'd finished collecting the samples, she turned her attention to the slit beneath Michael's belly button. It was barely noticeable, even up close. An inch long, it was like a soft tear in fabric caused by a shirt snagging on a thorn. But it wasn't the slit Vanessa was interested in. It was the inch length of silk protruding from the wound that captivated her. Soft, golden, and somehow untainted by blood. To the untrained eye, it looked like yellow thread. But, as Paul had suspected, Vanessa was pretty sure it was spider silk. She'd studied enough webs during her years to recognise it.

She peered up at Gordon. 'May I remove this piece of silk to take a closer look?'

Paul shot him a hard look.

'I suppose so,' Gordon grumbled.

She pulled on some new gloves, then took the end of the silk between her thumb and forefinger, watching in amazement as a full ten inches unravelled from the bloody wound. When it was all out, she dangled it in the rays of light filtering through the glass roof above. It looked very much like the silk produced by golden silk orb-weaver spiders with its distinctive gold coloration, thanks to carotenoid pigments in the spider's diet. Though it was thinner than human hair, it was incredibly strong, so strong it had been used in a wide range of applications, from bulletproof vests to biomedical implants. Vanessa never failed to be in *awe* of what creatures like this were capable of producing.

'What do you reckon?' Paul asked her. 'Was I right?'

'I'm pretty sure it's spider silk,' Vanessa said. 'Most likely the silk of a golden silk orb-weaver.'

Mio quirked a dark eyebrow in interest. 'Fuck me, this case is weird.'

'You'd have to get a spider expert in to confirm,' Vanessa quickly added.

'Aren't you one?' Paul asked.

'Well, yes,' Vanessa replied. 'I know all there is to know about them. But for the sake of the courts, you'll need a professional spider expert. My official area of expertise is forensic entomology. What I can say is, if it *is* from a golden silk orb-weaver, they're not native to the UK. So it seems an interesting choice considering how challenging it would be to get your hands on a spider like this, not to mention how difficult it is to extract silk from arachnids, if indeed that's what's been done here. It *does* look a little too neat to have been taken from a web. But extracting spider silk from a spider itself is quite a delicate process.'

'What does it involve?' Paul asked.

'Well, first anaesthetising the spider, to avoid harming it,' Vanessa murmured. 'Then, the silk is carefully drawn out from the spinnerets, the organs that produce the silk, using a tweezer before being attached to a spool with glue to begin the harvesting. It's the only method that could produce the continuous, unbroken threads we see here.' Vanessa cast her eyes over the bodies again. 'There's something else, too. The way the silk's been placed in their stomachs ... it makes me think of mate binding.'

Gordon grunted and shook his head in disbelief, but Vanessa continued to ignore him.

'*Mate* binding? What do you mean?' Paul asked.

'It could be nothing,' Vanessa said, chewing her red lip in the way she did when an idea came to her, 'but it's this trick male spiders, especially golden silk orb-weavers, use to calm their mates down.'

'Sounds kinky,' Mio said.

'This is ridiculous,' Gordon said. 'Mating rituals, honestly!'

'Here, I'll show you.' Vanessa retrieved her phone from the pocket of her coveralls and scrolled through it to find the video she'd recorded the year before while on holiday in Thailand. Paul drew in closer to watch it, as did the other forensics investigators. But Gordon remained stubbornly where he was. His eyes, however, betrayed him, straying over to the screen.

At first, it showed the vast, green-topped hills of Khao Sok National Park. Then the camera zoomed in to a golden web. The female spider was clearly visible in the middle of it with her inch-long black and white body, and eight black-and-yellow-fuzzed legs. Then the camera zoomed in on another spider at the outer edge of the web. Much smaller and now making his way carefully over to the female. When he got to her, he began frantically crawling over her.

'What's it doing?' Mio asked.

'Mating,' Vanessa explained. 'The large spider is the female.' On the screen, the small male spider paused, hovering close to the abdomen of his mate.

'Are we watching the money shot?' Mio asked.

'No, we're watching the "how to stop my mate eating me" shot,' Vanessa explained. 'The male is actually depositing silk soaked in hormones into the female spider's stomach to placate her before mating with her.'

'So, you're suggesting the man – or woman – who murdered these men was inspired by this mating ritual?' Heena asked, clearly entranced.

Gordon wasn't entranced though. He was shaking his head, his loose-fitting mask falling down to expose his crooked nose.

'It might be a coincidence,' Vanessa replied. 'But look where we are.' She gestured around them. She didn't add the suggestion of the small voice inside her also noting how the men seemed to be posed in a Y shape . . . the same shape that species such as the golden silk orb-weavers used to begin their webs. She couldn't be sure that was the intention, and voicing that now really would send the senior CSI over the edge.

Vanessa stood up, wiping the bark from the knees of her trousers as she noticed Gordon saying something in a low voice to one of his male colleagues.

'We'll know of course once we get any test results back. The evidence doesn't lie, after all,' she said curtly as she picked her kitbag up. 'Well, the evidence that's still of any use, anyway,' she added, peering towards the forensic bag containing the dead larvae. 'At least you have my thoughts. Do what you want with them. I'm staying at the pub, Paul,' she said as she passed her friend. 'Maybe see you there later? Oh, and something else.' She paused, turning to Heena specifically, trusting this CSI was actually approaching everything with an open mind. 'I suggest you check out the bright green beetle shell under Simon's shoulder. At first glance, I'd say it's from a tansy beetle, an incredibly rare beetle that happens to be popular with illegal wildlife traders. Of course, being in a venue once dedicated to interesting insects, that might not be a surprise. But it seems too new to have lasted the years since the place was shut down. It might provide a clue to where these men were before they died.'

Then she quickly signed out from the scene and shoved her way through the plastic sheets, yanking her PPE off as she walked through the gift shop and outside. As the fresh air hit her, she leaned down and gulped in deep breaths, letting her professional persona evaporate for a moment, the true feelings she'd kept bottled up taking over.

Three men dead, just like that. Three men she'd once known.

She took a moment to compose herself, then walked towards her truck. The wind swept around her and over the wild glades beyond the broken fences. She looked up and instantly thought of her brother, Vincent. It was among that long grass that she'd last seen him twenty-five years ago.

She remembered him running through it. Heard his voice, too, as he asked her to slow down and wait for him. But she hadn't been listening. She'd been too intent on catching up with Damon Oberlin. Too focused on the way Damon's dark hair lifted with each step. The way his T-shirt rode up to reveal the soft hair and the tan of his lower back. When he disappeared from sight, she'd run ahead, leaving her twelve-year-old brother behind as she called out Damon's name. Then she'd felt a hand grasping hers and yanking her away from the path, down into the tall grass. Hidden from everyone. Hidden from Vincent. Damon placed his hand over her mouth, blue eyes dancing with mischief as they watched her brother run past them, still shouting their names. Then suddenly, Damon's hand was replaced with his lips, and nothing else mattered.

Nothing else.

If only she'd known that would be the last time she would see her brother. He'd simply seemed to disappear into that tall grass, never to return.

'You're thinking of Vincent, aren't you?' Vanessa turned to see Paul walking towards her, his eyes on the grasslands too. Without the PPE shrouding his face, she could see he'd aged a little; having twin toddlers and a promotion to the Major Crime Unit would do that to a man. But he still somehow looked like a children's TV presenter with his token bow tie – today's a sombre navy to match his suit.

'I always think of him when I drive past these grasslands. Reg says the same too,' Paul added, referring to his stepfather, the detective who'd been in charge of Vincent's case. Paul smiled sadly, the lines around his tired eyes crinkling. 'I know it's difficult being back, mate. Difficult delaying your flight too.'

'Just for forty-eight hours. I'll have to leave Wednesday.'

'I know. I appreciate it, really. You've helped so much already.'

Vanessa smiled too as she placed her kitbag in her car. 'Gordon doesn't seem to think so.'

'Ignore the old goat. He's always like that.' Paul watched the tall grass sway in the summer breeze. Then he cast his eye towards Oberlin Manor. 'You know Damon's working on a new TV series about the cannibalistic mating rituals of insects? After what you said about the mate binding thing . . .'

Vanessa thought of the Damon she'd once known. Reckless, yes. Wild and defiant, too. But a killer? 'I don't know, Paul. Sure, he's always loved the weird and wonderful. Doesn't make him a killer though.'

Footsteps rang out across the car park. They both looked up to see a police officer jogging over, radio in his hands, cheeks flushed from the exertion of running in the cloying heat.

'Boss,' he said when he got to Paul, panting slightly. 'They've found another body.'

'Where?' Paul asked.

'In the grounds of Oberlin Manor,' the officer replied. 'They reckon it's Benjamin Oberlin.'

Vanessa and Paul exchanged shocked glances. Benjamin was Damon's older brother, the man who'd taken over the reins of the butterfly farm after Arthur Oberlin grew too ill to look after it.

'They said some really weird stuff was done to his body,' the officer said.

'Like with the three guys on the butterfly farm?' Paul asked.

'No, different.' The officer swallowed, looking uncomfortable. 'They said his eyes were removed and . . . and stuffed with some kind of substance. It's in his nostrils too, his ears and, erm, other orifices,' the officer added, cheeks flushing.

'A mating plug,' Vanessa said.

'Mating *what*?' Paul asked.

'It's another mating ritual used by some insect species,' she explained. 'They deposit secretions in genital tracts, which form a plug to stop their mates from being inseminated by others.'

Paul took a sharp breath as the young officer looked like he was about to be sick.

'Come on,' Paul said to Vanessa. 'We're going to Oberlin Manor.'

Vanessa stayed where she was, imagining the grand house she'd once so loved . . . and then so hated. Was this really happening?

'Vanessa?' Paul asked. 'You with me?'

She nodded, resolve filling her. 'I'm with you.'

4

Paul drove Vanessa down Oberlin Manor's long gravel driveway, several police and forensic vehicles following like a macabre motorcade. In the distance, the Oberlin family home stood tall and imposing, its once cream facade now obscured by ivy vines and weeds. It shocked Paul to see it like this. He hadn't been to the manor in years, not since he'd been called in as a newly qualified officer to deal with some complaints about Arthur Oberlin getting too handsy with his staff. Back in the day, Paul remembered his stepdad joking about how the manor's windows were so gleaming, you could probably see them twinkle all the way from Scotland. Now they were coated in grime, and the surrounding gardens clearly hadn't been tended to in a while either, long grass and wildflowers reigning supreme.

Paul turned to look at Vanessa, noting how those red-painted lips of hers were set in a grim line. She might have changed her look, but all that fancy make-up, hair the colour of black ink and letters after her name didn't fool him. She was still the same girl who used to drink cider with him in the fields and cry on his shoulder whenever Damon let her down . . . which was a lot.

'You OK?' Paul asked her now.

'Yep,' she said. 'Just thinking about the last time I saw Benjamin. He was drunk and dancing in that very fountain.' She gestured to a large fountain that adorned the manor's drive. It had once been the centrepiece of the manor – a nod towards Oberlin opulence and the family's insect obsession. A large stone butterfly emerged from its circular centre, a plethora of insects engraved into its wing. Now those once elaborate wings were green with moss, the water below murky and odorous.

Vanessa remembered how, as kids, she and Paul would come to this place each year for the Oberlin Summer Ball, the grand

Tracy Buchanan

event the family would throw for the butterfly farm's staff and their families. As teens, they'd sneak alcohol away from the party and would inevitably end up dancing in that fountain with the Oberlin brothers and their friends.

'Right,' Paul said, snapping her back to the present. 'Let's do this.'

They walked over to Mio and the CSI team. Ideally, Paul would want separate CSIs on each scene. But resourcing, as ever, was making that impossible. While the rest of them got changed into new PPE, Paul didn't. He'd seen enough bodies up close. He'd let the forensics guys focus on that side of things. His focus had to be talking to Damon Oberlin.

Paul noticed Gordon refusing to acknowledge Vanessa as they walked towards the manor's garden. Vanessa being Vanessa made sure to walk right beside him, throwing her presence in his face. She'd always been like that. Gutsy. Unafraid. He sometimes thought Vanessa was more suited to policing than him. But watching her in action earlier highlighted just how perfect forensics was for her. Sure, he knew how revered Vanessa was in the forensics world. But to watch her in action was something else. He was proud of his friend . . . now he just needed to crack this case to make *her* proud. But four dead bodies in the space of three hours? That was a tall order.

Looking up, Paul saw DS Harry O'Sullivan appear from around the corner. The twenty-nine-year-old looked like a rugby player who had taken a wrong turn into police work. Built like a brick shithouse, he had biceps like tree trunks and a chest that seemed to take up half of any room he entered. His nickname was OS. Easier to spit out in a rush than O'Sullivan. Plus, as Selma had once pointed out, he had shoulders like an oak tree. 'OS for Oak Shoulders', as she'd put it. But despite his imposing exterior, OS was a softy at heart, especially after a recent break-up. He'd often regale Paul with tales of his heartache over a beer or two. But judging from the attention he got, he'd soon find new distractions.

Paul had sent him to doorstep some neighbours, but he must have heard news of another body and hotfooted it over. Typical OS. As Paul walked towards him, he could see the sergeant's clean-cut face was pale and waxy, his blue eyes haunted. Paul couldn't help but wonder what kind of scene awaited them.

'All right, Boss, was just coming out to see if you were here,' OS said, giving Vanessa a curious once-over. 'It's this way – we've just secured the scene,' he said as he led them around the side of the manor. 'The Damon bloke is a bit of a twat,' he added under his breath.

Paul raised an eyebrow as he fell into step beside him. 'I can confirm he is.'

Vanessa didn't seem to react, just kept her eyes straight ahead as they all walked into the gardens at the back and quickly signed in with the officer standing at the hastily organised outer cordon.

'It's changed,' Vanessa remarked as she took the garden in.

She was right. No herb rows carefully curated and loved. No immaculately mown lawns and distinctive gravel paths. Just overgrown weeds and grass. The stream had long dried out and the once pretty white iron rails of the bridge that crossed it had rusted.

They passed the orangery. Arthur Oberlin was in there, sitting in his wheelchair with a blanket over his thin legs, his wizened old face expressionless as he observed the crime scene. Paul would have to talk to the old man, something he wasn't particularly looking forward to. Arthur Oberlin had always hated Paul's stepfather, ever since he'd questioned him in relation to Vanessa's brother going missing. Now he hated Paul too after his visit a few years back.

'Anything interesting come up from residents, OS?' Paul asked.

'Nothing to note,' OS said as he led them over the bridge towards what had once been a neat circular patch of lawn with a sundial standing in its middle. Now it was the scene of a crime, two officers already standing guard over an overgrown thatch of grassland and a body Paul couldn't yet see. Damon Oberlin was nearby, outside the outer cordon, crouched down in the long grass with his head in his hands.

If the sight of her old flame made Vanessa take pause, she didn't show it. She just continued walking to the scene with Mio, face expressionless. But Paul could see that for Damon, it was a different story. His face instantly changed when he took Vanessa in, obviously recognising her despite the PPE she was wearing. His blue eyes widened in surprise. What a time to see her again after all these years, at the scene of his brother's death. Paul even felt a hint of sympathy for him, especially when Benjamin came into view.

He lay face up among the wildflowers, flies and butterflies buzzing around him. Some kind of white material had been crudely crammed into his nostrils, his ears and his mouth, so much so, his lips yawned open with the stuff, his cheeks bulging. Most horrifying of all was the way the substance had been stuffed into the sockets where Benjamin's eyes had once been.

No wonder OS had looked so disturbed. He noticed Vanessa flinch.

As they all watched, Damon jumped up and shoved past the officer guarding the inner cordon to get to his brother's supine body, reaching his hand out towards his brother's mouth.

'Stop right now,' Mio called over to him.

But Damon ignored her, instead plucking some of the substance from Benjamin's mouth.

'Didn't you hear the doctor?' Gordon shouted, face red. 'You're contaminating the goddamn scene.'

Damon stood and shoved past Paul, walking straight towards Vanessa. Paul noticed his eyes were glassy, desperate. His pupils seemed dilated too. Was he on something? The entire country had seen the exposé about him in one tabloid: *Oberlin BUGGED out on coke.*

Paul exchanged a look with his sergeant. OS could see it too.

'You're back,' he said to Vanessa.

'I'm helping with the case.'

'Makes sense. How long will you be here?'

'I don't know. Look, Damon, I'm so sorry—'

'It looks like sphragis.' Damon cut Vanessa off, holding the substance out to her. Up close, it looked like cotton wool specked with yellow earwax.

'What are you saying, Damon?' Paul asked.

'It's the official word for mate plugs,' Vanessa explained, her voice calm, measured. 'I wondered the same. May I?' she asked Damon, observing him over the top of her mask with her watchful brown eyes. Damon nodded. She placed her kitbag on a rusting bistro table and pulled out some forceps and a magnifying glass. Then she carefully took the cotton wool from Damon's fingertips with her forceps and lifted her magnifying glass to observe it under the sunlight.

'The yellow fragments are tiny,' she murmured. 'About a millimetre wide and curled like the aperture of a small shell.'

'Like the mating plugs produced by the regal Apollo butterfly,' Damon said.

Paul felt like a teenager again, watching the way these two seemed to communicate in a different language when it came to their shared love of insects. OS looked bemused, the other officers too. Most of them lived in large housing estates in the nearby town of Cranleigh, so this creepy-crawly camaraderie must have seemed strange. But to the people of Greensands, it was normal.

'So your theory could be right,' Paul said to Vanessa. 'Whoever did this is trying to recreate mating plugs?'

Vanessa peered over at Benjamin's body as Mio and the other CSIs attended to it, a faint flicker of sadness in her eyes. 'Yes.'

'It's a warning sign to other potential mates,' Damon said, his haunted blue eyes still on Vanessa. 'Whoever did this is saying, this one is mine. Nobody *else* shall cross the threshold. Nobody *else* shall have him.' He turned to Paul. 'Was the same done to the other three?'

'You know about the other men?' Paul asked.

'*Everyone* knows about them,' Damon replied.

Paul shook his head. The village was like a leaky tap, the way secrets dripped from it so easily.

Damon's eyes travelled over to his brother's body again, his annoyingly handsome face crumpling. 'Who the *fuck* would do this?'

'We're working as hard as we can to find the answer to that question,' Paul said. 'Speaking of which, I'd like to ask you a few questions, if I may?' Paul got his notepad out and gestured to the bistro table outside the cordon area, while Vanessa walked over to join Mio, Damon's blue eyes following her.

'You don't mind, do you?' Damon said as he took the seat across from Paul, pulling a packet of Pall Mall cigarettes from the pocket of his tan chinos. 'I'd say this occasion calls for a promotion from once-a-week social smoker to once-a-day mourning smoker.'

'I'd rather you didn't,' Paul said.

Damon ignored him, lighting the cigarette with a golden lighter and putting it to his lips, taking a deep, desperate drag before exhaling slowly. Paul noticed the way some of the female officers – one of the male officers too – watched Damon. How had the *Daily Mail* described him once? 'The only man handsome enough to hold the nation's attention while describing the digestive habits of a wood-feeding roach.' It had always been the way with the Oberlin brothers, having the girls in the village swooning. It was partly why Paul had been so disappointed when Vanessa had fallen for Damon. He'd thought his best friend was different from the other girls. He thought she wouldn't be taken in by good looks.

'So, let's begin with the last time you saw your brother,' Paul asked Damon.

'Saturday night, about ten,' Damon replied in his Etonian drawl, watery eyes back on his brother's body as he puffed on his cigarette. 'He was drunk after a boozy dinner, arguing with Dad as usual.'

'Arguing about what?' Paul asked.

'Same old thing. The secret funds Benjamin's so sure Dad has squirrelled away somewhere. Dad denies it. Benjamin accuses him of lying. *Exceedingly* tedious.'

'I'll need to speak to your father,' Paul said, looking towards the orangery.

Damon tilted his head back and blew smoke up into the air. 'I'm not sure he'll want to talk to *you*, will he, Detective Truss? Not after the way you were with him a few years back. He's never forgiven you for that. Best get one of your minions to question him.'

Paul ignored the comment. Only a fool would blame him for following up on the complaints he'd got about the old man. Not

Paul's fault it got into the local paper. 'What were you doing while the two of them argued?' he asked Damon.

'I was in my study, doing research for my next show.'

'The one about the cannibalistic mating rituals of insects?' Paul asked pointedly.

'Ah, so now I see what this is about,' Damon said with a bitter smile as he tapped some cigarette ash into a coffee mug, the congealing liquid at its bottom squirming with flies. 'You think I murdered my brother because of the subject of my next series?' He rolled his eyes. 'Seriously, you think I'm that stupid?'

Paul resisted the desire to punch him in his square jaw. 'If you were in your study, how could you hear them arguing?' Paul asked through gritted teeth. 'Were their voices raised?'

'You'd be surprised how thin the walls are in the manor.' Damon's eyes slid over to Vanessa, then back to Paul, a small smile on his face. Paul narrowed his eyes at him. He knew Damon was thinking about the time Paul stumbled in on him and Vanessa tangled up in each other during a Christmas party.

He was tempted to scribble 'twat' on his A4 notepad, but couldn't risk it in case it was used in evidence.

'Did you see your brother again after the argument?' Paul asked.

'Actually, I did, now you mention it,' Damon said. 'He popped his head into my office to tell me he thought our father was a cunt. Imagine if that was his last word – *cunt*? *So* Benjamin.' There was a subtle faltering of his expression as he gazed once more at his brother's lifeless form.

'So the next time you saw your brother was here, like this?' Paul asked.

Damon nodded. 'I came out here about an hour ago. I sat right here, actually. I didn't even notice him at first.' He sighed, raking his fingers through his dark hair. 'Jesus, he was lying there all that time. I checked his pulse . . .' He shuddered as his voice trailed off, blinking back tears.

'So that's nearly forty-eight hours since you last saw him. And yet you didn't report him missing?' Paul asked.

Damon sighed. 'He's an *adult*, Detective. We don't keep tabs on each other. We can go *days* without seeing one another. This place isn't exactly small, is it?' he added, peering up at the manor.

'Can you think of anyone who might want to do this to your brother?' Paul asked.

Damon laughed bitterly. 'Better to ask who *wouldn't* want to do this. You know what Benjamin's been like the past few years. Drinking too much. Getting into people's faces. Fucking people's husbands *and* wives.'

'I'll need a list of people,' Paul said. 'Can you do that for me?'

Damon shrugged. 'Sure.'

'To your knowledge, was Benjamin experiencing any personal problems?'

'Just the usual alcoholism and sex addiction.'

Paul sighed. 'Did that lead to any specific issues with people?'

'Not from what I know.'

'And what about work? Last I knew, Benjamin was on the board of some wildlife parks and charities.'

Damon smiled slightly. 'It was all for show, really. He didn't do actual work for them. Certainly didn't get paid for it. Look,' Damon added with a sigh, 'with all due respect, this is not the work of a loan shark. Whoever did this is clever, calculated, cruel.'

Like you, Paul thought.

Damon stubbed his cigarette out and threw it down onto the cracked paving slabs below.

'Pick that up, please,' Paul said.

'I can litter where I want. You don't own this place.'

'Neither do you – your father does.'

'For now.'

Paul narrowed his eyes at Damon. Of course, that was something else to factor in. With his oldest son gone, Damon would be the main benefactor of the Oberlin estate.

'Pick. It. Up,' Paul said again. 'Don't want one of our forensics investigators finding it and assuming it belongs to your brother's *killer*, do we?' he added.

Damon sighed and picked the cigarette stub up, adding it to the ash-and-fly-riddled mug.

'What I don't understand,' he said, 'is why place Benjamin here and the other men at the butterfly farm? And why target *Benjamin*, too? He's not friends with them.'

It was a question that had crossed Paul's mind, as well.

Another question was: was Damon Oberlin capable of murder?

5

Vanessa was aware of Damon's eyes on her as she carefully examined Benjamin's body with Mio. Arthur Oberlin was also watching her from his spot in the orangery. What was going through his mind? It was hard to tell with the old man. Hard to tell with Damon, too. He'd had a complicated relationship with his brother. Still, it *was* his brother. This was bound to be tough, especially with Paul seeming convinced Damon was involved with all this in some way.

Vanessa looked down at Benjamin and his cotton-wool-clogged eyes, his bulging cheeks. Not just bulging, but moving too as larvae squirmed in the crevices of his gums and under his tongue. There was a lot of larvae at this crime scene. It could just be because Benjamin was out in the open and more likely to attract flies quickly. Or it could suggest Benjamin died before the other three men. Olivia would have to factor that in, in her report.

'What's the deal with famous TV presenter dude over there?' Mio asked Vanessa in a low voice as she peered over at Damon. 'He can't stop staring at you. You got history?'

'Long story,' Vanessa said. '*Ancient* story.'

Truth was, it had been tough seeing him again in such awful circumstances. He hadn't changed much. More dark stubble around his chiselled features, yes. More creases around his startling eyes and full lips. But still breathtaking to look at.

How did *she* look to him? More padding on the bones. Darker circles under the eyes.

Jesus. Why did it matter?

'So New York, hey?' Mio said as she opened a pack of sterile, pre-packaged swabs. 'Are you heading up a whole department there?'

'Nope. I *am* the forensic entomology department,' Vanessa replied. 'You know what it's like, not as in demand like some other disciplines.'

'*Yet,*' Mio said. 'Not everyone understands the potential of your field but that'll change with you in charge. So, when are you leaving our plastic-clogged shores?'

'I was supposed to fly out today.'

Mio raised an eyebrow as she gently rolled a swab over Benjamin's cheek. 'You've delayed it for the case?'

Vanessa nodded as she began to take her own samples, carefully using forceps to extract some larvae from Benjamin's belly button and placing them in a container. She wouldn't know for sure what stage they were at before looking at them under a microscope. But they were very small larvae, which suggested they were possibly first instar and only recently emerged from eggs.

'I'll need some boiled water,' she told the young, muscular officer Paul had referred to as OS. 'Can one of your officers get some from the manor?'

'Why?' OS asked, grimacing as he looked at the squirming maggots.

'It's imperative we kill the larvae first with hot water to destroy any bacteria, and keep them in the same state as they were found here at the scene for examination,' Vanessa explained.

'Stopping the clock, so to speak,' Heena called over, as she set up the data logger Vanessa had given her.

Vanessa smiled beneath her mask. The girl was a quick learner.

OS called over an officer. 'Go to the manor, get some boiling water, stat.'

The officer stared at the maggots Vanessa was collecting.

'Run, then!' OS instructed the officer. He did as OS asked and Vanessa continued collecting more samples, being careful to ensure they were stored and labelled separately depending on what part of the body they'd been found in.

'Is that cat food?' OS asked as she placed some cat food from a pouch in one of the containers holding live larvae.

She nodded. 'Larvae are hungry little beasts.'

'Why not just cut a patch of skin off for them to feed on?' OS asked. 'I saw one of the CSIs do that once.'

Vanessa shook her head. 'That is just plain *wrong*.'

'Help me turn him over, will you?' Mio asked Vanessa.

They both eased Benjamin onto his side, and Vanessa noticed

right away what she had suspected: his rectum was stuffed with the cotton wool substance found in his other openings. A bluebottle fly took the opportunity to squeeze into a small gap between Benjamin's puckered skin and the cotton wool as she watched, beginning her journey to find a place to lay her eggs.

'The indignity of death,' Mio murmured.

Vanessa nodded in agreement. As grotesque as it was, she couldn't help but be fascinated, too. The truth was, after death, the body became a paradise for animals. A place to dine. A place to breed. A place to set up home. A final resting place too, as she could see from the dead fly nestling in the crease of Benjamin's bottom as well.

'Sorry, Benjamin,' Vanessa said with a sigh as she extracted the dead blowfly with her forceps. It was so undignified for a man who used to pride himself on his neat appearance. She placed the fly into a container of ethanol, labelling it and handing it over to Heena. This one was a greenbottle, suggesting two species had colonised the body.

The officer she'd sent for boiled water was making his way over to them with a kettle in his hands. 'Just boiled,' he said, face red from the heat and the exertion.

Vanessa took the kettle and poured water into one of the containers of squirming larvae as the officer screwed his nose up. She waited thirty seconds to ensure they were dead.

'Does it hurt them?' the officer asked.

'Maggots probably don't feel pain,' OS said. 'Like fish when you hook 'em.'

'You know that's bullshit,' Vanessa said as she sieved the dead larvae out and placed them in a phial filled with ethanol. 'Just something made up by the fishing trade to make people feel better. Fish are like any other species with a complex enough nervous system, using pain as a survival tool.'

'Shit, now you're making me feel bad about my monthly fishing trips,' OS said. 'Probably making *you* feel bad, too, about your boiling-water pool party for the maggots.'

Vanessa labelled the phial and handed it to Heena. 'Actually, chances are, larvae don't feel pain because of their rudimentary nervous system. But it's still not nice. You just have to weigh up the benefits to the deceased.'

She sighed as she looked at Benjamin. As she did, she noticed a raised bump on his right foot with a tiny hole at its centre.

'A sting,' she murmured.

Gordon looked up from his notepad with interest, then walked over, crouching down beside her. She could smell the potent aftershave that did little to cover the stench of his body odour.

'Yes, I noticed that already,' he said dismissively.

Vanessa and Mio exchanged a look.

Liar.

'The stinger's still in it,' Heena remarked. 'That'll be why it's so swollen, right?'

Vanessa nodded as she carefully extracted the tiny sting with her forceps and stared at it. 'It could be from a mining bee. They usually like to nest in the sandy banks of the ridge here.'

'How on earth can you tell that?' Gordon asked.

Vanessa shrugged. 'I wouldn't know for sure until getting it under a microscope, but I just recognise the shape and size. My dad's academic insect books were my favourites as a teen. Plus, look,' she added, pointing to a small black hair. 'That could well be from a black and white miner bee.'

'Detective Truss!' Gordon called out.

Paul strolled over from where he was standing with Damon. 'What have you found?' he asked.

'A bee sting on the deceased's sole,' Gordon said. 'I suggest you send some officers to search along the banks of the ridge first thing in the morning, when we have better light,' he said, peering up at the dark clouds Vanessa hadn't even noticed gathering above. 'Based on the sting I found, it's possible the deceased was killed near some mining bee nesting sites located there.'

I found. So it was official. He really was taking credit.

Mio went to open her mouth to correct Gordon but Vanessa quickly shook her head.

'OS, can you set up a search for tomorrow morning at seven?' Paul asked OS. The officer nodded. 'Vanessa, you should join us,' Paul added.

'Of course,' she replied, eyes still on Gordon.

Paul clapped his hands. 'OK, everyone, let's leave the forensics team to continue their work. We've got four victims now and a whole load of questions that need answering. I'm going to talk to Benjamin's father. Those of you not on scene guard, head back to the station with Detective Sergeant O'Sullivan. He'll get an incident room set up.'

As the officers dispersed and Paul strolled towards the orangery, Vanessa set about packing her gear away beneath a caterpillar-infested apple tree.

'Sorry about the boss,' Heena said, casting her brown eyes towards Gordon. 'I noticed he took credit for your find. He does that a lot.'

'He's not the first and won't be the last. In fact, did you know, Heena,' Vanessa said, raising her voice loud enough for Gordon to hear, 'that mining bees *imitate* the behaviour of a competitor to win a mate? I suppose you could call it a form of *taking credit* for behaviour that isn't theirs?'

Gordon pretended not to have heard her, but Vanessa could tell he had from the way his broad shoulders tensed. Mio suppressed a smile as she took some blood samples from Benjamin.

'Boss!'

They all turned to see the young female officer with platinum-blonde hair calling out from the other end of the garden. 'We've found something.'

6

Paul turned, and began to walk down the overgrown pathway that cut through the extensive gardens to see what Selma had found. As he drew closer, he could see instantly there were tyre tracks pressed into the dry mud leading from a large gate at the back.

'Damon,' he called over to the TV presenter. Damon strolled over, hands in his pockets. 'Do you use this gate to drive your car in and out?'

Damon shook his head. 'Never. These are new,' he said, gesturing to the tyre marks.

'Can you do some casts?' Paul called over to Heena.

Heena grabbed her kitbag and headed over. As she passed Gordon, Paul couldn't help but smile. He'd heard what Vanessa had said just now. Her way of saying the old goat had taken credit for the sting she must have found on Benjamin's foot. Hopefully Gordon was beginning to see you don't mess with Vanessa Marwood. She'd always outwit you.

'These look like particularly large tyres,' Heena observed when she got to them. 'Deep, too, so a decent-sized vehicle.' She took out her tape and began measuring the marks. 'Yep. Unusual tyre size. Tyres like this aren't common. They usually belong to supercars like Ferraris.'

'Sounds about right,' Paul said, looking over at Damon.

Damon laughed. 'I am *not* that flash. I prefer small vintage numbers. Not beasts with tyre marks like this.'

'Know anyone who owns a car that might have tyres like this?' Paul asked.

'Oh, I know plenty of Ferrari owners. But none who have visited us lately.'

Heena took some photos with a small camera then pulled out the items she needed from her kitbag to take casts of the tyre marks.

'There are more tyre marks outside, leading in,' Selma observed as she peered through the cobweb-clad bars of the gates. 'Looks like the gate's locked, though,' she added, rattling the bars.

'Damon,' Paul called the presenter over. 'Have you got a key to these gates?'

'We don't use this gate,' Damon said. 'Not anymore, anyway.'

'What about your staff?' Paul asked him.

Damon laughed. 'Staff? What are those? We don't have staff anymore, Detective Truss. Just my father's nurse.'

'Let's check CCTV and doorbell cameras from the area,' Paul said to Selma. 'OS, can you radio the guys at the butterfly farm and ask them to pay close attention to any tyre marks? It'll be difficult to tell on the concrete slabs of the car park, but worth a look.'

His thinking was, maybe the killer had murdered all four men at the same time, then transported them to two different scenes. Maybe they targeted Benjamin first, then took down the other three as they walked home from the pub, Benjamin's body lying in the car boot as it happened.

More theories. He preferred to let his imagination run wild, so every possible scenario was there to consider.

He took a deep breath as he looked towards the orangery. 'Right, I'm going to talk to Mr Oberlin,' he said to the surrounding officers. 'Hold the fort here, will you, OS?'

OS nodded.

Damon laughed to himself. 'Good luck with interviewing my father, Detective.'

Paul gave him a hard look, then walked towards the orangery. It seemed in decent nick with its stained-glass ceiling depicting various insects in an almost reverential way. Paul walked through the ornate double doors which were flanked by symmetrical pillars. As he entered, the intoxicating fragrance of blooming citrus trees and exotic plants hit him. It felt almost suffocating in the unbearably warm room. And yet there Arthur was, sitting in his wheelchair with a blanket over his legs. But then he was nearly ninety, not quite the powerful physical presence he once was. Frail and gaunt, with thinning white hair and deep-set blue eyes, he seemed lost in thought as he stared out at the activity around his son's dead body, hardly seeming to notice Paul.

Paul paused a moment to take everything in. Various artefacts were scattered among the exotic plants, showing the man's obsession with insects, from intricately detailed sketches of butterflies on the walls to beautifully carved sculptures of insects, which Paul recognised as the work of Vanessa's mother. The strangest object was an eighteen-inch-tall mahogany moth which was emerging from what looked like a cocoon, its circular base carved with interwoven insect symbols and arcane glyphs. Paul couldn't help but think of all the rumours that used to circulate about Arthur Oberlin's involvement in some kind of insect-worshipping cult.

'Mr Oberlin,' Arthur's young male nurse announced, breaking the old man's reverie. 'Detective Truss is here to see you.'

Arthur turned his gaze towards the detective, his eyes suddenly piercing and intense.

Looks like there's life in the old man yet, Paul thought.

'Thank you. Please leave us,' he said in a raspy voice.

The nurse nodded and left the orangery, closing the glass door behind him. Paul made a mental note to talk to the nurse later about whether he'd noticed anything suspicious over the past day or two. He went to take the seat across from Arthur. But the old man quickly shook his head. 'The seat is new,' he snapped. 'I'd rather you didn't sit on it.'

Paul resisted the urge to defy the old man and sit anyway, reminding himself that Arthur had lost his favourite son to a brutal murder.

'I'm sorry for your loss, Mr Oberlin,' he said.

Arthur grunted.

'As I'm sure you understand,' Paul said, getting his notepad and pen out, 'I need to ask you some questions about Benjamin's last few hours.'

'Is that the Marwood girl?' Arthur said as he watched Vanessa stride by. Paul was surprised he recognised her, she looked so different.

'Yes, it's Doctor Vanessa Marwood. I've brought her in to help with the investigation. She's a forensic entomologist now.'

Tracy Buchanan

Arthur's eyes shot over to Paul. 'I don't need a forensic entomologist to tell me, in this heat, my boy's probably been dead a day or two. The blowflies around his head tell me that. The filthy buggers are attracted to the post-mortem gases already beginning to gather within him.'

Paul frowned. He supposed this was the way an insect enthusiast would process death. 'So you've seen your son's body?'

'Of course I have.'

'When was this?'

'Is it relevant?'

'Everything could be relevant.'

The old man took in a deep, rattly breath. 'I heard Damon on the phone to the police. I had my nurse bring me out. I had to see for myself.'

'I see. Can you run through the last time you saw your son alive?'

'Before bedtime Saturday night. He was intoxicated, as usual.'

'I believe you had dinner together here?' Paul looked towards the grand dining room through the glass doors that led into the manor.

'We did.'

'How did he seem?'

'No different from his usual self.'

'And his usual self was to be intoxicated of an evening, as you just suggested?'

Arthur gave Paul a hard look. 'You know the answer to that. My son had an issue with alcohol in recent years, and I imagine that proclivity for alcohol lies at the heart of his sad demise.'

'Why do you say that?'

'You and I *both* know the effect alcohol has on the brain's neurotransmitter systems, specifically gamma-aminobutyric acid.' Paul didn't know, but that was exactly why Arthur was delivering the information like a university professor: it was all part of the power play he enjoyed. 'Not to mention,' Arthur continued, 'how it impairs the functioning of the prefrontal cortex and dampens the amygdala, all leading to a perfect storm of reduced inhibitions and increased risk-taking behaviour.'

A very Oberlin way of saying, 'Drinking alcohol makes you act crazy.'

'I am aware of that,' Paul said. 'But the circumstances of your son's death, and the wider context, do not suggest to me this is a simple case of him drinking too much and getting himself into a spot of bother.'

'Oh, I'm sure you'll come up with your theories,' Arthur said, waving his hand about. 'After all, it's important the constabulary continue to appear important and busy. But I think you will find my son got drunk, partook in one of his strange sexual games, and found himself dead by accident.'

The old man was delusional. Did he really think his son plucked his own eyes out? Or maybe this was part of *not* thinking about that awful fact. Easier to think Benjamin did it to himself than a stranger.

'What do you mean by strange sexual games?' he asked.

'I've seen the filth on his computer. Whipping. Bondage. That kind of thing. I presume your digital forensics team will be all over that?'

'Yes, we will be taking a look at Benjamin's devices. But I think it's very unlikely your son did this to himself, Mr Oberlin,' Paul said carefully. 'We found three other bodies, too.'

Arthur's watery eyes widened. 'Three? Who?'

So the village grapevine hasn't quite travelled as far as the Oberlin orangery yet.

'Michael Regan, Simon Taylor and Tim Holmes,' Paul replied. 'All former employees of the butterfly farm. In fact, they were found in the *grounds* of the butterfly farm.'

Arthur blinked rapidly, but then seemed to pull himself together. 'Everybody here worked for the farm in some way or another. Is there even evidence these three other deaths are connected with my son's?'

'There are . . . some similarities.'

'Like what?'

'We can't disclose that right now.'

'Then we are done here. Nurse!' he called out.

'We're not done,' Paul said. 'I have more questions.'

'I'm exhausted,' Arthur said.

His nurse stepped in then. 'All done?'

'I need to sleep.'

'If I can just have a few more minutes,' Paul said.

'Mr Oberlin is ninety next month, Detective,' the nurse reminded him. 'This will be taking a great toll on him.'

Paul sighed. 'Fine. I'll be in touch. And again, I'm sorry for your . . .' What was the point? Arthur was already being wheeled out of the orangery. Paul shoved his notepad in his pocket and strolled out.

'That looked fun,' Vanessa said sarcastically as he joined her outside.

'Still the same stubborn old man.'

'So, what are your next steps?' Vanessa asked.

'Got a roomful of officers to brief. Did you book yourself into the B&B at The Monarch and the Grasshopper, like I suggested?'

Vanessa nodded. 'I did it online.'

'Good. I'll get one of the officers to give you a lift to your truck, then why don't you go and check in, rest up?' He pulled his phone out, looking at the screen. Vanessa could see he had a few messages and missed calls. 'I'll get Helen to drop you a text. I know she'd like to see you, even if I'm too busy to join you later. Then I'll meet you in the morning at seven, at the ridge?'

Vanessa nodded. 'Not a problem, but I *will* have to leave the day after that.'

Paul sighed. 'I understand.'

'Good luck with everything.'

'I'm gonna need it.' He went to walk away then paused, turning back round. 'Be aware, the entire village is likely to be at The Monarch and the Grasshopper tonight.'

Vanessa peered towards the pub in the distance. 'Maybe I should just check into the Premier Inn.'

'You think Sharon would forgive you if you did?'

Vanessa sighed. 'I guess not. I'll just have to soften the edges with some alcohol.'

'Oh, there'll be plenty of that going around.'

Then he headed off towards his officers, hoping it wouldn't be too tough on his old friend being thrust back into the grieving, messy heart of Greensands village life.

7

The Monarch and the Grasshopper pub sat halfway up the village's main road, nestled between houses and overlooking the wildest of the grasslands. As Vanessa pulled up into its car park, she wasn't surprised to see the pub had been renovated since she was last there. Its once dirty cream exterior had been replaced by a lick of bright white paint and black Tudor cladding. Ivy crawled over one side of the wall, and each of the windows was lined with plant pots filled with vibrant black-eyed Susan flowers throbbing with bees. There was a new outdoor area too, with picnic tables overlooking the grasslands.

Vanessa parked up, then jumped out with the very suitcase she was planning to take to New York with her, wheeling it towards the entrance designated to B&B guests. She narrowly missed some drying vomit on the ground, a swarm of flies dancing around it, their iridescent bodies shimmering in the sunlight.

She opened the door, a bell clanging to announce her arrival. As Vanessa walked down the hallway towards the reception area, she passed the archway leading into the main pub area. She could see it had changed too; no longer the 'old man's pub' she was used to with its sticky red carpets and scratched mahogany tables. Now the walls were shrouded in pretty dragonfly wallpaper and gilded mirrors, gold leaf lighting illuminating mango-wood tables. She spent so much time here as a kid, especially after her mother left. She remembered how the pub made her think of a beehive, the butterfly farm's workers pressed in close to one another most nights, buzzing with conversation about the day that had just passed. Sharon was the queen bee, of course.

Vanessa got to the reception desk to find a teenage girl glued to her phone behind it. She had an intense and almost ethereal beauty, her pale skin in stark contrast to her purple hair. Vanessa cleared her throat, and the girl looked up. She quickly shoved her phone away and stood up, eyes travelling over Vanessa's tattoos in fascination.

'You're the bug babe,' she said.

The bug babe. That was a new one.

Vanessa nodded. 'Or, as we like to call it in the forensics world, Doctor of Entomological Forensics.'

'So cool.' The girl reached behind her and grabbed a key from the wall. 'It's the first door on the right, up the stairs. Our biggest room. Sharon said she'll be behind the bar and you're to come and see her as soon as you're settled.' Vanessa went to take the key, but the girl paused, holding it hostage. 'You're going to find him, right? The one who killed them all? Or maybe it's a *her*. Though ninety-three per cent of killers in England and Wales *are* men, so probably not.'

'Good stat knowledge,' Vanessa said, grabbing the keys.

The girl smiled. 'I heard it on the *Dark Deeds Dissected* podcast last week. You know, you guys ought to check local phone masts to see where the victims were last.'

Vanessa felt like rolling her eyes, *hard*. Amateur sleuths given power by true crime podcasts and Reddit posts were part of the deal nowadays. She knew how much it wound police and forensic investigators up, to be told how to do their jobs by people fired up by podcasts like *Dark Deeds Dissected*. 'I'm pretty sure the police have done that already.' She gave the girl a quick smile, then headed towards the narrow staircase at the end of the hallway.

When she got to her room, Vanessa saw the girl was right. It was their biggest, which actually meant it was *small* rather than *tiny*. It was pretty though, one wall adorned with the same ornate wallpaper as downstairs, clogged with flowers and pretty insects. A large double bed dominated the room with an emerald bedspread draped over it.

The best part was the large window to the right of the bed, which looked out over the grasslands. The pub may have changed, but the grasslands hadn't. The village had been buying into the 'no mow' philosophy way before the rest of the UK caught on, letting the grasses and the wildflowers grow as tall as people's shoulders.

Vanessa opened the window and breathed in the rich, earthy scent of the grass. Then she set her laptop up on her desk, replying to some emails. Updates on cases. Emails of thanks. Interview requests. Newsletters. One email subject line stood out among it all from Dr Bronagh Thompson: *Looking forward to seeing you Sunday night!*

Bronagh was co-partner of the forensics lab Vanessa was joining, and had arranged a welcome dinner on the Sunday night. Vanessa imagined how it would feel, to arrive in a completely different city, meeting completely new people, after the horror of these murders in her home town. Maybe it would be the best remedy. A complete change of scenery.

After a long, cool shower, she changed into a pair of red and black plaid capri pants and a black vest top, tying her hair up into a bun – it was so *hot*. Then she made her way downstairs, trying to ignore the nerves flapping their wings within her stomach.

She recalled all the times she'd come here as a child. Her dad would usually be deep in conversation with someone from the butterfly farm at the bar, so it would just be Vanessa and her brother sitting at their usual table by the main bay window. Vincent would always be reading, nose down in one of their dad's books about the anatomy of some insect or another. Like Vanessa and their father – in fact, their mother too, as it was always insects she loved to create with her art – Vincent was fascinated by creepy-crawlies. But whereas the interest for Vanessa lay in their habitats and social interactions, for Vincent it was in their anatomy. Their exoskeletons and their alimentary canals and their proboscises. Words that easily tripped over his twelve-year-old tongue, unusual for a boy his age. But Vincent wasn't your usual boy. He was *her* boy, *her* unique brother.

God, she missed him.

She took in a calming breath, then walked into the busy pub. Every table was taken, the air stifling despite the French doors leading out on to the busy veranda being open. Vanessa knew these villagers weren't there for a typical summer evening outing to the pub, though. They were there to work through the horror that had struck at the heart of their community. This pub was their therapy room and their church, all rolled into one. It pleased Vanessa to see that this part of the town hadn't changed. With the closure of the butterfly farm, maybe she'd expected the ties of the community to loosen a little. But the beehive was still going strong.

As she walked in, people turned to look at her, the hubbub dying down. It reminded Vanessa of the first public talk she did at the university a few years back. It was on advances in forensic entomology and she'd thought there would be a small turnout, but she'd arrived to a packed lecture theatre full of hundreds of people staring at her silently.

Like then, she felt herself shrink a little. She preferred to be out in nature or in her lab. Not crammed inside, in front of a crowd.

She was saved by the sight of Sharon. Dear Sharon, her red curly hair now greying and shrouding her freckled shoulders. Her presence still filled the room, *commanded* it, and her red-rimmed eyes told the story of what she had lost. She manoeuvred out from her usual spot behind the bar and marched up to Vanessa, pulling her into a tight, desperate hug as everyone watched on.

'You're going to find the fucker who did this,' Sharon whispered fiercely into her ear. It wasn't a question. It was an order.

'We're going to try,' Vanessa replied. 'Sharon, I am *so* sorry about Michael.'

Sharon held Vanessa at arm's length as she looked into her eyes. 'Save your condolences. We need to find the monster who did this. And with your help, I feel like we have a fighting chance.'

A young girl of about seven came running up to Vanessa then, gawping up at her. She looked like Sharon, with her freckles and red hair.

'Is it true spiders put their webs in my daddy's belly?' the kid asked.

Michael's daughter. God, it was unbearable. The poor kid. The emotional weight of it anchored Vanessa down, making it hard for her to respond. Why should a kid know something like this about their father? Damn this village and its grapevine.

'Why would a spider put its web in my daddy's belly?' the girl continued. 'Did it poison him and the others?'

'Vanessa's going to find out for us, don't you worry,' Sharon said, steering the girl away towards a nearby table where several people sat, including a pregnant woman with short dark hair. Michael's wife? Next to her was another red-headed man who looked like a younger version of Michael.

'My brother always said how clever you were,' the man called over to Vanessa. 'Mum's right – it's good you're here. He'd be pleased.' As he said that last bit, his voice cracked, and he quickly gulped down some beer.

'The cleverest girl I know,' Sharon said. 'I won't be charging you for staying, of course. Not a penny. Take as long as you want. Weeks. Months even.'

Vanessa tried to keep her expression neutral at the idea of spending *months* in the village, but Sharon seemed to sense her hesitation. 'It's important you're right here in Greensands,' she said, jabbing her finger at the ground.

'I'm going to do everything I can,' Vanessa replied, unable to find the heart to tell Sharon she'd be leaving the day after next.

The pub door swung open then and, to Vanessa's relief, Paul's wife Helen walked in. Vanessa hadn't seen Helen for a couple of years. She had a look about her of a woman who'd had to simultaneously navigate the uncharted waters of being a mother to twins while also being the wife of a DCI. Vanessa had liked her from the moment they'd first met ten years ago, after Paul brought her to London for a theatre weekend. Tough, no-nonsense, funny. Her father had actually lived in Greensands after separating from Helen's mother when Helen was three. Helen lived in the nearest town, Cranleigh, all her life, and came to Greensands every other weekend to stay with her father.

But it wasn't until Helen was attending a protest in Cranleigh that Paul met her as a young officer trying to keep the peace. Helen was something of an activist, coming from a long line of union workers and lobbyists, now making a career out of using her design skills to create manuals and posters for various political clients.

Vanessa watched Helen pull Sharon into a tight hug. 'I am *so* sorry about Michael, Sharon. So sorry,' she said.

Sharon closed her eyes, nodding. Then she took a deep breath and scanned the pub. 'Move your butts,' she shouted to several young people sitting around a large table nearby. They all rolled their eyes, but did what Sharon asked anyway, moving out of the way as Helen and Vanessa took their places. 'You must be hungry,' Sharon said as she removed the empty glasses and wiped the table down. Amazing to think she was still working, despite what had happened. But Sharon had always been the kind of woman who needed to keep herself busy and in the midst of the community. 'Want Aggie to whip you up one of your mum's curries?' she asked Vanessa.

'Aggie still works here?' Vanessa asked. 'Surely she's a hundred by now?'

Helen laughed. 'Eighty-two and still the best cook in the county.'

'Two curries it is then?' Sharon asked. Helen and Vanessa nodded. 'What about drinks?'

'We can get them from the bar, Sharon,' Helen said, moving to get up again.

Sharon clamped her hand over Helen's shoulder and made her sit back down. 'As the wife of the man running himself ragged looking for my son's killer, you are not moving an inch. Drinks?' she asked again, her expression fierce.

Helen nodded. 'Usual for me.'

'You?' Sharon asked Vanessa.

'Rum and Cherry Coke, if you have it,' Vanessa replied.

When she left, Helen leaned back in her chair, blowing her blonde fringe away from her sticky forehead. 'I still can't get over it. Four Greensands men dead. Gone just like that,' she said quietly with a click of her fingers. 'So huge for a small village like this.'

Helen was right. With just two thousand residents, Greensands *was* small. In fact, it didn't exist before the butterfly park opened in the seventies, many of the homes specifically built by Arthur Oberlin for the farm's employees.

'To think the perpetrator could be someone sitting right in this pub,' Helen said, eyes scanning the room.

'Could well be,' Vanessa admitted. But who could possibly be capable of doing the things she'd seen today? One person caught her interest. A skinny teen with a shaved head and a black web tattoo dominating his right cheek. He was sitting with an older Severus Snape lookalike, with black hair down to his shoulders, and an older couple she recognised as the Wheatleys, who'd worked and met at the butterfly farm. As she scrutinised the Snape lookalike's face, Vanessa realised who it was: Ricky Abbott, her father's old assistant at the butterfly farm. He'd always been fascinated by spiders in particular, and it seemed he'd passed that on to the young man sitting with him.

His son?

Helen squeezed Vanessa's arm. 'Honestly, it's such a relief you're here. I was so pleased when Paul told me you'd delayed your flight for a couple of days. This is going to be a lot for him. Maybe too much. I need someone on the inside checking on him.'

'Paul can handle himself.'

Helen looked Vanessa in the eye. 'Can he?'

They both went quiet as Sharon brought their drinks over.

'Paul's OK, right?' Vanessa asked Helen when Sharon left, sensing something in her voice.

'It can just get a bit stressful, that's all.' Helen took a long, hard sip of her beer, avoiding Vanessa's gaze. She was hiding something, Vanessa could tell. But what? Maybe the stress had got too much for Paul. Vanessa had seen enough police officers weighed down by the job. She even knew of two who had taken their own lives. Just like any profession on the front line – nursing, teaching – the burden on workers' shoulders was huge. But Vanessa felt like the public often saw the police as having the broadest shoulders. It was part of their job, after all. Being strong, dealing with the harsher elements of life. It was easy to forget police officers were human, vulnerable, able to crack like any other person. They couldn't even go on strike like other professionals. It was tough.

As she took a sip of her rum and Coke, she made a note to talk to Paul before she left, *properly* talk to him.

'Who are the twins with?' she asked Helen.

'Paul's mum. She's a lifesaver.'

Vanessa had to agree. She'd brought Paul and his three brothers up alone before she met Paul's stepdad. Money had always been tight for them until then, and living in a small terraced two-bed hadn't been ideal. But Paul's mother always seemed to take it in her stride.

'How's it all going with the twins?' Vanessa asked. 'I can't believe they started school last September.'

'Oh, you know, hell in a playpen.' They both laughed. 'No, seriously,' Helen said, 'they're a delight. A *devilish* delight. Do you fancy coming for dinner tomorrow night? You can see them in action. You'll have to bring your riot gear, though.'

'Oooh, riot gear. I think I have a suitable outfit. Sounds fun.'

'You know, Paul was gutted when he found out you'd be taking that job.'

'I know – he told me.'

'Yeah, he's good at the whole guilt-trip thing. We will miss you though,' Helen said, squeezing Vanessa's arm. 'I enjoyed our annual London trips.'

'You'll just have to come to New York!'

'An eight-hour flight with the twins? Are you joking?'

Vanessa shrugged. 'Get the grandparents to have them.'

Helen smiled. 'Now *that's* an idea.'

Over the next couple of hours, they continued to talk and eat a pretty damn good curry made by Aggie as Vanessa kept half an eye on her phone, wondering how Paul and the other officers were getting on. Also, she had to reluctantly admit to herself, wondering how Damon was getting on. It was nagging at her, seeing him again. She thought she'd never come across him again in the flesh. Sure, she'd often see his handsome face smouldering at her from news-stands and TV screens. But to be within touching distance of him? It was doing all sorts of things to her, things she wasn't happy about. She tried to push the thoughts of Damon away, taking more sips of her drink.

Around them, the villagers grew rowdier. There were tears, cross words, even laughter mixed in. Vanessa had always found herself intrigued by the strange burden of grief, how it sat unsteady on mourners' shoulders, tipping from sorrow to anger to humour. She took a sip of her third drink and recognised she was getting tipsy herself. She was fine with that. She liked that whimsical stage between soberness and full-blown drunk. In control, but blurred around the edges, like honeybees after sipping on fermented lime, weaving happily and haphazardly back to their hive.

At some point, someone squeezed into the space next to Vanessa, bringing with them the overwhelming scent of floral aftershave. It was a man in his sixties, wearing a shirt peppered with exotic flowers and a bright blue tie. He slammed a hardback book onto the surface of the table, the author's name in bold type making her realise who it was: Clive Craviso, her father's old best friend. His sister, Emi, had been very close to Vanessa's mother too.

'I've signed it for you, Vanessa dear,' he said in his distinctive lisped voice. 'You'll love this one. It's set in your beloved London. A hardened detective, battling the bottle, returns one last time to track down a serial killer.'

'Very original,' Helen said as Vanessa smiled into her drink.

'Thank you,' Clive said. 'I do rather pride myself on finding unique ideas in what is a rather oversaturated market. How long has it been since I saw you last, Vanessa? Ten years?'

'Fifteen.' She knew the years like they were imprinted behind her eyelids.

'Ah, yes, of course,' Clive said. 'Your father's funeral. Our beloved Tony. What on earth would he think about today's events, I wonder?'

Vanessa nodded, solemn. What *would* her father think? She imagined he'd be upset about his beloved butterfly farm being used as a crime scene.

'Any theories?' Clive asked, eyes sliding over to Helen.

'You'll have to leave that question for the police, Clive,' Vanessa said.

'Dear Paul,' he said. 'What a burden on his shoulders. I still remember him as the little lad I would kick a ball about with. You know I lived next door to his mother for many years, before income from my writing was able to elevate me.'

'Elevate you?' Helen asked. 'What's that supposed to mean?'

Clive ignored her, eyes scouring the room before settling on Vanessa again. 'Must be strange being back here, after all this time. You know, one of your mother's sculptures is still on the mantelpiece.' He jutted his chin towards the other end of the pub to a small sculpture sitting above the fireplace. It was one of Vanessa's favourites, depicting a one-winged monarch butterfly made from wood and steel whose remaining wing was pinned down by a bejewelled pin. That was her mother's preferred subject right from when she was a child: wounded or distorted insects. She remembered the day her mother had finished that sculpture, standing in the garden barefoot before her outdoor work table, her thick black hair tied back into a messy plait.

'Have you seen her lately?' Clive asked.

'We don't keep in touch,' Vanessa said as Helen shot her a sympathetic look.

'Is she still in Brighton?' Clive asked.

'I really have no idea.'

The only clues she had that her mother was still alive were the new pieces of art that would appear on her website. Vanessa made a habit of checking once a month for a recent addition. She told herself that if there wasn't a new piece, that was when she'd worry.

'Such a shame,' Clive said with a sigh. 'I know your father was dismayed at the way your mother seemed to just cut off contact when she left. Have you ever tried to reach out to her?'

'No,' Vanessa replied, really not in the mood for this conversation. 'I don't feel the need.'

Of course she did. She yearned to see her mother. But she wasn't about to tell Clive that. The anger she felt at the way her mother had walked out on her and Vincent – especially Vincent, who was just four at the time and always clinging to her like a limpet – still burned strong.

Helen's phone buzzed, and Clive's eyes darted over to the screen. 'Update from the hubby?' he asked.

'Nope, just the Pornhub newsletter,' Helen replied.

Clive's eyes widened in shock as Vanessa smiled. Helen was such a wind-up merchant, and she loved her for it.

'You know,' Clive said, lowering his voice as his eyes travelled over to Sharon's husband, a tall man with a dark beard, 'I *did* wonder about Galinn. He always had something of a tempestuous relationship with his son and was a bit heavy-handed when he did security at the butterfly farm, if I recall. Then there's the handsome vet, Dr Keir Sinclair,' he added, pointing to a silver fox of a man sitting at the bar with a black Labrador by his side. 'He certainly knows a thing or two about the weird and wonderful world of the insects. Or how about the friendly schoolteacher?' His eyes glided to a large man with red hair and round glasses. 'It's always the nice ones, isn't it?'

'In your novels, maybe,' Helen said. 'But real life isn't quite like that.'

'I think you'll find truth can often be stranger than fiction, Helen,' Clive bristled.

'If that's the case, maybe *you* should be a suspect?' Helen asked, eyes twinkling with mischief. 'Writer obsessed with crime and butterflies. Living *alone*.'

Clive blanched. 'What a thing to say.' He quickly stood up. 'Well, just wanted to say hello, Vanessa.'

He walked off as Helen shook her head. 'Most deluded man I know.'

'Biggest fan of floral shirts too,' Vanessa said drily.

As she said that, a curvy black woman in her fifties wearing a smart grey suit walked in with a muscular man. A long silver pendant of a butterfly dangled over her ample chest, glinting beneath the pub's harsh lights.

'Why do I recognise her?' Vanessa asked.

Helen curled her lips. 'It's Indra Hudson.'

'Oh yes,' Vanessa said. 'She used to run marketing and PR at the butterfly farm. She had a penchant for buzz words like "leverage", "actionable" and "blue-sky thinking".'

'That'll be her,' Helen said. 'Weird she's here in the pub. In all the years I've lived here, I swear I haven't seen her set foot in the place. Must be here to feed on the drama, like the leech she is.'

'Not a fan then!' Vanessa remarked with a laugh.

Indra headed over to the bar with her husband, her heels clicking rhythmically on the wooden floor. People turned to look at her, clearly as surprised as Helen to see her there.

'She's planning to reopen the butterfly park, you know?' Helen said.

'Really?'

'Yep, she's currently in negotiations to buy the land off Arthur Oberlin. She will *not* be happy with three bodies desecrating her little business ambitions.'

'So sorry to interrupt.' Vanessa looked up to see the red-haired teacher Clive had pointed out earlier smiling down at them.

'Hello, Andrew,' Helen said. 'How are the twins behaving for you?'

'Very well,' Andrew replied.

Helen gave him a cynical look. 'Don't lie. This is Andrew Kirk,' she explained to Vanessa. 'He's the twins' teacher at Greensands Primary.'

'Brave soul,' Vanessa said.

'Oh, it's not too bad,' Andrew said jovially. 'They keep me on my toes. Actually, it's why I wanted to pop over, Doctor Marwood. I hope it's not too presumptuous to ask if you might be interested in popping into the school while you're here to give a brief presentation to our year sixes about what you do? Sanitised, of course, for a younger audience? If it's not too much to ask . . .' His voice trailed off.

'I'd usually be delighted,' Vanessa said, an outright lie. She couldn't think of anything worse than explaining the use of insect evidence to determine post-mortem intervals to a class of ten- and eleven-year-olds. 'But I'm afraid it's just a fleeting visit.'

'Ah, I see,' Andrew replied. 'Of course. Another time, maybe?'

'Sure. Here,' Vanessa said, digging her business card out and handing it over. 'Feel free to send over questions from the kids and I can do a video answering them.'

The teacher's face lit up. 'That would be wonderful.' He turned away, then paused, turning back and looking at Helen. 'Do wish your husband good luck with the investigation, Helen. Absolutely terrible business.'

'I will, thanks.'

The teacher nodded his head, then walked off.

'He seems nice,' Vanessa said.

'He's lovely. All the kids call him Mr McQuack.'

'Why?' Vanessa asked.

'The way he walks. He waddles.'

Vanessa laughed as she watched the teacher's hips shift side to side in yes, a waddle, before he sat down.

'Such a nice guy, though,' Helen said. 'Excellent actor too, pretending he's not deeply traumatised by teaching our girls.'

They both laughed. As they did, Vanessa noticed the young tattooed man watching them, brow creased.

Helen followed Vanessa's gaze. 'That's Abe,' she said. 'Our resident TikTokker. He's another bug collector, like you. Well, spiders anyway. He does all these TikToks about his little menagerie of eight-legged friends. You'd probably get on.'

'Is that his dad with him?' Vanessa asked. Helen nodded. 'He used to be my dad's assistant.'

'Yes, Paul told me. Ricky's a decent enough guy, keeps himself to himself. Wow,' Helen said. 'I sound *just* like someone being interviewed by a news channel about a suspect. "He was a nice guy, kept himself to himself."'

Vanessa watched Ricky Abbott as he sunk back a pint. She couldn't recall much about him except that he'd left abruptly. She couldn't remember why.

Helen's phone buzzed again, and she sighed. 'The twins have decided to wake up and cause mischief. I better get back.'

'Any news from Paul?'

Helen shook her head. 'You?'

'Nope. You better head back and rescue Paul's mum,' Vanessa said, downing her glass. 'I'm going to try to sleep.'

Helen gave her a quick hug as they both stood up. 'See you tomorrow evening, about six?'

'Sounds good. Will you be OK walking back alone?'

'We live a few doors down. I'll be fine.'

They went their separate ways, Vanessa heading back into the corridor as Helen stepped outside into the darkness. As Vanessa let herself into her room, her phone rang. A withheld number. Maybe it was Paul, calling from the station? She put her phone to her ear. 'Hello?'

'Vanessa.' It was Damon, his voice slurred and strained. 'I've done something stupid. Please, I need you.'

8

Paul trudged wearily down the dimly lit corridor of Cranleigh Police Station, his feet aching. He hadn't eaten anything other than crisps for fourteen hours straight, hadn't really sat down either, and he was bone-tired. He nodded at other officers as he navigated the bog-standard corridors that had been his maze for most of his police career, finally getting to the office he shared with his team: third floor, windowless, freezing cold in winter, stifling hot in the summer.

Before he headed inside, he paused, fishing out a small bottle of pills from his interior coat pocket. Helen would kill him for leaving it so late. He popped one into his mouth, washing it down with a swig of warm Diet Coke, then took a moment to compose himself, running his fingers through his curly hair and trying to shake off the weariness that clung to him like a shroud. He needed to be energetic, upbeat. He needed to be the best detective he could for his dead friends.

When he was ready, he pushed open the door and stepped inside. The room was a hive of activity, with officers huddled around tables covered in notes and photographs. Paul could see the strain on their faces, the same exhaustion he felt reflected in their eyes.

They all looked up when he walked in.

'All right, briefing time, kids. Gather round,' he said, clapping his hands.

The officers did as he asked, some perching on the edges of tables, others taking seats.

'Let's start with the door-to-doors,' Paul said. 'Anything of interest?'

'Yes, sir,' Selma said. 'Someone living across from the manor has some grainy doorbell footage of a car driving into the grounds in the early hours of this morning. We're currently trying to sharpen it up to see if we can get a clearer picture.'

Paul felt a flicker of hope ignite in his chest. 'Nice. Keep me updated.' He looked around, frowning. 'Where's PC Jenkins?' PC Kimberley Jenkins was dating Selma. She was a bit of a clumsy, disorganised officer who might've been fired by now if it weren't for her uncanny ability to needle the best kind of information out of unsavouries.

Selma shrugged. 'No idea.'

Paul rolled his eyes. 'OK, anyone else? OS?' He looked over at his sergeant, who somehow still looked as fresh as a daisy.

'Nope, nothing of interest, Boss,' OS said with a sigh. 'Unless you count the "suspicious-looking hedgehog" a certain Mrs Amersham saw the other day.'

The other officers in the room snickered. Paul allowed himself a small smile. 'Sounds like the old crow I know. Deano? What about you – anything?'

'Nothing. Sorry, Boss. But I did watch a TikTok video about golden silk orb-weavers. Their silk does look like the stuff found in the bodies, like your bug friend said.'

'Oooh, look at Deano,' Selma said. 'Down with da kids.'

'Maybe that's what he's planning to do after he retires,' OS added. 'I can see it now.' He put his hands in the air. 'Grandpa TikTokker Takes the World by Storm.'

'Shut your cake 'ole,' Deano said, throwing a half-eaten cupcake at OS as everyone laughed.

But Paul didn't join in with the laughter. Instead, he walked over to the incident board, taking in the symphony of photographs, notes and strings that told the tale of the four victims. It was on a grimy whiteboard at the front of the room. The force hadn't yet quite transitioned to the shiny new screens you see on TV crime shows. Paul preferred an old-fashioned approach anyway.

'Blimey, OS,' he said as he took it all in. 'It's a bloody masterpiece.'

'Art and crafts were always my thing when I was a kid,' OS said.

'Just make sure you don't get too carried away with the glitter and glue when dusting for fingerprints, OS,' Deano said. 'We don't want our suspects shimmering in the line-up, now do we?'

Everyone laughed. But the victims on the board didn't. Their four faces stared back at Paul, frozen in time, reminders of lives stolen by whatever monster was doing this. Below their images, the facts and details were meticulously arranged, like pieces of a macabre puzzle waiting to be solved.

'All right, quiet down,' Paul said. 'This looks good. But the fact is, it's all style and no substance. We have minimal leads right now. These men,' he said, gesturing to each of the victim's names, 'they deserve more than minimal. More than style. Plus, it won't just be The Banger and her seniors throwing themselves all over this case like an itchy rash soon. It'll be the media too. Right, Yasmin?' he said, looking over at the young, dark-haired media officer who had joined the briefing.

'They already are,' she replied with a sigh. 'I've put a statement out on our socials and website, saying we're investigating an incident in Greensands. I've also told any press who've been in touch that they'll get no concrete information until we hold a press conference. But honestly,' she said with a shake of the head, 'my phone's never been so busy. So I'm hoping to sort that press conference as soon as we can.'

'Oooh, the public might be treated to your mug on TV, Boss,' Deano said to Paul. Paul shuddered at the thought.

The door opened and Selma's other half, Kimberley, ran in, a half-eaten burger in her tanned hands. Selma glared at her partner.

'What?' Kimberley said mid-chew as everyone rolled their eyes at her. 'I was hungry. A woman has to eat.'

'Not when four men are dead,' Paul said.

'Yes, sir!' Kimberley threw her burger towards a nearby bin. It missed, ricocheting off a chair leg and onto OS's immaculate desk.

'Jesus, Kimberley,' OS said, shaking his head.

'Sorry,' Kimberley replied as she squeezed between two tables and walked over to Paul. 'I have something, though, Boss. Something good.'

Paul was all ears.

'I just spoke to one of the druggies I know,' she said. 'He witnessed Damon Oberlin having a right go at his brother outside the pub on Thursday night.'

Paul's fingers dug into his palms. He knew it. He bloody knew it. 'Tell me more,' he said.

'Apparently, Damon Oberlin slammed his brother up against the wall,' Kimberley said, now breathless with the excitement of the information she'd managed to glean, 'and then Simon, poor sod, tries to pull him back and gets a punch in the face from Damon for his trouble.'

The room fell silent, the air thick with tension.

'Is this witness really a reliable source?' Paul asked.

Kimberley nodded. 'His intel usually checks out. But just to be sure, I asked around and had it backed up by a woman walking by. She's a teacher.'

'Nice work. Looks like we need to bring Damon Oberlin in for questioning then,' Paul said. 'I'll give The Banger a call. If she's on board, we'll officially nominate him as a suspect for these murders.'

'You sure, Boss?' Deano asked in a low voice. 'He's famous. It'll be a shitshow.'

'Got any better ideas?' Paul asked him. 'We're several hours into a quadruple murder with fuck all to go on. No, let me correct myself,' he added. 'We have this fight to go on, *and* we have the fact that an expert on this case, Doctor Marwood, believes the murders are influenced by insect mating rituals – something Damon Oberlin specialises in.'

'Looks pretty suss to me,' OS said. 'Plus we only need a *suspicion* to arrest. Ten per cent rule and all that.'

Paul pointed at his sergeant. 'You got it in one, OS. Ten per cent suspicion is enough to arrest. We're bringing him in.'

9

Vanessa walked up the gravelled drive of Oberlin Manor, the soles of her DMs crunching each stone into submission. Two lights were fixed to the manor's walls, lighting the fountain up in a soft yellow bloom, caressing the moss and the cracks away so it almost looked like its old self.

Vanessa was about to lift the large, butterfly-shaped knocker on the front door when she paused. She'd done this so many times as a teenager. She still remembered that surge of excitement she used to feel at the thought of seeing Damon.

Now that excitement was replaced by trepidation and fear.

What *had* he done to insist she come here?

She slammed the knocker against the door and waited. Finally, she heard footsteps on the other side, and the door opened with a creak, two blue eyes staring out at her.

'You came,' Damon said, opening the door wide.

Her eyes travelled all over him, searching for any blood, any evidence he'd hurt himself . . . or hurt *someone*. But he looked fine. *More* than fine, dressed in a smart white shirt and tailored black trousers. She could tell he'd been drinking though, could smell the whisky on his breath and hear it in the slur of his voice. Had he just lied to get her to come here? She was about to ask him that very question. But then she remembered he was mourning. She knew how it felt that first night after someone you love dies. She'd felt the same after her dad had passed away from lung cancer with her by his side. Such a force of life, gone in the blink of an eye.

'What's wrong, Damon?' she asked gently. 'I was worried.'

'Your hair wasn't as dark as this before. Good to see you without that human-sized sandwich bag on, too. You definitely look different.'

'It's been over twenty years, Damon.'

'Twenty-two years, three months and four days.'

Vanessa rolled her eyes in exasperation. Was this all just a ruse to get her there? 'I can see you're fine. Call me when you've sobered up.'

'Wait!' Damon said. 'I need you.'

'Why?' She crossed her arms.

'I'm afraid I had a bit of a tantrum and tore my brother's office apart. In the process, I found something . . . interesting.'

She peered behind him into the large, dark hallway, the only spots of light coming from two lamps. 'Related to Benjamin's death?'

'I don't know. Maybe.'

'Then this is a police matter.'

'You are the police.'

'I am *not* the police. I'm a forensic scientist who helps the police.' She pulled her phone from her pocket and checked to see if Paul had called her back. She'd called him on the walk over to explain where she was going and why. Still nothing.

'Don't tell me you've called PC Pedestrian,' Damon asked.

'Yes, I thought you were in danger.'

'I told you not to. Since when did *you* become so pedestrian?'

Vanessa fixed him with a look. 'Since four men were murdered, including your brother.'

His face crumpled a little, and she felt herself softening.

'Come inside,' he coaxed. 'Please.' She'd never been able to resist that look he was giving her. It was all it took sometimes to make her forget his excuses.

I'm sorry I didn't turn up yesterday, Vanessa. Something came up. I didn't mean to be this late. Come here, give me a hug.

I wasn't flirting with that girl, I swear. She was the one all over me.

But she was different now. Stronger. Maybe she should just walk away this time?

'Honestly, Vanessa,' Damon said. 'You'll want to see what I've found. Trust me.'

She could see he was serious. So she stepped inside, following him across the hall, the echo of her footsteps on the marble floors bouncing between the walls. Was it her imagination or was there less *stuff* here than she remembered? Fewer paintings on the walls, fewer ornaments on the surfaces of the many tables scattered around.

Had they been sold over the years to address the mounting debts she'd heard rumours of?

Two corridors ran off to either side of the main hallway. Damon led her to the right, down the dark, narrow passage towards the second door. She paused. 'Isn't this your father's study?'

'It's Benjamin's now.' His face darkened. 'Or was.'

She followed him in, remembering when she would sneak into this very room with Damon, letting him spread her legs against the desk in defiance of his powerful father. The scent of spices and cigars, leather and wax still dominated the room, bringing with it heady memories of his tongue against her, his fingers pressing into her thighs.

Damon switched the light on and the shocking mess of the room came into view. Large armchairs turned over. Books ripped from the shelves and thrown around the room. Worst of all, the glass of one of the wall cabinets once holding dead, pinned butterflies and other insects was smashed, a morbid collection of invertebrate body parts scattered across the floor.

'What *happened* in here, Damon?' she asked.

'I was trying to find a key. I got a bit carried away.'

'What key?'

Damon gestured to a bookcase at the far end of the room. 'There's a hidden room behind that bookcase,' he said.

'How very Agatha Christie,' Vanessa remarked.

'The irony is,' Damon said as he led her to the bookcase, careful not to tread on broken glass, 'the key was in plain sight, lying on Benjamin's desk.' He pressed the spine of a dark red book. There was a mechanical sound, then a door clicked open. Damon pulled it wide and walked inside, disappearing into the darkness.

'Come on then,' he called out to her.

Vanessa peered in to see stairs leading down into the darkness. She knew there was a vast network of rooms and corridors beneath the manor. She'd never been down there, though. It had always been off limits to them as kids, intensifying rumours that Arthur Oberlin would hold rituals and sacrifices down there.

She peered over her shoulder. Was it sensible following Damon, who was clearly in a drunk and unstable mood, down those stairs?

'I'm not going to bury you in the cellar walls, if that's what you're worried about,' Damon called out to her from below.

Jesus. She knew Damon. Why was she so worried? She walked into the darkness, using the torch from her phone to light the way as she followed him, finding herself in a small, low-ceilinged room. In the middle of the room was a large table with a lamp providing light in the gloom. Shelves lined the walls, each of them heavy with dark boxes. On one of the walls was a round mural painted in exquisite detail, depicting a moth mid-metamorphosis. Surrounding the moth was a circular border made up of more insects and mandala-like symbols in fine lines and geometric shapes.

It felt oddly familiar to Vanessa.

'What is that on the wall?' Vanessa asked Damon who was standing at the far end of the table, next to one of the boxes. 'I feel like I recognise it.'

'No idea. But take a look at this,' he said, beckoning her over.

She walked over and carefully, slowly, opened the lid. Peeking inside, she expelled a small, sad sigh. A ghost mantis insect was nestled in a bed of soft moss. With its prominent, shield-like thorax and elongated, leaf-shaped head, it stood poised and still, as if sensing the precariousness of its situation.

'Poor baby,' she whispered.

'Indeed.' Damon was standing close to her, too close, his whisky-laced breath hot on her cheek. 'I think Benjamin was selling them illegally.'

Vanessa curled her lip. She hated the illegal insect trade with a fiery passion.

She moved away from Damon and walked around the room, taking in the labels on some of the boxes. Many species of tarantula. Praying mantis. All sorts of rare insects. 'You didn't know he was into this?'

Damon shook his head as he leaned back against the table and crossed his arms. 'I *knew* he was hiding something behind these doors, though. He always insisted the key was lost, but I heard him creaking about at night. Seems my brother had himself a nice little illegal earner. And you know what that means?'

Vanessa turned to Damon. 'What does it mean?'

'*Illegal* usually brings with it rather nefarious individuals, no? Individuals who might take pleasure in hurting Benjamin and the men who helped him.'

Vanessa frowned. 'You think the other victims were in on this enterprise?'

Damon shrugged. 'Maybe.'

'I don't know. The manner in which your brother and the other men were killed seems a little too *creative* for the usual thugs you see carrying out kill orders. Either way,' she said as her eyes scanned all the boxes, 'we need to get the police here and get some help for these creatures. I'll make some calls.'

Damon pushed away from the table. 'You won't get reception here. Let's head back up.'

'Strange to finally see what's beneath the manor,' Vanessa said as she followed Damon back up the stairs.

'Oh, this is just a fraction of it.'

'Have you seen the rest? I remember your father never let you and Benjamin come down here.'

'I managed to sneak down to the storage room a couple of years after you abandoned me.'

She rolled her eyes. 'I did not *abandon* you. In fact, from what I recall, you were the one who broke it off.'

Damon paused and turned around, blocking her way just before they got out into the study. 'I don't remember it that way.'

She held his gaze, then shook her head. 'What does it matter? It's all water under the bridge.' Then she lifted his arm and ducked under it, stepping into the study and checking her phone for a signal.

'I'll head to the kitchen and do us some coffee while you make your calls,' Damon said, picking books up and kicking glass out of the way as Vanessa tried calling Paul again. He didn't answer, so she left him a quick message. Then she called Cranleigh Police Station's main number, asking to be put through to the incident room. But the phone was engaged.

'They'll have to get *that* sorted before the murders become public,' she murmured.

She scrolled through her contacts, finding the name of a fellow insect lover she knew who worked at a local wildlife rescue place. It was late, but she was confident a phone call from her would get an answer. She was right, and they promised to be at the manor within half an hour to see to the live creatures. The rest would be evidence for the police to collect. Until then, she had just enough time to grab a coffee and sober up even more before everyone arrived.

While Damon was in the kitchen, she walked around the study, pausing by the Oberlins' vintage vinyl record player. It was a Garrard 301, and still in perfect condition, its sleek silver platter gleaming beneath the soft lighting above. Music had only truly come alive to her the first time she'd heard it being played on the turntable.

'Remember it, do you?' Damon asked as he walked in with their coffees.

She nodded. 'I have my own now.'

'Which one?'

'A Pioneer PL-518.'

'Ah, a seventies classic. What tunes do you like to play on it?'

'The latest vinyl I bought at auction was The Sisters of Mercy's *First and Last and Always*.'

'Always the strange stuff. At least you have the look to match your musical tastes now.'

Vanessa took her coffee and continued walking around, passing a solid mahogany coffee table strewn with old books about the insect world, bent at the spines and littered with colourful Post-it notes. Damon's research for his next series? She'd only managed to get through one episode of his *Zombie Killers of the Insect World* series. She didn't like the way Damon skimmed the surface of the whys and the hows. She didn't like the strange estuary accent he put on for the camera, either.

'Still have your animal graveyards, I see,' she said, stopping by a cabinet on the wall that showcased an array of pinned spiders, from a tiny black cave spider to a brown Goliath birdeater the size of a dinner plate. There was even a cobalt-blue tarantula in there, just like her own pet, and a golden silk orb-weaver, which looked elegant in its macabre resting place, its long, angled legs arranged carefully to stress the spider's length and highlight its bold, golden torso.

For a moment, she imagined *Damon* in a glass cabinet himself, his hands and feet pinned, his cobalt eyes open and fogged. 'I know, I know,' Damon said as he joined her, 'you prefer your creepy-crawlies alive.'

'That *is* preferable,' she said, shaking the image away, 'but I know how fond you Oberlins are of these entomological elysiums.'

'Do you remember how your brother used to refer to this cabinet as the "Spider Slumber Party"?'

'I do.'

He frowned. 'Something just occurred to me, actually. The way Benjamin and the other men were displayed is just like how a collector displays their insects.'

Vanessa's brow creased. 'You know how the other men were displayed?'

'I have my contacts.'

'In the police?'

He didn't answer, instead leaning close to stare at the golden silk orb-weaver. 'What's particularly impressive about these ones is the way the females devour their dwarfish counterparts post-coitus. *Very* sexy, don't you think?'

He turned to look at her. It was the same look he'd given her the first time he'd really noticed her at the Oberlin Christmas party when she turned fourteen. She'd been noticing him for years though. The untouchable, handsome boy who stood at his father's side at various events. Growing taller, more broad-shouldered, more handsome and confident with each year that passed, while she remained flat-chested, boyish, insecure. But then the chrysalis of clumsy youth had made way for curves and long lashes and a deep awareness of what an abundance of femininity can do to a heterosexual man.

As Damon held her gaze now, she felt an irrational urge to press her lips against his. That urge made her angry. She wasn't that naive teenager anymore. She saw Damon for what he was now: an arrogant, entitled dick. And yet still, he was just *so* beautiful to look at.

'Why are you talking like this?' she asked. 'Isn't it inappropriate?

Only a few hours ago, you were staring at your brother's dead, mutilated body.'

As if a switch had been flipped, the pretence of resilience gave way on Damon's face, replaced by a heart-wrenching display of sadness.

'I'm sorry,' Vanessa said, realising she'd taken it too far. Yes, he may be an entitled, arrogant dick but he was grieving and she still cared for him. She placed a hand on his arm. 'I shouldn't have said it like that.'

He looked up at her through tear-laced lashes. 'Look at us both, *brotherless*,' he said, the words twisting in his mouth.

Vanessa removed her hand.

'I often think of that day, you know,' Damon continued. 'The day we lost Vincent. How we were so wrapped up in each other, we didn't even notice.'

She could see what he was doing. She had hurt him, so now he had to hurt her with memories of the worst day of her life. It was the way it had always been for them and now his words were dragging her back in time as she walked through the maze of long grass, eyes scouring the place for her brother.

'Sorry, I shouldn't have brought it up.' Damon placed his cool hand on her shoulder, the message in his eyes clear as he looked at her: *we're even now.*

The doorbell went, breaking the spell. Vanessa stepped away from Damon, pleased for the distraction. Damon sighed, then walked out into the hallway as she followed, opening the door.

It was Paul, flanked by two officers.

'Damon Oberlin,' he said. 'We're arresting you on suspicion of the murder of Benjamin Oberlin, Michael Regan, Simon Taylor and Tim Holmes.'

10

Paul stood outside the interview room, rubbing his weary eyes.

'I told you to have that protein shake, Boss,' OS said. 'Mine perked me right up.'

'Honestly, mate, I'd rather drink my own piss.' Paul put his hand on the doorknob. 'Ready? Damon Oberlin can be a slippery little eel.'

OS gave Paul a nod, like he was about to head into the boxing ring, and they both strolled in to find Damon sitting at the table with his solicitor, a woman who made Paul think of the queen with her short curly grey hair. Damon sat straight-backed, exuding his usual arrogance. But Paul noted a slight quiver in his hands. He seemed out of place in the drab interview room with its magnolia concrete walls and faded blue carpet.

Paul switched on the recorder and went through the usual pre-interview preamble before launching into his questions: 'Let's start with your brother, Benjamin Oberlin. He was found dead on the grounds of your family's manor yesterday afternoon. You have already told us,' he said, looking down at his notes, 'that the last time you saw him was Saturday evening. Can you confirm your whereabouts after that?'

Damon sighed, leaning back in his chair. 'In my office, working. Then bed. Then back to the office again all day Sunday. Bed. And so it repeats.'

'Is there a way to corroborate this?' OS asked.

Damon turned to regard the sergeant with an unimpressed gaze. 'My phone, I imagine, which you've seized.'

'Let's rewind a few days,' Paul said. 'Specifically to Thursday, the third of August. Witnesses say you were arguing with Benjamin outside The Monarch and the Grasshopper pub that evening?'

Damon's face remained neutral. But Paul noted his fingers gripped the edge of the table.

'Arguing is a rather harsh word,' Damon said. 'I was trying to drag him back home, so he didn't make more of a drunken fool of himself.'

'How was he making a drunken fool of himself?' Paul asked.

'Stumbling around the pub, knocking over drinks,' Damon replied. 'Sharon called me to collect him.'

'So you *dragged* your brother out of the pub and then what?' OS asked.

Damon shrugged. 'He tried to go back in, so yes, maybe I slammed him against the wall in my attempt to stop him. Not all of us can carry a grown man like you seem to be able to, PC O'Sullivan.'

'It's Detective Sergeant,' OS said.

'What happened next?' Paul asked, keen to move away from the prospect of these two men getting their dicks out on the table to compare sizes.

'Simon Taylor came along,' Damon replied.

'Yes, Simon Taylor,' Paul said, drumming his fingers on the table. Damon's eyes focused on his fingers, and he frowned. 'The same man who was found deceased alongside Tim Holmes and Michael Regan.'

'In the grounds of the butterfly farm *your* father once ran,' OS added.

'Just a few hours before you found your brother,' Paul finished.

'Well, look at you both,' he said with a smile. 'We have quite the Little and Large act going on here, don't we? Did you practise this in the police academy?'

'Let's return to Thursday night,' Paul said, ignoring Damon's jibes. 'What happened when Simon Taylor *came along*, as you put it?'

Damon was quiet for a moment. 'He told me to take my hands off Benjamin,' he said eventually. 'He tried to pull me off. I reacted in an instinctive and, I have to confess, *stupid* way. I punched him, which I'm sure you're already aware of.'

OS leaned back in his chair and crossed his arms, the muscles in his forearms flexing as he fixed Damon with a glare. 'Why didn't you mention this to the police?' he asked.

Damon's expression darkened. 'It was a petty argument that had *nothing* to do with the murders. Simon's very punchable face combined with the fact he called me a "failed TV presenter" set something off in me.' He shrugged. 'What can I say? I'm a sensitive little soul.'

Paul quirked his head. 'I never took you for the type to get into pub punch-ups, Damon.'

'Neither did I,' Damon said with an exaggerated sigh, 'but it seems the combination of self-pity, humiliation and whisky does that to a man.'

'It also establishes a rather volatile connection between you and two of the victims in the days leading up to their deaths, doesn't it?' OS said.

'Officers,' Damon's solicitor said, 'there's a lot of conjecture here. Do you have actual evidence to present?'

'There's the manner in which the men were killed,' Paul replied. 'It is our belief their deaths were inspired by the mating rituals of insects.'

'*Vanessa's* belief, don't you mean?' Damon asked. 'Shame you had to cut our evening together short, by the way.' Damon looked right at Paul as he said that. He knew it would wind Paul up, knowing Vanessa was at Oberlin Manor so late. And he'd be right, but Paul wasn't about to give this prick the satisfaction of showing his unease.

'The mating rituals of insects are a particular area of expertise for you,' Paul stated. 'What can you tell us about this?'

'I'm sure you've seen my TV show, Detective. Insects have been a lifelong passion of mine.'

'I'm afraid I haven't had the delight of watching it,' Paul said, his gaze never wavering. 'Given your fascination with insects, though, you must admit the killings are quite unique.'

Damon pinched the bridge of his nose, suddenly looking as exhausted as Paul felt. 'I didn't kill my brother or those other men. *Yes*, I had an argument with Benjamin, and *yes*, I punched Simon. But I would never murder anyone. The person who did this,' he said, leaning forward and tapping his finger on the table, 'is creative. Clever. Focused. These aren't murders carried out after a seedy pub bust-up. Come on, Paul. Deep down, you know I didn't do this. That I couldn't *do* this to Benjamin, my *brother*. He was a fucking annoying twat, but I loved him.'

His voice cracked then, his eyes filling with tears. Paul studied

Damon's face, searching for any signs of deception. The TV presenter's eyes held a flicker of vulnerability, and for the first time since the interview began, Paul wondered if Damon might well be telling the truth.

OS didn't look convinced though, his expression glacial as he regarded Damon.

'Let's talk about the underground room you found beneath the manor containing rare insects,' OS said. 'What can you tell us about that?'

'I knew nothing about it,' Damon replied.

'Are you sure?' OS asked. 'Perhaps both you and your brother were running this business with the other three men, and you all had a falling-out?'

Damon let out a frustrated growl. 'No, our argument had *nothing* to do with that. I had no idea Benjamin was involved in anything illegal, let alone illegal insect trading.'

'So despite living in the manor with him,' Paul said, 'you didn't have an inkling?'

'No, that's obviously what the secret underground room was for: to keep me out of it,' Damon replied through gritted teeth. 'But I'm sure your officers are tearing the place apart as we speak, *trying* to find something to connect me to it all. I can tell you now, you won't unearth anything. And I doubt the three men found murdered yesterday morning were involved. They were decent family men . . . right?'

Paul agreed. He just couldn't see the three men being involved.

'Any other people you think might have been involved?' Paul asked.

'You know, now that you mention it, Benjamin *had* been going out for more lunches lately. He always came back with a scent of perfume on him, *women's* perfume. Specifically, Black Ophelia. My ex-wife used to wear it,' he added with a look of contempt. 'It's not her, before you suggest it. She's been in Paris the past few weeks. Anyway, when I asked him about it, he was very mysterious.'

'Might have been a lover?' Paul suggested.

'No, Benjamin loved boasting about his conquests. This felt . . . different.'

Paul and OS exchanged a look, noting this new piece of information.

Damon looked at the clock on the wall, the exhaustion clear on his face. 'Look, I'm all for helping you catch my brother's killer, even if that means you taking desperate measures and arresting me. But it's nearly one in the morning, and although your colleague here looks like he eats durable batteries for breakfast, you, my old friend, look like you're about to nod off any minute. It's clear I'm not your man, so are we done here?'

Old friend. They had *never* been friends.

'*I* will say when we're done,' Paul said in a voice that could cut glass.

Damon rolled his eyes. 'So this is a power play.'

'No, Damon, this is a very, very serious case.'

'And you think I've been a very, very naughty boy?' Damon replied. 'I mean, I *can* be naughty. Vanessa will tell you that.'

The solicitor gave her client an exasperated look.

Paul imagined losing control then. Really losing it and taking out all the years of anger he felt at the smug git sitting across from him with a full-fisted smack to the face. But that would just get him thrown off the case and make Damon even more smug. So he did something better. He stood up and walked from the room, leaving OS scrambling for his files to stand up and follow, too.

'What's going on?' Damon shouted after him. 'You're not letting me go?'

'We need to corroborate what you said,' Paul called over his shoulder.

'Some way to treat the family of one of your victims,' Damon snapped back.

'Don't worry, we'll get in some Earl Grey for you,' OS promised, turning to give Damon a smile that didn't reach his eyes before stepping out of the interview room with Paul and closing the door.

'He really is a slippery little eel,' OS said as they walked back to the incident room. 'Or a wily little maggot, if we're keeping with the insect theme. Not sure he's the man we're looking for though, Boss, I've got to admit.'

Paul sighed. 'Yeah, maybe. Still fun keeping him in for a few more hours though, right?'

'Hell, yeah. The mysterious lunches Benjamin was having sounded interesting.'

'I thought the same.'

'An ex of mine used to wear Black Ophelia,' OS added, wrinkling his nose. 'It's gross. Smells like flowers and truffles. Maybe we should get a sample or something, have the officers give it a sniff, then if they notice anyone wearing it, we can question them about the lunches?'

'Yeah, good idea.'

'So, him and the Bug Lady . . . ?'

'Ancient history,' Paul quickly replied. 'I think we better head back, get some kip, so we're all fresh for our little team outing to Greensand Ridge tomorrow. The sting on Benjamin's foot isn't exactly a mind-blowing lead, but it's something.'

'Cool, I'll see you there, Boss. That's if there isn't another murder overnight.'

Paul frowned. He hoped to God there wasn't.

11

Greensands Ridge, which ran through the centre of the village, wasn't much of a ridge, especially in the summer. It was more like a long, flat sandy plain that ran down one side of the road through the main part of the village and out towards the manor and butterfly farm. Once it left the main street, it was flanked on one side by the woods and on the other by the grasslands that stretched across to the manor. The part of the ridge that was most enjoyed by mining bees was in that quieter section on the outskirts of the town, just before the butterfly farm and manor. In the earlier part of the last century, a railway line ran beside it, as evidenced by the brick railway arch that loomed in the distance. The arch had now been converted into offices, the space between the arches bricked up with glass doors and windows revealing a large office with desks and side rooms within.

Vanessa pulled her truck up into the car park. As she stepped out of her car, she could see several officers were already there, including Paul. They all looked pretty tired, despite supposedly having got a few hours of sleep the night before. Paul looked particularly tired. Was that because he'd been up even longer interviewing Damon?

It had been a shock, watching Damon get arrested like that. But she knew Paul would have his reasons. The Damon Vanessa remembered wouldn't be capable of murder, let alone killing his own brother. But she knew people changed.

'Damon's still in custody, if that's what you're wondering,' Paul said as she walked up to him. Did she detect a hint of coldness in his voice? Knowing Paul, he was probably annoyed he'd found her with Damon so late. But she *had* called Paul to tell him she was going there. It wasn't like it was some secret tryst.

'I'm actually wondering if you're doing OK?' she asked, remembering Helen's request to keep an eye out for him. 'Must've been a late one?'

'Not bad considering I'm in the middle of a four-body-count shitstorm.'

'You know you can always talk to me.'

He gave her a quizzical look, then rolled his eyes. 'Helen put you up to this, didn't she?'

'Maybe.'

'She gets worried when I'm busy – that's all. Moans I'm not sleeping enough, not eating enough.'

'*Just* that?'

'What do you mean?'

Vanessa shrugged. 'I don't know. I got the impression it was more than that.'

'Your impressions are shit.'

She shook her head, smiling to herself. 'So what happened to the railway arch?'

'Indra Hudson owns it,' Paul said.

'She was at the pub last night.' As Vanessa said that, the young, muscled detective sergeant she'd seen the day before strolled over, giving her an appreciative look.

'I didn't get the chance to introduce you both properly yesterday,' Paul said. 'This is Detective Sergeant O'Sullivan, or OS as he's known. OS, this is the Bug Lady, as you called her.'

'I like the Lady addition,' Vanessa said.

'Get much sleep last night?' Paul asked his sergeant.

'A few hours.'

'You must all be tired,' Vanessa said.

'Tired isn't in my vocab,' OS replied with a mischievous smile.

'Liar,' Paul said. 'You should've seen him at his birthday drinks the other month. Was curled up like a baby on the sofa at the pub by midnight.'

OS rolled his eyes.

'I saw the case got on the national news,' Vanessa said. 'Saw a few media vans this morning too. Just what you need.'

'Like a giraffe needs a necktie,' Paul said.

Vanessa smiled. 'Or a cactus needs a raincoat.'

'*Now* I get it,' OS remarked as he looked between them.

'Get what?' Paul asked.

'Why you two are friends,' OS replied. 'She's got the same lame sense of humour as you.'

'I just pretend I do to make him feel better,' Vanessa said, pulling on some latex gloves and flexing her fingers as OS watched, his cheeks reddening slightly.

'So, where do your little mining bee friends hang out so we can let our specialist search team know?' Paul asked her.

'Here.' She led them towards the edge of the ridge, which was actually more pronounced there, like half a shallow tunnel carved into the sandy ground.

'Right, gather round,' Paul said to the dedicated team, all of whom were wearing gloves and masks. 'For those who don't know, this is Doctor Vanessa Marwood,' he said, gesturing to Vanessa. Some of the officers she'd met the day before smiled at her. Others took in her tattoos and piercings with the usual predictable stares. 'Vanessa is my old friend,' Paul continued, 'a former Greensands resident, and most important of all, a forensic entomologist and bug geek.'

There were some confused looks among the gathered officers. Vanessa was used to it. Whenever the word 'entomologist' was used, most people were confused, thinking it had something to do with fossils or even gynaecology.

'For those with an IQ of minus one,' Paul said, 'that's a forensics investigator who has a particular expertise in insects and other arthropods. It should be pretty clear by now why she might be of use in this case. The reason we're here is Doctor Marwood found a sting on the fourth victim, Benjamin Oberlin's, foot. Why don't you explain a bit more, Doctor?'

Vanessa turned to the officers. 'The stinger I found in the deceased's skin, and the small fragment of hair, suggests it may have been made by a mining bee. Mining bees particularly like these sandy ridges.' She gestured towards the sandy banks nearby. 'This means there's a chance Benjamin was here before he died.' She turned to look towards the main part of Greensands. 'If he was walking back from the pub, it would have been along the path through the grasslands,' she said, pointing towards a path which stretched through the grasslands towards the manor. 'Being here would have meant a bit of a detour. So Detective Chief Inspector Truss and I believe it would be prudent to search along these banks for evidence. Bonus points for those who find any dead mining bees. One of them could be the very creature that came into contact with Benjamin Oberlin's foot.'

'Your job, my lucky people,' Paul continued, 'is to do a thorough fingertip search of this part of the ridge. You know the drill. Find anything, mark it with an evidence flag and call me over if it's of particular interest.' He looked at his watch. 'Nearly ten past seven. Let's begin before the press descend on the village, because descend they surely will.'

The officers organised themselves into three groups – one to follow the middle of the ridge and the others to follow down the sides. They then got on their hands and knees like a line of centipedes carefully traversing the land. It felt surreal to Vanessa. Sure, she'd seen this before plenty of times. But to witness it in her childhood village felt all kinds of wrong.

'I thought bees didn't like to sting,' one of the police officers watching the search said. She was the platinum-haired young woman Vanessa had seen earlier.

'I don't like to hurt people either,' Vanessa said, 'but if someone trod on me, I might.'

'Oh yeah, makes sense. I'm Selma, Selma Traynor, by the way. You used to babysit me.'

Vanessa's mouth fell open. '*Little* Selma?' she said, remembering the rosy-cheeked, blonde-haired kid she used to babysit for the butterfly farm's office manager. 'Now I feel *really* old. I bet I was a terrible babysitter.'

'No, you were the best,' Selma said with a huge smile. 'You let me stay up super late *and* I could have pudding before dinner.'

Vanessa quirked an eyebrow. 'Like I said, a terrible babysitter.'

Selma stared at the pockmarked, packed sand that sloped downward before them. 'So this is where the bees burrow, then? Do they all meet up underground?'

Vanessa watched as a couple of mining bees zigzagged lazily across the sun-dappled sand. 'No, each of these holes represents a solitary nest. The females create them. Tough little buggers. They actually use their jaws to break up the sand.'

'Awesome.'

'Insects *are* awesome.'

Selma sniffed the air. 'I like your perfume. Damon Oberlin told the boss his brother was meeting up with someone for mysterious little lunches and would come back smelling of Tom Ford's Black Ophelia. Apparently it's got *truffles* in it. I got *obsessed* with looking up perfumes last night and I'm thinking my Tesco's Own body spray might be doing me a disservice. What do you think?' She shoved her wrist under Vanessa's nose.

'Smells fine to me,' Vanessa replied.

'Found a dead bee,' an officer called out. He was part of the group searching the right side of the ridge, over the grassier bit. Vanessa stood up and walked towards him. As she did, she noticed movement in the trees to her right. It was a woman walking her dog, watching the scene with curiosity. Vanessa recognised her. She was older, her long hair greyer. But she was pretty sure it was Clive Craviso's sister, Emi Craviso, or – as she was known around Greensands back in the day, due to her habit of foraging for herbs and plants to make strange concoctions – the 'Butterfly Witch'.

Emi had once managed the gift shop at the butterfly farm many years ago, working closely with Michael Regan. She was fired when she was caught getting down and dirty with one of the farm's groundsmen. That had never seemed fair to Vanessa, especially considering the number of work-based affairs Arthur Oberlin was suspected to have had. Emi didn't find it fair either, bringing some of her feminist friends down to protest with phrases like *He's a Stud, She's a 'Slut': Smash the Stigma!* painted on their placards. Vanessa suspected her mum would have joined them too – she was close to Emi – if she wasn't worried it would risk her husband's job at the farm.

The woman disappeared out of sight and Vanessa strolled over to the officer who'd called out. She crouched down to look at the tiny black and grey mining bee he'd found lying on its back and carefully picked it up with her forceps, placing it in a phial and turning the phial around in her fingers to examine it. 'It's still pliable so it probably only died within the past hour, meaning it's unlikely to be the one that stung our victim. Nice find though,' she said, smiling at the officer. 'Let's continue looking.'

A few more dead bees were found, several scraps of rubbish too, including a used condom, which was taken in for evidence. Finally, though, something interesting *did* come up. Another dead bee, but this one had been dead longer than the other one judging by the stiffening up of its body parts. Most telling though, was that its stinger was missing.

'Could it be the bee that stung Benjamin?' Paul asked, leaning over Vanessa's shoulder to look at it.

'Maybe,' she replied. 'We should get it tested. Might be a trace of blood or skin fragments on it, if we're lucky.'

'Great. Let's carry on looking for another hour, shall we?'

Over the next hour, in the growing heat, the officers scoured that part of the ridge for any further clues. But there was nothing else. When they headed back to the car park, a sleek-looking silver car had joined the collection of police cars.

'That's a Porsche Panamera,' OS observed. 'And guess what? They have a larger than average tyre size, much like supercars.'

'Like the tyre marks found in the manor gardens.' Paul went up to the car and peered inside at its immaculate interior.

'Looks new,' OS said as he joined him. 'Bloody expensive too.'

'Could it be Indra Hudson's?' Vanessa asked as she eyed the warehouse.

'Let's find out.' Paul walked towards the offices. But when he tried the door, it was locked. Vanessa looked at her watch. It wasn't even nine in the morning yet. She watched as Paul got his police radio out. 'Can I get a PNC check on a—'

'Why are you all so interested in my car?'

Vanessa turned to see Indra Hudson emerging from the office, her keys in her hands. As she passed Vanessa, a small breeze carried along a whiff of the perfume she was wearing, a strange truffly-floral scent.

Tom Ford's Black Ophelia.

12

'Nice car,' Paul said to Indra. 'Don't you usually drive a Jag?'

'It's new,' Indra replied. 'I had delivery of it at the beginning of this week.' Paul exchanged a look with OS as they both caught a whiff of her distinctive perfume.

'You know, I've always liked this model of Porsche,' OS said as he appraised it. 'Decent amount of space in the boot, too,' he added meaningfully. 'Maybe I'll consider one as my next ride.'

Indra raised an eyebrow. 'You *do* realise how much they cost?'

'No, no, you're right,' OS said, 'too much of a luxury for plebs like us, hey, Boss?'

Paul smiled.

Indra looked at her watch. 'If this is about the break-in on Sunday then—'

'Break-in?' Paul asked, interrupting her.

'Well . . . yes. Isn't that why you're here?' Indra replied. 'I reported it yesterday morning, but understandably police attention was diverted elsewhere on Monday. Those *murders*. Just terrible.' She shook her head, her glossy sheen of long black hair barely moving as she did.

'How was this missed?' Paul asked his sergeant. 'I asked you to check on any reports from the weekend.'

'It wasn't missed, Boss,' OS replied, looking slightly panicked. 'But we didn't think it was something to flag.'

Paul suppressed his frustration. 'I think we're going to have to have a look inside your offices.'

Indra frowned. 'Really? Nothing was actually stolen.'

Paul matched her frown. That made it even stranger. 'Yes, really.'

'You don't think this is related to the murders, do you?' Indra asked in a horrified voice.

'Could be. It's a complex case, and we're having to explore every single avenue.'

'But I can't see how a break-in at my offices could be related.'

Paul's eyes glided over to Indra's car, then towards the ridge. 'Can I ask where you were on Saturday evening and overnight?'

Indra looked taken aback. 'Can *I* ask why you want to know?'

'Because I'm a police detective asking you, a member of the public, a question.'

Indra took in a breath, composing herself. 'I was sleeping, then I was in the office the next morning.'

'Can Tom verify you were at home overnight?' Paul asked, referring to her husband.

'He was away until yesterday morning. Look, this is ridiculous. If you want to question me further, I'll have to call my solicitor.' As she went to do just that, Paul noted her hands were trembling slightly. Was she hiding something? Convenient that Tom was away around the time the men disappeared, too. But Indra Hudson, a suspect? He couldn't see it.

'No need to disturb your solicitor,' Paul said. 'Not now anyway. We'd just like to look inside. With your permission, of course?'

Indra considered it, before nodding. 'That's fine, I suppose. It's quiet at the moment, just me and my PA, Avery. But more people will arrive soon. Shall I ask them not to come in?'

'Might be worth it.'

Interesting how she was being so helpful now. She hurried towards the offices as Paul gestured for Vanessa and the other officers to follow. Indra held the door open for them all, watching Vanessa with interest as she passed.

'Please, come in,' Indra said. 'There's a water cooler and a coffee machine. You can all help yourselves.'

Paul led the way in, taking in the floor-to-ceiling windows and exposed brickwork. Some money had clearly been spent on the place. He wondered what Helen would think about it all. She hated Indra and all the capitalist values she stood for.

'Look around,' Paul instructed his officers as Indra strode over to an androgynous-looking wisp of a person with blue hair cropped close to their head and unnaturally long eyelashes. Paul always felt on edge around people like this kid, as though he might say the wrong thing or refer to them with the wrong pronoun. Helen teased him about it, telling him he'd better catch up with the twenty-first century considering he had two girls who'd be teenagers in a few years.

'We need to make some calls,' he heard Indra say as she pulled her PA into a room, slamming the door shut behind them.

'See if you can find any blowflies or maggots,' Paul asked Vanessa in a low voice. 'Basically, any evidence of a body being kept here.'

Vanessa nodded. 'It would make sense. A place to kill and keep bodies in the dead of night. But Indra Hudson? Unless she had help . . .'

'Yeah, I'm not sure either. But it's something. You noticed the perfume she was wearing too, right?'

Vanessa nodded. 'Tom Ford's Black Ophelia. Selma mentioned Benjamin's mysterious lunches.'

'Quite. Right, let's get on with it.'

Paul began strolling around, casting his eyes over the state-of-the-art desks and high-spec computers. Glass-fronted offices sprouted off from the main area with large-screen displays and touchscreen whiteboards within. While passing by one room, Paul noticed dozens of sketches pinned to the walls that looked like proposed layouts for a revitalised butterfly farm. So she really was serious about it. Helen wouldn't be happy. It *would* explain lunches with Benjamin, though. Maybe he was trying to negotiate a buying price for Indra?

'Boss!' a voice called out. OS was standing by a large office, which looked directly out over the view at the back. Paul walked over. It was clearly Indra's office, the walls painted in soft pastels with accents of silver adding a touch of glamour. In the centre of the room was a large, ornate desk. Several framed photos sat on it, including graduate photos of Indra's grown-up children.

OS led him to the desk where a beautifully engraved hardback booklet lay. 'It's got a bunch of photos in it of insects,' he said. 'Pages of them. There are prices on each page too, like the insects are being *sold*?'

'Where did you find it?'

'There.' OS gestured to a small gap between the desk and the filing cabinet beneath it.

'Think it's related to illegal insect trading?' OS asked.

'There's one person who might know.' Paul leaned his head out of the door. 'Bugs!'

13

Vanessa strolled into Indra Hudson's plush office to find Paul and OS standing over the booklet, its embossed cover adorned with a wreath of flowers imprinted with insect symbols.

'We found this,' Paul said. 'Could it be related to illegal insect trading?'

Vanessa picked the brochure up with her gloved hands, noticing it had a waffle feel to it. She then opened the booklet, finding page after page of high-resolution photographs of insects and cocoons. Among the photos was one of a tiny emerald-green tansy beetle, the same rare breed the fragments of shell she'd seen under Simon Taylor's shoulder might belong to. A small symbol was etched into the back of the brochure: a moth emerging from a cocoon, like the mural she'd seen on the wall of Benjamin's secret room.

'These are *rare* insects now, sadly,' Vanessa murmured. 'And totally illegal to sell in the UK.'

'Have you seen anything like this before?' Paul asked.

'Not a brochure quite like this, but I have come across some illegal insect trading cases.' Vanessa paused on a page featuring a photo of a silky cocoon the colour of sand with a bulbous body and tapered end. 'This is the cocoon of the giant atlas moth. They're illegal to sell in the US. The species is already in rapid decline because of habitat loss.'

'Going pretty cheap then,' OS said. 'Just a hundred quid.'

'Not when you're selling thousands to unethical hobbyists,' Vanessa replied. 'It mounts up.'

'How does it work?' Paul asked, looking over her shoulder, lip curled in disgust as he took in the insects. 'Is it like a mail-order catalogue?'

Vanessa shook her head. 'There won't be any clue within of who produced this catalogue, or how to procure the creatures. See the codes beneath each photo, though?' She pointed to the line of numbers and letters beneath a photo of a blue morpho butterfly. 'I wouldn't be surprised if they correspond with codes on the dark web.' She looked through the door towards the room Indra had disappeared into with her assistant. 'Looks like we have an illegal insect trading issue in Greensands, and our local marketing entrepreneur could be involved. It would explain the clandestine lunches with Benjamin.'

Paul picked up the booklet and walked towards the office Indra was in, gesturing for Vanessa to follow. He knocked on the door, and Indra answered, her eyes alighting on the brochure. Vanessa couldn't read her expression.

'We just found this in your office,' Paul said, holding it up. 'How did you get your hands on it?'

'It came in the post the other day,' Indra replied without missing a beat. 'I have *no* idea why.'

Bullshit, Vanessa thought.

'Pull the other one,' Paul said.

Indra sighed. 'Honestly, as a highly respected marketing leader I get stuff like this *all* the time.'

Highly respected marketing leader. Vanessa now understood why Helen wasn't a fan of the woman. The disdain obviously showed on her face because Indra looked at her sharply.

'Who *are* you, by the way?' she asked Vanessa.

'This is Doctor Marwood,' Paul explained. 'She's helping with the case.'

Indra's eyes widened. 'As in, Tony Marwood's daughter?'

Vanessa nodded. 'Hello, Indra.'

'You're a forensics officer now?' Indra asked.

'Forensic entomologist,' Vanessa said. 'Hence why this brochure advertising rare insects is of *particular* interest to me,' she added.

'Have you ever bought exotic animals illegally, Indra?' Paul asked.

'Of course not!' Indra replied in an indignant tone. 'I'm a legitimate businesswoman.' She made sure to stare at Vanessa as she said that. Vanessa didn't react, just pinned Indra down with an impenetrable gaze. Indra looked away. 'I don't know what you're trying to achieve with all this—' Indra gestured around her at the officers searching the building. 'But should one strange little brochure really take you away from doing what's most important: tracking down the person who killed four of our beloved villagers?'

'Yes, it should,' Paul replied, 'when those beloved villagers were killed using techniques inspired by insects.'

Vanessa was intrigued to see Indra didn't look shocked by that revelation. But then, knowing Greensands, the details would have already got out about the nature of the murders.

'And you think I'm involved?' Indra asked incredulously. 'Because of *this* little book?'

'Not just that,' Paul said. 'A car similar to yours was seen on Oberlin Manor land the day Benjamin was believed to have been killed.' He looked over his shoulder at the ridge outside. 'A potential clue linking his body to the ridge outside has been found too.'

Indra's dark face turned grey.

'Plus we believe you enjoyed a few lunches recently with Benjamin Oberlin?' OS asked.

'Yes, of course. We've been discussing the reopening of the butterfly farm.'

'When's the last time you saw him?' Paul asked.

'Saturday, for lunch.' Indra's face hardened. 'Is this an official interview? Do I need to call my solicitor after all?'

Paul's expression matched hers. 'I am trying to put together a picture of a murder victim's last hours. You're not willing to help with that?'

Vanessa was enjoying this, watching her old friend at work. He really had come a long way from that annoying little bug-killing kid in the playground.

Indra blinked. 'Of course I'm willing to help. But I'd rather this all be done officially. I will definitely call my solicitor now.'

Paul smoothed his palm over his stubbled cheek. He looked exhausted. 'Fine, call them,' he said.

Indra walked away, putting her phone to her ear.

'So, what do you think?' OS asked Vanessa when Indra was out of sight. 'My bet's on her and Benjamin getting involved in some clandestine creepy-crawly commerce.'

'Looks likely,' Vanessa replied as she watched an officer bag the brochure up as evidence.

'But how would that link to the three other men being murdered?' Paul mused.

'The insect trade isn't like selling a dodgy designer bag on eBay,' Vanessa said. 'It's often bigger than that, pulling in gangs from overseas.'

'Yeah,' OS said. 'Maybe something kicked off that meant these men ended up paying the consequences?'

Vanessa frowned. 'Even so, I still think the way the men were posed is too carefully planned for gangs like that. And can you really see Michael, Simon and Tim getting caught up with anything shady?'

OS shrugged. 'Times are tough.'

'I think their families would have had an inkling, though,' Paul said. 'Nothing came up when I talked to them yesterday. But there's definitely something here.'

Indra walked over again. 'My solicitor is advising me to say nothing else without him. We'd be happy to come down to the police station to talk at your convenience, though, Detective Truss. But unless you have a search warrant, I'd like to get on with my very busy day.'

Vanessa could see Paul grappling with what to do. It was a precarious line to tread between making sure all potential witnesses and suspects were questioned, but also ensuring he didn't step out of place, especially with a woman as connected and moneyed as Indra.

'Fine,' he said. 'I'll be in touch.' As Indra walked away, Paul's phone buzzed. He got it out to read a text, then peered at Vanessa. 'Mio says the Home Office forensic pathologist has carried out the post-mortems. That's bloody quick, to be honest, but this is a suspected triple murder. Mio was with her when she did it. She suggested we visit her to go through the findings. Makes sense you tag along, what with the spider silk and mate plugging stuff.'

Vanessa took in a deep breath. She'd been to a few post-mortem suites in her time. Even enjoyed some of them. The human body was fascinating, after all, especially when it intersected with the insect world.

But this was going to be tough.

'Of course,' she replied. 'Let's go.'

14

The aluminium table. The whitewashed walls. That acidic stench of chemicals and bleach. Paul could never quite get used to the sight of a post-mortem examination room, no matter how many times he'd had the misfortune to find himself observing one. The worst part was always the brutal way the chest cavities were opened. It just didn't feel right, watching something so terrible being done to another human, even in death. It was going to be worse now. He knew these men.

He sighed heavily as he swung through the doors of the viewing room. Vanessa was already in the examination room with Mio, both of them talking animatedly. As Mio gestured, a strand of her blunt, ear-length grey bob peeked out. 'I'm giving the middle finger to hair dye,' was how she'd put it last time Paul had seen her without her PPE on. It was a strange sight, seeing the two women together. Vanessa was half a foot taller and several times curvier than the petite Mio. It was interesting to see someone from Vanessa's life post-Greensands, too. Seeing the camaraderie between the two women, it was clear they were great friends.

Mio gestured at the hint of spider's web on Vanessa's neck as Vanessa adjusted the neckline of her scrubs. 'New tattoos, I see,' Paul heard Mio say through the sliding window dividing the two rooms.

'I got it for my thirty-ninth birthday,' Vanessa replied.

'You know this one gets a new tattoo for every birthday,' Mio said to Paul.

'I didn't,' Paul replied, feeling that gap between the Vanessa he once knew and the one he saw before him now.

'I was there for her first,' Mio said with pride.

'She fainted,' Vanessa added with a lift of her dark brow.

'Oh come on, it was only for a brief moment! So, let's get on with it, shall we? The post-mortems have already been carried out on each of the deceased individually. I thought it would be useful to have them together now.'

They all grew quiet as they took in the four bodies that lay on the aluminium slabs, their dignity covered by white sheets.

'You OK, Detective?' Mio asked him. 'I know they were friends of yours. You could have sent that beefy sergeant instead. I need some eye candy.'

'Na, let's do this.'

Mio walked over to Tim Holmes, the butterfly farm's former truck driver and Paul's drinking buddy. He lay still and silent – his greying hair neat against his head, his once non-stop talking mouth slack. Some officers said bodies looked like mannequins in situations like this. But to Paul, they almost felt more human in their vulnerability.

Vanessa gave Paul a sympathetic look. It made him feel worse in some ways, reminding him she hadn't seen the man Tim had become. All she could see now was how he'd changed physically over the years, not how he'd developed into a great friend and father.

Paul shook his head. What a waste of a good man. He made a silent vow: *I'm going to find the fucker who did this.*

'So, I have five things to tell you,' Mio said, holding up her small hands, her fingers splayed out as her brown eyes regarded Paul and Vanessa. 'One, we think a muscle relaxant drug was used on all four men.'

'You've already had toxicology results back?' Vanessa asked.

Mio laughed. 'Are you fucking joking? You know these things take weeks.'

'In a quadruple murder case?' Paul asked.

'Of course I've asked for toxicology to be expedited. But I can't promise anything. In the meantime, I noticed this.' She pointed to some discolouration around Tim's mouth. 'I've seen it before, specifically in a suicide case where someone took an overdose of atracurium. It's a neuromuscular blocking agent commonly used in anaesthesia. I think it may have been used to incapacitate all three men, possibly Benjamin Oberlin too. The Home Office pathologist agrees with me. It explains how the incisions and the orifice stuffing were done while the men were still alive.'

Vanessa and Paul exchanged an appalled look.

'They were still *alive* while it happened?' Paul asked.

'Yes,' Mio replied with a sigh. 'It's pretty clear from the tissue reaction, clotting and bruising around the incisions in the first men's stomachs, and a wound on the fourth man's lips. It all suggests the likelihood their hearts were still pumping when the cuts were made.'

'They would have been aware of it, too,' Vanessa said sadly. 'Atracurium paralyses the body, but not the mind.'

Paul curled his hands into fists as he imagined the horror and helplessness the men must have felt to be fully aware of what was being done to them.

'Number two,' Mio said, gently lifting Tim's arm and pointing to a red mark on the skin at the back. 'There are skin indents like this on the back of each of the four men's limbs. Signs of mud, too, on the back of their bodies. This points to them having been wheeled via something like a wheelbarrow to their resting places.'

Paul nodded. 'That makes sense. Your favourite jock sergeant called me earlier to say they found some small tyre indents at the butterfly farm. What about time of death?'

'That's point three. Once your assistant reports back on her findings from the insect specimens you collected, Vanessa, and any temperature data, we'll have a better idea. But I know that can take weeks.'

'Weeks?' Paul asked. 'Jesus, you scientists need to speed up.'

Vanessa rolled her eyes. 'And you coppers need to be more patient. Olivia will need to rear any eggs and larvae found at the crime scene in the lab until they're adult flies. Depending on species, this can take anything from weeks to even a couple of months. The full report won't be ready until that rearing process has finished.'

'Can't you just pop the maggots under a microscope to identify their species?' Paul asked.

'Some,' Vanessa said. 'But most maggots and eggs look alike. It's not until they've grown into adult flies that we're able to officially identify their species.'

'And we need to know the species because . . . ?' Paul asked, looking slightly confused.

'So we can figure out when the eggs were first laid on the bodies, and therefore when the bodies were placed at the crime scene,' Vanessa replied. 'Each species of fly has a different life cycle. So in summer temperatures, eggs can take ten to thirty hours to hatch depending on species, and larvae can take three days to thirty days to develop, again depending on species. If we can confirm the eggs we collected, and the larvae that hatched from them in the lab, are from a species *known* for developing quickly, then that would suggest the bodies were there some time after the men left the pub.'

'She's right,' Mio said. 'If the right scientific rigour isn't applied, you'll be the ones moaning to us when our reports don't stand up in court. What Vanessa won't tell you, though, is that someone as experienced as her will deep down have a sense of time of death just by looking at the insect evidence at a crime scene. But officially, she can't tell you until she knows for sure. In fact, I'm sure she knew early on what I'm guessing now from rigor mortis and tissue degeneration.'

Vanessa couldn't help but smile. Mio was right.

'And that guess is?' Paul asked.

'All these men died a day, maybe more, before their bodies were found,' Mio replied. 'Maybe all four died around the same time, too.'

'So they *were* most likely killed in the early hours of Sunday, a couple of hours or so after witnesses say the first men left the pub on Saturday night?' Paul asked.

Mio nodded. 'And if Olivia's report can confirm that in a few weeks, then we can be even more sure.'

'And Benjamin is likely to have been killed with them, but placed at a different crime scene?' Paul asked.

'I can't say for sure,' Mio replied. 'But that would be my guess. Now on to point four. Cause of death. Our suspicion for the first three men is an overdose of atracurium. At least it wouldn't have been too traumatic in the end. Not for this poor man though.' Mio gestured to Benjamin's naked, pale body. The infested cotton wool had been removed from his mouth so he looked more like himself. Paul noticed Vanessa close her eyes briefly. 'His cause of death was asphyxia by suffocation due to obstruction of respiratory orifices.' Mio pointed to four separate evidence bags featuring wads of yellow-flecked cotton wool. 'Cotton wool found in his eyes, mouth, throat and anus. Judging by some superficial wounds around the orifices, they were rammed in.'

'The stuffing of substances,' Vanessa said, eyes still closed. 'The muffling and the wadding and the smothering. The *ultimate* control.'

'Yes, that's what this is usually about.' Mio's voice was soft as she regarded her friend. 'Control. Another interesting point related to that, point five: initial observations suggest there was no sexual interference, including no sign of semen. I know that was a question you had, Detective Truss, considering the connection with insect mating rituals?'

Paul nodded. That was something, at least. No further violation before death.

Mio turned to Vanessa. 'So, I know you've preserved samples from the crime scenes. But I managed to preserve more maggots – or larvae as you would call them – from the bodies here and took a quick look myself.'

Vanessa followed her gaze towards two microscopes. 'Don't usually see microscopes in the post-mortem suite.'

'We wheel them in for special guests,' Mio replied. 'There's something interesting I want to show you. Shall we do some maggot wrestling? Let's see if you notice it before I do my big reveal.'

Vanessa smiled at the challenge. 'You're on.'

15

Vanessa followed Mio towards the metal table at the end of the room, her mind still reeling with the knowledge the men had been *alive* as they were cut into . . . and Benjamin had still been alive when he was stuffed. The horror he must have felt. The confusion. She dreaded to think how Damon would react when he found out.

'Let's look at the maggots I obtained from Benjamin Oberlin's body.' Mio opened a secure cabinet and pulled out a labelled container, carefully opening it to reveal another container with several maggots inside. Good. Vanessa liked it when specimens were placed in a secondary container. There had been an incident or two in the past where specimens from a crime scene had been damaged when someone dropped the tube.

Vanessa lifted the clear tube out and held it up to the light, examining the larvae within. They were at a later stage of their development than the ones she'd retrieved from the scene, left to feed on the deceased flesh here in the post-mortem room and grow. The live maggots that had been transported from Benjamin's crime scene to Olivia the day before with some cat food would most likely be this size too, around five millimetres long with a creamy white hue to them.

She carefully used forceps to take one squirming larva out, placing it onto a white tray as Paul regarded it with a look of disgust. 'Christ, they're minging little beasts.'

'I prefer to think of them as one of the most important creatures on planet Earth,' Vanessa said as she placed some under the microscope. 'They're the clean-up crew of the natural world, breaking down dead plant and animal material to give soil a nutrient boost.'

'Plus, they're a vital food source for many species of animal,' Mio added. 'The actual kings and queens of biodiversity, really.'

Paul rolled his eyes. 'OK, admins of the Larvae Lover Club. I get it.'

Vanessa smiled, shaking her head as she lowered her face towards the microscope.

'I'm afraid my state-bought microscopes won't do as good a job as the magnifying mystery machines you'll have in New York,' Mio said. 'I bet they have scanning electron microscopes there.'

'They do have one, apparently.'

'Ergh.'

'See, this is why you should have taken up that offer of a Skype chat with Bronagh,' Vanessa said. 'You would have got the chance to work with many magnifying mystery machines.'

'No thank you, honey,' Mio quipped back. 'I'm quite happy with my government-issue peek-a-boo peepers.'

'Don't forget the cut-back pension plan that could rival a rusty tin can,' Paul said.

Vanessa fiddled with the focus knobs until the larva came into focus. There. She could see *exactly* what Mio was referring to. She smiled.

'She's fucking figured out my reveal already,' she heard Mio whisper to Paul.

'I have,' Vanessa confirmed. 'We'd need to get an entomotoxicologist to confirm. I can recommend someone. But from what I can see, these larvae fed on something toxic.'

'The atracurium?' Paul asked.

'No. Come and look.' Vanessa beckoned Paul over to the microscope and he squinted, clearly trying to make sense of the tiny creatures before him. 'I see . . . a maggot,' he began, a hint of scepticism in his voice.

'Look closer,' Vanessa said. 'Notice anything peculiar about its body?'

'There's something on it,' he replied. 'Little markings, like it's been in some kind of scuffle?'

Vanessa nodded. 'Exactly that. Those markings suggest it's ingested something toxic, especially around the mouthparts and spiracles. Now, let's take it a step further.' She upped the power of the microscope. 'Look closely at the body. Do you notice any unusual structures or substances?'

'Yeah, there are these tiny hair-like structures all over it.'

'Yes,' Vanessa said. 'They're called trichomes. They're found on plants, often as a defence mechanism.'

'Particularly toxic plants,' Mio added.

'Specifically,' Vanessa said, '*Atropa belladonna*. Commonly known as deadly nightshade.'

Paul moved away from the microscope lens. 'I see. But that's pretty common around these parts, right?'

Vanessa shook her head. 'Not in the places where the four bodies were found. I know for a fact Arthur Oberlin went to great lengths to ensure it didn't grow in the butterfly farm or in the manor's ground. Gastrointestinal distress and seizures aren't good PR for a tourist attraction.'

'But it's been years since the farm and manor have been tended to,' Paul said.

'I remember my dad saying Arthur used some quite radical techniques,' Vanessa said. 'Plus, I would have noticed if there was any deadly nightshade at the crime scenes. It's very distinctive. Maybe the men were located where deadly nightshade is prevalent before they were moved to their ultimate resting places? The plant would have somehow got into whichever orifice this was found in.' She turned to Mio. 'So, which orifice was it?'

Mio nodded. 'The mouth. It wasn't noticeable at first but after seeing the evidence on this pretty little maggot, I took another look.'

She reached over for an evidence bag and laid it on the surface. Inside was a small, drooping, soggy branch of deadly nightshade, its glossy, asymmetrical leaves playing host to purple-black flowers and glistening berries.

'It appears to have been shoved down Benjamin's throat,' Mio said.

'Jesus,' Paul whispered. 'But he definitely didn't die from ingesting it?'

'No,' Mio said. 'I am certain cause of death was asphyxia.'

It occurred to Vanessa that Benjamin may have preferred death by deadly nightshade, joining an illustrious group of kings and emperors who had succumbed to its deceptive allure.

Then she noticed something. 'It looks like it's newly plucked, judging by the roots and mud.'

'Yes, I noticed that too,' Mio said.

'So whoever did this could have done it while next to some deadly nightshade?' Paul suggested.

'Well, the plant could have been uprooted in advance for the sole purpose of doing this,' Mio mused, 'but if I had to place a bet, I think you're right – it would have been within reach.'

'Is there deadly nightshade along the ridge with the mining bees?' Paul asked Vanessa.

'I didn't see any deadly nightshade there,' Vanessa said with a sigh. 'Though there could be some in the forest.'

'Anywhere else?' Paul asked.

Vanessa thought of the woman she'd noticed watching them from the forest earlier. 'Why not ask Emi Craviso?' she suggested.

'The Butterfly Witch?' Paul asked.

'A witch?' Mio said. 'This case is definitely one for my autobiography.'

Vanessa nodded. 'From what I recall, she was pretty knowledgeable about the plants and foliage around here.'

'OK, I'll get Selma on it. She loves all that witchy stuff.' Paul's phone buzzed. He quickly put it to his ear. 'OS, what's the latest?' He listened, then shook his head. 'Fucking great.'

'What's up?' Vanessa asked.

'The media have arrived in full force in Greensands. It's a nightmare, apparently.'

16

Vanessa steered her car down the main road off Greensands. Already she could see several camera crews gathered on the green in the distance, some talking to camera. *Great.*

She wasn't a fan of the media, especially after the way they'd acted when her brother disappeared. Even back in the nineties, before twenty-four-hour news and online reporting had really swung into action, the attention had been ferocious. A sweet-looking twelve-year-old boy seeming to disappear into thin air was juicy fodder. Even better, the fact his mother wasn't living in the family home at the time *and* she didn't come to Greensands to help with the search whipped up a great deal of drama and speculation. It was tough for Vanessa. Fifteen and full of teenage hormones had made it even worse.

A small voice wondered now: maybe part of Vanessa had enjoyed that element of the coverage? Maybe it reflected how *she* felt. Why *had* her mother not rushed to Greensands after learning Vincent was missing? Sure, she was being kept up to date over the phone and she sounded reasonably frantic during the times Vanessa spoke to her. But she wasn't frantic enough to leave Brighton, was she? It was wrong. The press knew it . . . and Vanessa knew it. It was why Vanessa had pulled away from her mother, refusing to take her calls anymore, not even opening the birthday and Christmas presents she sent in the post.

Now the press was back in Greensands. Would they join the dots and realise the forensic entomologist working on the case was the missing boy's sister? Eventually. In fact, maybe they had already. The longer she could avoid them, the better. So when she stepped out of her car, she quickly walked across the car park towards the B&B entrance, hoping none of the journalists hovering outside the car park noticed her. But it was too late. She could already see the shadow of a camera-holding journalist stretching across the ground like a three-headed cyclops.

'Doctor Marwood!' a young female voice called out.

In the reflection of the glass of the door ahead of her, Vanessa could see a young woman wearing a pair of denim shorts and patterned vest top walking towards her, holding out a microphone, not a camera. Vanessa frowned. She didn't *look* like your usual reporter. But then Vanessa didn't look like your usual forensic entomologist, either.

She sighed and turned around. 'Yes?'

'It's Heather Fala from *Dark Deeds Dissected* podcast. Do I have permission to record this conversation?'

Ah, *now* Vanessa understood the casual attire. It didn't matter if you wore a bin bag or a prom dress when presenting a podcast. It was all about the *voice*, and Heather Fala sure had the perfect voice for podcasts: confident, clear, *loud*. Vanessa had only listened to the show once, when an old colleague had been a special guest to explain the nuances of being a forensic botanist. In response to his brief mention of forensic entomology, Heather had referred to the field as 'maggot whispering'. Not exactly the most flattering description.

'No, you don't have permission.'

Heather lowered her microphone. 'Oh. Well, I live a few villages away,' Heather said, slightly out of breath. 'Literally jumped in my car and steamed up here – *so* sorry about the clothes.' She gestured down to her ripped shorts. 'Though I didn't expect a forensic entomologist to be wearing green velvet creepers and a skull-patterned blouse, but here we are. *How* have I not heard of you before?'

'I prefer to do my work behind the scenes.' Vanessa opened the door to the pub and stepped in. 'Speaking of which, I need to make some calls.'

Heather grabbed the door before it fully closed. 'I've always been dead keen on the field of forensic entomology!'

'Didn't you once refer to it as "maggot whispering"?'

'Oh my gosh, no offence intended! You guys are absolute legends and in a case like this, your work is bloody essential. I'd be over the moon if I could just grab a quick chat with you about The Cobweb Killer.'

Vanessa paused, looking over her shoulder at the girl. 'The Cobweb Killer? Isn't that a bit . . . hammy?'

'Hammy? Catchy, more like! So, about that chat . . .'

'I'm afraid I can't.'

'But we've spoken to other residents. It'd be great to add your voice.'

'I'm not a resident.'

'But you *were*,' Heather said. 'Wasn't it your brother who disappeared, like, twenty-five years ago?' Vanessa grimaced. 'That's got to be tough,' Heather continued, 'coming back after all these years? And the word on the street is you're tight with Damon Oberlin, so double whammy.'

Vanessa turned to face the woman, crossing her arms and enjoying the full four inches of height she had over her. 'I'm trying to be polite. But seriously, can you just go away?'

Heather sighed, reaching into her pink Panda-shaped backpack. For someone who loved the dark stuff, she sure liked her accessories fluffy and pastel-coloured. 'I get it. But if you ever want to talk, hit me up.' She handed Vanessa her business card with a wink.

Vanessa shoved the card into her pocket then headed inside, leaving the enthusiastic podcaster smiling slightly manically at her through the glass panes of the door. At least she didn't come in. Vanessa walked up to her room, noticing the bed had been made and the pillows were fluffed. A vase of fresh flowers sat on the bedside table too, bright violet lilies filling the room with a pleasant fragrance. Even her clothes from the night before, which she had left in a pile on the floor, had been neatly folded and placed on a chair. Sharon must have done all this. She knew violet lilies were Vanessa's favourites. For a moment, Vanessa allowed herself to imagine what it would have been like to have someone like Sharon as a mother.

How *lucky* Michael had been.

Her phone beeped with a message from Paul. She opened it to see he was sharing a link to a *Daily Mail* article about the murders. Vanessa clicked on the link, shaking her head when she saw a photo of her near the bottom of the piece. The caption:

Glamorous forensics bug expert and former Greensands resident Doctor Vanessa Marwood has been brought in to help.

Her phone let out a loud ring as though protesting the headline. Vanessa put it to her ear. 'Hello?'

'Vanessa!' It was Helen. 'Still on for dinner?'

'Absolutely.'

'Great. I can't guarantee you'll see Paul. He's about to hold a press conference. But you'll get to see me and the twin tornadoes. And—' She paused.

'What's up?'

'I need to talk to you about something. Six still good?'

Vanessa frowned. That didn't sound good. 'Sure. Six is perfect.'

17

Paul watched the journalists waiting for the press conference to begin. They reminded him of a swarm of flies hovering over a pile of rotting fruit, buzzing and jostling for the best position.

Beside him, Fiona scanned the crowds, her blue eyes sharp and focused. 'You ready for this?' she asked him.

He gave her a grunt back. He was still angry with her for releasing Damon Oberlin. The sight of that smug bastard walking out of the station earlier had made him feel sicker than the four-day-old croissant he'd wolfed down in a hurry earlier.

'You're still brooding about us letting Damon Oberlin go, aren't you, you stubborn bastard?'

Paul didn't answer. Truth was, he knew he didn't have enough to keep Damon in. But still, he hadn't been delighted to come in that morning to discover Fiona had released him.

'You know there wasn't enough evidence to charge him,' Fiona said. 'Anyway, he was causing more damage than good being here with this lot slinking all over the place.' She gestured to the room full of media. 'Trust me, you'll be thanking me in a minute. Speaking of which.' She looked at her watch. 'Let's do this so we can get back to what we do best: investigating.'

They both walked out to face a barrage of flashing cameras and shouting reporters. It took a while for Fiona to get to her seat. She was what Paul's mum would call a 'generous build'. So generous, she had her own chair for occasions like this. When they were finally seated, a hush fell over the room.

'Good afternoon,' Fiona began, her enjoyment of amateur dramatics showing in the way she projected her voice around the room. 'I'm Chief Superintendent Fiona Wright, and this is the detective in charge of this case: Detective Chief Inspector Paul Truss. As you all know, we're currently investigating the tragic murders of four men in the village of Greensands, Simon Taylor, Tim Holmes, Michael Regan and Benjamin Oberlin. Our deepest sympathies go out to the families and friends of the victims during this difficult time.'

She paused for a moment, that unnerving stare of hers surveying the room. 'We understand that this is a deeply troubling time for the people of Greensands, and we want to reassure residents that we're doing everything in our power to solve these crimes quickly and effectively. We ask for your continued support and patience as we work *tirelessly* to bring an end to this devastating chapter in the village's history.'

Paul had to give it to her. She knew how to command a crowd. 'We urge anyone who may have information about these murders,' she continued, 'no matter how seemingly insignificant, to contact the police immediately via our incident hotline.' She gestured to the number displayed on the screen behind her. 'Your cooperation is vital in helping us bring the person responsible for these crimes to justice, and ensuring the safety of this close-knit community.' She turned to Paul. 'DCI Truss will now give an overview of what we know so far. Then we can take some questions.'

Resisting the urge to start with 'fuck all, frankly', Paul gave some brief details about the crime scenes, ending with: 'To confirm, we have reason to believe that these heinous crimes are connected, and are currently pursuing several leads while working closely with residents and businesses to gather crucial information that will assist in our investigation. Questions?'

The questions came fast and furious, with reporters shouting over each other to get themselves heard. The media relations person who'd briefed Paul earlier pointed at each of the journalists in turn.

'Jimmy Thyme from *The Sun*,' a middle-aged man with a round face and a receding hairline said. 'Can you comment on rumours that Damon Oberlin was brought in for questioning over the murders late last night?'

Paul tried not to roll his eyes. He knew Damon would be the first topic to come up. In fact, he bet this was the very question each journalist in the room would have asked if they'd been chosen first.

'As a key witness to his brother Benjamin Oberlin's last hours,' Paul said, 'he has been helping us with our investigation.'

Jimmy gave Paul a cynical look. 'He still *helping* you with the investigation down in the cells, Detective Truss?'

'I have no idea where Damon Oberlin is, but he isn't here,' Paul answered, noticing how smug Fiona looked to be proven right. The journalist frowned, clearly annoyed the little scoop he thought he had was now outdated.

'Next,' Paul said, keen to get this over with.

More questions were thrown at Paul, most of which he couldn't answer.

What is the suspected motive behind these murders?

Can you provide any details about the method of murder? Were any weapons or specific techniques used?

Have you found any forensic evidence that could help identify the killer?

Are there any indications of a possible serial killer or organised crime involvement in these murders?

Are there any updates on the timeline of events leading up to the murders? Have any witnesses come forward with new information?

As the questions were thrown at him, Paul felt the weight of the investigation pressing down on him. This whole thing just made him realise how many questions he *didn't* have an answer to. The sooner he could get back to the investigation, the better. In fact, once the big names had got their questions out, he began to stand up, the frustration of having to deal with these goons too much. But Fiona grabbed his arm, forcing him back down as the media officer pointed to a woman with brightly dyed hair and denim shorts. How the *hell* had she got in? And what was that hair colour supposed to be: blue rinse for millennials?

'Yep, go ahead,' he said with a sigh.

She held a large microphone out, the recording light blinking on and off. 'Heather Fala from the *Dark Deeds Dissected* podcast,' she said proudly.

Paul noticed Fiona purse her lips. 'How the *hell* did a podcaster get in here?' she hissed under her breath.

'This is what happens when you hire millennials, Boss,' Paul whispered back, eyeing the young media relations officer.

'First, I want to say thanks for all your hard work trying to track down The Cobweb Killer,' the podcaster said.

Paul exchanged a look with Fiona. The bloody Cobweb Killer?

'Are you aware that a local resident named Abe Abbott was in a relationship with Benjamin Oberlin?'

Paul tried to hide his surprise at the question. Ricky Abbott's son? He'd heard nothing about this. Clearly the other reporters hadn't either, as they exchanged surprised looks. Fiona kept her gaze straight ahead, but Paul could tell from the way she was curling her meaty hands that she wanted to slam her fists down on the table and ask why the hell the team didn't know this already.

'As I said,' Paul replied carefully, 'we are investigating all leads in this case, and will follow up on any information we receive. I think that's enough questions now; we have a lot of work to do.'

Paul walked out of the room with Fiona and headed over to the young media officer. 'Get that podcaster to stay behind for a bit, yeah? Do it discreetly.'

'And next time, check with me before inviting a podcaster in, Ella,' Fiona snapped.

The girl's cheeks reddened. Fiona turned to Paul. 'Let me know what she says. Let's hope it's bullshit otherwise—'

'—you'll kick my arse from here to Inverness?' Paul finished for her. 'Yeah. I get it.'

When the room emptied, Heather was waiting for him by her chair. As soon as Paul walked over, she stuck her microphone in his face. He shoved it to the side. '*Off* the record,' he snapped.

She sighed, putting her microphone down. 'Fine.'

'Can you tell me what information you have to suggest Abe Abbott was having an affair with Benjamin Oberlin?'

She crossed her arms and smiled. 'What's in it for me?'

'Excuse me?'

'I'm thinking an exclusive interview with you, in exchange for some exclusive intel from me?'

Paul felt his blood pressure rising. 'Ms Fala, this is a serious case. I will *not* be giving you an interview.'

Heather shrugged, looking unimpressed. 'Fine. How about a tiny titbit of info?'

Paul thought about it. 'I *can* give you something.'

Her eyes lit up. 'What's that?'

He leaned in close, lowering his voice. 'A guarantee you won't get arrested for withholding information. You know that's a criminal offence, right?'

'Don't play me, Detective,' Heather said with a bored sigh. 'I can't get arrested for that. You'll just have to wait until I release the information on my podcast, then.'

'Oh sure, I'll wait a day,' Paul said. 'I'll go let the families know they'll need to wait a day too, shall I? Like Michael Regan's seven-year-old daughter who was actually hugging a panda bear teddy that looks just like your backpack while she was crying for her daddy yesterday.'

That was a lie. It was a Barbie doll she'd been holding. But Paul needed something to make this girl stop and think about this as more than just a story for her podcast. It seemed to do the trick as she blinked, unsure what to say.

'Look,' he said, voice softer. 'We're knee-deep in an important investigation here and can't afford to play games. So, spill.'

'Fine. I'll give you the information for free . . . *this* time. But only because you asked so nicely.' She pulled her phone from her pocket and scrolled through it. 'It all started with *this* comment.' On her screen was one of Abe Abbott's TikTok videos. Heather clicked into the comments section and pointed at one comment from a user called Chomajo_GS from a week ago:

I like the way you handle your spider. Is it the same way you handle your posh new lover? it read.

Paul frowned. *Posh new lover.*

'Click on the name,' he asked the podcaster.

She did as he asked, revealing a profile. Keeper of ancient secrets, the profile read, eco-feminist and protector of winged wonders. Unveiling the mystical realm of butterflies and their hidden powers for the feminine form. 🦋✦⁺

Paul didn't even need to look at the profile picture, which showed a heavily filtered photo of a white-haired woman in her fifties.

It was Emi Craviso, the Butterfly Witch.

So now it looked like he had two people to question: Abe Abbott and Emi Craviso.

'OK, we're done,' Paul said, ignoring the podcaster's spluttering protests as he walked out of the media room and towards the incident room, finding several officers gathered around the TV.

'Presume you saw all that?' he asked them. They nodded. 'Selma and Deano, go chat to Emi Craviso. OS!' he called over to his sergeant. 'We're going to pay Abe Abbott a visit.'

18

Paul walked with OS towards the Abbotts' small red-brick house, his eyes scouring the front garden for any signs of deadly nightshade. But all he could see were poppies and weeds. Ricky Abbott was already standing outside the house, his arms crossed.

'He's not here,' he said.

'OK, Ricky,' Paul said. 'Where is he then?'

'Manchester. Gone to see some band.'

Paul examined his face. Was he lying?

'What band's that?' OS asked.

'I don't know, do I?' Ricky replied. 'Listens to all this weird alternative stuff.'

'Know what venue they're performing at?' Paul asked.

'No idea,' Ricky said.

OS crossed his arms to match Ricky's stance. 'When's he due back?'

Ricky shrugged. 'No clue.'

'Any idea where he's staying?' OS asked.

'Nope.'

'You don't know how long your seventeen-year-old son's going to be away?' Paul asked. 'Or where he's staying?'

'He's not a kid, Paul,' Ricky said. 'He can handle himself.'

'Can you call him?' Paul asked.

Ricky frowned. 'Now?'

'Yeah, now,' OS said.

Ricky sighed and pulled his phone from his pocket, scrolling through his numbers before putting it to his ear. 'Gone to voicemail,' he said. 'Abe, it's Dad. Police here looking for you. Call me back ASAP.'

OS got his notepad out. 'Can I take Abe's number, please?'

Ricky read it out to him and Paul got out his phone, trying the number himself as Ricky rolled his eyes. But Ricky was right: it rang through to voicemail. He'd try to get a trace on it when he got back. 'Mind if we come in?' Paul asked.

He could see Ricky thinking through his answer. 'Fine,' he eventually said, opening the door wide. Paul and OS walked in, and Paul realised how much it reminded him of the house Vanessa had grown up in, with its vibrantly coloured walls and insect-inspired artwork. In fact, one of the sculptures sitting on the side was by Vanessa's mother.

'How's business going?' Paul asked. 'Ricky runs an online store selling food for exotic pets,' he explained to OS.

'Not bad,' Ricky replied as he watched OS peer up the stairs. 'He's not here, you know.'

'We just need to be sure,' Paul said. 'You know how serious this is.'

'I saw the press conference,' Ricky said. 'The thing with Benjamin wouldn't have been serious. Not best pleased about it though. Abe's only seventeen, for Christ's sake. You know he's not capable of murder, Paul. Problem is, people like us . . .' He gestured at his tattoos. 'We're always misunderstood. We're just like spiders, man. They're misunderstood too. People think they're all creepy and gross, but they're more shit-scared of us than we are of them. Tony's girl, Vanessa, would understand.'

'Vanessa also understands we need to follow any lead we get to find the person responsible for the deaths of *four* of our fellow villagers,' Paul countered. 'No matter how tenuous,' he quickly added.

Ricky sighed. 'Fine. I get it. Knock yourself out, then. Abe's room is the second one on the right.'

Paul walked upstairs, OS close behind. 'Check the other rooms,' Paul told him. 'I'll check Abe's room.'

Paul stepped into the room, immediately struck by how tidy it was, a stark contrast to the typical teenage chaos he often encountered. The walls of the room were adorned with various artworks featuring spiders, many of them detailed illustrations. On a desk in the corner, there was an imprint where a laptop would have been. He must have taken it with him . . . wherever he was. Paul flicked through some folders, but the paper within mainly seemed to be related to his TikTok channel, including some tax forms, which revealed he earned a decent buck from sponsorship.

Then his eyes were drawn to a corkboard hanging above the desk. Pinned to it was a newspaper article highlighting a recent community garden Benjamin had been involved with setting up, in one of the less privileged estates in Cranleigh. Paul was intrigued to see Indra and Tom Hudson standing on either side of him. Benjamin had clearly had more than just a casual acquaintance with the Hudsons. Even more intriguing: why would Abe have a photo of them in his room?

'Found anything?' OS asked, walking in.

'Not much, though this is interesting.' Paul gestured to the article cutting.

OS walked over and examined it. Then his eyes strayed over to the window overlooking the back garden. 'Boss, is that deadly nightshade?'

He was pointing to a shrubby plant with purple bell-shaped flowers. 'Looks like it,' Paul said.

19

'I'm sorry, it's a *complete* mess,' Helen said as she led Vanessa through the Trusses' three-bed semi-detached house, one of the newer builds that sat back from the main road in Greensands. Helen picked up a discarded child's cardigan with one hand from the sofa and kicked a squeaky toy away with her foot, sending their Blenheim King Charles Cavalier running after it in excitement.

'I'm surprised it's as tidy as it is with the twins to look after,' Vanessa said.

'Don't lie,' Helen said with a wry smile. 'So, did you see the press conference?'

'I did. I think Paul did well, considering.'

'He looked a bit surprised about the Abe Abbott revelation. I listen to that podcast, you know. *Dark Deeds Dissected.* The host can be annoying as hell, but she has good stuff to say.'

Vanessa followed Helen through to the open-plan kitchen. 'I can confirm she is annoying as hell. She accosted me earlier.'

'Oooh, I bet the media loves you. I saw the *Daily Fail* article. Looks like you're going to be their cover girl for this case.'

Vanessa put two fingers in her mouth and pretended to puke. 'I hope not.'

As she did, two little humans came ploughing through the middle of the living room, one crying, the other giggling as she flung a fluffy centipede teddy up and down in the air as the dog jumped up at her. They pummelled past Vanessa and the crying girl flung herself into Helen's arms, barely noticing the new addition to the room.

'Didn't I tell you they're like two tornadoes?' Helen said as she hugged her crying daughter.

Vanessa caught the fluffy centipede before it was catapulted into a glass of squash. 'Isn't that one of the gifts I sent for Christmas?' she asked.

'Yes, Celia the Centipede,' Helen replied. 'Summer lost Wilma the Worm, so now it's all about Celia.'

'Summer keeps stealing Celia,' the crying girl moaned.

'Girls, this is Vanessa, Daddy's friend,' Helen explained to her girls. 'She's the one who sent you Celia and Wilma!'

Molly clung tight to her mother's thigh as she eyed Vanessa suspiciously. The antagonist twin, on the other hand, stared up at Vanessa in amazement, her mouth hanging open as she took in Vanessa's tattoos and chunky green velvet shoes. The twins were so different. Vanessa and Vincent had been different, too. Like Molly, Vincent was clingy and oversensitive whereas Vanessa was more independent and thick-skinned, like Summer seemed to be.

'Is that a *blue* spider?' Summer asked, pointing to the large spider tattoo that dominated Vanessa's right shoulder.

Vanessa crouched down, letting the kid take a closer look. 'It's a replica of my pet, Nancy.'

'You have a blue spider?'

Vanessa nodded. 'Yep, it's a cobalt blue.' She thought of Nancy, currently being looked after at a facility near the airport before flying out the next day. While spiders didn't possess emotions in the way humans understood them, they did have acute sensory perceptions, honed to interact with their environments in complex ways. In the confines of her container, Nancy would most likely be attuned to the absence of familiar stimuli – Vanessa's scent, the vibrations of her footsteps, the specific pattern of light and shadow that fell across her enclosure each day. She would be missing Vanessa, but not as much as Vanessa missed her.

'Is she a good pet?' Summer asked, interrupting her thoughts.

'Not as easy as other tarantulas,' Vanessa admitted. 'They're quite particular about their surroundings. But a bucketload of roaches and a cuddle every day keeps them happy.'

Summer's brown eyes, so like her dad's, widened. 'Cuddle?'

'OK, cuddle isn't the right word. But she likes to climb up my arm sometimes.'

Even Molly seemed interested now. 'Does Nancy bite?' she asked quietly, tears still falling down her cheeks.

'Only if someone's naughty. Now,' Vanessa said, looking between the two girls, 'I think I have a solution to the centipede situation. Why don't you cut it in half?'

Molly looked at her in horror, but Summer seemed interested in the idea.

'It's fine, honestly,' Vanessa said. 'They can survive being cut in half. Look.' She pulled her phone out and found a video of a centipede being cut in half and still moving. Molly burst into tears, but Summer continued to look delighted.

'Erm, maybe keep the centipede-slaughtering videos to a minimum around the kids, hon,' Helen said.

Vanessa shrugged. In her experience, kids could handle this kind of stuff far better than adults. They had an endearing fascination and constitution for the macabre and beautiful. She found it interesting how desperately some parents tried to hide their offspring from the more disgusting and brutal parts of life. But what did she know, really? She rarely interacted with kids, bar the occasional visits from colleagues' children to the offices.

So she took Helen's advice and dug around in her black leather studded bag to find the two wooden jitterbug toys she'd got from a service station on the way up, hoping the gifts would make up for the video.

'One for you,' she said, handing one to Summer, 'and one for you,' she said, giving Molly the other one. The two girls squealed in delight.

'What do you say?' Helen shouted over their squeals.

'Fank you!' they both said as they grinned up at Vanessa.

'I hear these toys *love* being outdoors,' Vanessa suggested. The girls took her advice and darted outside with their new toys as the dog followed, doing just what she hoped they would: disappear for a bit so she could find out what Helen wanted to talk to her about.

'You are my *saviour*,' Helen said. 'You always manage to discover things with just the right amount of *yuck* to appeal to them.'

'I'll take that as a compliment,' Vanessa said, stepping over an upended toy pram to follow Helen.

'I got some rum in especially. Want some?'

'Yes, please.'

Helen sloshed some rum into a Disney *Frozen* mug. 'Sorry, dishwasher's still going with the glasses inside.' She quickly grabbed a beer for herself from the fridge. 'Look, confession time. I was going to pop the barbie on, but frankly, I can't be arsed. So I've shoved some pizzas and garlic bread in the oven and grabbed some salad from the local shop. That OK?'

'Sure, you know me. I'll eat anything and everything.'

'Oh, you are *so* easy.' Helen slumped down onto a nearby stool and took a large gulp of beer.

Vanessa joined her, enjoying the sweetness of the rum as it hit her tongue. 'So, you wanted to talk to me about something?'

Helen checked the girls were occupied, then turned back to Vanessa. 'You can't tell Paul I told you this.'

Vanessa wasn't sure how she felt about that, keeping something from her friend.

'Please,' Helen insisted, noting her hesitation. 'He'll go mad. But you need to know, even if he thinks you don't.' She sighed. 'Last month, Paul was diagnosed with AFib, a heart rhythm disorder.'

Vanessa was silent, letting what Helen had just said sink in. *Don't you dare, Universe. Don't you dare take Paul Truss away from me,* she thought. But she couldn't help also wondering: why hadn't Paul told her?

'And before you think badly of Paul for not telling you,' Helen quickly added, 'he was planning to, before all this kicked off.'

'This case won't help, will it?'

Helen took another deep sip of her beer. 'Nope, the case certainly won't help. He takes meds every day, but stress can exacerbate the condition. Big time.'

'Do his seniors know about the condition?'

Helen's eyes filled with tears as she silently shook her head.

'God, he's a stubborn fucker,' Vanessa said.

'You know him well. I tried to convince him to hand the case over when he got in this morning, looking exhausted. He was hearing none of it.'

''Course he wasn't. He's a stubborn bastard.'

Helen raked her fingers through her messy blonde hair. 'I even thought about telling his chief superintendent behind Paul's back. But I actually think Paul would file for divorce if I did.' She laughed, but Vanessa could see from her expression she really was worried he might.

'Don't be silly,' Vanessa said. 'Paul adores you and the girls too much to do something as dumb as that.' She sighed. 'But he *would* be pissed off.'

'Like he'd be pissed off about me telling you. So please promise not to say anything to him to indicate you know?' She clutched Vanessa's hand. 'Please?'

'Fine.'

'I mean, I wouldn't have told you. But you being here means I have someone who knows him – *really* knows him – to watch over him, you know?'

'I'm flying out to New York tomorrow though, remember? I was only ever staying until Wednesday.'

'I know, it's just—' Helen chewed at her lip. 'Could you delay your flight a bit more? Paul said you don't start your job until Monday. I could even pay for the service charge – I have some savings.'

'Helen, I can't. I just . . . I can't.'

Helen sighed. 'I understand.' A timer went off and Helen jumped up, going to the oven.

'Can I help?' Vanessa asked.

'No, no, stay there.'

As Helen tended to the food, a sense of trepidation gripped Vanessa. Paul felt so permanent in her life. So consistent. So strong. The very thought of him being vulnerable unravelled her slightly. What would she do without him?

She also felt a tonne of guilt too for leaving him to deal with this case while she'd be thousands of miles away in New York. But what choice did she have?

After Helen served the pizzas up, they walked out into the garden, taking seats at a large table overlooking the lawn. Helen gave the girls their pizzas on a picnic blanket, distracting the dog with a large bone to stop her from stealing their food. Vanessa leaned back in her chair, drawing in the last rays of sunlight that peeked through the wooden slats of the pergola above.

'How's the love life, then?' Helen asked, clearly keen to move the topic on to lighter stuff.

'Casual.'

'Like casual, passionate sex every night?'

Vanessa laughed. 'More like every few months. Honestly, I just don't have time for a relationship.'

'That old cliché. You think *Paul* has time? Somehow we produced these two,' Helen added, gesturing to the twins.

'You only needed to do it once,' Vanessa joked.

'True. What about Damon? Seeing him again must have stirred up some old memories.'

Vanessa's gaze drifted towards the manor in the distance. Paul had texted her to say Damon had been released. He didn't seem happy about it, but it felt right to Vanessa.

'So?' Helen pushed.

'I can't deny there's a certain chemistry between me and Damon. But you must have heard what he's like. I'm too grown up now to be pulled in by all that crap.'

Helen leaned back to take in the sun. 'What was he like back then? In the sack, I mean? You did the deed, right? Back in the day?'

Vanessa laughed. 'What is it with you married types, always so desperate for salacious details from your single friends? It was a long time ago, Helen.'

'You remember though . . . I can see it in your face.'

Vanessa remembered, all right. Every detail. There hadn't been a man or woman since who could make her feel the things he had. 'No comment,' she said.

'Do you think you'll act on it while you're here, a little holiday romance?'

Vanessa gave Helen a look. 'Holiday romance? I'm here working on a quadruple murder, you nutter.'

'You can't blame an exhausted mother of twins for trying.'

'How about we talk about *you*,' Vanessa said, leaning over to touch the pretty mustard-coloured bracelet Helen was wearing. 'I like this.'

She peered closer as she noticed the glimmer of orange and black within. 'Is that part of a monarch butterfly wing?'

'That's right,' Helen said. 'After Dad died, I found a massive collection of preserved butterfly wings in his house. He collected all the dead butterflies he could find after the butterfly farm closed down. Never found out why, there was box after box of them, carefully preserved between glass slabs. I made a load of resin jewellery from it when I was on maternity leave.' She shrugged. 'A nice little earner.'

'You know, my dad used to fix broken butterfly wings.'

'Really?'

Vanessa nodded, thinking of the time she watched her father tend to a blue morpho whose wing had been injured during the breeding process. He was tending to it in his lab, a place Vanessa had spent countless hours as a child. She remembered watching in awe at her father's skill and precision, his hands moving deftly with years of practice. Despite the delicate nature of the task, he seemed completely in control. He'd once told her how her mother reminded him of a butterfly wing: delicate and feathery on the surface, but strong inside.

He couldn't fix her when she broke, though. And Vanessa couldn't fix her father . . . or the way he looked at her after Vincent went missing.

As Vanessa thought of that, a shadow fell over them. She looked up to see Paul standing at the garden door.

'You're here!' Helen declared, giving a Vanessa a quick 'remember what you promised me?' look before jumping up to give her husband a kiss.

'How's it all going?' Vanessa asked as Paul leaned over to grab a slice of pizza, fielding leg hugs from his girls.

Paul shoved a piece of pizza into his mouth. 'Ball-ache now the press are all over the case. Plus none of the people we want to talk to are around, including Abe Abbott.'

'I saw his name mentioned at the press conference,' Vanessa said. 'He's just a kid, isn't he?'

Paul nodded. 'Seventeen.'

'Want a beer?' Helen asked.

'Nope. Can't stay long,' Paul replied. 'Just coming back for some sustenance. I promised I'd be back in an hour or so. I need to check we've got permission from Abe's phone network to track it.'

'You don't need to be in the station to get that sorted,' Helen said. 'Stay here. You need sleep.'

'Na, sleep's for amateurs,' Paul replied dismissively. 'Right, can we talk about something other than this case while I shove some food down my gullet? I need to make the most of this one being in the same time zone as me,' he added, gesturing to Vanessa.

Over the next hour, they all ate pizza and talked about the good old days, like Paul and Vanessa's antics at primary school, and Helen and Paul's first disastrous date at a restaurant that got flooded. As they all talked and laughed, Vanessa watched Paul with a sense of trepidation. Despite his easy laughter, there was a lingering pallor to his skin, an almost imperceptible tightness around his eyes. Even when he was joking and seemed relaxed, Vanessa noticed a subtle rigidity in his posture.

When the girls grew sleepy, rather than taking them up to bed, Helen let them fall asleep in the still-warm garden, curled up on the outdoor sofa. After a while, Summer gravitated her little head to Vanessa's lap and Vanessa gently stroked her soft hair as she slept, feeling a bittersweet yearning for the children she'd never had.

'Right,' Paul said. 'I better get going. I'll walk you back.'

'Walk me back?' Vanessa said with a laugh. 'I think I can handle the five-minute walk.'

'We've had four people killed in two nights. I'm walking you back.'

'Admit it, babe,' Helen said. 'It's actually *Vanessa's* protection you need. Greensands men in their forties seem to be more the killer's type, remember?'

'She's right, you know,' Vanessa said. 'Come on, let me be your security guard.'

When Vanessa and Paul got outside a few minutes later, the air felt heavy, not just from the cloying warmth of being in the middle of a heatwave, but also the presence of more than the usual number of people scurrying through the streets like nocturnal beetles. Paul needn't have worried about her walking alone. The main street leading from the Truss house to the pub seemed even more busy than usual with not just residents, but police officers too. There were also unfamiliar faces – journalists no doubt.

'I'm going to miss you, Bugs,' Paul said.

'I'll miss you too. But remember—'

'—you can stay at my apartment any time. Yeah, yeah, I know, so you keep telling me. It's not the same though. The idea of you being in another country, in another time zone . . .' He let his voice trail off, shuddering. She understood. She felt the same, especially now she knew about his heart condition.

Just before they got to the pub, there was a quiet patch flanked by trees and grasslands. Paul's eyes scoured the darkness. He was no doubt thinking what she was thinking: the killer could be out there right now, stalking their prey.

But who *was* it?

As she thought that, a faint scream polluted the silent air.

'Did you hear that?' Paul asked.

Vanessa nodded. 'I did. It *is* pub closing time though, could just be—'

She was cut off by another scream, strangled and high-pitched, coming from the direction of the dark grasslands.

Paul instantly started running towards the noise.

'Damn it,' Vanessa hissed as she took off after him through the tall grass, the light from her phone bouncing up and down as she tracked Paul's distant figure.

'Need backup in the grasslands behind the village hall,' she heard him shout into his phone. 'Screams heard.'

Two figures suddenly appeared in the distance, their forms outlined by the moonlight. One was hooded with their back to them, the other crouched down in the grass.

'Police!' Paul shouted. 'Stop.'

The hooded figure jumped up and darted into the darkest heart of the grasslands.

'I'm going after them,' Paul shouted to Vanessa. He pointed down to the prone figure. 'Check on this one.'

Vanessa watched her friend running off alone, defenceless, into the dark . . . with a heart condition. Part of her wanted to forget the person lying in the grass and instead, continue running after her friend. But she couldn't do that. She needed to tend to whoever it was.

There was a soft moan, and she ran to the figure as Paul disappeared from sight.

20

Paul's heart raced as he gave chase through the thick grass, trying to ignore the voice inside that told him he was no match for the hooded figure's speed. That his ailing *heart* was no match.

His breathing grew ragged, and his chest ached with every step. He could feel sweat dripping down his forehead as the figure moved quickly, weaving in and out of the grass. At least his mind was working as he pressed the details into his memory.

Tallish. Maybe a couple of inches away from six feet.

Navy hoodie.

Dark trousers that looked like combats.

Likely to be a man.

Maybe a seventeen-year-old boy.

'Stop!' Paul shouted again, his whole body shaking with the effort of trying to keep up with the figure. A cloud crossed over the moon and the figure was swallowed up in darkness. Paul could hear his own wheezing breaths, so took a moment to slow to a jog, trying to catch his breath. He scanned the area, looking for any sign of movement, but everything was still.

Suddenly, the figure appeared out of nowhere, slamming into Paul with all their weight. Paul stumbled backward, falling heavily onto his butt. He quickly tried to scramble back to his feet, but the figure was on him, shoving him back down before disappearing into the night again, leaving Paul alone in the long grass, gasping for air, his heart beating erratically . . . too erratically.

More figures approached from the opposite direction. One of them was Selma.

'Boss, you OK?' she asked, trying to help Paul up as sirens whined in the distance.

But he shoved her away. 'That way,' he said, pointing towards where the figure had run off.

131

The two officers with her darted off in that direction and Paul placed his head between his legs, taking gulps of air as he tried to calm his fumbling heartbeat. 'There was someone hurt,' he got out between breaths. 'Vanessa's with them.'

'Emi Craviso,' Selma replied. 'She's the one who's hurt. It's crazy, I only spoke to her an hour ago.'

'Jesus. She OK?'

'She was stabbed. An ambulance is on its way.'

Paul lifted his hand towards Selma. 'Help an old man up, will you?'

Selma grabbed his hand and pulled him up. 'Hardly old, Boss.'

'Feel like it.'

'You just need to lay off the stale croissants.'

'True. Come on, let's see what's going on.'

They both trod back through the grass to see a small crowd of people standing around Emi Craviso. She was lying on her side in the grass as she whimpered. Vanessa had untied her black cardigan from her waist and had it pressed against Emi's side.

'It's a stab wound to the stomach,' Vanessa explained to Paul when he got over.

He crouched down. 'Did you see who did it, Emi?'

Emi shook her head, her eyes large and scared. 'It was too dark. I was walking by when I heard someone calling for help. They-they just jumped out at me in the darkness and grabbed hold of me.' She craned her head to look down at her wounded side. 'Then they just-just stabbed me. I don't understand. I don't understand what I did wrong!'

Her eyes started to close.

'Emi,' Vanessa said loudly, tapping her cheek firmly to try to rouse her. 'Emi, can you hear me?' But it was no use. She'd lost consciousness.

Blue lights flooded the field and two paramedics made their way through the long grass with a stretcher, more police officers in tow. A female paramedic crouched down beside Emi, gently removing Vanessa's cardigan from the wound as the other, male paramedic directed some torchlight over it.

Vanessa frowned as she noticed something. 'What's that?'

Paul followed her gaze to see an off-white, creamy substance oozing out of the wound.

'I'll take a sample for the CSI guys,' Vanessa said quickly, pulling a container from her bag. Paul could tell from the look in her eyes that she knew what it was.

The paramedic frowned.

'She'll be quick,' Paul said.

After she'd carefully taken her sample and Emi was placed into the ambulance, Paul went up to his friend, who was looking at the contents of the container using the light from her phone.

'What do you think it is?' Paul asked.

Vanessa lifted her gaze to meet his, a look of disgusted horror on her face. 'Semen.'

21

'*Semen*? In a wound,' Paul said to Vanessa. 'What the fuck? Do you think he . . .'

'No, I don't think the suspect penetrated the wound,' Vanessa replied. 'I think, in the context of these cases, it's more likely an attempt to replicate traumatic insemination.'

'Traumatic what?'

'It's where the male bedbug inseminates his mate by piercing her body wall with his penis, depositing his semen directly into the cavity.'

Paul felt like he was going to throw up. 'Shit. Nature sure has got some kinky stuff going on.' He took the phial from Vanessa and stared at the soapy substance within. 'This could be handy if it *is* the suspect's semen.'

'I don't think they'd be that stupid, using their own semen.'

'True.'

'What's that you're holding?' a bright voice called out.

Paul peered over to see his least favourite podcaster watching from behind a police cordon that was being set up. Heather Fala shoved her microphone out towards them. 'My listeners are desperate to know. We have over twenty thousand tuning in to this live cast right now. Is it true the person being taken away in the ambulance *also* worked at the butterfly farm? Do we have a serial killer targeting former employees of the farm, Detective Truss? And is it true you just had the suspect within arm's length, but couldn't keep up with them?'

He glared at the podcaster and walked away without answering. She was right though: he'd had the likely suspect within his grasp. If it hadn't been for his stupid heart condition, he might have been able to stop them. Now they were free to hurt more people. More villagers. More *friends*.

Selma walked over, her young face drawn with worry, Emi's blood on her white shirt. 'This is getting crazy.'

'It is,' Paul replied. 'I think we need to thrash this out back at the station until Emi's ready to talk to us. I'll do a call-around, see who can come in.'

Paul walked down one of the many corridors of Cranleigh Police Station, noticing the way officers he passed regarded him with a mixture of envy and sympathy. This was a big case now. They'd all be aware of it. He headed into the incident room to see it was already filled with clusters of officers, some sitting in chairs, others leaning against the walls, most of them fixated on the whiteboard at the front of the room, which OS had updated. The air was thick with the smell of stale coffee, too. They all went quiet as Paul walked to the front of the room.

'First of all,' Paul said, 'I want to thank each and every one of you for coming in at such short notice. We've got a potential fifth victim, and we need all hands on deck.' The room buzzed with anticipation. Paul turned to face the board, his hand resting on the edge. 'First, let's take a moment to absorb all this.' All the officers did as he asked, eyes homing in on the board.

Victims:
Victim 1 (deceased):
Michael Regan
Age: 45
Suspected cause of death: overdose of atracurium
Insect-pattern: mate binding (spider silk in stomach wound?)
Victim 2 (deceased):
Simon Taylor
Age: 46
Suspected cause of death: overdose of atracurium
Insect-pattern: mate binding (spider silk in stomach wound?) / rare beetle shell under shoulder?
Victim 3 (deceased):
Tim Holmes
Age: 45

Suspected cause of death: overdose of atracurium
Insect-pattern: mate binding (spider silk in stomach wound?)
Victim 4 (deceased):
Benjamin Oberlin
Age: 44
Suspected cause of death: asphyxia by suffocation because of obstruction of respiratory orifices
Insect-pattern: mating plug (cotton wool mixed with sphragis?) / bee sting
Also: deadly nightshade shoved down throat
Victim 5 (hospitalised):
Emi Craviso
Age: 58
Injury: stab wound to the right of abdomen
Insect-pattern: traumatic insemination (semen in wound?)
Connections Between Victims:
Worked at Greensands Butterfly Farm at same time
Live in Greensands
Insect mating ritual-inspired injuries / poses
Suspects / Key POI:
Abe Abbott (spider enthusiast / rumoured sexual relationship with Victim 4 / conveniently missing / deadly nightshade in garden)
Damon Oberlin (fight witnessed, questioned and released)
? Indra Hudson (owns similar-looking car seen at Victim 4's house / last person to see Victim 4 / offices based near where Benjamin's body may have been)
Awaiting:
Toxicology
Entomology
Web and cotton wool analysis
Bee analysis
Digital forensics (illegal insect trade)
Abe Abbott interview
Clues:

Crime Scene 1 – Butterfly Farm
Unusual beetle shell (possibly tansy beetle?)
Wheelbarrow tracks
Deadly nightshade in Benjamin's throat and on maggots (?)
Crime Scene 2 – Oberlin Manor
Tyre marks
Illegal insect trading room
Greensands Ridge
? Bee that stung Benjamin Oberlin
Indra Hudson offices
Illegal insect trading brochure
Dead bee on ridge

'Nice job,' Paul said, nodding at OS, who gave him a curt nod back. He pointed at Abe Abbott's name. 'So this is a person of interest to us right now, *especially* because he's conveniently missing. We've had permission to track his phone. We now just need his service provider to agree.'

'Wouldn't be surprised if we discover he was in the grasslands in Greensands an hour ago,' Selma said.

Paul sighed. 'Maybe. In the meantime, let's go through what else we have. An update from me: I visited the post-mortem suite with Doctor Marwood.'

'The Bug Lady,' he heard Deano explain to one of the officers in a low whisper. 'You should see her. She looks like she's just come from a Halloween party.'

'You look like you raided the lost property box at clown college,' Selma snapped back.

'She's right, Deano,' OS said. 'I hope you have an alibi for that outfit choice.'

The officers around the room burst into laughter.

'Enough about Deano's questionable fashion style,' Paul said. 'Back to what's important. To sum up: it's likely the four men died in the early hours of Sunday morning. Then their bodies were moved in the night. Maybe by car, maybe by wheelbarrow too, judging from tyre tracks found at both crime scenes. They were alive when the silk and other substances were put inside them.' The officers around the room flinched. 'And it's highly likely a substance called atracurium was used to placate them. Plus deadly nightshade was found in Benjamin Oberlin's throat.' He turned to OS. 'Did you do the list of all the people who worked at the butterfly farm at the same time as the victims?'

'I did, Boss,' OS replied. 'Me, Dodds, Wayfair and Truby have plans to pay them all visits first thing.'

'Good,' Paul said. 'It's the one obvious thread that connects them all: the fact they worked together at the farm in the years before it closed, and now this hook is even stronger with what happened to Emi Craviso this evening.' Paul turned to the officers he'd assigned to the victims' families. 'Anything interesting to share from the families? Any grudges, strange incidents, indications they might have been involved in the illegal insect trade . . . apart from Benjamin Oberlin, of course?'

They all shook their heads.

'Anything from our digital forensics guys?' Paul asked Deano who'd been put in charge of liaising with Gordon's team.

'Nothing to link any of the Oberlins with illegal insect trading yet,' Deano said. 'Or Indra Hudson.'

'Apart from the underground insect bazaar,' OS said.

'Yeah, apart from that.'

'So the past is what continues to really connect these people.' Paul looked at each of the victims' faces.

'How are we doing with doorbell footage around the manor and butterfly farm, Deano?' he asked the older officer.

Deano sighed. 'Painfully, that's how. Most of it's grainy as shit and we're still waiting for one family to send us their footage. They're getting back from holiday today according to a neighbour. I was planning to visit tomorrow.'

'Call them now,' Paul said.

Deano looked at his watch. 'It's past midnight, Boss.'

'Call them,' Paul said again.

Deano sighed and went to his desk, picking up his phone.

'Right, let's move on to our latest victim: Emi Craviso,' Paul said.

'While what happened to her was nasty, she's going to survive as far as I can tell. Great for her. But also great for us. So as soon as she's well enough to talk, we'll get an official statement from her. In the meantime, you said you talked to Emi earlier, Selma, before she was attacked?'

Selma nodded.

'How'd she seem?' Paul asked.

'Fine. I mean, a bit loco, you know? But she seemed totally chill. I noticed nothing unusual.' She looked down at her notepad. 'I asked her how she knew about Benjamin Oberlin and Abe Abbott, and she said she saw them doing the deed in the grasslands behind the butterfly farm once. She was also going on about Jupiter being near the moon or something, and how it creates this weird energy so she's not surprised about the murders. Honestly, Boss, most of the stuff she said wasn't of much use. But she did give me a list of places around Greensands where there might be deadly nightshade.'

'Great,' Paul said. 'Can you coordinate some officers so we can do a search first thing tomorrow?'

'Will do,' Selma said. 'Will Doctor Marwood come?'

'I'll see. She's due to fly to New York later tomorrow,' Paul said with a sigh. Paul looked at his watch. 'Right, let's get back to work.' He clapped his hands, sending the officers racing to their desks like worker ants on a mission. Paul took the chance to go over all his notes again. After a while, Deano appeared, eyes alight.

'What you got?' Paul asked.

'Video footage from a very pissed-off and jet-lagged Mr Barrowman. But it's good.'

He held his phone up to show a video featuring a Porsche Panamera being driven in via the back entrance of what was clearly Oberlin Manor. The timestamp showed it was 1.08 a.m. on Sunday morning.

'Can we get the licence plate?' Paul asked.

Deano zoomed in but it was blurry. 'It's exactly the same make as Indra's though, and Porsche Panameras aren't a common sight in a place like Greensands.'

'It looks like I'll be paying Indra Hudson a late-night visit then,' Paul said.

22

Vanessa was standing in the middle of Greensands' grassland, bathed in the moonlight's ethereal glow. As she looked up, the sky stretched into an endless expanse, the stars above like fireflies in flight. Suddenly, the ground quivered beneath her, and a swarm of enormous butterflies flew over her head, their wings spanning the horizon. Then ladybugs the size of dinner plates scurried through the grass, their tiny spots molten-ruby glows in the darkness. But then a darkness loomed ahead as a colossal praying mantis emerged from the foliage, its delicate forelimbs extending towards Vanessa. She approached cautiously, a mixture of fear and fascination intertwining within her.

But then she noticed something hanging from its mouth. A boy wearing a bright green T-shirt with a spider on the front.

Her brother, Vincent!

The praying mantis began rubbing its limbs together, making a loud thudding nose that reverberated through the meadow.

Startled, Vanessa's eyes fluttered open, the remnants of her dream fading into the recesses of her mind as an urgent knock on her hotel room door rang out.

She frowned, peering at her clock. It was nearly one in the morning. Another knock. Maybe it was Paul? She jumped out of bed and peered through the viewfinder to see Damon standing in the corridor. She looked down at what she was wearing. A skimpy black vest top with red skulls and roses all over it and a matching pair of shorts.

She opened the door with a creak. 'Damon, have you seen the time?'

'Are you OK? I just heard what happened with Emi.' He looked frantic, his blue eyes red-rimmed as he searched her face. 'Did they touch you? I swear if they—' He sucked in a breath, curling his hands into fists.

140

Vanessa didn't know what to think about this moment of chivalry from Damon. 'I'm absolutely fine.'

'Can I come in?'

Vanessa hesitated.

'Vanessa, please,' Damon begged. 'It'd be good to talk. Wasn't I there for you when your brother disappeared?'

Damon was right. He had been there, joining in with the search, visiting her even when she refused to see anyone. She sighed and opened the door, grabbing a long black nightgown covered in red bats and pulling it on.

'Drink?' she asked, flicking on the small kettle.

Damon nodded, going to the minibar and grabbing a small bottle of vodka.

'I meant coffee,' Vanessa said.

He slumped down at the table, twisting open the lid and downing half the bottle. 'I missed out on a night of drinking last night, thanks to your police buddy. Completely pointless them pulling me in. Makes me worry, how much they're wasting their time.'

'They would have had good reason to arrest you.'

'Clearly not,' Damon said, shaking his head. 'You should have seen the way his chief inspector apologised to me. So do you think it was The Cobweb Killer who stabbed Emi?'

'I see the moniker sits well with you.'

'I've tried to think of alternatives, for the sake of my brother. He always liked a bit of a flourish. The Venomous Weaver. The Arachnid Assassin. The Silkstrand Slayer. But none of them sound quite right. So.' He leaned towards her. 'What was the *pièce de résistance* this time? I heard she was stabbed in the stomach.'

'You know I can't tell you that.'

'Then I will have to guess.' He bit his lip before a smile spread across his face. 'I've got it. Traumatic insemination.'

Vanessa said nothing. How did he know these things? She knew there was an obvious answer to that. But he'd already been questioned and released.

'So it is then,' he said. 'It's one of the subjects I'll be exploring in the new series, actually.'

'Has anyone had access to your notes for the series?'

'Just my editor. But trust me, he's no killer. Unlike Abe fucking Abbott,' he hissed.

'You saw the press conference, then?'

'And had a visit from one of Detective Dullard's minions, asking me if my brother ever mentioned the spooky little shit.'

'Did he?'

'My brother fucked anything with a pulse, Vanessa.' Damon threw his head back to take another sip of vodka. 'Might as well have half the village considered suspects if that's the route they're going down. Though Abe Abbott *does* know a lot about insects,' he mused. 'That's one thing we can be sure of when it comes to The Cobweb Killer: they certainly know a *lot* about creepy-crawlies.'

'It's spiders he's passionate about and spiders aren't *insects*, remember?'

'Pah. Semantics.'

'Well, it doesn't rule that many people out in Greensands,' Vanessa remarked. 'The people here were drawn here for their passion for arthropods. It's in their blood, which means it's in their children's blood, too. In *our* blood,' she added, gesturing between the two of them. She poured herself a black coffee and sat across from him.

'The techniques are getting more violent, wouldn't you say?' Damon said. 'First mate binding, which is gentle enough. Then on to the more invasive mate plugging. And now this. I don't think you can get much worse than stabbing a woman to insert your semen into her.'

Vanessa frowned. He was right. But then that was the way with most serial killers. They got more frantic with each new victim.

Damon leaned back in his chair, sipping at the vodka. 'What's the message this sicko is trying to send?'

'That they're in charge. Even the binding is a way of forcing power over their mate. The meticulous and intentional placation to ensure reproduction.'

'Pretty standard for serial murderers – the power trip.' Damon was quiet for a few moments. 'Something I'll be talking about in the traumatic insemination episode is how the female bedbug is *erased* from the process by the male. She has no choice, no active role. She is just a bag of reproductive organs for the male.'

'That *is* interesting,' Vanessa said as she took a sip of her coffee. 'We talk about power, but what if this is more about the killer *erasing* their victims?'

'Isn't that what all killers want? Erasure through the method of murder?'

'Not necessarily. It's rarely the *after* that's of importance to serial murderers. Not the gap left behind, but the very act itself.' She shrugged. 'Of course, murders of convenience occur where the removal of a victim *is* important to the murderer. But for serial murderers who pose their victims like this, it's the *act*. In this case, it's the *act* and the *absence*.'

Damon regarded her with a smile. 'You're enjoying this, aren't you?'

Vanessa frowned. 'Four people have been murdered, Damon, including your brother. So no, I'm not enjoying it.'

He examined her face. 'You can't lie to me. Didn't we once discuss the fine line between disgust and desire? Between pain and ecstasy? Between death and . . .' he paused, his gaze dropping to her cleavage '. . . lust?'

Vanessa didn't dignify his question with an answer.

Damon sprawled his legs out in front of him. 'My ex-wife messaged me, you know, fuming. She saw the photo of you in the newspapers, knows we have a past. Apparently, I should have *warned* her about how attractive you are. She's always been the jealous type. She even gets jealous when I pay our son too much attention. Speaking of children, I'm surprised you haven't had any. I never took you for the type to be a stay-at-home housewife, but still.'

Vanessa shrugged, the casualness of that shrug belying how tense the question made her feel. 'It's just the way it's panned out.'

'Don't lie,' Damon said. 'We both know you've never stopped blaming yourself for what happened to Vincent. You couldn't protect your brother, so you sure as hell can't be trusted with any other children. I bet that's the way you feel. The way your *dad* made you feel, anyway.'

'Wow, amazing you could pin the reason for my lack of children down in *one* sentence.' Vanessa stood up, having had enough of his mind games. 'I have a flight to catch in the evening. I need sleep.'

'The New York job. I read about it in *Nature* magazine.'

'Yes. I was due to fly out Monday night and then all this happened.'

'You're still going to leave after what happened with Emi?'

'I have to.'

'Do you? This is a serial murderer, Vanessa. In your home town too, involving people you know, *and* the investigation is headed up by your little buddy Paul. You're just going to up and leave and abandon us all when we need you most? Who's to say there won't be more victims added today?'

Vanessa wrapped her arms round herself, remnants of her dream still buzzing around her mind, the limbs of the praying mantis clicking together like the arms of a clock counting down to when the next victim would be claimed.

'Like I said,' she repeated, 'I'm flying out tomorrow night.' She walked up to the door and held it open for him. He sighed and dragged himself up from the chair, brushing past her as he left the room.

'That scent of yours,' she heard him say as he walked down the hallway. 'You know it haunts my dreams at night, Doctor Marwood.' Then he disappeared down the stairs.

She closed the door and leaned against it. *Would* there be more attacks the next day? She hoped not. But as the room darkened, a grim realisation washed over her: if they were dealing with a serial killer, it wasn't a question of if there would be more victims, but when.

23

Paul sat with OS across from Indra and her husband in their plush living room. Tom Hudson was an imposingly large man, at least six foot three, his bulging muscles covered by a dark tailored suit. A match, finally, for OS, who was eyeing up those muscles with a mixture of admiration and envy, no doubt making plans for a shift at the police station gym later.

Paul's tired eyes scanned the couple before him. They'd recently returned from a dinner party, so were dressed in their usual immaculate designer clothes. They were both intelligent people. *Powerful* people. He knew he'd have to tread carefully, especially now the media were all over this.

'We appreciate you letting us in for a chat,' Paul said, 'especially at this time of night. We've come across some new information that I hope you can help us with.'

He nodded at OS, who opened the folder before him, pulling out a still image from a doorbell camera's footage, enhanced even more now to reveal a light-coloured Porsche Panamera, *just* like Indra's new car. 'Mrs Hudson, this car was recorded entering the Oberlin estate in the early hours of Sunday morning.'

Though Indra seemed to give off her usual self-assurance – chin up, hands relaxed as they rested on her knees – Tom looked uneasy. Maybe even . . . angry? Paul knew he'd feel the same if he'd learned Helen was visiting a man known for his promiscuity in the dead of night. Especially when that man ended up dead the next morning.

'Though the number plate isn't visible, it is the same model and colour of your car,' Paul said. 'Did you visit Oberlin Manor in the early hours of Sunday?'

'No,' Indra said. 'But I visited during the day on Saturday, as you know.'

'So to clarify,' OS said. 'You're saying this is *not* you driving this car at 1.08 a.m. on Sunday morning.'

'No. I haven't even *driven* my car at night since I got it brand new a week ago,' Indra protested.

'And to confirm,' OS said, 'nobody can verify your whereabouts during the times of midnight and 6 a.m. on Sunday, Mrs Hudson?'

'No,' Indra admitted. 'As I've said before, Tom was away on business, weren't you, darling?'

Tom nodded. Paul noted the flare in his nostrils as he did.

'Do you have your own video footage from the exterior of your property to show your car on the drive during the hours we mentioned?' OS asked.

Indra sighed. 'We *did* until my husband disposed of the old cameras we had before the new cameras arrived.'

OS gave Paul a cynical look. Paul knew what he was thinking: *very convenient.*

'This is ridiculous!' Indra said, catching the look they exchanged. 'I can absolutely, definitively tell you I did *not* drive my car that night. Somebody is clearly trying to set me up with this footage. You can even take the car if you want, I don't care.'

Tom placed his hand on his wife's arm. 'There's no need for that, darling.'

'Well, it could help,' Paul said quickly. 'Just for our forensics guys to give it the once-over.'

'Forensics? Come on, why is that necessary?' Tom said.

'A car matching the description of your wife's car was seen driving into the Oberlin grounds the same night Benjamin Oberlin is suspected to have died,' Paul shot back.

'But my wife is not a suspect, is she?' Tom retorted. 'We have been good enough to invite you into our home at—' he looked at his watch '—one in the morning. But unless you have proper evidence that this is indeed my wife's registered car, and that she was driving it at the time you say, then we are absolutely within our rights to ask you to leave now so we can get some sleep.'

Paul couldn't argue with that. They would just have to regroup and gather more information before making any further moves. With a resigned nod, Paul stood up, OS doing the same. 'We'll be in touch if anything else arises.'

'If we can get the doorbell images sharpened up even more, that would be useful,' Paul said as they walked out of the house.

'I'll see what we can do,' OS replied.

'We really need to get on the digital forensics guys' backs with the illegal insect trading stuff, too.'

As he said that, his phone buzzed with a text from Vanessa:

You up?

'Give me a moment,' Paul said to OS, suddenly desperate to talk to his friend as he called her.

'There's my answer then,' she said, her wary voice echoing how he felt.

'What the hell are *you* doing up?'

She hesitated a moment. 'Damon paid me a visit just now.'

Paul squeezed the phone between his fingers as OS looked at him sideways. 'I don't want to know, Vanessa.'

'He just needed to talk. He's grieving.'

'Hmmm.'

'That's not why I'm calling, though. Have you heard anything about Emi's condition?'

'She's going to be fine. We're hoping to get a proper statement from her in the morning.'

'Thank God.'

'We just paid the Hudsons a visit.'

'Oh. Why's that?'

He told her about the doorbell footage and his interview with Indra.

'So she's insisting she hasn't even driven the car at night yet?'

'Yes, but that's difficult to verify.'

Vanessa was quiet for a moment. 'Actually, there might be a way to tell if she's being truthful.'

'How?' Paul asked as he stopped by the very car they were talking about.

'I could check the car's air filter to see what kind of insects have been sucked into it,' Vanessa replied.

'I don't understand.'

'You really are tired, aren't you?'

'Yep, if I auditioned for the role of a zombie in a film, I'd get it.'

Vanessa laughed. 'Well, let me explain. If the car's *never* been driven at night, as Indra claims, then there will be a low percentage of nocturnal insects in the air filter. Maybe none at all.'

'Interesting,' Paul said, his tired mind trying to grapple with it all. 'Indra did offer to let us take her car, though her hubby didn't seem too keen.'

'Well, if what she's saying is true, *she* might be keen if you tell her we can confirm what she says? If she doesn't agree, then that speaks volumes.'

'Good point. If she does agree, I can ask the CSI guys to get you into the vehicle compound as soon as they can in the morning and have the air filter ready for you? You'll have time before you leave for your flight, right?'

'Sure.'

'OK, I'll let you know.' Paul hung up and walked back towards the house, ringing the doorbell.

Tom answered, giving the two officers an exasperated look. 'What now?'

Paul peered behind him to see Indra watching from the hallway. 'We might have a way to prove you didn't drive the car at night, Indra,' he said. 'That's if you let us take the car in tonight, anyway.'

Tom opened his mouth to protest but Indra interrupted him. 'Fine. Take it. I have nothing to hide.' She grabbed the car keys and handed them to Paul. 'Do what you want with it.'

Paul nodded and took the keys. As Indra shut the door, he noticed some moths buzzing around a light on their wall. It was amazing how useful insects could be. Did The Cobweb Killer love insects, like Vanessa did? Or did they hate them? His stepfather had once said there was a fine line between love and hate.

Paul made a promise to himself: soon, very soon, he'd be sitting across from the fucker to ask.

24

Indra's car had been taken to a special compound housed at a local vehicle recovery centre in Cranleigh on Wednesday morning. Vanessa walked into the sterile, well-lit room. Workbenches lined the walls, and hydraulic lifts stood ready to elevate vehicles. Vanessa sniffed the air, taking in the mixture of cleaning agents, gasoline and metal. Among it all, Indra's smart silver Porsche Panamera took centre stage. Already, two CSI investigators were tending to it, one standing over the boot as they carefully sprayed forensic luminal inside, another gathering items from the floor on the passenger side. As Vanessa walked over, she realised Heena was the CSI by the boot, and Gordon was the one inspecting its interior. His large figure was unmistakable. He peered over his shoulder at the sound of Vanessa's heels.

'I heard you were coming,' he said in a less than delighted voice as Heena peered up from the boot and gave Vanessa a smile. He jutted his chin towards a nearby metal table where the car's air filter was. 'Good luck extracting the insects. They're completely wedged in.'

'I have my methods.' Vanessa walked over to the table where she found an air filter and cabin filter from Indra's car, both designed to purify the air for the engine and the vehicle's interior, trapping leaves, dust . . . and insects. Already, Vanessa could see the remains of some insects were glued into the fibresof both, the beginnings of a gruesome melting pot of insect death. The number of insects made a depressing sight for Vanessa. The four horsemen of the insect apocalypse – climate change, habitat destruction, habitat fragmentation and pollution – meant insect numbers were drastically reducing as each year went by, and now here the evidence was, before Vanessa's very own eyes. A few years ago, many more insects would have clogged those grilles in a hot summer week.

She sighed and pulled a tray from the lower shelf of the table, placing it next to the items. Then she popped her AirPods in, finding The Horrors' latest album. Over the next couple of hours, she meticulously dampened the interiors of both filters with a gentle soapy solution, making sure to approach from the reverse side to dislodge the insects almost intact. After the bugs had loosened, she gently washed the filters to remove any remaining debris, then sieved through the dirty water to retrieve any other parts. After, she lay the sodden miniature creatures on the table, examining them all first by sight, then through her microscope.

'Wow, and there was me thinking paperwork was the most brain-numbing part of forensics,' Heena said loud enough for Vanessa to hear over her music. Vanessa took one of her AirPods out and gratefully took the mug of coffee Heena was holding out to her.

'Crime scene cleaning at a micro level,' Vanessa conceded, taking a sip from her coffee.

Gordon walked over too. 'Surely it would have been better, and far speedier, to use compressed air to dislodge the insect debris?'

'In my experience,' Vanessa replied, 'compressed air can be too forceful and may inadvertently scatter the insect debris rather than remove it entirely. I find this a much more thorough method.'

Gordon didn't look convinced. But she had a feeling he'd say the sky was green if she said it was blue.

'Notice anything of interest?' Heena asked.

'The usual collection of Pterygota – flying insects,' Vanessa said, gesturing to an assortment of drenched insects in the tray: delicate caddisflies with their slender bodies and intricate, cylindrical cases. Moths of various sizes and colours, their powdery wings now matted and subdued by the moisture. 'Including nocturnal species, the number of which suggests the car *has* been driven at night.'

'Bit tenuous, don't you think?' Gordon asked. 'I know it's a brand-new model, but it would have had to get to the dealership from the manufacturing plant somehow, and during that time, it would probably have been exposed to night-time air.' Vanessa imagined he'd been practising these lines since the moment he'd heard she'd be turning up that morning.

'Yes, it's something I've factored in,' she replied, trying to keep the wariness from her voice. 'One officer did some checks and discovered that while the car *was* transported at night here, the engine wouldn't have been on. So the air filters would have sucked nothing like this number of nocturnal insects in. This,' she said, gesturing to the tray, 'suggests the car has been driven at night-time, in the past couple of days too, judging from how long these creatures have been dead.'

Gordon sighed audibly and crossed his arms.

'I better call Paul,' Vanessa said. She looked at the time. Nearly one in the afternoon. Hopefully, he'd be awake by now. As she made the call, Gordon leaned against a nearby wall, observing her.

Paul picked up straight away. 'So?'

'I've examined the insects found in the car grille,' Vanessa said. 'There are lots of nocturnal species. In my estimation, this suggests the car was driven at night.'

'Great work, mate. I better pay Mrs Hudson another visit.'

'Wait!' Vanessa said.

'Yeah?'

'Did you get some sleep?'

'A few hours. Helen took the girls to her mum's so I wouldn't be disturbed by them.'

'Great. You've got to look after yourself, you know, for the sake of these victims. They need their detective at his best.'

'Jesus, you sound just like Helen.'

'Have you heard anything about Emi's condition?'

'I took an official statement from her just now. She's better, but remembers nothing about the person who attacked her.'

'Damn.'

'Actually, she was asking after you. Might be worth you paying her a visit before you leave? She was close to your mum.'

Vanessa looked at her watch. 'I could swing by.'

Paul was quiet for a moment. 'So you really are still going to fly out tonight?'

'I have to. I've done what I can here. Olivia, my PhD assistant, is on the case back at the uni lab, so she'll send you a report when it's ready. Depending on the species of fly, that could take a couple of weeks or more. I've given Heena a list of other experts to call on, too. I'll swing by before I go, to say goodbye.'

'You better. Right, chat later.' Then he hung up.

Vanessa frowned. How could he expect her to stay? She'd already delayed her flight once. She shook her head and walked back over to find Heena looking at the soaked remains of the insects. 'You know, I really am finding the entomological side of things fascinating.'

Vanessa smiled. 'Maybe you should specialise?'

'Maybe I should.'

'Well, you have my number now if you ever need any advice.' Vanessa looked at her watch. 'I better go. I said I'd pop by the hospital to see Emi.'

Heena smiled. 'It's been great meeting you, Doctor Marwood.'

'You too, Heena. Keep in touch.'

'Will do.'

Vanessa peered over at Gordon. 'I'm off now,' she called over to him. 'Heena is preserving the specimens for me and I'll get a report over today.'

He looked up. 'That's it then?'

'What do you mean?'

'You're leaving, just like that?'

She crossed her arms. She was sick of people making her feel guilty. 'I have a flight to catch.'

'So what?' Gordon shot back. 'A serial murderer's on the loose in your childhood village, killing your old friends.'

Vanessa's mouth dropped open. 'You didn't even want me here in the first place!'

He shrugged. 'It's nothing personal. I just think bringing lots of experts in overcomplicates things. I've been in this job now for thirty years. In that time, I've seen the world of crime scene investigation change drastically. It used to be simpler, more straightforward.' He sighed. 'We could follow our instincts, trust our expertise and present our findings with confidence. But now, we're caught in the crossfire of conflicting opinions, battling through a maze of red tape and bureaucratic hurdles.'

Vanessa got it. She herself had experienced the increasing complexity of forensic investigations first-hand, with multiple specialists, consultants and stakeholders involved in the process.

But most of them were dead wood. She wasn't.

'Your decomposing eggs didn't seem to enjoy your instincts,' she shot back at him. Then she headed out, readying herself for visiting Emi in hospital.

Vanessa walked down the hospital corridors towards the ward Paul had told her Emi was in, unable to stop herself remembering her father's final moments fifteen years ago. He'd got confused a lot in those final days, thinking Vincent was still there. At first, she would remind him Vincent was missing, but it would just bring back all his pain again.

And his anger.

'Why did you let him go?' he'd scream at her. 'It's your fault.' She soon learned to go along with his confusion, telling her dad Vincent was at school; that he'd be joining them soon.

As she walked down the hospital corridors now, the memories dispersed. She got to Emi's small private room in the ward, finding a police officer standing guard. Paul had called ahead to let him know Vanessa was visiting, so he stepped aside when she arrived.

Taking a deep breath, Vanessa pushed open the door and entered the room. The sterile scent of antiseptic greeted her as she spotted Emi lying in the hospital bed, her long white hair cascading over the pillow. She had her face turned to the side, looking out towards Greensands in the distance with a whimsical expression.

'Emi,' Vanessa said softly. 'It's Vanessa Marwood.'

Emi turned to look at Vanessa, her face lighting up with recognition. 'Vanessa! I told Paul I wanted to see you.'

'Yes. How are you?'

'Alive. You know the knife penetrated an ovary.' *Penetrated an ovary.* Traumatic insemination, just like Vanessa suspected. 'They said I should be a lot worse off but here I am,' she added with a weak smile.

'Clearly you're made of strong stuff.'

'Us independent women are though, aren't we?' Vanessa smiled in agreement. 'Not happy about this though,' Emi said, gesturing to the drip attached to her arm. 'God knows what they're pumping into me.'

'It'll be helping your body heal.'

'Pah! Knowing big pharma, half the stuff's making me worse, so I'll have no choice but to come back for more.'

Vanessa pulled up a chair and settled next to Emi's bed.

Emi's smile softened. 'Look at you, all grown up. Your mum must be so proud of the woman you've become, Vanessa. The three of us, we're cut from the same cloth, you know. Independent, passionate . . . unwilling to conform to society's expectations.'

Vanessa tensed at the mention of her mother.

'You haven't heard from her either, then?' Emi asked, noticing her look.

'Not for years. I know she's OK though.'

'Yes, as long as her art still appears on that website of hers.'

So Emi did the same as Vanessa, regularly checking in on her old friend's online gallery.

'I bet she's doing the same with you,' Emi said. 'Keeping an eye on you from afar.'

Vanessa couldn't help herself – she gave a dismissive snort. Emi grasped Vanessa's hand, her grip strong despite her injuries. 'I promise you, she will be, Vanessa. She loved you, so much. Will still love you.'

'Funny way of showing it.'

Emi searched Vanessa's face. 'We women, we're complicated creatures. Like those insects you love, there's more to us than men can *possibly* understand.' Her face darkened. 'And your mother, she was more complicated than most. But what I do know is that she *will* be keeping tabs on you. I bet, for example, she knows you're off to New York.'

'Well, you certainly know,' Vanessa said with a wry smile.

'I like to keep up to date with the warriors of this world. When are you going?'

'Tonight. I was supposed to be flying out there the night before last.'

'So you delayed it for this case? For Greensands?'

Vanessa nodded. 'It's hard saying no to Paul Truss.'

Emi was quiet for a few moments. 'Are you sure it's a good idea to leave tonight?' she asked eventually.

154

Vanessa rolled her eyes. 'You sound like Paul. Like half the people I've been in contact with the past couple of days, in fact.'

'No, they're all thinking about what those poor dead men need. *I'm* thinking about you. Maybe you need some closure before you go. *Proper* closure, so you can start your new job all fresh and ready.'

Vanessa frowned. Maybe Emi had a point. She fiddled with the dragonfly ring on her finger.

Emi went to sit up, wincing.

'Emi, don't.'

'I need to.' Emi clutched Vanessa's hand, looking her in the eye. 'Closure is the brush that paints the canvas of your future. Without a strong brush, how can you make the most of this next phase in your life? You need to stay and see this through for *you*, Vanessa.'

Vanessa thought about what Emi was saying. Maybe she really was right. Also . . . what if there were more attacks, more murders, and she was on the other side of the world? Could she really throw herself into her new life, without feeling like she'd done all she could to help her childhood village? To help Paul?

She looked at her watch. Nearly two in the afternoon. She really should be leaving soon. Then she looked towards Greensands. Why couldn't this all have happened a week ago?

No, she couldn't delay her flight again. She just couldn't.

'Enough about me,' Vanessa said as she smiled at Emi. 'I want to hear all about you.'

After her visit with Emi, Vanessa headed outside to her truck, driving back to Greensands and the back of the butterfly farm. She just needed to say a proper goodbye. She parked up by the grassland and stepped out, taking in the vast expanse of grass that stretched out before her. This was the very spot where Vincent had disappeared all those years ago. It looked so sorry now, with rubbish and broken furniture scattered across the grass.

As she took it in, she noticed something leaning up against the back of the butterfly atrium: the huge wooden sculpture her mother had created that had once dominated the car park. Now it lay abandoned and rotting in the very place where Vincent had disappeared.

'Strangely fitting,' Vanessa murmured to herself.

She turned away from it and closed her eyes, letting the stillness of the moment envelop her. In the solitude of the grasslands, she felt a connection to Vincent, as though his presence lingered in the whispers of the wind and the rustling of leaves.

'Vincent,' she whispered, her voice barely audible. 'I hope you've found your peace, wherever you are. I love you.'

When Vanessa opened her eyes again, her gaze fell upon a figure in the distance. Her heart almost stopped when, for a small moment, she thought it might be Vincent. But as the figure drew closer, she realised it was Abe Abbott.

Wasn't Paul trying to track him down?

Vanessa glanced at her truck, the engine still warm, her suitcase in the back seat packed for her new life. A flight was waiting for her, a whole new chapter to her life. And yet there was Abe, a stark reminder of the village she was leaving behind. A place that had also given her roots, however gnarled and twisted they might be.

Vanessa wavered, torn between two worlds. Her fingers twitched involuntarily towards her car keys – she could still make her flight, leave behind this mesh of complications and pain. But then she thought of Paul – of all the people in this village, the dead and the living – and she wondered how her expertise, her presence, could tip the scales towards tracking down the killer stalking these people. Her hand moved away from her car keys and, with a sigh that carried the weight of her decision, she started walking towards Abe.

25

Paul walked up to the reception desk at Indra's office. He flashed his badge. 'Detective Chief Inspector Truss here to see Indra Hudson, please.'

The receptionist narrowed her eyes, giving his ID a proper look. Then she sighed and picked up the phone. 'Sorry to disturb, hon. But I have a Detective Truss here for you.' She gave a slight quirk of an eyebrow, then put the phone down. 'She'll be out in a moment.'

A few moments later, Indra strode out into the reception area. 'If this is about the complaint I made—'

'What complaint?' Paul asked.

'Against you barging into my place of work yesterday and dragging me out of bed last night. Frankly, it's an outrage! If you wanted to search my premises, you should have made it official and got a search warrant. If you wanted to *interview* me, you should have had the decency to wait until daybreak.'

Paul was going to enjoy this. *Really* enjoy this. 'Nope, it's not about that. Can you step outside a moment?' He at least wanted to give her a chance at some privacy.

She gave him an incredulous look. 'No, I won't, Detective. I'm rather busy and so you should be too. Why on earth are you wasting time with me when you could be out there, catching the person who committed these heinous crimes?'

'That's exactly why I'm here, Mrs Hudson. You lied about not driving your car at night.'

She frowned. 'I did not.'

'We have proof you did.'

'Well, that's impossible.'

'Then how can you explain the presence of nocturnal insects in the car's air and cabin filters?'

Indra blinked. 'I-I have no idea. I mean, it's kept in the garage at night. But insects can get into the garage. And what about the dealership? They could have driven it at night.'

Paul watched her. He couldn't decide if this was all bravado, or she was genuinely confused about why he was suggesting she'd driven the car at night.

Then her eyes widened as something seemed to dawn on her. 'I've just remembered something. Wait here a moment. Let me just check.' Paul watched as she strode to her office and went to her desk, opening a drawer and looking inside. Then she shook her head and came back to Paul. 'Follow me.'

'Where?' Paul asked.

'Just come.'

She walked through the office as Paul followed, people peering up in curiosity from their screens. Then she stopped in front of the desk of her androgynous, blue-haired PA. 'Avery, do you know where the spare key for my new car is? It was in my desk drawer.'

The tops of Avery's cheeks went red. Instantly, Paul's antennae went off. 'I-I don't know.'

'Are you sure about that?' Indra said. She leaned close to her PA, her brown eyes sparking with anger. Under her hard gaze, Avery suddenly burst into tears.

'OK, come on,' Paul said with a sigh, gesturing to a free meeting room and marching in as Avery and Indra followed. He slammed the door shut. 'Sit,' he instructed them both. 'What's going on?'

'My car was delivered here, to the offices,' Indra said. 'I completely forgot there was an extra set of keys, which I put in my drawer . . . while *he* was with me.'

So Avery was a *he* then.

'You think Avery might have them?' Paul asked.

'Avery has form,' Indra said. '*Don't* you, Avery?'

The tearful PA just sank his head down.

'What do you mean?' Paul asked.

'Avery was accused of stealing one of the social media girls' blazers. He always denied it, but considering this car nonsense . . .' Her voice trailed off.

'Fine,' Avery said. 'I stole the blazer. But I did *not* take your car keys, I swear! But . . . I know who did. He came here when we went out for lunch last week and he-he took the spare set when I told him about the new car.'

Paul leaned his palms on the table and stared at the blue-haired PA. 'Who took the spare set?'

Avery blinked up at Paul through his long fake lashes. 'Abe Abbott.'

26

As Vanessa drew closer to Abe, she noticed the intricate tattoo on his cheek. It was a typical 'dartboard' orb web, apart from the thick, elaborate pattern that twisted down its middle. His head was closely shaven, just a hint of black fuzz. In his left earlobe were two earrings: one large circular stud, the other small and silver. His face was angular, eyebrows curved high, the stare of his dark eyes bleak. But most interesting of all was that he was holding a carrier with an enormous spider inside.

He certainly looked the part. No wonder the media were salivating at the thought of this young, unusual, spider-loving, possibly gay man being The Cobweb Killer. It had been all over the tabloids that morning, the love affair between Benjamin Oberlin and Abe Abbott. But Vanessa had long learned not to judge books by their covers.

'Abe?'

He turned at the sound of her voice, eyes widening in surprise.

She looked down at the small, transparent carrier case he was holding. It wasn't just any carrier case either, but a bloody expensive one with multiple ventilation holes on the sides and a sophisticated lid with a secure locking mechanism to prevent any accidental escapes. The kid really took his spider ownership seriously. She regarded him. He seemed like a good kid. Maybe he even reminded her a bit of Vincent with his awkward manner and fascination with insects.

'Is that a Mexican redknee?' she asked, peering inside the carrier to see a large, velvety black spider with vibrant red-orange leg joints.

Abe nodded, still regarding her with a slightly boggle-eyed look.

'How old is she?' she asked, able to tell the sex of the spider from size and abdominal marking as it climbed up the transparent wall of the carrier.

'Twelve.'

'So you've had her since you were a boy?'

Abe nodded.

'Any reason she's out of her usual terrarium?'

'Taking her to the vet,' Abe replied, his tone subdued. 'Hasn't been acting like herself lately.'

'My cobalt blue was the same a few months back. It turned out to be a digestive issue. She's fine now. The vet will help.' She gestured to his tattoo. 'That's a wasp spider web, right?'

Abe nodded, eyes lighting up. '*Argiope bruennichi*,' he said, using the official term for the black and yellow patterned spiders that frequented British gardens in the south. 'My mum used to like them.'

'Used to?'

'Died last year. Cancer.'

Poor kid. 'I'm sorry,' Vanessa replied. 'I lost my dad to cancer, too.'

Abe shrugged. 'It shouldn't really matter, being motherless. I mean, these guys are cool with it.' He gestured down to the spider. 'Only, like, one per cent of insects show parental care as it's not biologically needed. Their offspring are usually independent from birth. We should be the same. Would save a lot of pain.'

He was right. It would save a world of pain.

'The stabilimentum's nicely done,' she said, referring to the pattern that ran down the middle of the web tattooed on his cheek.

'Yeah, the guy I use is pretty sick. Wasp spiders are cool, right? Especially their mating habits. Did you know the dude breaks off their own cock and leaves it in the female's vag to prevent competitors from entering her?' Vanessa raised an eyebrow, and Abe laughed. 'Shit,' he said, ''Course you know that. You're, like, the goddess of arthropods.'

'That's very kind.' She paused a moment. 'You know Paul Truss is looking for you, right?'

Abe's face faltered. 'I didn't kill Benjamin Oberlin, if that's what you're trying to imply.' It was a statement delivered in monotone, a contrast to the passion he'd shown when talking about spiders.

'I'm not implying that. But you ought to talk to Detective Truss, he—'

As she said that, there was the sound of tyres screeching as a police car pulled up beside the grasslands. Paul jumped out, flanked by two uniformed officers, and ran over to Abe and Vanessa.

The young man's face turned pale. He hugged the carrier case close to his skinny chest, like a security blanket. Then he suddenly broke into a run, darting through the long grass.

Vanessa sighed. This really would *not* help his case.

Paul and the other police officers sprang into action, giving chase through the grasslands. A couple walking their dog nearby paused to watch as the commotion disrupted the serene atmosphere. In the chaos, Vanessa noticed the carrier case slip from Abe's hands, hitting the ground with a loud thud and bouncing. The see-through walls cracked, exposing the startled Mexican redknee tarantula that hopped out of the carrier and scurried away through the grass with surprising speed towards the couple.

A cry of alarm pierced the air. 'A spider!' the woman screamed. Vanessa ran forward, heading towards the fleeing and undoubtedly terrified tarantula. The creature made a beeline for safety, attempting to disappear under a large rock. It wouldn't survive out here, not for long. Vanessa swiftly moved, kneeling down to block its escape route with her hand.

The spider hesitated, its multiple eyes fixated on Vanessa's hand. Then it stepped onto the tip of her forefinger, its delicate legs clinging to Vanessa's skin as it sought refuge on her palm. With careful precision, Vanessa rose to her feet, the tarantula nestled safely on the palm of her hand. She locked eyes with Abe for a brief moment as Paul placed handcuffs on the young man.

'Abe Abbott,' Paul announced. 'I'm arresting you on suspicion of taking a vehicle without the owner's consent.'

Vanessa furrowed her brow, her mind racing to connect the dots. Was this about Indra Hudson's car?

'You do not have to say anything,' Paul continued, his voice firm and authoritative. 'But it may harm your defence if you do not mention when questioned something you later rely on in court. Anything you say may be given in evidence. Do you understand?'

Abe nodded, his expression resigned, as if he had expected this moment to come. As he was led away, he twisted around to steal a final glimpse of Vanessa. 'Look after Amy Lee!' he shouted out, his voice carrying through the air. 'My dad's useless at it.'

Vanessa nodded in acknowledgement, her eyes following Abe's retreat as he was shoved into the back of the police car.

She looked down at Abe's cherished companion, the dog walkers continuing to watch on in horror at the spider in Vanessa's hand.

Could its loving owner *really* be capable of killing four men and injuring one woman?

Once again, she thought of the flight she had to catch. There was still time. But as she watched the police car drive off, she realised she'd already made her mind up a few moments back when she first saw Abe. She had to stay to see this case through.

27

Abe Abbott sat slouched in his chair next to his bored-looking solicitor, his gaze shifting between Paul and OS.

'We've been looking for you since yesterday, Abe,' Paul began. 'We went to your house, didn't we, DS O'Sullivan?'

'We did indeed,' OS confirmed. 'Your dad said you were at a gig in Manchester. Which gig was that?' He held his pen over his notepad, waiting to write the answer down.

'Gig?' Abe replied, looking confused. 'What's he talking about? I wasn't at a gig. I was with a friend.'

'What friend?' Paul asked.

'Devon.'

'We'll need to corroborate that. Do you have Devon's number?'

'Yeah, sure. But good luck getting hold of him – he never picks up.'

Paul wasn't too concerned about that. There were always other ways of verifying if Abe had been in Manchester.

Paul leaned forward, his eyes locked on Abe's face. 'Let's move on to the reason you're here. We believe you stole Indra Hudson's car in the early hours of Sunday.'

Abe put his head in his hands and groaned.

'Is that a confirmation?' OS asked.

'I just borrowed it,' Abe said, his voice barely discernible.

'Can you repeat that?' OS asked.

Abe looked up, beads of sweat forming on his pale forehead. 'I just *borrowed* it. I wanted to go clubbing in Cranleigh. Taxis cost a fucking fortune. Cost of living crisis, and all that.'

'This is where proper jobs come in handy,' OS said under his breath.

Paul shot him a look. He was a good interrogation partner, except when he decided to make little digs like that.

'So you just steal someone's car keys from their office?' Paul said. 'Then sneak back in the night to take the car for a little joyride, too?'

'Indra Hudson can afford it,' Abe said. 'Anyway, she treats Avery like shit. She deserved it.'

'I noticed you had a photo of her in your room,' Paul remarked. 'Why is that?'

Abe looked confused, then he rolled his eyes. 'The article. Yeah, I was planning on doing a TikTok about her plans to reopen the butterfly farm. Was part of my research.'

'Tell us more about Saturday night,' Paul said. 'You said you went clubbing in Cranleigh. Which club is that?'

Abe named a club-cum-casino that had just opened in the city.

'So much for cost of living,' OS said. 'Pretty pricey to get into, so I've heard.'

'Who did you go with?' Paul asked.

'Some friends from college,' Abe replied.

'I need names,' OS asked, pen still poised.

Abe reeled off three names Paul recognised as being other kids from the village.

'And you stole Indra Hudson's car before heading out to give them a lift?' OS asked.

'Kind of,' Abe mumbled.

'Kind of?' Paul asked.

'I didn't *steal* it,' Abe replied.

'How else would you describe taking someone's car keys without their permission, then using them to drive their car?'

Abe didn't answer.

'Where did you drive the car to after leaving the club?' Paul asked.

'You clearly know the answer to that already,' Abe grumbled. 'That's why I'm *really* in here, isn't it? So yeah,' he said, putting his pale hands up, 'I admit it, I drove Indra Hudson's car to go and see Benjamin. And for the record, he was alive and well when I left him. I didn't harm a fucking hair on his head. It's more likely to be the other way around.'

'What's that supposed to mean?' OS asked.

Abe sighed. 'Benjamin had this kink for saying snarky stuff when he was fucking. You know what I mean, right?'

'No, explain,' Paul said.

'Like, I dunno, "you fucking skinny little scrounger with your fucking tiny little dick". That kind of thing. The closer he got to, you know, coming, the harsher his words got. He did it with all the people he fucked.'

'You all meet up to discuss it then, do you?' OS asked.

Abe rolled his eyes. 'Funny.'

'So you're confirming you were in some kind of relationship with Benjamin Oberlin?' OS asked.

Abe shrugged. 'It was casual. We were just having fun. Nothing serious.'

'Fun?' Paul asked. 'What kind of fun?'

'S-E-X, if you need me to spell it out.'

'How often did you see him?' Paul asked.

Another shrug. 'Every now and again. Maybe once or twice a month.'

'How did it make you feel, hearing him abuse you like that?' Paul asked.

'I blocked it out.'

'You sure?' OS asked. 'Maybe it made you so mad, you lashed out.'

'Please remember, officers, you have not arrested Abe for murder,' his solicitor said as he stifled a yawn. 'He has been arrested for taking a vehicle without the owner's consent.'

'Yeah,' Abe said. 'And anyway, I told you, no fucking way did I kill him.'

'You got to admit, it's strange, though,' Paul said, pushing his luck with Abe's solicitor, 'that just a few hours after you see him, he turns up dead?'

'I'm telling you,' Abe said, leaning across the table and tapping his black nails on its surface, 'I didn't off Benjamin. It was just sex. Pleasure. No big deal. I didn't *feel* enough to do anything but fuck him. Killing him would mean I *felt* something.'

'Bit heartless,' OS said.

'Officers,' the solicitor said in a warning tone.

Abe rolled his eyes. 'Whatever, man. I didn't kill him or stuff his mouth with cotton wool – that's all I'm trying to say.'

Paul's eyebrows rose in surprise. 'Cotton wool? Nobody said anything about cotton wool.'

'Come on, everybody in this tiny Hicksville town knows about that,' Abe said. 'Like the spider silk being found in the first three dudes' stomachs. Fucking crazy,' he said, shaking his head.

'You own a number of spiders, don't you?' OS said. 'In fact, I was just checking your TikTok channel out, and you own a golden silk orb-weaver?'

'Is that what silk was used?' Abe asked.

'Answer the question,' Paul snapped.

'No, he doesn't need to answer it,' the solicitor drawled. 'This line of questioning isn't related to taking the vehicle, and if you had evidence of murder, you would have surely arrested my client.'

'It's fine,' Abe said to his solicitor. 'I've got nothing to hide. I did own a golden silk orb-weaver.'

'Did?' Paul asked.

'Yeah, until Friday. But someone stole it.'

Paul exchanged a look with OS.

'Are you saying someone broke into your shed and stole it?' Paul asked.

'Yeah, that's right,' Abe replied.

'And you didn't think to report it?' OS asked.

Abe laughed. 'Why bother? As if you guys are gonna care about a fucking spider being nicked.'

'Every piece of information is crucial in this investigation,' Paul said. 'How did you get your hands on a golden silk orb-weaver, anyway? They're not the kind of thing you find in Pets at Home, are they?'

'It's all legit via a US website,' Abe said.

'Got proof of that?' OS asked.

'Might have receipts in my shed.' Abe smiled. 'So it really was spider silk from a golden silk orb-weaver that was put in their stomachs, wasn't it? Doctor Marwood would have recognised it. Jeez. This dude is *sick*. Using Sharon den Adel to do something like that.'

'Sharon den what?' Paul and OS asked at the same time.

'My golden silk orb-weaver. She's named after the lead singer of Within Temptation. I guess if you find my stolen *Nephila*, you'll find the twisted fucker who did all this.'

'Maybe you just offed your spider to hide the evidence and are pretending it was nicked,' OS suggested.

'Fuck, I'd never do that!'

Paul searched the kid's face. He looked genuinely aghast at the idea. But the evidence was mounting up. Not enough to charge him for anything but taking a vehicle without the owner's consent. Paul peered up at the clock. Maybe they'd get enough evidence by the time they'd need to apply for more time to hold him?

A thought came to him then. 'Where did you stash the car key?'

'In my shed.'

'OK. We're going to keep you in a little longer as we're just waiting for an official statement from Indra, Abe. In the meantime, I'd like to head to your shed and retrieve the key. In light of the break-in too, I can get our forensics guys to check it out, see if we can figure out who took your spider. Do you give us permission to do that?'

Abe thought about it. 'Only if Vanessa Marwood is there. She can make sure my kids are OK.'

'Kids?' OS asked.

'He means his spiders,' Paul explained. 'And I'm afraid Doctor Marwood will be on a flight to New York soon, so she won't be available.'

Abe groaned, sinking his head down onto the table. It was the same way he felt about Vanessa leaving.

'I promise I'll be extra careful,' Paul said. 'So, do we have permission?'

'Sure, I've got nothing to hide,' Abe said.

'Fine. Now go and have a nice long rest. You look as knackered as I feel,' Paul said as he stood up with OS.

'Looks like a visit to this kid's spider emporium is next on the list, then?' OS said as they walked out. 'Shame your Bug Lady's getting a flight out tonight; she'd be in her element.'

Paul sighed. 'Yeah, she would. I better give her a quick call, actually, before she leaves.' OS strolled away as Paul dialled Vanessa's number.

'Hey,' she said when she picked up. 'How'd the interview with the kid go?'

'We're about to search his spider shed.'

'Wow, you must be *delighted* at the prospect.'

Paul shuddered. 'You know me too well. Where are you?'

She hesitated. 'Still at the grasslands,' she said eventually.

'With the spider?'

'Yep, she's hanging out with me.'

Paul smiled. He could imagine Vanessa sitting in the middle of the grass, that huge spider crawling over her. 'Don't you have a flight to catch?'

'I did.'

'Did?'

He heard her let out a sigh. 'I can't leave, Paul. Not yet.'

Paul felt like punching the air in victory. 'So my emotional blackmail worked?'

'Actually, it was something Emi said.'

'Well, God bless the Butterfly Witch. What did she say?'

There was a pause. 'Long story.'

'So, I'll text you the Abbotts' address? See you there in half an hour for the shed search?'

'An hour. I need to go and buy a travel terrarium.'

28

Vanessa stood outside Abe's small shed with Paul, OS, Selma and Heena, and two other officers, still not quite able to believe she'd delayed her flight *again*. She couldn't even get one for tomorrow night – they were fully booked. So she'd be flying out the day after, on Friday. She had to remind herself these weren't normal circumstances. With a serial killer on the loose in her childhood home, she could sacrifice a few settling-in days in New York to try to help Paul.

To try to help herself, too.

Abe's shed was nestled at the edge of his father's messy backyard, its worn wooden panels adorned with patches of moss and ivy. One dusty window showed glimpses of a dimly lit interior. Vanessa felt a tingle of anticipation at the thought of seeing Abe's pets. The others didn't seem to feel the same though, one of the officers casting anxious glances towards the shed.

'You really think the kid's a killer?' Vanessa asked Paul now in a low voice. He was looking towards the shed, a slightly horrified expression on his face at the prospect of having to be so close to spiders.

'We haven't arrested him for murder,' he said.

'*Yet*,' OS added.

'I can't see him being a murderer,' Vanessa remarked.

'You've got a soft spot for him,' Paul said as he pulled some latex gloves from his trouser pockets. 'A fellow spider worshipper.'

'A *Doctor Marwood* worshipper too,' OS added. 'He talked about you like you're a god.'

'Oh please,' Vanessa said. 'I'm just someone who knows that strange little tattooed insect worshippers aren't always the psychopaths people think they are.' She didn't add that Abe reminded her of her brother Vincent. Not just those dark eyes and hair, but also the vulnerability he exhibited, mixed in with a strangeness that set him apart from other kids his age. It had always been a struggle for Vincent at school, and

Vanessa imagined it was the same for Abe. Just him being arrested, even if it was for taking Indra's car and not murder, would have the villagers whispering, wondering, presuming. 'I always knew he was a wrong 'un,' they'd be saying.

'Bit dumb of him to take Indra's car either way,' OS said.

'I think he saw it as some kind of revenge for the way Indra treats his friend Avery,' Paul explained.

'Bit extreme,' OS remarked.

Paul nodded. 'Yeah.' He pointed at the officers milling nearby. 'Check the garden, will you?'

'Speaking of extreme,' OS said. 'Benjamin having a kink for verbally abusing his partners while doing the deed wasn't ever going to help him, was it?'

Vanessa remembered how Benjamin used to have a bit of a spiteful tongue. He'd disguise it as banter; tell you that you were being 'oversensitive' if you reacted with anything other than a laugh. But there was always an undertone to it.

'Was it consensual?' Vanessa asked. 'Some couples like to indulge in a bit of negative banter.'

OS gave her an interested look.

'I got the impression it was *endured* rather than enjoyed,' Paul said. 'Benjamin's never exactly been the most honey-tongued of individuals. Didn't realise he'd turned it into a kink.'

'Did you ask Abe how he got hold of a golden silk orb-weaver?' Vanessa asked. 'They're not easy to buy . . . unless you're on the dark web.'

'We did,' OS replied. 'He insists it was all legit, said we might find the receipts in his shed.'

'OK, let's take a look then.' Using the key Abe's father had given them, Paul opened the padlock protecting the latch, and they all walked inside. Vanessa couldn't help but smile to herself as Paul swallowed nervously, eyes scanning the area. Like Abe's bedroom, it was tidy inside. Several shelves lined the walls, each one housing a variety of terrariums of different sizes and shapes. At the back of the room, there was a sofa with a blanket and pillow flung over it. Vanessa imagined Abe spent so many hours in the shed, watching and caring for his beloved spiders, that he sometimes slept there. There was also a small desk with a lamp and a laptop computer on its surface, the screen covered in notes and research papers on spider behaviour and biology. In the corner of the room was a tripod and fuzzy-headed microphone where Abe must have done his TikTok videos.

Vanessa took in the array of different spiders in the shed. In the smaller terrariums were a variety of jumping spiders, including a zebra jumping spider with its distinctive black and white stripes. Vanessa also noticed a regal jumping spider, its vibrant green, orange and blue hues standing out in the gloom. In the larger terrariums were several tarantulas. One was a Chilean rose tarantula, about six inches in size with a brown and pinkish-red coloration on its body that made Vanessa think of sweet potato skin. The other was a Goliath birdeater tarantula, like the one pinned in the Oberlins' manor. But this one was very much alive, all eleven inches of it lounging in the terrarium's corner.

'Aren't they gorgeous?' she whispered as she peered into the terrariums.

'Not sure I'd use that expression,' Paul said, shivering with disgust and blinking rapidly as he watched the Goliath birdeater tarantula lift one of it brown legs.

'He obviously cares for his little eight-legged friends,' Heena murmured.

She was right. Abe had created custom-built habitats for each spider, with an abundance of thick substrate for the spiders to burrow in, several hiding spots and shallow water dishes.

One terrarium that sat in the corner of the room drew particular interest from Vanessa. It was medium-sized, around twenty centimetres in diameter and thirty centimetres in height, tall enough for arboreal spiders like golden silk orb-weavers, which preferred to spin their webs in trees or high up in vegetation. But the most noticeable aspect of this terrarium was the fact that the top had been removed. This must have been where the golden silk orb-weaver had once resided.

Vanessa felt a pang of sadness. If Abe's golden silk orb-weaver had been used to extract spider silk – a fact Vanessa still struggled to wrap her head around considering how awkward it was to do – what was its fate now?

Then she noticed another terrarium that was empty, one of the larger ones. A crack zigzagged down the glass. She walked over to it and peered inside. Something *had* been in there. She could tell from the arrangement of the bark and scrubs. But what?

'Is this *really* necessary?' a voice asked.

They all turned to see Abe's father, Ricky, standing in the doorway. He was wearing a Mötley Crüe T-shirt over skinny grey jeans. The same get-up he'd preferred when he helped Vanessa's father, too.

'You know the kid's not capable of murder, Paul,' Ricky said. 'He's a good boy. You can see that from the way he cares for our beloved house lodgers. He might prefer arachnids to humans, but that doesn't mean he'd *kill* someone.'

'Who said anything about murder?' Paul replied. 'Abe told us this place was broken into the other day. So we're just doing due diligence, Ricky. He gave us permission.'

'Oh come on, Paul. You lot suspect my boy, admit it.' Ricky turned to Vanessa. 'From one insect aficionado to another, you know it's not him, right? You know what it's like to be one of us.' He rolled up his sleeve to reveal his own tattoos, mainly featuring drawings of what Vanessa presumed was his late wife. 'Freaks on the edge of society. It's always us they cast their suspicious eyes over, right?'

'I really can't comment on the investigation,' Vanessa said, aware of the various police officers' eyes on her. 'Nor on your son's role in it.'

Ricky laughed. 'You sound like you've regurgitated a police manual, Vanessa. Surely you're not a detective yourself?'

'I just know my place. Speaking of which, do you know what spider was kept in this terrarium?' She gestured to the large, broken terrarium.

Ricky followed her gaze. 'Nope.'

He was lying. Vanessa could tell.

'Are you sure?' she asked.

'Yep.' He backed away. 'I'll leave you all to it now.'

As he disappeared from sight, an officer who'd been searching the garden poked their head around the side of the shed door. 'Think I've found something, Boss.'

Paul gestured for Vanessa and Heena to follow him around the back of the shed towards a strip of overgrown bushes. Another officer was crouched down by some barrels, holding back a large branch as he looked at something beneath the bush.

'Didn't notice it at first,' he said as he moved out of the way for them to see.

It was a clear footprint, pressed deep into the soil. Vanessa crouched down to look.

'Nice find,' Paul said.

'I'm guessing Abe Abbott's got smaller feet than this print, judging by his height and size,' Heena said. Paul nodded. 'Maybe it's his dad's?'

'Could be,' Paul agreed, 'but he's on the small side, too. This one looks average-sized, maybe a nine? Can you measure it, Heena?'

Heena nodded and pulled a vernier calliper out, moving its sliding jaws to measure the footprint. 'You're right,' she said. 'It's a size nine, which *also* happens to be the UK's average shoe size for a man.' Then she frowned. 'Doctor Marwood, look at this.'

Heena was pointing at a shiny, metallic green shard, about five millimetres long.

'Tansy beetle,' they both said at the same time.

'What's that?' Paul asked.

'It's the same kind of shell we found under Simon's shoulder,' Heena explained. 'I had it tested and it's definitely a tansy beetle. I've emailed you both the findings.'

'Great, I thought as much. And from what I can see here, this is an entire forewing from a tansy beetle. It's unusual to see one as they're so rare now . . . and sold in the booklet we found in Indra's offices, too,' Vanessa added. 'My guess is the wearer accidentally – or purposefully – trod on one or more of the poor things, carrying and distributing their remains from one place to the next. Maybe they were at Benjamin's little insect emporium . . . or there's another place where these creatures are being kept? I'd like to take a proper look at the two fragments,' she said to Heena. 'Do you have any microscopes in your lab?'

Heena nodded. 'If you can call it a lab. But yes, we do. You're welcome to use it. But haven't you got a flight to catch?'

Paul and Vanessa exchanged a look. 'I've delayed it,' Vanessa said.

Paul stood up, stretching. Vanessa examined his face. He looked particularly pale today. 'Heena, take a cast of this footprint, will you, and get some pics. I think we've got what we want from here.'

After they finished their search, turning up nothing new, they headed back to their cars.

'What are your plans tonight?' Paul asked. 'Helen would love to have you for dinner again.'

'I need a night in, to be honest, Paul. I need to juggle a bunch of stuff around in New York. Plus I'm spider-sitting, remember?'

'I couldn't think of anything worse,' Paul said. Then he squeezed her arm. 'You're a good egg for staying, Vanessa.'

'What, runny in the inside and hard to crack on the outside?'

'Something like that.'

'What about you? You should get yourself a proper dinner, have some rest.'

'That's the plan.' Paul looked out over the grasslands behind the Abbotts' garden, frowning. 'As long as we're not pulled into another attack tonight.'

Vanessa sighed. 'Let's hope not.'

29

The Crime Scene Investigation Unit at Cranleigh Police Station felt more like an office, with staff seated at their desks hard at work. There was a door leading to a small, glass-fronted lab at the back though, and that was where Heena led Vanessa.

'A brand-new forensics facility is being built,' Heena explained. 'But that won't be ready for a while, so for now, we make do with this.'

When they walked in, the first thing that hit Vanessa was the familiar odour of chemicals. To most people, that smell could be overwhelming. But Vanessa had grown so used to it over the years, she barely noticed it now. In fact, there was something about the combination of disinfectants mixed with the earthy, biological scents of blood and mud, combined with the hum and whir of lab equipment, that felt like a strangely macabre lullaby to her.

Vanessa imagined what the New York lab would look like. It had only opened a few weeks ago and she'd seen photos of its sleek interiors and top-of-the-range equipment online.

'This won't be anything like what you're used to at the university,' Heena said. 'We mainly do fingerprints here, and less serious crime. A lot of the samples from these murders have been outsourced to private forensics firms, and your PhD student, of course. I'll get these beetle fragments sent to an expert but we can take a look first, especially now we've found another.'

'Sounds good.'

Heena gestured to two small glass boxes where the fragments lay in some acid-free tissue paper. Vanessa removed her forceps from her kitbag and carefully extracted the first fragment from its container, placing it under a microscope.

'Yep, it really does look like it's from a tansy beetle. They're usually mixed up with other leaf beetles. But I can tell this is a tansy beetle from the lip running down the full length of its forewing.' Vanessa shook her head. 'Jesus, these creatures have no place being in stamping distance of humans. They're so rare now.' She placed the fragment back in the container and got the other, smaller one out, laying it on a fresh glass to examine. 'Yep, this looks like it's from a tansy beetle, too. The pitting is pretty distinct.'

'Same one?'

'Hard to tell.'

'So whoever was wearing the size nines stepped on one or two very unlucky—'

'And very rare,' Vanessa said.

'Yes, very *rare* tansy beetles.'

Vanessa frowned. 'Wait a minute. What's that?' As she adjusted her microscope, she noticed something purple stuck to the underside of the most recent shell fragment.

'Look at this.' She moved out of the way so Heena could see.

'Is that a wool fragment?' Heena suggested.

'Looks like it.'

'*Very* purple too.'

'Yep.'

'So chances are our suspect not only has size nine feet,' Heena said as she took some photos with the microscope, 'but they also have a purple carpet or rug?'

Vanessa nodded. Gordon walked into the main office then, frowning when he noticed Vanessa.

'So you took my advice and stayed?' he called through to the lab.

'Yes, it was all down to you, Gordon,' Vanessa called back sarcastically.

He ignored her comment, instead walking over to the lab door. 'Mio called. We have some preliminary toxicology findings in.'

'They really did expedite things,' Heena said.

Gordon nodded. 'First, the dead bee you found in the ridge outside Indra Hudson's offices? Benjamin Oberlin's blood was indeed detected on it.'

'That's something,' Heena said.

'Yes,' Gordon said. 'It might suggest Benjamin was at the ridge, barefoot, at some point before his death. We've also had it confirmed that atracurium was found in the blood of all four men.' He frowned. 'Weird extra detail. A trace of resin was also noticed. Very small though, so might just be incidental. The most interesting fact to me was the substance we found in the cotton wool from Benjamin's body. The first substance he noted was human semen.'

'They think semen was found in Emi Craviso's wound,' Heena said.

Gordon nodded. 'Yes, I have the results from that, too. They really are rushing things through for this case. Turns out, like the semen found on the cotton wool, it's from three different DNA make-ups.'

'The first three victims?' Vanessa asked.

'That's right,' the CSI lead confirmed.

Heena took in a sharp breath. 'My God.'

Vanessa frowned, trying not to think how that semen would have been extracted from the men.

'There were no signs of sexual assault though, right?' Heena asked. 'So how could it have been extracted?'

'They may have been forced under the threat of death to, erm, produce it,' Gordon said with a shudder. 'It doesn't end there though. There's another substance mixed in with it too, which backed up your theory about it being an attempt to mimic mating plugs,' he added begrudgingly to Vanessa. 'A hydrocarbon called ocimene?'

Vanessa nodded. 'That makes sense. Some species of butterfly such as the postman butterfly produce ocimene to repel competition.' She remembered her father telling her that and how fascinated she'd been. 'You can *buy* ocimene. I guess it's just another way for this killer to show their calling card.'

'That he's a sick bastard?' Gordon suggested.

'Don't need ocimene to show that.' Vanessa looked at her watch. 'While it's been a pleasure, I think I better head back now and check on Abe Abbott's pet.'

'Are you keeping it in your hotel room?' Heena asked.

Vanessa nodded. 'Yes, but I've arranged to take it to the vet's tomorrow morning. Unless you need me here, I'm going to head back?'

'We never needed you in the first place,' Gordon snapped. But he was smiling, so she smiled back.

'Gordon, you are such a charmer,' she said. Then she grabbed her bag and headed out.

Vanessa stepped into the small room above the pub an hour later, feeling the weight of exhaustion settle on her shoulders. As she went to close the door, she noticed an envelope on the floor. She picked it up to see her name was written in elaborate calligraphy on the front, the back sealed with a butterfly-shaped circle of wax. She tore it open to see a thick invite inside featuring a delicate pencil drawing of vivid blue and white Doris longwing butterflies.

Dearest Vanessa,
*   You are cordially invited to a luncheon on Thursday 10th August at 1 p.m. at my apartment as my guest of honour.*
*   Your father's friend and your long-time admirer,*
*   Clive Craviso*

Vanessa frowned. That was tomorrow. Strange time to be holding a 'luncheon' considering the murders *and* his sister being injured. It also sounded like other people would be there, what with her being the 'guest of honour'. Who on earth would want to attend a luncheon during such an awful, scary time? But then she remembered: this was Greensands, with residents preferring to gather in their beehive during moments of crisis. Well, she wasn't a Greensands resident anymore. Clive would just have to do without his special guest.

She threw the invite in the bin and walked straight over to the terrarium where Abe's spider, Amy Lee, sat crouched in the corner among some bark. She really was beautiful with her striking patterns and imposing stature. It made Vanessa miss her pet Nancy even more.

Her rumbling stomach reminded her she hadn't eaten since lunch. So she reached into her bag and pulled out a sandwich she'd grabbed from the newsagents on the way back. The thought of heading downstairs to eat in the bustling pub held little appeal that evening. Instead, she sat at the desk watching Amy Lee as she opened her sandwich. Abe Abbott would probably be eating a Maccy Dees. That was what prisoners usually got, from what Paul had told her. She couldn't help but feel sympathy for the kid, now even more of an outcast in a town grappling with this tragedy.

She'd sometimes felt like an outcast as a teenager. Motherless. Darker-skinned than the other kids. Still, she'd had a knack of blending in. Her father had told her she was like a katydid insect, which merged with its surroundings. Not Vincent, though. He'd had no desire to fit in, and that was why she loved him.

She pulled her laptop out and opened her email. There was an update from Olivia.

Dear Vanessa,

I hope this email finds you well. I'm so very sorry to hear about what's happening in your childhood village. I know the people there will take comfort in you being there. I just hope I can do your reputation justice here in the labs! I must admit, the attention this case is receiving in the press is a bit overwhelming, and I'm slightly nervous. However, I'm grateful for your trust in my abilities.

Anyway, you left a message asking me to update you on the progress of the insect rearing from the samples you collected at the butterfly farm crime scene. I've attached some initial findings but to summarise, the eggs hatched into first instar within a few hours of arriving, and the larvae you collected are developing at a good rate. By my estimation, considering the developmental stages and the environmental conditions in the lab, they should pupate soon. So possibly the usual suspects, such as *Calliphora vicina* and *Lucilia sericata*? Of course, we won't know until they have been reared to adult size. But that should hopefully be by the end of next week when I'll send over a full report and photos. I suppose you'll be in New York by then?

Best regards,
Olivia

New York. It seemed a world away right now. Just as Vanessa was about to bite into her sandwich, there was a gentle knock at the door. For a moment, she wondered if it might be Paul or one of his officers here to inform her of another attack. Maybe even Damon. But when she opened the door, it was Sharon, a tray of food in her hands. She looked watered down by the tide of her grief – her usually vibrant curls greasy and lank, her green eyes red with exhaustion.

'My friend Dawn saw you buying one of those godawful sandwiches from the newsagents,' Sharon said. 'I couldn't let you subject yourself to that. I had Aggie make you one of her Thai curries.'

'Sharon, you are an *angel*.' Vanessa took the tray, then paused. 'Fancy joining me while I eat?'

'Are you sure, love?'

'Absolutely. I've been wanting to chat properly, anyway. See how you are.'

Sharon closed the door behind her, following Vanessa towards a small table by the window and taking the seat across from her. A breeze came in through the window, the dim early evening light casting a warm glow across the room.

Vanessa reached over and clasped Sharon's hand. 'I'm always thinking of you and Galinn, and the other families, too. I won't ask how you are. I imagine you're constantly asked that.'

'Thanks. I might just get "coping" tattooed across my head.' Her eyes snagged onto the terrarium in the corner. 'You do know we have a no-pet policy,' she said with a small smile.

'It's Abe Abbott's,' Vanessa said.

'Abe who is currently under arrest, I hear,' Sharon said tightly.

'For taking a vehicle without permission.'

'Still, timing's interesting. People are talking.' She shook her head. 'Jesus, he went to the same college as my oldest granddaughter.'

'Don't get carried away, Sharon,' Vanessa said softly. 'He hasn't been arrested for murder.' Vanessa popped a forkful of curry into her mouth. It sure beat a stale sandwich. 'Paul and the entire team are working their arses off to uncover the truth though, whoever's done this.'

Sharon nodded, her eyes welling up with tears. 'I know they are. I dropped some food off at the station earlier. It's the least I can do.'

'Good way to keep busy, too?' Vanessa asked gently.

'You know me too well.' Sharon suddenly let out a sob, pressing a fist to her mouth. Vanessa got up and crouched down in front of her, putting her arms around her.

'My boy,' Sharon gasped. 'The things that were done to him.'

Vanessa thought of what she'd learned earlier about his semen being used. Sharon didn't even know the *least* of it.

'I'm so sorry.'

'When they find out who did it, I swear . . .'

Vanessa recognised that swerve from sorrow to anger. She'd felt it herself after Vincent went missing.

'I thought I knew what grief was when my mum passed away,' Sharon continued. 'We were so close, you remember?' Vanessa did remember. She'd often see them together around the village. 'It changed me, losing my mum. But this . . . God, this. This is another level.'

'I can't even imagine.'

Sharon pulled away, wiping at her tears. 'Get back to your food before it gets cold.'

Vanessa did as she was told, taking her seat again.

'You're no stranger to grief, of course,' Sharon said as she watched Vanessa eat. 'Vincent. Your dad. Your mum, too. Still a form of grief when someone leaves like that.'

Vanessa scraped her fork through the mound of sticky rice on her plate, searching for the right words. 'You're right,' she admitted. 'When Mum walked out, it was like the ground beneath me shifted. It was worse for Vincent, though. He was only four at the time.'

'I remember. He clung to you like a little limpet after.'

Vanessa nodded. 'Nights were the hardest. He'd cry himself to sleep, asking when Mum would come back and why she didn't love us anymore. I got so frustrated sometimes. Looking back, I wish I'd done more for him.'

'Don't be so bloody stupid,' Sharon said sternly. 'You did all you could! Anyway, you were a kid yourself. It takes strength to deal with something like that at such a young age. But now look at you. An eminent forensic entomologist. Your mum should be proud.'

Should be.

'Ever hear from her?' Sharon asked carefully.

Vanessa shook her head.

'Always struck me as being so strange,' Sharon said, 'the way she just upped and left. She loved your dad so much, and goes without saying how much she adored you and Vincent. Even worse, the way she didn't even keep in touch properly. It just seemed . . . so out of character. She was always such a mumsy mum, you know?'

Vanessa supposed Sharon was right. Her mum had always been there for her and Vincent when she *was* living at home. But then suddenly, that love and compassion just seemed to disappear when she walked out on her family.

'I still think something happened that night, at the party,' Sharon said, biting her lip as she looked out towards the manor.

'What party?' Vanessa asked.

'The big party the Oberlins held for Benjamin's tenth birthday.'

Vanessa did remember the party. It was an extravagant affair, like all the Oberlin parties back then. She leaned forward. 'What happened?'

'One minute, your mum was her usual self, life and soul of the party, dancing around and chatting. Next, she's inconsolable and in floods of tears. People put it down to her being drunk, but I swear she'd only had a glass or two of champagne. The next week, she left, just like that,' Sharon added, clicking her fingers.

'So you think something happened at the party to make my mum leave?'

'Maybe. Maybe not.'

They both fell into silence as they contemplated it.

'Let's talk about Michael,' Vanessa eventually said. 'Tell me about him.'

Over the next half an hour, Vanessa let Sharon reminisce about Michael. When Sharon left with Vanessa's empty tray, she seemed in a better place. Vanessa knew it wouldn't last though. In the patchwork of grief, there were moments when it weaved its threads in unexpected patterns, catching you unaware. But for now, it was something to see Sharon smile.

Vanessa yawned, a reminder she needed sleep and a clear mind for tomorrow's tasks. So she got ready for bed and slipped between the sheets, doing a last check of her phone. Helen had messaged as she'd been talking to Sharon. How did Paul seem today? she'd written. He's gone straight to bed. He's exhausted.

I'm the same, Vanessa typed back. So try not to worry. He actually seemed fine today. She didn't add that he looked pale. She didn't want to worry Helen too much.

Good, Helen replied. He was getting himself wound up about some podcast episode that dropped today, so I'm actually pleased he's managed to fall asleep. You doing OK?

Vanessa frowned. Podcast episode? She'd bet a million pounds it was *Dark Deeds Dissected*. She quickly wrote back:

Doing fine. Going to sleep now. Night. X

Then she went to her podcasts app and searched for the show. The title of the latest episode said it all: *In the Lair of The Cobweb Killer: Exclusive Interview.*

Interview? With whom?

Vanessa knew she shouldn't, but she did it anyway: she put her AirPods in and clicked on the play button. The host, Heather's voice erupted into Vanessa's ears.

'Welcome to another episode of *Dark Deeds Dissected*, with your host Heather Fala. As you know, we provide on-the-scene coverage of high-profile cases hitting headlines. So sit back, relax and grab your favourite beverage because I've got an *amazing* exclusive today from the tiny village of Greensands, where a killer is on the loose. For those living under a rock, some background: this isn't your average run-of-the-mill killer, no. This guy's got a signature move – weaving silk into his victims' cavities. How twisted is that? Four men are already dead, and one woman is badly injured in hospital. So grab your bug spray and join me as we delve into the bizarre world of The Cobweb Killer with an exclusive interview with a woman who's right in the middle of this case: local resident Indra Hudson.'

'Shit,' Vanessa whispered.

'Indra is a local businesswoman, who was visited by the detective leading the case, Detective Chief Inspector Paul Truss, in the middle of last night to be questioned. And now here we are, on the doorstep of what is frankly the most *beautiful* house I've ever seen. Ms Hudson, welcome to *Dark Deeds Dissected*.'

'Yes, hello.'

'So, as I was just explaining to my listeners, you were questioned by the police last night, I believe?'

'I was, Heather, all over a *complete* misunderstanding, after my car keys were stolen by the very man they have in custody now.'

'That's Abe Abbott, listeners. Abe Abbott who I exclusively revealed was involved with one of The Cobweb Killer's victims, Benjamin Oberlin – brother of TV-presenting hottie, Damon Oberlin. So, Ms Hudson, I know you can't discuss the details of your police interview, but what are your thoughts on the investigation so far?'

'It's been an absolute disgrace. Everyone knows the first few days after a murder, let alone *four* murders, are crucial and they waste time interviewing me? It's *obvious* Abe Abbott is behind these murders.'

'Let's remind listeners that Abe Abbott has not been arrested for murder, but for stealing a car. We have no idea if he's involved with the actual murders. But let's focus on what we *do* know. I believe a forensic entomologist has been brought in to work on the case, a Doctor Vanessa Marwood?'

Vanessa groaned.

'That's right, Heather. She used to live in Greensands. Her father looked after the butterflies at the farm. As you already know, her brother went missing when they were children.'

'What's she going to tell them next?' Vanessa hissed to herself. 'My bloody bra size?'

'Also, I believe she was once in a relationship with Damon Oberlin.'

Vanessa yanked her AirPods out and threw them across the room. 'Damn it.' She'd been hoping, maybe naively, that wouldn't get out. But now the intimate, painful chapters of her life were suddenly laid bare, turning her from a background player to one of the centrepieces of this unfolding horror.

Vanessa plumped up her pillow and laid her head down, twisting herself around in bed so she could watch Abe's spider to calm herself. It didn't matter, she told herself. All that mattered was that the night passed without another victim being claimed by The Cobweb Killer.

As she thought that, there was a knock on the door. Vanessa sighed. Would it be Damon again? Maybe part of her liked that idea. For a moment, she imagined losing herself in him. His touch. His taste. His scent. Just forgetting the horror of what was happening in Greensands and wrapping herself up in pure physical sensation, something she'd done many times before to unwind. So she got out of bed, quickly checking herself in the mirror, then opened the door.

But it wasn't Damon standing in front of her. It was Ricky Abbott . . . with blood all over his hands.

30

Vanessa's eyes were wide with terror as she struggled to break free from the sticky strands of the web that held her fast. A huge spider with a twisted, humanoid face crawled towards her, its sharp mandibles clicking menacingly. Paul tried to run to help his friend, but just as he was about to get to her, he suddenly fell, landing in a large, grotesque heart. He struggled to break free from the folds of bloody flesh. But the more he struggled, the deeper he seemed to sink. As he watched in horror, the spider crawled closer and closer to Vanessa, its eyes fixed on her with cold, calculating malice. Vanessa's face was contorted with fear as she tried to scream, but her voice was choked off by the spider's web.

Paul woke up with a gasp, his heart racing. He sat up and glanced around the dimly lit room, trying to shake off the remnants of the nightmare.

Beside him, Helen reached out a hand and placed it gently on his arm. 'You OK?'

'Just a nightmare. Go back to sleep, babe.'

Helen stroked her husband's face. 'You always have nightmares when a case gets to you. You have to be careful. The long hours, the stress . . . it's taking a toll on you, I can tell.'

'What do you want me to do? I can't just pull myself off the case, Helen. Anyway, I've got my tablets, haven't I?'

'The cardiologist said the tablets alone aren't a quick fix. That there need to be other lifestyle changes. You were doing so well before this case.'

'So were the bloody victims. Stop fussing!'

How could Helen expect him to just walk away from a case like this? To abandon his team and leave the community vulnerable to this bloody killer? He couldn't simply step aside, even if it meant putting his own health at risk. In fact, the thought of doing that was enough to make him *have* a damn heart attack.

He noticed Helen's face harden in the semi-darkness. 'That's what my dad said to me before he had his heart attack. "Stop fussing over me!" He would still be alive today if he'd just listened to us.' Her eyes filled with tears. 'He'd have got to see his granddaughters grow up, too. I don't want to lose you like I lost him, Paul. It's not fair to me, *or* the girls.'

Paul sighed and reached out for his wife's hand. 'I know. I'm sorry. You and the girls are always my number-one priority. And that's why it's so important I catch this killer. They injured a woman. A vulnerable woman in her sixties. Who do they have their sights on next? A child?'

Helen shuddered. 'Don't even go there.'

'But it's true. It's the people of Greensands who are being stalked, and that could include kids too. *Our* kids.'

Helen frowned, peering towards the girls' room.

'I'll be more careful,' he said, voice softening, 'I promise. I'll listen to my body. I'll get more sleep. I'll eat better. But this case is important, for *all* of us.'

Helen nestled her head against his chest. As she did, Paul's phone buzzed. His face fell.

'I have to get it,' he said.

'I know.'

He picked it up, seeing it was Deano. He put his phone to his ear. 'What's happened?' he asked, dreading the answer.

'Two bodies have been found,' Deano answered. 'A couple.'

31

Paul stood in the semi-darkness of the ridge where he'd been only the day before, searching for mining bees.

Now, instead of the dead body of a bee, he was standing over two dead human bodies.

A couple in their fifties. Harvey Wheatley, the butterfly farm's old maintenance manager, and Harvey's wife, Natalie, the last horticulturist who'd worked at the farm. They'd met at the farm and had been popular with the staff, often inviting workers back to their house. Now they were dead.

The couple had been posed together, Harvey's arms in a death grip around Natalie's shoulders, her leg hooked over his thigh. He was naked, but she was fully clothed. It made for a morbid scene beneath the moonlight. So morbid, the drunk teens who'd stumbled upon them would probably need counselling for the rest of their lives. It took all of Paul's tired resolve to hold himself together. If he felt like he was losing a grip on the case before, now it felt like it had completely run away from him.

Mio was crouching down beside the bodies now, quiet as her eyes travelled over their prone forms. Paul counted his blessings that Mio lived nearby. He needed someone with her expertise on the scene. Heena took photos, the flash of her camera casting the bodies in a harsh light each time she did. There didn't seem to be any visible cause of death, but then there hadn't been for the other victims of The Cobweb Killer.

'They only welcomed their first grandchild a few months ago,' Paul said.

'Fuck,' OS whispered. Even he was looking wary now, his jaw stubbled, his hair dishevelled. 'You said they worked at the butterfly farm?'

'Yep.'

'Did you know them well?'

'Reasonably,' Paul replied. 'I'd see them in the pub every now and again. They were popular. So, what do you think, Mio? How long have they been here?'

Mio stood up. 'My guess from the rigor mortis that's set in and the presence of eggs and larvae in their wounds, that they've been dead a day or two.'

'A day or two?' OS said. 'It's pretty open. Wouldn't they have been seen?'

'They would have been moved here, like the others were moved. Check for any wheelbarrow tyre marks.'

OS nodded. 'Will do. Wouldn't they have been reported missing?'

'Their son doesn't live in Greensands. He might not have noticed if they didn't talk every day,' Paul said. 'Their cottage is slightly out of town too – no direct neighbours. So what shall we do, Mio? Is it best we transport them together, or try to part them here?'

'I'd like to try to keep them together,' Mio replied. 'Makes it easier to catch any evidence as they're pulled apart. We're just a few steps from my van so we should be able to manage it. I'll need help though.'

'Gordon! Heena!' Paul called over to the CSI lead who was setting up a floodlight. 'Come and help lift the bodies, will you?'

Gordon and Heena headed over.

'Ready?' Mio said to them.

They nodded, their gloved hands poised to begin the delicate operation.

Paul watched with bated breath as the three of them crouched to lift the bodies together, trying to maintain the twisted form. Gordon, clearly the strongest of the three, crouched by Harvey's back, scooping his gloved hands carefully beneath him. Mio was by the couple's legs and Heena stood at Natalie's head.

'One . . . two . . . three . . .' Mio said.

They began to slowly lift the two bodies. But the sun-baked earth beneath was brittle and uneven. As they lifted the bodies, a puff of dust rose, and a clump of dry soil crumbled, shifting their balance.

'Shit,' Gordon grunted as the weight of Harvey's body pulled free from Natalie, revealing the most disturbing sight Paul had witnessed in his career.

A gaping, bloody hole just below Harvey's waist.

OS flinched and turned away as Paul closed his eyes, shaking his head.

'Well, at least we now know the likely cause of death for the deceased male,' Mio said in her no-nonsense bellow. 'Severe loss of blood from penectomy and castration.'

32

Vanessa took in Ricky's bloody hands as he stood before her in the corridor. All sorts of thoughts ran through her mind. Was he The Cobweb Killer? And had he come to claim his next victim?

She clenched her fists behind her back, ready to fight if she needed to.

'What the hell have you done, Ricky?' she asked.

'They won't believe me,' he said. 'I need to talk to you first. You can try to make them see sense.'

'*Who* won't believe you?'

'The police.'

Her eyes dropped to his hands again. 'Where's the blood from?'

'My room. It was starting to smell. I was trying to find the source of the stink and found—' He swallowed. 'It was under my bed.'

'What was under your bed?'

'Someone's . . . body part. It's in here.' He gestured to a rucksack she hadn't even noticed until now, slung over his back. 'It's-it's someone's, you know,' he said, gesturing to his crotch area.

Vanessa recoiled, remembering what Abe had said earlier about wasp spiders. *Did you know the dude breaks off their own cock and leaves it in the female's vag to prevent competitors from entering her?*

'You must go to the police,' Vanessa said. 'Now.'

'No! They won't believe me. They'll blame my son, use it against him. I know you think he's innocent, I can tell. If you can just *talk* to Paul Truss. He'll listen to you, not jump to conclusions.'

'You're right,' Vanessa said carefully. 'I'm just going to reach for my phone and I'll call him.'

She went to slowly reach for her phone, but then a tall figure appeared behind Ricky.

It was Damon.

Ricky slowly turned, his bloody hands held out.

'Damon, no!' But it was too late. Damon had seen the blood. He ran at Ricky, pummelling him with his entire weight.

'My boy didn't do it,' Ricky said as Damon tackled him to the ground. 'Vanessa, he didn't do it!'

33

Paul sat across the table from Ricky Abbott and his solicitor, trying to keep his gaze steady. Deano was with him this time. OS had felt 'queasy' and was currently convalescing in the incident room with a strong cup of coffee. Paul wouldn't mind doing the same himself. But the need to stop this twisted rampage was burning too strong inside him. It felt like one by one, these villagers – some of them friends, all of them familiar faces – were being picked off in the most heinous of ways and he could do fuck all to stop it. Fiona no doubt felt the same. He'd had several missed calls from her. But he didn't want to talk to her, not until he had something concrete to say.

What would that concrete something be?

Paul looked at the man before him. Was Ricky responsible? Maybe it was him and his spider-loving son? Some sick family hobby? Mio said the couple had possibly been dead a 'day or two'. If that proved to be true, then Abe wouldn't have been behind bars then. He'd have been free to kill. Sure, he said he was in Manchester but if his phone and banking activity proved otherwise, then that would speak volumes. Having two killers responsible for these murders would certainly make sense. The movement of bodies. The grotesque manipulation of those bodies.

'Do you know about the mating behaviour of the wasp spider, Ricky?' Paul asked. He'd spoken to Vanessa on the phone. It made him sick to his stomach to think she'd possibly been standing across from The Cobweb Killer, alone and vulnerable.

It made him sick Damon was the one to save her too.

Ricky shifted uncomfortably in his chair, his eyes darting away for a moment before meeting Paul's gaze again. 'I . . . I've heard of it.'

Paul leaned forward, his eyes narrowing. 'Interesting, isn't it? How the male spider detaches his own body parts, leaving them behind as a gruesome deterrent to other potential mates.'

Ricky's eyes widened slightly, a flicker of realisation crossing his face . . . but also fascination. 'Jesus. You think that's what's happened? The Cobweb Killer's copying wasp spider mating habits?' He smiled slightly. Paul noticed Deano frowning, probably thinking the same thing Paul was: *weird reaction*. 'My wife loved those creatures,' Ricky added.

'Did she now?' Deano asked meaningfully.

'It's a fascinating parallel, isn't it, Ricky?' Paul said. 'A way to mark one's territory, to claim ownership. To eliminate rivals.'

Ricky's unease grew more palpable, and he shifted in his seat again. 'It's got nothing to do with me.'

'You sure?' Paul asked. 'Nice little game for you. Maybe you and your son, in fact. A chance to truly bond.'

Ricky's face paled, beads of sweat forming on his forehead. 'Abe? No, no way. And why the hell would I come to you with the body part if it was me, for Christ's sake?'

'But you didn't come to us, did you?' Deano said. 'You went to Doctor Vanessa Marwood. Was she supposed to be your next victim?'

There was that sick feeling in Paul's stomach again.

'I wouldn't hurt a hair on that girl's head!' Ricky said. 'You know how much I looked up to her dad.'

'I do,' Paul said, 'and maybe that's part of it. Part of *everything*.' He looked down at his notes featuring some information OS had dug up. 'Tony Marwood fired you, didn't he?'

Ricky blinked.

'Can't find any records showing why,' Paul continued. 'But three years and two months after being his assistant, you got the chop. Why was that?'

'Maybe you were witnessed doing something you shouldn't have,' Deano said.

'And maybe you're picking off those witnesses now, one by one?' Paul added.

Ricky shook his head, looking distraught. Was it an act?

'Let me ask you again,' Paul said, 'why were you fired?'

Ricky was quiet for a few moments. 'I was selling insects illegally,' he finally said.

Adrenaline rushed through Paul's body. 'What do you mean?'

'I was skint and dumb,' Ricky said. 'eBay was becoming popular. I heard about other people selling insects on there so—' He shook his head. 'Man, I still hate myself for this. I'd take some of the rarer butterflies we got at the farm and sell them. I don't know why the hell I thought Tony wouldn't find out.'

'Do you still dabble in illegal insect trading now?' Deano asked.

'No,' Ricky said. 'The lecture Tony gave me before he fired me put me off for life.'

'Really?' Paul asked, glaring at him. 'I imagine you made decent money from it before you got caught. Maybe you took it up again? Maybe you're running this little enterprise with your son?'

'Yeah,' Deano said. 'Makes sense. A nice little business, hidden behind the website you run now. What's it called, Boss?'

'ExoGourmet: Culinary Delights for Exotic Pets,' Paul said. 'Deano's right. It's the ideal cover. A perfect little business for you and your son.'

'I don't do it anymore, I swear!' Ricky said.

'Maybe Indra Hudson is involved, too,' Paul said. 'Maybe Benjamin Oberlin as well.'

'No,' Ricky said. 'No.'

'Bet it still winds you up that Tony Marwood nearly put a stop to your enterprise,' Paul said. 'Even all these years later. Maybe other people found you out too, then and now. People like Michael Regan, Simon Taylor, Tim Holmes.'

'Emi Craviso?' Deano added. 'The Wheatleys?'

'The Wheatleys? What have the Wheatleys got to do with all this?' Ricky asked. Then his eyes widened. 'Harvey. It's his-his . . .' He put his hands to his cheeks, shaking his head. 'No. Not him. Not Natalie, too. They're my *friends*.' He took in a few deep breaths then looked at the two officers across from him. 'Why the *hell* would I hand in his body part if it was me who did it?' he asked again. 'Even if it *was* to Vanessa. She's part of your team, isn't she?'

That was a question that kept playing on Paul's mind, too. But he felt closer than he ever had to cracking this case . . . and he felt even more sure that the Abbott men held the key to solving it. In fact, with the body part being in Ricky's possession, it wouldn't take much to convince the Crown Prosecution Service to allow him to charge the man. The question was, was his son involved too?

34

Greensands Vet Practice was a single-storey brown-brick building tucked away in a quiet corner of the village high street. Vanessa had never been inside. She didn't have any pets as a kid. Their pets were the butterflies and other insects at the farm. But the sight of the vet practice's entrance, framed by a neatly trimmed hedge that led to a small gravel parking area, took her back to the days when she walked past it to get to school each morning, Vincent dragging his feet behind her.

She carried Amy Lee's carrier case inside now and approached the reception area where several people were already sitting or queuing with their pets in tow. They stopped talking when she walked in. No surprise. News had broken already about Harvey and Natalie Wheatley. Vanessa herself had woken to a Sky News alert about it, and a text from Paul to say they were keeping Ricky Abbott in for more questioning, alongside Abe. He'd also shared his suspicions about the two men running the illegal insect trading ring. Vanessa didn't really know the father and son. But the thought of them working together to kill their fellow villagers so brutally was sickening . . . and to trade in the creatures Abe seemed to love so much. One of which she was in possession of now.

'Doctor Marwood,' a voice said. It was Dawn, the woman who ran the newsagents. She was in the queue in front of her, holding a tiny Pomeranian on a lead. 'Can you believe it about the Wheatleys? Such a lovely couple.'

'It's terrible,' Vanessa agreed.

'I heard they took Ricky Abbott in. No coincidence his son's still in custody too. The two Abbott men, hey? Do you think it's them? I always thought that Abe boy was strange.'

The door opened and Andrew Kirk, the teacher at Greensands Primary, walked in with a carrying case like hers, a tarantula within.

'I can't really comment on the case,' Vanessa said to Dawn. 'But Paul has it under control. He's a brilliant detective.'

She finally got to the front to see a harassed-looking receptionist. 'Sorry, we're a vet down this morning so it's been rather hectic.' She took in Vanessa's tattoos. 'Oh, you must be Doctor Marwood.'

'I am, and this is Amy Lee,' she said, placing the carrier on the reception desk.

The receptionist looked at the spider in fascination. 'We always love it when Abe brings in his spiders. Or used to, anyway.' She frowned. 'Do you really think him and his father could be behind the murders?'

'I can't comment on the case, I'm afraid. I'm just here for Amy Lee.'

'Of course,' the receptionist said. 'Take a seat. I'll let Doctor Sinclair know you're here.'

She took her seat and Andrew joined her after he checked in.

'What a beauty,' Vanessa said as she took in the tarantula that spanned at least six inches across the container Andrew was holding. She could see from the distinctive red-orange bands on its legs and abdomen, which contrasted sharply with its black body, that it was also a Mexican redknee tarantula, like Amy Lee.

'It's our classroom pet,' Andrew said. 'Her name's Moana. It's actually Abe who recommended we get this species for the classroom and put me in touch with a breeder.'

'Ah. Yes, they can make good pets. So Moana, hey? Like the Disney character?'

Andrew smiled. 'Yep. The kids had the final vote.'

'Of course.'

'What a creepy classroom pet,' Dawn said, curling her lip.

'Actually, a tarantula like this is an ideal classroom pet,' Vanessa remarked. 'They're so docile.'

'Unless you're a cricket or grasshopper,' Andrew said.

'Or a small rodent,' Vanessa added, as Dawn went slightly pale and turned away. 'Is Moana OK?' Vanessa asked Andrew, pleased for some conversation that didn't involve dead bodies and seventeen-year-old suspects.

'Just her annual check-up,' Andrew replied.

'I bet the kids adore her.'

He smiled, pushing his glasses up his freckled nose. 'They do. She's educational too, helps them understand how to treat animals with care. Having said that,' he added with a grimace, 'I *did* have to rescue one of the millipedes we once had. One of the kids was about to start cutting it in half with some scissors to test whether they can regenerate lost limbs.'

'Ouch. Typical kid move there,' Vanessa said, '*especially* boys. My brother used to do stuff like that.'

Andrew looked at her with interest. 'Really?'

'Sure. It was never malicious on his part. He was just always so *curious*, you know? He needed to know insects inside out.'

'And you were the same?'

'I wasn't cutting millipedes in half to see if they'd regenerate, if that's what you mean.' They both laughed. 'No,' she continued. 'For me, it's less about the anatomical structure of these creatures and more about their behaviours, ecology and evolution, in particular how they interact with the environment and with humans.'

'So your brother is more like a doctor or pathologist, and you're the anthropologist? Sounds like you make a great team.'

Vanessa nodded, surprising herself as her eyes filled with tears. 'Yeah.'

'Did I say something wrong?'

'No, it's just . . . he-he went missing years ago, when he was twelve.'

'Oh no. That's awful.'

They were both quiet for a moment, watching as Moana moved around the container to look in at Amy Lee.

'I lost a sibling too,' Andrew said in a low voice. 'My sister. So I get it.'

'I'm so sorry.'

'She was in an abusive relationship. The guy she was with was domineering, powerful. He isolated her from her friends and family. I rarely saw her in the last year of her life.'

'That must have been tough.'

He nodded, and they fell into another sombre silence.

'I know you can't talk about the case,' Andrew eventually said, 'but do you really think Abe Abbott is involved with these murders? He's such a good kid.' His eyes slid over to Dawn. 'I worry people judge him just because of the way he looks.'

'I don't know, Andrew.'

'Of course, of course, I shouldn't have asked. But—' He sighed. 'Well, I just can't see it myself. Actually, now I think about it, there's something I probably should have mentioned to Paul.'

'What's that?'

'I sometimes meet up with Clive Craviso at the pub. I'm a bit of an aspiring author, so it's good to chat to another writer. Anyway, he was very intrigued when he discovered we have a tarantula for a class pet and was asking me many questions about spiders and spider webs for his new novel. Interesting, no?'

Vanessa frowned. 'Very interesting. What kind of questions was he asking?'

'Which spider silk is the strongest, that kind of thing. I directed him to the "Entomological Enthusiasts" subreddit on Reddit.'

'You should mention it to Paul,' Vanessa said. 'It's probably nothing, but in a case like this, I know Paul is keen to leave no stone unturned.'

'Absolutely. I'll make a call to the incident line right after this appointment.'

As he said that, Vanessa heard a commotion down the corridor. She craned her neck to see a gorgeous grey kitten darting down the corridor as a nurse and vet – a man in his late thirties with salt-and-pepper hair – chased it. Vanessa smiled as she watched the kitten jump up onto the reception desk, the receptionist trying but failing to grab it before it jumped back down.

Vanessa calmly stood up and scooped the mass of fur up, holding it out in front of her as it scratched and snarled. Honestly, she didn't understand why more people didn't own tarantulas. They were *so* much more agreeable than these felines.

The nurse gave Vanessa a grateful smile as she handed the kitten over.

'My next client, I presume?' the vet said to Vanessa. 'I do apologise. It isn't really a proper workday if one of our animals isn't trying to make an escape. Please, come through.'

Vanessa picked Amy Lee's carrier up, waving goodbye to Andrew before following the vet down the corridor.

'I was in the same class as your brother, you know,' he said as he stepped into a small room.

Vanessa looked at him with interest. 'You were?'

'Yep. I'd like to say we were friends, especially as we both loved animals. But—'

'Vincent preferred friends with exoskeletons instead of endoskeletons?'

'Precisely,' the vet said. His face darkened. 'It was tough for the class when he went missing. Of course, tougher for you,' he quickly added. He placed the carrier on the aluminium table. 'No leads since?'

'Just some random sightings that have come to nothing.'

'Shame, such a sad turn of events. And now we have these horrendous murders, with two more last night. A truly awful time for the village.'

'It certainly is.'

'Still, life goes on for the rest of us, including our beloved arachnids. So, you've come today to drop Abe Abbott's Amy Lee off, have you?'

Vanessa nodded. 'I think it's for the best as I'll be leaving tomorrow. Abe said she's been acting lethargic lately? It would be good to stay and see what you think is wrong with her. Then I can leave her in your capable hands, Doctor Sinclair.'

'Please, call me Keir. Good of you to bring her in for Abe. It's not this gorgeous creature's fault if it turns out her owner is one of the people behind these heinous acts, is it?' He carefully opened the carrier. 'Back to the matter at hand though.' Vanessa watched as Keir's experienced hands manoeuvred around the enclosure and carefully scooped Amy Lee out. 'Fascinating little creature,' he said as Amy Lee carefully crawled up his arm, his eyes observing its movements and inspecting its body as she did. 'And it seems we will welcome even more of them, because I believe Amy Lee is pregnant.'

Vanessa frowned. 'Abe was breeding her?'

'Looks like it.'

He carefully turned the spider over. 'See her stomach? It's swollen.'

'Dystocia,' Vanessa said. 'I can't believe I didn't notice.'

'You'd had other things on your mind, Doctor Marwood.'

'Call me Vanessa.'

'Vanessa,' he said. 'Yes, it's dystocia. The poor thing hasn't been able to lay her eggs properly. I suggest, what with Abe's . . .' he paused '. . . *predicament* – we keep her here. I can have a go at manually extracting the eggs, but if that doesn't work, we have some medication we can use.'

Vanessa felt a twinge of disappointment at losing out on her little buddy's company. But she knew it was for the best. 'Thank you, Keir,' she said.

'I'll make sure Amy Lee is looked after and will keep you posted. Maybe I can have your number?'

'Sure.' She retrieved her business card from her bag and handed it over. 'My mobile number is on there, too.'

'Forensic entomologist,' Keir said as he looked at it. 'Quite the mouthful.'

'Isn't it just? Thanks for your help.'

Keir smiled warmly. 'It's my pleasure. Thank *you* for your work on the case.' He gently placed Amy Lee back in her carrier, then paused. 'Another thing that struck me as odd about Abe's possible involvement in the murder is the extraction of spider silk. I just couldn't see Abe subjecting his golden silk orb-weaver to such a difficult procedure. Sorry,' the vet said when he noticed the look on Vanessa's face. 'Shouldn't have brought it all up. You're in a tough position.' He opened the door for her and she walked out. 'The fee's on me,' he explained to the receptionist when they got to her.

'Oh,' Vanessa said, 'I was planning to pay.'

'I insist,' Keir said with a charming smile.

Vanessa smiled back. 'I'm sure Abe will be grateful.'

'No, this one's for you. Pleasure to meet you properly, Vanessa. I'll be in touch. Andrew?' Andrew stood up and followed the vet down the hallway. Vanessa was about to turn around, then paused. Lying behind the reception desk was a stack of brochures advertising the clinic . . . all glossy, with a similar design she'd seen on the front of the illegal insect trading brochure they'd found in Indra's offices.

'Who designed those brochures?' she asked the receptionist.

'Oh, Doctor Sinclair does them himself. He's multitalented, that one.'

'May I take one?'

'Of course!'

Vanessa took the brochure from the receptionist and walked outside. When she was out of view, she found the photo of the brochure Paul had sent her on her phone and compared it to the clinic's brochure. Yes, they were very similar.

She peered in through the clinic window. Could the handsome vet be involved with this village's illegal insect trading ring? And what about Andrew's comment about Clive Craviso's sudden curiosity about spider silk?

When she got to her truck, she googled the subreddit Andrew had mentioned. It was popular, with over fifty thousand members. She clicked on it and searched for Clive's name. Nothing came up, so she searched for spider silk. Several results popped up this time. Vanessa scrolled through them until she found what she was looking for: a post by a user calling themselves The Silken Scribe entitled: *Help needed with crime novel set in abandoned butterfly farm.*

Vanessa shook her head. That really *was* a bit too close to home. She clicked on the post and read it.

Hello, my fellow arachnid enthusiasts! I am a BESTSELLING AND AWARD-WINNING AUTHOR working on a thrilling new novel set in a fictional butterfly farm that becomes embroiled in an illegal insect trading ring. Now, the question I want to ask you all: which spider silk is the strongest? And by strong, I mean strong enough for a human psychopath to bind a victim's wrists?

Spider silk. Abandoned butterfly farm. Illegal insect trading. A *psychopath*. Plus, it was posted four weeks ago, *before* all these murders happened. Could it just be a coincidence?

Vanessa quickly did a search for more posts from The Silken Scribe, who she presumed must be Clive. But the only other ones that came up were in various writing-related subreddits with no mention of insects or butterfly farms. Plenty of murder though, but then he *was* a crime novelist. Still, it didn't feel right. So she tried calling Paul, but he didn't pick up. No surprise; he had six murders and an attempted murder to solve. She took a quick screenshot of the post and WhatsApped it to him.

She then thought of the invitation she'd received from Clive. Maybe she should go, after all?

35

Paul stepped into the bustling incident room, feeling like the entire world was on his shoulders. He noticed Fiona was in there too, studying the board at the end of the room.

'So, this could be the breakthrough we need then,' she remarked as Paul walked over, Selma passing him a steaming coffee as he did. 'It would make sense,' Fiona continued. 'A father-and-son team, working together to run an illegal business, and murder, too.'

Paul chewed at his lip. 'Maybe.'

Fiona gave him a look. 'You're doubting it?'

'I just want all the loose ends tied up, you know? Motivations and so on. Finding the knife used on Harvey would be useful, too. Mio reckons it would have had a serrated edge.'

'What did Abe Abbott say when you questioned him again?'

Paul thought of the hour he'd spent questioning Abe after he'd questioned his father. The kid had looked visibly shaken at the news that two more murder victims had been found, *and* that his father might be a suspect. 'Denied any involvement,' Paul said. 'Seemed genuinely shaken but who knows? If someone's capable of murder, they're capable of lying too.'

'Exactly,' Fiona said. 'We just need to gather more evidence. Speaking of which.' She gestured towards the waiting officers.

So Paul turned to face the room. 'Right, everyone, we've got work to do.' He looked at his watch. 'Is OS back from searching the Abbotts' property again?'

'On his way,' Deano said.

Paul nodded. 'So, let's make this case watertight, OK? Let's talk to anyone who knows the Wheatleys, and figure out when they were last seen. I've had it confirmed their son is on holiday. Can't get hold of him yet but hopefully soon. Also need to chat to people about Ricky Abbott, get a sense of his behaviour and movements in the past week or so. We need to talk to Abe's friends today, too, the ones he claims went to the club with him?'

Deano nodded. 'On it, Boss.'

'Pay a visit to the nightclub too,' Paul said, 'see if there's any CCTV footage of Abe. I'd like to get a feel of his behaviour that night.'

'What about Benjamin Oberlin's derogatory remarks during his sexual encounters?' Fiona said. 'We should try to track down his other lovers and get a sense of just how far he went with his verbal abuse. Will all help with building a motive if Abe is involved.'

'Good idea,' Paul said.

'I'll look into it,' Deano said.

Paul turned to a tired-looking Kimberley, who'd been working with the team assigned to picking up calls to the incident line at night, calls still going on in the room's corner. 'Get any interesting calls in the night?'

'Nothing concrete,' she replied, looking down at her notepad. 'Just the usual time-wasters, like a Mrs Tonbridge, who suggested we investigate the ghost that haunts the newsagents.'

'Looks like we've got a real Scooby-Doo mystery on our hands,' Deano said.

The officers around the room laughed.

'All right, you can head home to sleep,' Paul said to Kimberley. 'Good work.'

'Thanks, Boss.'

The door opened then and OS walked in, looking better than he had earlier. He had something in his hand. 'Found this at the Abbott house.' He walked up the middle of the room and handed it to Paul as Fiona looked over his shoulder. It was a card featuring a sketch of a blue and white butterfly. Paul turned it over.

Dearest Ricky,
You are cordially invited to a luncheon on Thursday 10th August at 1 p.m., at my apartment.
Your friend,
Clive Craviso

* * *

Paul looked at his watch. 'That's in an hour.'

'Yeah, and guess what?' OS said. 'It's printed on that weird waffle card like the illegal trading brochure.'

'Interesting,' Paul said. 'We should gatecrash.'

36

Clive lived in a church that had been converted into four apartments. It sat on the edge of the forest, not far from Indra's workplace and the quieter part of the ridge. Both the church and the manor had been constructed in the same year – 1565 – meaning they both enjoyed a similar light-coloured limestone facade. But the one feature the manor *didn't* share with the church was its beautiful, circular rose window made up of seven interlinking floral patterns.

Vanessa walked up the path and knocked on the bright blue door that marked the entrance to Clive's flat, hearing voices behind the door. How many people were *in* there? Vanessa looked down at what she was wearing: a grey and black collared dress etched with insect patterns. She hadn't really packed for a luncheon, but at least it was a dress.

Clive opened the door. 'You made it!' he declared before pulling her into an enormous hug, overpowering her with the scent of his floral aftershave.

As he pulled away, she examined his face. Was he capable of killing? Was he even capable of being involved in an illegal insect trading ring?

'I thought about cancelling after the terrible events overnight,' he said, face clouding over. 'But I knew Harvey. He always loved a good dinner party, so I see this as a way of showing my appreciation of him.'

'Did you know him well?'

'Just from some chats at the pub. He is – I mean, *was*,' he added with a sigh, 'an avid reader. Come in, come in. They're all waiting.'

'How's your sister doing?' Vanessa asked as she followed him up the stairs leading to his apartment.

Clive's cheeks coloured slightly. 'I haven't seen her yet. We aren't exactly . . . close. But I did send her flowers. It could have been *so* much worse. It's been a troublesome time.'

Not so troublesome he couldn't hold a luncheon, Vanessa couldn't help thinking.

She felt something brush past her cheek and was surprised to see it was a large white and black Doris longwing butterfly.

'Do you keep butterflies here?' she asked in surprise.

'Oh, just a few. They're my little pets. And before you say butterflies shouldn't be kept as pets in sixteenth-century apartments, these are rescues. That one there, for example—' he gestured to the butterfly that had brushed against Vanessa's cheek '—had a broken wing, which I fixed, the same way your father taught me.'

'Where do you find them?'

'I just go out with my net. Of course, sometimes the perfectly healthy butterflies jump in too, so it would be churlish not to bring them back.'

So they weren't just rescues, then. Instead, Clive had taken these beautiful creatures from their natural habitat. Even worse, she could see an overweight, snow-white cat chasing a butterfly around the landing at the top. It certainly showed a disregard for these creatures. The same disregard illegal insect traders took.

Murderers too.

'I'm not sure this is the ideal environment for them, Clive,' she said.

'They're perfectly happy, Vanessa,' he replied dismissively.

As they got to the top of the stairs, Vanessa saw even more butterflies, some flitting around and landing on tiny bowls of water Clive had laid out for them, others feeding from the exotic plants and flowers adorning the surfaces of the furniture dotted around the vast open-plan room. Paul would hate it here with his dislike of butterflies.

Vanessa pulled her attention away from the butterflies and looked towards a large, claw-legged dining table in front of the stained-glass window, several familiar faces sitting around it. Andrew and the vet, Keir, who she'd only seen that morning. Even Indra Hudson with her husband, Tom, both eyeing Vanessa suspiciously. Arthur Oberlin had somehow been wheeled in too, looking ancient and foreboding at the head of the table. And then Damon, who was giving her a bemused smile from his place at the end of the table, clearly finding this strange little luncheon odd too.

Vanessa examined each of their faces. Who else among them was involved in the illegal ring?

'Here she is,' Clive said as he placed his hand on Vanessa's shoulder. 'Our guest of honour.'

'I should have brought my cloak and crown.'

As everyone laughed, Clive led her towards the empty chair at the other end of the table, directly opposite Arthur Oberlin, with Andrew and Damon on either side of her.

'Arthur,' she said, looking at the old man. 'I'm so very sorry about Benjamin.'

Arthur blinked, as though taken aback by her condolences. Then he shook himself, like he was shaking away the grief, and just ignored her, taking a gulp of his red wine. It reminded her of how he used to treat her as a teenager when she turned up at the manor to see Damon. Barely even noticing her presence.

'You OK?' she asked Damon quietly.

'Better now you're here,' he replied. 'Though I'm surprised to *see* you here.'

'Me too.' She was beginning to regret coming to the luncheon, especially with the likes of Indra Hudson there. But Paul hadn't returned her call yet, and it had just been too tempting to see Clive up close and personal after what she'd discovered. Even better, the vet was here too, which could be useful considering the brochure she'd seen.

Maybe she was driven by a desire to help the Abbott men, too, especially Abe. She just couldn't wrap her head around *him* being behind the murders. Was she being naive, though? Just because you couldn't sense the lurking darkness within people, it didn't mean it wasn't there.

'Drink?' Clive asked Vanessa, gesturing to an old-fashioned globe drinks holder.

'Just a soft drink, please,' she said, trying not to be swayed by the sight of a nearly full bottle of RL Seales rum in the globe.

Clive smiled as he picked up the distinctive wonky blue bottle of rum. 'Your father gifted me this, you know.'

'Really?'

'Yes, really. Sure I can't tempt you?'

'No, but thanks.'

Clive poured himself a glass, then walked to the kitchen. 'Chat among yourselves while I see to Vanessa's *soft* drink and the entrées,' he called over his shoulder as he disappeared behind the door.

Arthur leaned forward, narrowing his blue eyes as he looked down the table at her. 'Yes,' he said in a gum-filled, barely discernible voice. 'I see her in you.'

'Her?' Vanessa asked.

'Delilah,' Arthur said.

'Who's Delilah?' Andrew asked Vanessa.

'My mother.'

'She escaped this godforsaken place many years ago,' Damon said.

'Where does she live now?' Keir asked.

Vanessa felt her cheeks flush. 'Brighton.'

'She's a sculptor,' Indra said in a bored drawl.

'Yes, she made that over there.' Arthur pointed his wrinkled, shaky finger to the large sculpture sitting on a table beside Clive's brown leather Chesterfield sofa. It depicted an ornately detailed oak tree with iron butterflies of all colours and sizes clinging to its branches. Vanessa couldn't quite tell from that distance which butterflies were real and which were sculpted. Beneath sat a wooden sculpture of a girl reading a book. It had once been in their own living room and gave Vanessa a pang as she took it in.

'I didn't realise you had this,' Vanessa said to Clive as he came back with two small plates of savoury tarts topped with purple flowers. Edible flowers, Vanessa presumed.

'Your father gifted it to me before he died,' Clive explained to Vanessa as he placed the plate before her. 'There were *so* many pieces of art that your mother left behind.'

'Is that you in it?' Keir asked her.

Vanessa nodded. 'I think so.'

'Actually, I think we might have one of your mother's sculptures displayed at the school,' Andrew said, smiling. 'And didn't I see a similar one at the pub? She's very talented.'

'And generous too,' Clive added.

'Very,' Arthur murmured to himself.

Vanessa frowned.

'So, it looks like The Cobweb Killer has been caught?' Indra said, dark eyes drilling into Vanessa's. 'Or should I say, killers?'

'I wouldn't know,' Vanessa said. 'Detective Truss is the man in charge.'

'But you were searching the Abbotts' shed yesterday, no?' Indra asked.

This village and its relentless rumour mill.

Vanessa picked up the petal on her tart and examined it. 'I'd rather not discuss an ongoing case.'

'Ms Hudson seemed happy enough to discuss the case with the gutter press,' Damon said, narrowing his eyes at Indra.

'A true crime podcast isn't *quite* the gutter press, Damon,' Indra said in a voice of restrained politeness. 'Anyway, what choice did I have in the matter? My many years in media relations have shown me it is *far* better to get one's side of the story across first, before someone else does.'

'And what side is that?' Damon asked. 'The side that absolutely needed to expose the fact that Vanessa and I once dated?'

Andrew's face flushed, and he looked like he wanted the ground to swallow him up. Vanessa gave him a sympathetic look. He was one of the newer members of the village, so probably didn't understand how everything was thrown out onto the table and examined here.

'I can't be alone in thinking this is a deeply inappropriate conversation,' Vanessa said, finally having had enough of it. 'I know this village likes to air anything and everything in the open, but considering the present company, I think we should change the subject.'

'I agree,' Andrew said.

'So, Clive, tell us about your work-in-progress,' Vanessa asked the host, keen to focus on why she was enduring this luncheon from hell.

The author's cheeks flushed slightly. 'Oh, I won't bore you with that,' he said, waving his hand about as a butterfly swirled in the air around him.

'You're usually quite *happy* to bore us with every detail of your books,' Arthur said.

Clive gave the old man a hard look. 'Well, if you *insist*. It's actually a new series.'

'About . . . ?' Vanessa asked.

'You know, the usual,' Clive said dismissively. 'Victims. Police. Clues. Angst.'

'You're being *very* mysterious, Clive,' Damon said. 'That's not like you.'

'Fine, truth be told, I might have a book deal in the works,' Clive said, throwing the words out in rapid succession. 'So I have reasons to be secretive.'

'You think one of us will steal your idea and snatch that book deal from your sweaty palms?' Damon asked.

'No,' Clive said, shooting him daggers. 'I've just been asked by the interested party to keep the idea under wraps for now.'

'So you're not independently publishing the next one?' Andrew asked.

'Let's see what the publisher offers first, shall we?' Clive answered with a nervous laugh.

'Admit it,' Arthur said. 'The deal hasn't been sealed yet, has it? If not, you'll want to get it confirmed soon.' He gestured to his son. 'This one here thought he had a half-a-million-pound advance in the bag. Even put a deposit down on a house before the deal was pulled out from under him once his issues with narcotics were exposed.' Damon closed his eyes, pinching the bridge of his nose. 'And now he's back at home, humiliated and berated.' Arthur laughed as he shoved some bread into his mouth.

Vanessa regarded the old man with disdain. He'd always been like that with Damon. Little digs about his flamboyance – 'surprised you've got yourself a girlfriend; I always thought you were a poofter' – and his struggle with numbers and the business side of things – 'if you were more like your brother, you might actually be a millionaire by now. Such a waste'. It was probably worse now that Arthur's favourite, Benjamin, was gone.

The room went quiet as Damon sighed. 'Thanks for that, *Father*. I think you'll find I *did* get the contract. I just hadn't checked the morality clause about acceptable author behaviour, which feels ironic to me considering the number of authors I know with *all* sorts of kinks and addictions in their pasts *and* present'. He gave Clive a look when he said that.

'You have a new TV series in the works though, I hear,' Andrew quickly said, clearly also feeling sorry for Damon. 'Fascinating topic.'

'Yes, I bet the publishers will come running back,' Keir added.

'Oh I don't know,' Indra said. 'In my experience, publishers aren't the tastemakers they pretend to be. Any scent of risk and—' she clicked her fingers '—they bow out.'

'I wouldn't say that,' Vanessa said. 'I bet there are publishers out there willing to take a chance, especially if there's increased attention around it.' She turned to Clive. 'Wouldn't you agree, Clive? I mean, I imagine the fact you're living in Greensands, the centre of a real-life crime, would appeal to publishers?'

Clive looked uncomfortable, squirming in his chair. Damon frowned at her. He could tell she was up to something.

'I've thought about writing a novel,' Andrew said, saving Clive from answering. 'They say we all have a novel in us, don't they?' he added with a nervous laugh. Poor man, trying to bring some normality to a group of individuals who were anything but.

'What would you write about, dear boy?' Clive asked, clearly pleased the attention was off him.

'I don't know, maybe a *Percy Jackson* type of novel,' Andrew replied.

'Percy who?' Arthur shouted down the table.

'It's a series of children's books, Father,' Damon explained. 'Josh reads them.'

Arthur huffed. 'How would you know? You barely see the boy. *I* barely see the boy!'

Damon's jaw clenched as he looked down at his plate. Again, Vanessa's heart went out to him. She was almost tempted to clutch his hand, which was curled into a tight fist beneath the table. But she didn't.

'Do you have any children, Vanessa?' Andrew asked, ever keen to massage the awkwardness away.

'No,' Vanessa replied, taking a long sip of her drink.

'I suppose you're too busy, what with your job,' Clive said.

'That's no excuse,' Indra said with a laugh. 'I'm the busiest person I know and yet I still managed to be a hands-on mum with my two before they headed off to university. Didn't I, Tom?'

Tom nodded, but Vanessa noticed some hesitation on his face.

'It surprises me you haven't had children, Vanessa dear,' Clive said. 'I remember that little baby doll you'd carry everywhere with you. Plus, the way you were with your brother, always so attentive, so kind.'

'Isn't that the one who went missing?' Indra asked in a too-loud voice.

Now it was Vanessa's turn to curl her hands into tight fists beneath the table. This time, Damon did what she'd been tempted to. He gently covered her fist with his palm, offering his silent support.

'So sad,' Clive said, shaking his head. 'Tore your poor father apart, that did. Never forgave himself.'

Never forgave me, Vanessa thought. It was under her watch that Vincent disappeared. And boy, did her father like to remind her of that during his less sober times. 'There'd be more presents under the tree if you hadn't taken your eye off your brother that day,' he would say after one too many rums, those first few Christmases. Or: 'Vincent would be the same age as that one over there if you hadn't lost him,' when he saw one of Vincent's old school friends in the pub.

'We all know the reason too,' Arthur said as he gestured to Vanessa and Damon. 'It was all because these two weren't watching Vincent like they were supposed to.'

Vanessa took in a sharp breath.

'Weren't there rumours *you'd* taken him, Father?' Damon snapped back. 'Snared him away from us and kept him in your dungeon for your strange little cult?'

Arthur's eyes turned to fire. 'Ridiculous thing to say!'

As he said that, Vanessa noticed a large distinctive butterfly fluttering past his head with iridescent green and black wings.

'Is that an Allotei's birdwing butterfly?' she asked.

Clive followed her gaze. 'Why yes, it is.'

'Another one of your strays?' Andrew asked.

Clive hesitated, looking at Vanessa. He knew she'd be well aware that particular breed of butterfly wasn't native to the UK. In fact, it was incredibly rare. So rare, they were known to be listed for thousands of pounds on eBay. It would certainly make a catch for a butterfly enthusiast embroiled in the illegal insect trade.

'No, this one wasn't a stray,' Clive said carefully. 'It was a gift from a friend.'

'Where did your friend find it?' Vanessa asked. 'I mean, *Ornithoptera allotei*,' she added, using the butterfly's formal name, 'are native to the forests of New Guinea. So it would be rather hard to transport it here, alive.'

'She's right,' Damon said. 'Strange addition to your flock.'

Vanessa noticed Clive give Keir a quick look.

'I have a contact at a butterfly farm,' Clive quickly said. 'Anyway, let's move on to mains, shall we?'

Vanessa stood up abruptly. 'Just popping to the ladies' room.'

'It's upstairs and to the right, dear,' Clive said.

She walked up the stairs, butterflies fluttering their wings around her. Of course, it wasn't the bathroom she needed, but a chance for some snooping, her resolve fired up by the thought Clive might have obtained that beautiful creature illegally. It was Clive's study she was looking for and after trying some doors, she struck gold as she entered a room that was about as typical a writer's study as you could get, with a vintage manual typewriter and walls lined with bookshelves laden with leather-bound books of various sizes and colours. The fact that the spines of those books weren't well worn revealed Clive probably hadn't even opened most of them.

Vanessa walked over to the neat pile of manuscript pages on his desk and flicked through them, stopping at one passage.

> He nestled beautifully and sadly among the overgrown grass of the butterfly farm, just as the other victims had. His face was a thing of utter beauty, like a cross between a young Ernest Hemingway and Mark Twain. His bronze skin and awesome muscle mass made me, yet again, think of Alexander the Great, and my memories instantly took me back to that utterly delicious evening we spent exploring each other's bodies like a hungry Marco Polo exploring the Silk Road. Except the only silk today was the spider silk that was wrapped around his wrists.

'Wow,' Vanessa whispered to herself. 'Clive loves his similes.'

She carefully flicked through the other pages, which revealed much of the same. Essentially, this was an erotica novel disguised as a crime novel. But what was most interesting were the victims: all men in their forties. All found dead in a butterfly farm. All bound in spider silk . . . and all involved with the illegal insect trade. It made her heart beat faster, and not in a good way. She quickly took some photos with her phone, just in case Paul needed to see the evidence for himself.

'Are you moonlighting as a reporter for the *Daily Mail*?' a voice asked. She spun around to see Damon watching her from the doorway, an intrigued smile on his handsome face. 'No, it's not a reporter you're moonlighting as,' he said as he stepped in and closed the door softly behind him. 'It's a police detective. *You* suspect Clive, don't you? I could tell by all those questions you were asking him. *Very* Paul Truss of you.'

Vanessa said nothing.

Damon smiled. 'Your silence speaks a thousand damning words.' He strolled towards her, standing close as he flicked through the pages of the manuscript she'd just been looking at. Vanessa thought about stepping away from Damon. She *knew* she ought to. But his scent, that leather-and-musk scent so familiar to her, was intoxicating. She peered at the back of his bare neck as he bent over the pages, took in the fine dark down of hairs and the curve of his strong shoulders. She thought about placing her fingers on his skin, pressing her nose against him, breathing him in.

'Now I see why you were snooping, Doctor Marwood,' Damon said. 'I think our celebrity author has based one of his characters on me. "Tall, dark and handsome, his muscles flexed beneath the moonlight as he pummelled into me, his length filling me to gasping point."' He turned to her, eyes deep in hers, challenging and mischievous. 'What do you think, Vanessa? Does that sound like me, if memory serves?'

She held his gaze. 'Sure, maybe the bit where his mate wants to kill him after, anyway.'

Damon's lip quirked up. 'Oh come on. Don't be like that. Did you really want to kill me after our sessions?'

Vanessa rolled her eyes. 'You are incorrigible.'

'Just the way you like it.' The smile slipped from his face. 'Seriously, though. Butterfly farm. Dead bodies. *Spider* silk? Not to mention the illegal insect trade, where the likes of Clive's birdwing butterfly would be enjoyed. All a bit too familiar, wouldn't you say?'

Vanessa sighed. 'Yes, I thought the same.'

'So, what do you suspect Clive of? Being an illegal insect crime lord? Even The Cobweb Killer himself? Old gay targets dead men because that's the only way he can get his kicks?'

'I don't think it would be as simple as that, if it *is* him.'

'Then let's make it simple. Let's ask him.' Damon began walking towards the door.

Vanessa reached out and grabbed his wrist. 'No, Damon.'

He looked down at her long fingernails, which were digging into his skin. 'Kinky.' Then he raised his eyes up to hers and took a step towards her. They were close again, almost chest to chest.

She shoved him away. She didn't have time for all this sexual chemistry nonsense. 'I'm going to talk to Paul, OK? Leave it to the professionals. Anyway, it's the Abbotts they have in custody.'

'I don't think it's them. I can tell you think the same. Anyway,

I don't think the professionals have a chance of hunting down this killer,' he added. 'This psychopath will not be caught by good old-fashioned police work, Vanessa. This goes deeper than musty interview rooms. This is about the stuff *we* know about, you and me.' He jutted his fingers softly into her collarbone. 'Greensands. Insects. *Sex.*'

'Yes, all the things you're an expert in,' Vanessa said, heart thumping as she held his gaze. 'With that argument, you could just as well say *you're* the perfect suspect.'

'So I'd kill my own brother?' Damon shot back. 'The *one* thing in my life that I hadn't quite destroyed yet? I'm not like you, Vanessa. I didn't take my eye off the ball with Benjamin, like you did with Vincent. As much as I sometimes hated the fool, I was always looking out for him, *always.*'

Tears sprang to Vanessa's eyes. She let go of Damon's wrist, but not before she'd dug her fingernails even deeper into his skin. Then she shoved her way past him, heading down the stairs and walking into the dining room, grabbing her bag.

'I've had a call,' she said. 'I need to go.'

'Something related to the case?' Clive asked.

'Yes. New evidence,' she could not stop herself from saying to him. Then she made her way outside.

Fucking Damon. How could he still get to her, even after all these years?

As she walked by a unit of garages, she noticed a woman standing in the forecourt, jogging a toddler up and down on her hip.

'Can you see that?' she asked when Vanessa walked by.

Vanessa paused. 'See what?'

'All those flies. They're coming from that garage.' The woman gestured towards a red-doored garage ahead of them, nestled in the middle of a row of four. Vanessa walked towards it, noting dozens of bluebottle blowflies squeezing through the gaps in the garage door. Judging from the number of them, there had to be something in there, something interesting enough to attract them in these numbers.

'Do you know who this garage belongs to?' she asked.

'My neighbour,' the woman replied.

'Who's your neighbour?'

'Clive Craviso.'

Vanessa went to dig her phone out then caught sight of something at the base of the garage. She leaned down to look at it.

It was part of a shell from a tansy beetle.

37

'I haven't used the garage in months, Detective Truss,' Clive stammered out as Paul walked towards the door. Two officers stood at the entrance to the garage area, blocking the view of gathering neighbours . . . and stopping Clive from disappearing. Vanessa and Gordon stood ready on one side of Paul in their PPE, OS on the other as Selma and Deano hovered behind them.

When Paul had got the call from Vanessa, his stomach had sunk. Sure, he didn't think the case was all sewn up yet. But it had felt close, with all the evidence stacking up against the Abbott men. This now felt like a fly in an already complicated ointment. But combined with all the other information Vanessa had given him – the rare butterfly, the manuscript, even the goddamn brochure at the veterinary clinic – he knew it couldn't be ignored. He just needed to hope that whatever was attracting those flies wasn't human.

He pulled up the front of the garage, and some more flies instantly came buzzing out. He batted them away. There was also an unpleasant smell that wafted out with them. Paul exchanged a concerned glance with Vanessa. As he did, he noticed some deadly nightshade bursting up from a patch of weeds nearby. The evidence was mounting up.

He cautiously stepped inside, switching on the lights.

The whole garage lit up, revealing shelves full of glass tanks housing exotic-looking insects, their vibrant colours contrasting with the shadowy corners. Many of them looked dead. Paul curled his lip. It still felt unbelievable to him that people paid good money for these things.

'Recognise any of these insects?' he asked Vanessa as he noticed Clive shrink back.

'Yes,' Vanessa said, her eyes glassy with tears. 'I do recognise these dead creatures,' she said, casting a cold, sideways glance towards Clive, who was watching from outside. 'Many of them are endangered.'

Paul strolled over to a nearby desk, shaking his head as he took in a pile of dusty brochures just like the one they found in Indra's office. There were also some letters addressed to Clive, featuring invoices for various terrariums, one of which was dated from three months ago.

'Boss,' he heard OS call out. 'We found something.'

'Take him to the car,' Paul instructed Deano, before walking over to one of the shelving units that had been pushed aside to reveal a crude-looking door.

'This was hidden behind the shelving unit?' Paul asked.

OS nodded. 'Yeah, like a hidden bookcase door or something. I could tell from the imprint on the floor that the unit had been slid over recently so thought I'd give it a look.'

'Not just a pretty face,' Paul said as he opened the mystery door to reveal what looked like a makeshift lab within the garage next door. Paul and OS exchanged raised eyebrows, and walked in. The garage was dominated by a large table, with aluminium trays lining workbenches around the sides. There was another door at the back of the garage.

'I bet that leads right onto the alleyway,' Paul said.

'Perfect way to transport bodies without people noticing,' OS remarked. 'Especially if you have an expensive tipping wheelbarrow to do it,' he added, gesturing to a large green wheelbarrow in the corner.

'That alleyway runs right to the butterfly farm area,' Paul remarked. 'It would only take five minutes to wheel bodies there, unnoticed at night. The manor and ridge would just be a dark field away.'

Paul's eyes snagged on a purple rug that lay on the concrete floor at the back.

'Bugs, come and check this out,' he called over to Vanessa. She walked into the second garage, eyes widening as she took it all in. 'You said you found purple wool on one of the beetle shells?'

'I did.'

They both went to walk towards the rug, but Paul paused when he noticed parts of it were *moving*.

'Larvae,' Vanessa said.

The sight was grotesque, a macabre dance of wriggling bodies among the rotten remnants. Paul fought back a wave of nausea.

'Take a proper look, will you?' he asked Vanessa.

Vanessa nodded and approached the rug with cautious steps, crouching down to look closer. 'Looks like they're feeding on blood,' she confirmed. 'Bits of flesh too.' She got her magnifier out and hovered it over the maggots. 'The larvae are most likely in their first, possibly early second, instar.'

'In layman's terms?' Paul asked.

She peered up at him. 'I'd have to get it confirmed in a lab, but based on their size and appearance, I'd estimate they hatched from their eggs in the last few hours. In fact, here's one of those eggshells,' she said, gesturing to a tiny broken eggshell nearby. 'Those eggs, in these conditions, might have taken under twenty-four hours to hatch. But again, it all depends on what's found at the lab, like what species the eggs belonged to.'

'So the insects could've found whatever was here around twenty-four hours ago?' Paul asked.

'I can't say that for sure yet,' Vanessa replied.

'Judging from the amount of blood, Harvey and Natalie's bodies could have been here,' OS said in a low voice. 'Harvey could have been . . .' He paused, wrinkling his nose. 'Well, castrated here.'

'Let's not rush to conclusions,' Gordon, who had also now joined them, said. 'Who knows, blood may have leaked from a rubbish bag filled with meat. We won't know until we get it all tested.'

'Get some samples,' Paul said. Gordon nodded and opened his kitbag, laying treadplates on the floor before gathering up samples of blood as Vanessa carefully collected some of the squirming larvae, killing some and gently putting others into an aerated vial with a small amount of cat food to feed on. It still looked so odd to him, the way she used everyday items like airline spoons and cat food to deal with these creatures. Strange science, forensic entomology.

Paul noticed something on a small table nearby: a tray with a tiny spool, some glue and tweezers. 'Bugs, didn't you say spider silk is extracted using a spool, tweezers and glue?'

Vanessa peered up, her brown eyes travelling over to the items Paul had found. 'Yes, I think you've just found the killer's spider silk extracting factory.'

'Jesus, look at all this,' OS said. He was standing by the large table, staring at a large, bloody knife with a serrated edge, just like the one Mio suspected had been used to mutilate poor Harvey. Even more damning was what lay on a tray next to it: two dead butterflies, their black wings adorned with vibrant red bands and spots, sitting right beside some yellow-flecked cotton wool. Next to it all was a long tube wrapped with spider silk, as well as tubes of what looked like semen.

'Postman butterfly,' Vanessa murmured as she gestured to the dead creatures. 'They produce the same substance found on the cotton wool that was used on Benjamin. And this,' she said, pointing at the silk, 'I suspect tests will show this is from golden silk orb-weaver spiders, but it's been purchased rather than extracted judging by how it's presented.'

'I think we have our killer, Boss,' OS said.

Paul sat across from Clive Craviso and his solicitor in the interview room, OS at his side. Clive's white hair was unkempt, strands falling across his forehead, while sweat formed in the armpits of his once-pristine shirt. His blue waistcoat, creased and rumpled, matched the askew bow tie.

Could Clive, the kind man Paul had lived next door to as a boy, really be The Cobweb Killer? Could Abe Abbott? Could Ricky Abbott? Maybe all three of them were in on it, running a nice little earner in the illegal insect trade, which then somehow led them to darker things.

'Mr Craviso,' Paul began, 'you are here because we have evidence connecting you to the murders of Michael Regan, Simon Taylor, Tim Holmes and Benjamin Oberlin, plus Harvey and Natalie Wheatley.'

'Paul, this is preposterous!' Clive said, brown eyes filling with tears. 'I wouldn't murder anyone. Couldn't!'

Paul clenched his jaw. 'Let me run through the evidence. In the garage next to yours, accessed by a hidden door on your property, we found a bloodstained and maggot-infested rug, as well as several pertinent items linking you to the murders – in particular a bloody knife.'

'Not to mention the blood-and-maggot-infested rug,' OS added.

Clive's mouth dropped open. 'What are you talking about? I know nothing about a hidden door. Which garage?'

'To the right of yours,' Paul replied.

'Dear old Mabel Barnes at number three owns that garage. I have never set foot in it, and as far as I know, neither has she. It is empty.'

Paul knew Mabel. She used to be the headmistress at Greensands Primary School, but was now a ninety-year-old woman who probably couldn't walk downstairs, let alone use a garage.

'Handy,' Paul commented, 'that she never uses it. Easy for someone else to secretly use it, no?'

'You can't seriously think *I* knocked a hidden doorway into Mabel's garage without detection, Paul?'

Paul shrugged. 'There was lots of work being carried out on the road outside the flats a few weeks back. Lots of drilling, from what I recall. The sound of a wall being knocked through wouldn't be noticed.'

Clive shook his head. 'No, I swear I know *nothing* of this garage.'

'What about your little illegal insect trading enterprise then?' OS asked.

'Interesting set-up you have in there,' Paul added.

'Ancient history,' Clive said, putting his hands up. 'I swear to you.'

'What's ancient history?' Paul asked him.

Clive swallowed. 'My little . . . side hustle. That's what they call it now, isn't it? I helped Arthur, then Benjamin when he became more involved in it all.'

So Arthur spearheaded his son's little enterprise? Maybe that was where all the cult rumours had come from . . . perhaps Arthur had been running the business from his cellar. He'd certainly have had the contacts to get his hands on rare insects.

'I gave it all up a few months ago,' Clive said, interrupting his thoughts. 'In fact, I haven't been in my garage since.'

'So you just left all those creatures to die?' Paul said.

'I-I was on my cruise, remember?' Clive said.

'That was just a month-long cruise, Clive. I'm guessing you didn't leave your precious butterflies to rot?'

Clive sank his head.

'So,' Paul said with a heavy sigh, 'we're talking about an illegal insect trading business then?'

Clive took in a deep, shaky breath. 'Yes. Money can be tight. I had to explore other options.'

'That include extracting silk from spiders?' OS asked. 'We found your little spider silk factory, Clive.'

'Spider silk factory? If you're referring to the batch I procured for Indra, Indra has that now, not me.'

'Indra?' Paul asked.

'Yes, she asked me to acquire some for her for a dress she was having made for an awards ceremony. In fact,' he added, 'she told me it had been stolen during an office break-in the other day, so she wanted me to order more. But I refused. As I told you, I do *not* want anything to do with that business anymore!'

Paul and OS exchanged confused looks. Indra hadn't told them that.

'Let's move on,' Paul said. 'Let's discuss the subject of your novel-in-progress about dead men found in an abandoned butterfly farm—'

'We live near an abandoned butterfly farm, for God's sake,' Clive interrupted. 'Write what you know, that's what they say. My writing is purely fictional! It's an exploration of the dark side of humanity. I would *never* act upon those ideas in reality.'

OS interjected, his tone sharp. 'It's not just your writing, though. Lab results reveal that the substance found on Benjamin Oberlin's body is a substance sometimes produced by postman butterflies – the very butterflies found on the tray in your little secret area next door to your garage, according to Doctor Marwood. The area you deny any knowledge of, and yet there we found butterflies just like the ones you so love. All so very convenient.'

Clive's face went pale, his hands trembling. 'No, I told you, I have never stepped into that garage. And I would never harm anyone. You know that more than most, Paul.'

Paul took in a deep breath. He couldn't let his personal affection for Clive get in the way.

'How about I give you some names?' Clive said in a desperate voice. 'To show you I am fully cooperating and I am *not* lying. Keir Sinclair, there's one! He, too, became a recent partner. And Indra Hudson, she's a client! Back in the day, even Delilah Marwood was involved.'

Paul frowned. 'Vanessa's mother?'

'Yes! She grew close to Arthur. There were even rumours they . . .' His voice trailed off. 'Anyway, she was present for our regular meetings about the business. She used her contacts in the arts world to procure clients.'

Paul sighed. How would Vanessa feel about that?

'But murder?' Clive continued. 'No. Never! Paul, my dear boy.' Clive leaned across the table to look at Paul. 'I can see the exhaustion etched on your face. Perhaps it's clouding your judgement? I understand. You're grasping at straws, looking for a culprit where there isn't one. But not your old neighbour. Not the man who taught you to ride a bike. I've been set up! The evidence has been planted. Paul, *please.*'

Paul suddenly felt his heart race, the room closing in around him as his vision blurred at the edges. The thud of his heartbeat echoed in his ears, drowning out all other sounds. It was as if time had slowed down, each second stretching out, magnifying the discomfort. Beads of sweat formed on his forehead, a clammy sensation that intensified with each passing moment.

He'd had this before, just before he was referred to a cardiologist.

He pushed back his chair and rose unsteadily to his feet. 'I need a moment,' he managed to get out. 'OS, take over, will you?'

Paul left the room, his steps heavy and unsteady. Once outside, he leaned against the corridor wall, taking deep breaths to calm himself.

'You all right?' an officer asked as they passed.

'Yep, just taking a moment,' Paul got out.

The officer nodded, but still regarded Paul with worried eyes. Did he really look that bad? As he thought that, Fiona appeared, moving down the corridor like a bulldozer.

Great.

'I hear you have a new suspect in?' she asked. Then she paused. 'Blimey, you look a right state.'

'Just need a coffee.'

'You sure?' She scrutinised his face. 'I know this is close to home for you. As I said before, if—'

'No!' Paul quickly said. 'I'm fine.' He straightened his shoulders, forcing his body to cooperate. 'As you said, we have a new suspect in.' He gave a rundown of the evidence against Clive.

'He got any previous?' Fiona asked.

Paul shook his head.

'Well, the evidence is clear,' Fiona said. 'Maybe he's been working with Ricky and Abe Abbott. Let's really pin these men down. What's your gut telling you?'

Paul wasn't clear about anything right at that moment. The thump of his heart was clouding any rational thought.

Fiona frowned. 'You really OK?'

Paul closed his eyes, nodding. 'Ah-huh.'

'Maybe you should go home, get some proper rest? I can get DCI Mitchell to join OS, get the interview wrapped up and reinterview the Abbott men. Might be good to get a fresh perspective on it all anyway.'

Paul quickly shook his head. 'Not a chance. I'll be fine.'

Fiona leaned close. 'I insist, Paul. I know about your condition. I don't want you collapsing on me, all right?'

Paul pulled away in shock. 'You know?'

'I had a chat with your wife earlier.'

'Fuck's sake. Helen told you?'

'She's just worried, that's all. And so am I!'

'She had no right!' he shouted.

Fiona's face hardened. 'She had every right, as a wife concerned for her husband *and* the father of her children. And *I* have every right to know if one of my detectives has a heart condition, all right? Now get home. You hear me?'

Paul thought about protesting, but when Fiona got that look in her eyes, he knew it was her way or the highway. So he stormed down the corridor, ready to blow a fuse at Helen.

When he got home, he found Helen at her desk, working on a

new poster for one of her clients. She twisted around to look at him when he walked in.

'Is it true Clive Craviso was arrested?' Helen asked.

'Ah-huh,' Paul said tightly.

Helen examined Paul's face. 'What's wrong with you?'

'You.'

She frowned. 'What?'

'I know you told The Banger about my condition.'

Helen swallowed, averting her gaze.

'You had no right,' Paul snapped. 'That was my decision to make, not yours. I don't need you to fight my battles for me.'

'Actually, I bloody *do* need to,' Helen countered. 'You've been promising me you'd tell them, but you haven't. It scares me to think of what could happen if you pushed yourself too hard. I just want to protect you.'

'You had no right,' Paul said again, jabbing his finger at her. 'Now The Banger's getting Anita bloody Mitchell to reinterview Ricky and Abe, meaning she'll be the one to wrap the case up, taking all the bloody glory.'

'Oh babe,' Helen said, getting up and going to give him a hug. But he stepped away.

'Don't be like this,' Helen said, as Paul's phone rang – piercing the tension between them. It was Deano. He quickly put it to his ear, walking away from his wife.

'What's up?'

'According to his phone and bank records, it looks like Abe Abbott *was* in Manchester when he said he was, Boss,' Deano replied. 'That means he wasn't around when Emi Craviso was attacked, and maybe when the Wheatleys were killed, too. Plus that friend he was staying with confirmed he was there.'

Paul started pacing back and forth. Just because Abe wasn't there when Emi and the Wheatleys were attacked didn't mean he wasn't around for the other murders. But it *did* prove he hadn't been lying about being in Manchester.

'Make sure you get this information over to OS stat, all right?' Paul said.

'Sure.' A pause. 'Oh, another thing. Selma spoke to the old bird who owns the garage next to Clive's. She confirmed she's never used it, it's just been sat there empty for years. She had no idea about the door between the garages, swore there wasn't one. No family, and Selma said she was pretty immobile. So easy enough for Clive Craviso to break in and use it.'

Paul nodded. 'Good to have it confirmed.'

'Pretty sloppy of Clive to leave all the murder weapons and other evidence out though, right Boss?'

'Not if he didn't think anyone would find his secret little lab,' Paul said.

'True.' Deano was quiet for a few moments. 'Is it true you've been kicked off the case?'

Paul curled his hand into a fist. 'I haven't been *kicked* off it, you numbnut. The Banger just reckons I need a bit of a rest.'

'Mitchell better not be working on it.'

Paul didn't answer.

'Shit,' Deano said. 'She is, isn't she? She's a bloody witch.'

'Yeah, well, you can complain to The Banger about that. I better go. But keep me posted, yeah? Unofficial like.'

'Will do.'

Paul put the phone down and walked over to his favourite battered armchair, sinking down onto it. Helen followed and knelt beside him, putting her warm cheek against his hand. 'Sorry, babe. I just do it because I care.'

'I know you do.'

'So what was that call about?'

'I don't think Abe Abbott's involved.'

'Me too. He's so young.' She frowned. 'I hope one of the people you have in custody is responsible though. At least it means the killer will be off our streets tonight.'

Paul peered out of the window. 'Me too.' He felt his eyelids drooping.

'Have a nap, babe, before the girls get back in an hour.'

Paul nodded, his eyes already closing.

An hour later, he woke to the sound of giggling girls and a message from Deano.

Abe Abbott's been released. The Witch said there's not enough evidence to keep him in any longer.

Bloody Mitchell. She was probably right though. Paul's gut was telling him Abe wasn't involved. At least he hoped so, anyway.

If not, they'd just let a killer back on the streets.

38

Vanessa drove her truck down Greensands' main road, feeling a heady sense of relief. Surely it was over now? Though she still wasn't convinced about Ricky and Abe's involvement, the evidence against Clive was too much. Once the bloodwork came back, it would be confirmed. Maybe the people of Greensands could sleep safe tonight.

It made the prospect of catching her flight to New York tomorrow so much easier.

As she drove past the Abbott house, she caught sight of Abe walking towards his shed. So Paul had released him? Good. She never thought it was him. She imagined how he'd feel, taking in his beloved shed. Fingerprint powder, books dishevelled, muddy footprints on his rugs. It was his sanctuary. The place where he would have felt most at home.

Vanessa used to feel that way about her father's tiny lab on the butterfly farm . . . The hours she would spend there with him, learning from him or one of his books as she curled up in the old armchair while he worked. She used to yearn for the same kind of involvement with her mother's art. But she was always so cagey about it all. Preferred to hole herself up alone in her small art room if she wasn't outdoors. So it was nice to be involved with her dad's work. Vincent had liked it too.

Vincent, who Abe so reminded her of.

Without really thinking about it, Vanessa pulled up outside Abe's house and got out, walking towards the shed. Even before she got there, she could see it was a mess. One of the smaller, empty terrariums had been knocked over, its glass smashed on the floor. Why couldn't the officers have taken more care? Abe was crouched down beside it, carefully picking the glass up.

'Hey,' she said when she entered. 'Can I help you clean up?'

He looked up at her, surprise registering on his pale face. 'You sure?'

"Course.' She grabbed some old newspaper from the side, using a nearby book to sweep the glass up onto it. 'So they released you then?'

'They had to, really. My twenty-four hours was up. They didn't have enough evidence to keep me in longer.'

'But your dad's still inside?'

Abe nodded. 'He didn't do it, though.'

Vanessa didn't comment. She *couldn't* comment. She didn't want to risk jeopardising the case. She *did* think about how tough it would be for this kid if his dad was charged with murder though. One parent dead. One parent absent. She knew how that felt. They worked in silence for a few minutes, removing the glass from the rug and tidying the books away. Vanessa couldn't help but notice the way Abe whispered to each spider as he passed them.

'I'm picking Amy Lee up later, by the way,' he said. 'Thanks for sorting.'

'It was a pleasure. I've been missing my Nancy, so it was nice to have her around for a bit. You really love these guys, don't you?'

The young man nodded. 'They're my entire world. I know you get it.'

'I do.'

'Dad thinks they're substitutes for my mum.'

'Maybe he's right.' What did her pet, Nancy, substitute? Maybe Vincent. Maybe her mum. Maybe her dad. Maybe the whole damn family she now didn't have.

As she thought that, her eye caught on the large, cracked terrarium. 'What was in that? Your dad didn't know.'

He got the same look his father had when she'd asked him.

'Abe, come on. Tell me,' she pushed.

'Don't tell anyone.'

'I can't promise that. What was it?'

'*Phoneutria*,' he whispered, in so low a voice she needed to ask him to repeat himself.

Her eyes widened. 'Brazilian wandering spider? What the hell?'

'Benjamin gave it to me as a gift,' Abe said. 'I should've questioned him more about how he got it.'

'You bloody should have.' Brazilian wandering spiders were

incredibly venomous and, as a result, illegal to own in the UK. Clearly, Benjamin had got it via his illegal insect trading gig.

'Where is it now?' she asked.

'It was stolen with my golden silk orb-weaver.'

Vanessa looked at him with disapproval. 'You really should have told us, Abe. Brazilian wandering spiders are *extremely* dangerous. I'll have to tell Paul.'

'I know,' Abe said with a sigh as he watched her pull her phone out. She called Paul but it went to voicemail so she left a message for him. Then she caught sight of the camera stand in the corner of the shed. 'How'd you get into TikTokking?' she asked, desperate to get the look of dejection off his face. He knew he'd done wrong, no need to hammer it home after a tough couple of days with possibly worse to come.

'I guess I was looking for my tribe, and I found it on TikTok,' he said. 'I've never really . . . fitted in.'

'My brother was the same.'

'Dad said I remind him of Vincent.' He paused for a moment. 'You know, the police thought Dad had something to do with your brother's disappearance at one point.'

Vanessa looked at Abe in surprise. 'Did they?'

'Yeah. No way he did though,' Abe quickly added. 'He had a proper solid alibi. But it's always the way with people who look like us.' His face lit up. 'Hey, I've got a crazy idea. Let's film a TikTok video together.'

'God, no. I can't dance to save my life.'

He laughed. 'TikTok's not all about dumb dance moves, you know. We can make it all about forensic entomology.'

'How?'

Abe's excitement was palpable as he explained. 'We can create a mini skit that explains how insects help solve crimes. Think quick cuts, cool transitions, and a bit of humour to keep people hooked. I can post it after the case is wrapped up.'

Vanessa couldn't help but smile at Abe's enthusiasm. Though the idea of making a TikTok video horrified her, she suddenly had an urge to do something to help this kid who reminded her so much of her brother. 'All right, let's give it a shot.'

Over the next hour, they worked on creating their video, experimenting with different angles and props, finding creative ways to demonstrate forensic entomology concepts using everyday objects. After a few attempts and bursts of laughter, they finally nailed it. Abe hit the play button, and they watched their creation unfold on the screen. Vanessa cringed through most of it. She really *wasn't* a natural. But it made Abe happy, and right at that moment that was her main aim. He was a good kid. She imagined Vincent would have been the same. She left with her business card in his possession and promises to send him links to some courses he could do.

As she drove back to the pub, she noticed the village green was crammed with people holding up candles as the sun set. An impromptu vigil. She sighed and parked up, then walked over towards them. Time to finally say goodbye to this village . . . and the victims it had claimed.

39

Paul and Helen walked side by side along the dimly lit street, their footsteps echoing in the silence as the twins ran up ahead, drawn to the lights from the vigil. The sun was setting, a sea of candles creating a warm glow on the faces of the gathered crowd. It seemed like every single villager was there, from the girls' teacher, Andrew, to the local vet, Keir.

Paul could see some of the families of the victims huddled together, arms linked, tears streaming down their faces. He moved through the crowd with Helen and the girls, offering words of condolence and comfort. People turned and watched as they passed.

As they got to the front, Sharon appeared, Michael's heavily pregnant wife at her side.

'So is it true, Paul?' Sharon asked him. 'Are Ricky Abbott and Clive Craviso responsible for my boy's death?'

'You know I can't confirm that yet,' Paul said.

'What about this illegal insect ring they were running?' Michael's wife asked. 'People are saying the victims might have been involved, and their deaths were part of some crime stuff. Michael had nothing to do with anything like that – you know that!'

Paul placed a comforting hand on her shoulder. 'I know. As soon as we have all the details, we'll let you and everyone else know. I'll do whatever it takes to bring closure for you and your family.'

Sharon nodded. 'You've worked hard, Paul. We appreciate it.' She looked around. 'Vanessa with you?'

'No. Not sure where she is.'

'Hope she hasn't flown to New York already,' Sharon said. 'I want to thank her too.'

'She's flying out tomorrow,' Paul said. 'I'm sure she'll say goodbye before she does.'

Simon Taylor's father, Gareth, headed over to them then. He was a short, stocky man. 'Got anything to say about this tweet by that podcast girl, Paul?' He held his phone up to show a tweet from Heather Fala, the host of *Dark Deeds Dissected*.

> 📢 Breaking News: Exclusive revelations on The Cobweb Killer case! Damon Oberlin, brother of victim Benjamin, assaulted Benjamin and attacked other victim Simon when he tried to intervene. Stay tuned for more updates! #CobwebKiller #TrueCrime #Greensands

'That was why your officer was asking us if Simon had been in any kind of altercation, wasn't it?' Gareth asked, raising his voice as people turned to look. 'Now we know why. He punched my son. We all know he hated his brother, too. And all the weird stuff done to my son and the others. That's the kind of weird shit Damon Oberlin's into, isn't it? Shouldn't he be in custody with the other two? I bet he was involved, a weird little ring of psychos. There's always been those rumours about the Oberlins. Even that one of 'em took the Marwood kid and held him in their basement.'

There was a murmuring from the crowd, some getting their phones out and no doubt looking the tweets up. Bloody Heather Fala. How'd she got that info, anyway?

'It's an ongoing investigation, mate – you know that,' Paul said to Gareth. 'Anyway, we've already spoken to Damon.'

As he said that, the very man they were talking about walked towards the green: Damon.

His eyes were bloodshot, and his usually confident posture seemed slumped, burdened by the weight of his loss. All eyes turned on him as he stepped into view, and the murmurs of conversation died down to an uncomfortable silence.

'You're not welcome here,' one villager shouted out to Damon, his voice quivering with anger.

Damon paused, looking surprised as he tried to detect the source.

'You think you can get away with anything, don't you?' someone else yelled.

Some villagers hesitated, unsure of how to react. Others nodded in agreement. Damon regarded everyone with confusion, and Paul couldn't help but feel a pang of sympathy for him.

A young man then stormed through the crowds towards Damon, shoving people out of the way. It was Nathan, Simon's son. Just sixteen, but already in a world of trouble at school, thanks to his angry outbursts. And now it looked like he was about to have another, aimed squarely at Damon's perfect jaw.

Paul went to run towards them, but it was too late.

'This is for my dad!' Nathan shouted, his fist connecting with Damon's face and sending him stumbling back as cheers rang out in the crowd. Paul stepped between the two men, facing Nathan with his hands on the kid's chest.

'Nathan, calm down,' he said.

Nathan tried to shove Paul away, but Paul grabbed hold of his arm, carefully twisting it behind his back. 'Don't do this to your family, kid,' he whispered in his ear. He peered over his shoulder at Damon. 'You all right?'

Damon wiped some blood from his nose, observing it on his fingers with an expression of alarm. Then he glanced up at Paul, suddenly looking like the young teenager Paul had once known. 'Yes, I'm—' He swallowed, frowning. 'I'm leaving.' He turned and walked away, some villagers shoving their shoulders into him as he did.

Paul caught Helen's eye. He knew she could feel it too: the palpable sense of anger and chaos in the air. He just hoped they really had solved the case that was tearing this village apart, otherwise God knew how much worse things could get for everyone.

Vanessa appeared then. She was wearing a long grey dress with black insect patterns all over it, her red lips in stark contrast. She smiled when she noticed Paul and headed towards him. But then she noticed Damon stumbling away with blood on his face and her expression changed. Just like always, it was as though Paul and everyone else disappeared as she went to follow him.

40

Vanessa caught up with Damon by the graveyard as he leaned against a wall, pinching the bridge of his nose, blood on his fingertips.

'What happened?' she asked when she got to him. 'Are you OK?'

Damon touched his bleeding nose gingerly, his voice strained. 'Just a stupid scuffle with a child.'

She steered him towards a nearby bench that overlooked the graveyard. 'Let me take a look at you.'

He gave her a dubious look. 'OK, Nurse Marwood.'

They both sat down and she reached into her bag for some tissues to stem the bleeding.

'Who did it, then?' she asked as he flinched.

'Simon Taylor's son. Seems news has broken about my little fracas with Simon.'

'Oh.'

'Oh, indeed.'

He kept his eyes on Vanessa as she soaked up all the blood. 'Hold the tissue there,' she instructed.

'Will you stay with me for a bit?'

She hesitated. Then nodded. 'Sure.'

'So, do you really think Clive Craviso and Ricky Abbott could be responsible for my brother's death and the others?'

'The evidence is there, especially for Clive,' Vanessa admitted.

'And there we were, having lunch with the fucker.'

'Yeah. But it's the lunch that helped catch him.'

'True.'

They sat together in silence, the weathered tombstones emerging, a sombre scene against the fading light.

'So you're off to New York tomorrow, then?' Damon asked eventually, his voice a bass note in the silence.

'I am.'

'That's a shame. You'll miss Benjamin's funeral. I was at the funeral home today.'

'That sounds tough.'

'Yes, especially with my father present.' His lips quirked into a small smile. 'He asked the funeral director if there were special discounts for being a repeat customer, as he was pretty sure he'd be leaving this mortal coil soon.'

Vanessa smiled. 'Your father certainly knows how to make an impression. *Do* they offer a discount? I mean, you *are* skint, what with that half-a-million-pound publishing advance falling through.'

Damon gave her a sideways glance. 'Cheeky bitch.'

She smiled. 'Seriously though, did it go OK?'

'If you call being surrounded by suffocating floral arrangements, and awkward small talk about coffins and embalming techniques "OK",' Damon replied.

'Sounds fun. When is the funeral?'

'In a couple of weeks. You'll be the toast of New York's forensics community by then. You know, I'm surprised you're moving there of all places. In fact, I was surprised when you moved to London.'

'Really?'

'You used to love rolling around in the mud and the grass.'

She gave him a look. She knew what he was trying to do, resurrect memories of their times exploring each other in the grasslands.

'If I were a therapist,' Damon continued, 'I'd say being in the city is a way of getting yourself as far away from the grasslands that claimed your brother as you can.'

Vanessa followed his gaze towards the swaying shadows of grass in the distance. 'I don't need a therapist to tell me that,' she said quietly. 'You know, we never had a funeral for my brother.'

'That's because your father never gave up hope of finding him. You did though.'

'Why would you say that?'

He shrugged. 'You left Greensands, didn't you?'

'Didn't you as well?'

'Not like you did. Leaving us all behind, leaving *me* behind.'

Vanessa clenched her jaw. 'I had a place at university.'

'But we'd always talked about studying Zoology at Edinburgh together. Then you go and accept an offer at Imperial.'

Vanessa thought of those years in Greensands after Vincent went missing. Three years of pain and guilt. She'd somehow got through it, knowing she'd be off to university when she was eighteen. The idea of Damon joining her had felt as though the past would be following her. No matter how much she'd felt for him, she'd known that being somewhere with him wouldn't be the clean break she so yearned for.

'At least this time we can have a proper goodbye,' Damon said. He was right. After she'd told him she'd accepted an offer at Imperial, he'd lost it, refusing to talk to her. She'd left Greensands without saying goodbye. 'I feel like we need a farewell drink,' he added. 'A strong one.'

She watched as the mourners dispersed from the fields. 'I'm not sure the scores of villagers heading to the pub now would welcome your presence.'

'I don't mean in the *pub*.' Damon retrieved a hip flask from the pocket of his navy-blue blazer and held it out to her. 'I mean a good old-fashioned Greensands piss-up in a graveyard.'

Vanessa smiled. They'd often enjoyed getting drunk on this very bench from rum out of that very hip flask.

'A Ron Zacapa special?' she asked.

Damon nodded, popping open the top of the hip flask and holding it out to her. The caramel and oak aromas brought back memories of that sun-and-rum-drenched summer after Vincent disappeared, when Vanessa muffled her guilt and her grief with drunken oblivion and the feel of Damon's lips and fingers and more on her and inside her.

She took the hip flask and caught Damon's peacock-blue eyes. She saw the memories in those eyes of his, too. She quickly sank back a mouthful of the stuff, closing her eyes as the velvety taste lingered on her tongue. Over the next hour, they drank and reminisced. Intoxicated by the alcohol, they even did a tour of the graveyard in the darkness, greeting the names they recognised as though the people themselves were there before them.

Vanessa stumbled upon a weathered tombstone. 'Well, hello there, Mr Thompson,' she slurred, feeling herself sway slightly. 'Thank you for spending most of my maths classes telling me off for not grasping the Pythagorean theorem while staring at my breasts.'

Damon pointed to another grave and said, 'Ah, Mrs Higglesworth, always the gossip queen of the village. I hope you're keeping everyone in the afterlife updated on the latest scandals. Rest in peace, dear, and try not to spread too much juicy news up there.'

Their laughter echoed through the quiet graveyard as they continued their tipsy tour, sharing humorous memories and raising their glasses to the departed souls. Vanessa knew it was childish, but something in the back of her mind reminded her how, in many ways, her teenage years had been cut short by her brother's disappearance. Maybe she was making up for it.

As they returned to their bench, their laughter eventually subsided into a comfortable silence.

'I miss this,' Damon said. 'I miss *us*.'

His eyes met Vanessa's and suddenly, her hand reached out and grabbed the lapel of his blazer, pulling him slowly towards her. Their breaths mingled, their faces drawing closer, until their lips collided. It was as though they were back in those fields again. Two teenagers torn to bits by circumstance: a lost brother, a dead mother. Hands and lips entwining to find some kind of meaning, some kind of light. But the two of them were too filled with darkness then; too shredded with urgent desire for any light to slip in.

It was the same now. Lust swirling with frantic shadows of feeling. Vanessa felt it sucking her all in, away from the city and back in the – what had Damon called it – the mud and the grass of Greensands. To the place that had pushed her mother away and hidden her brother. The place where her heart had broken in two, just as much as Damon's had, to turn her back on him. The place that, over the past few days, had claimed six lives in its macabre grip.

With a sudden surge of clarity, Vanessa gently pushed Damon away. 'I'm sorry,' she whispered. 'I can't . . . I just can't.'

'Bullshit,' Damon hissed, pulling her back towards him.

But she shoved him away. 'No.'

Damon's face hardened. 'What are you going to tell me? That you value our friendship too much?'

'Friendship? Jesus, no, Damon. I value my *sanity* too much.' She stood up, swaying slightly as she did. Then she bowed. 'It's been fun,' she said before walking away, leaving Damon watching her in the darkness, the gravestones an ominous, silent audience behind him.

The night enveloped her like a shroud as she walked down Greensands' narrow backstreet lanes. She wanted to avoid the main streets. The police presence was heightened there, and she didn't want to risk being seen in her current state of intoxication.

She shook her head as she smiled. God, she really was pissed. How thoroughly unprofessional! But the smile disappeared from her face as she heard footsteps behind her. She turned, expecting it to be Damon . . . but nobody was there. *Nothing* was there. The darkness had swallowed everything. A sense of unease settled over her as every creaking sound, every rustle of leaves, made her heart race. She couldn't shake the feeling of being watched, of unseen eyes tracing her every move. The hair on the back of her neck stood on end.

Footsteps again. Quicker. Closer.

Her mind sank to murky depths, imagining her fate, suspended from a ceiling, her lifeless body entangled in intricate strands of silk.

The footsteps grew louder. Fear gripped her tightly, threatening to suffocate her.

She darted into an alleyway, seeking refuge in its narrow confines. Her heart pounded in her chest as she leaned against the cold brick wall, desperately trying to catch her breath. Should she call for help? She cautiously peered around the corner. The street remained deserted, bathed in an unsettling stillness.

'You're being ridiculous,' she hissed to herself.

'Yes, you are,' Damon's voice announced behind her. She turned to see him at the end of the alleyway, arms crossed, dark hair in his eyes. Beneath the glow of the streetlight, he looked unbearably handsome. Ominous too.

'You've been following me,' she said.

'Just to make sure you got back safe.' A wicked smile crossed his face. 'You were scared, admit it.'

'Of strange men following me in the dark, yes.'

He laughed. 'Come on, Vanessa. I'm not a strange man.'

She quirked an eyebrow.

'Let me walk you the rest of the way,' he said. 'We can't leave it like that, you shoving me away. It'll be too similar to how things were left twenty-two years ago.'

He was right. 'Fine. But keep your head down. If the kid who beat you up earlier clocks you, God knows how you'll end up.'

They both walked in silence up the street and into the pub's dark car park. She paused, turning to look at Damon.

'So this is it,' Damon said. 'At least something good came of Benjamin's death. I got to see you.'

'Damon . . .'

'It's true. Benjamin would be pleased. He knew I never got over you.'

Vanessa looked down at the ground, fingers on the door handle.

'Can I come up?' Damon asked, voice barely a whisper. 'A proper goodbye, for old times' sake.'

'Best not to.'

'A hug then?' Damon opened his arms to her and Vanessa sighed, stepping into them, finding comfort in his familiar smell, his familiar touch. It was just like all those years ago when he'd found her crying in her room the day after Vincent had gone missing. He'd held her like that then. So much pain, so much worry. She thought it couldn't get any worse, but it had over recent days. *So* much worse.

She didn't know how it happened, but soon that embrace turned into more. A brush of Damon's thumb on her cheek. The press of her lips against his exposed collarbone. Feet stepping backward, clumsy, through the doorway and up the stairs, careful not to be seen. Then, when they were safely behind the door to her room, lips meeting in a bittersweet dance, clothing removed. Little bites and hair tugs, their familiar repertoire. It felt frantic, urgent, almost feral. This need for a momentary escape from the horror and the chaos. A chance to dissemble the moment into two simple things: touch, need.

She lay back on the bed, curling her hand around the back of Damon's neck, pulling him onto her. She felt his bare chest pressed hard, too hard, against her breasts. Felt his lips trailing down her neck, teeth sharp against her skin as his fingers jabbed at the buttons of her dress. He slipped one hand around her neck, the other between her legs, finding the place he'd once known so well, moving his fingers in the way she remembered. First teasing her, drawing her to the edge, then cruelly moving away again.

She moaned, arching her head back as his lips travelled down her tummy, kissing the flesh that wouldn't have been there twenty-two years ago. He yanked the hem of her dress up and pressed his face between her legs as she tangled her fingers in his dark hair, pulling at the strands as he winced against her, watching him as he circled his tongue in a way that left her gasping.

Damon. My Damon.

Then he sank into her a few minutes later and they moved together, the years slipping away. She didn't remember falling into an exhausted sleep after. She just knew they were staring at each other in the darkness as she did, Damon's blue eyes watching her with a mixture of pain and longing.

She woke just as the sun rose, its harsh rays seeping through the flimsy curtains. She felt the weight of Damon's arm over her, like a clamp stopping her from leaving. She was happy to stay there a few moments, watching him sleep. His thick, dark hair was tousled, hints of grey showing in the glare of the morning light at his temples. His long lashes fell over his high cheekbones. He was beautiful. Always had been. She thought about tracing the lines on his forehead with her finger and brushing the faint stubble on his jaw. But didn't want to wake him. She just needed to watch him for a few moments before the reality of leaving him behind yet again hit her.

Eventually, she removed his heavy arm from her chest. He groaned and opened his eyes. At first, he looked confused when he took her in. But then he must have remembered the night before, and a lazy smile spread over his handsome face. He went to pull her towards him, but she softly pushed him away.

'You have to go,' she said. 'I have a flight to catch.'

'Surely you can't deprive a man of a lazy morning fuck with the most beautiful forensic entomologist in the world?'

It was tempting, she had to admit. But she wanted to get on the road after swinging by Paul's to say goodbye.

'Sorry, Damon,' she said.

Damon let out a heavy sigh and sat up, yawning as he raked his fingers through his hair. 'Same time next year?' he asked, blue eyes sparkling with mischief. 'There's bound to be some kind of commemoration.'

'You're awful.'

'But damn good in bed.'

She picked his shirt up and threw it at him. 'Arrogant too.'

'But so good with my tongue.'

'Damon, stop it.'

He sighed, slowly getting out of bed and pulling his shirt and jeans on. 'Come on, Vanessa, you know my attempts at humour are a way to cover for my deep-seated emotional issues.'

'Oh, I know all right.'

He grabbed his phone from the side and flung his blazer over his shoulder, standing face to face with her, the expression in his eyes growing serious. 'I never stopped loving you.'

She flinched. 'Damon, please.'

'Never.' Then he gently kissed her cheek and opened the door. But instead of stepping out, he recoiled back, bumping into Vanessa as he let out a gasp.

'What's wrong?' she asked.

He didn't answer, just continued staring, his hand clutching at his chest as if trying to steady his heart. Vanessa looked around him and went very still.

There, lying motionless on the floor, was a lifeless body tightly wrapped in silky strands.

Abe Abbott.

41

Paul jogged up the stairs of the pub, taking deep breaths to stop his heart beating out of control. When he got to the landing, he was greeted by a flurry of activity. Uniformed officers had already cordoned off the area in front of Vanessa's room, and Deano was talking in hushed tones to a pale-looking Damon nearby. Paul didn't stop to think why Damon Oberlin was there at six in the morning, hair dishevelled. Instead, he walked over to the body. Abe Abbott's body, tightly wound in what looked like silk.

How the hell had another body ended up here, when The Cobweb Killer – or killers – were supposedly in custody?

'Where's Vanessa?' he asked Deano, who'd been one of the first officers on the scene. The one to wake Paul, too, with the horrific news twenty minutes ago. Deano jutted his chin towards the door to her room. Paul's eyes darted over to the corner where Vanessa was sitting on a chair, clad in a dark, patterned dressing gown, looking more vulnerable than ever without her make-up on.

'You OK?' he called through to her.

She looked up, and he was surprised – maybe *pleased* – to see a steely determination in her eyes. 'No, but I will be when this fucker is caught.'

Paul nodded and crouched down beside Abe's body, noting how thin and delicate the strands wrapped around him seemed, woven together in a complex pattern that must have taken hours to create.

Was it spider silk?

'How could someone carry a body up here without being noticed?' he asked Deano. 'The place has CCTV, right?'

Deano shook his head. 'Not in the stairwell. They only have cameras in the lobby and the parking lot. And he's not a big lad,' he added, gesturing to Abe. 'Most decent-sized people could haul him over their shoulder and carry him for a few minutes. The owners,

248

Sharon and Galinn, didn't hear anything and there aren't any guests other than Vanessa in. But Sharon just noticed one of the larger windows in the kitchen is slightly open. She said they're usually really careful about that, so it's odd.'

Paul sighed. 'CSI lot on their way?'

'Yep.'

'We can get them to look at that.' Paul stood up, carefully stepping over the body with his plastic-covered shoes as he approached Vanessa, Damon watching from the hallway.

'It's a present,' Vanessa said when Paul got to her.

'What do you mean?'

'Balloon flies bring their mates carcasses wrapped in silk as a present. It's a way to show their strength and desirability.'

'Right,' Paul said, feeling slightly sick as he looked back at the poor kid. 'You only saw him yesterday, didn't you?' he asked her softly. 'I got your message about his poisonous spider being on the loose.'

'Yes. I saw him just before the vigil. Eight thirty? Nine?'

'Did he say where he was going after?'

She shook her head. 'No. I presumed he was just going to stay in.' She looked down at what she was wearing. 'I'd like to get ready.'

Paul nodded. 'Of course.'

'You can come back to the manor,' Damon called through to her, 'get ready there?'

Paul shook his head. 'We need to have the CSI guys check your truck as well, just in case. I'll get you driven back to mine. Helen can take you to the airport.'

Vanessa seemed to look surprised at the reminder she had a flight to catch. 'I can't go. Not now. I can't leave until I know who did this.'

For the first time since she'd told him about the New York move, he actually wanted her to go. To get her away from all this. Let her start anew without the horrors of Greensands clinging to her.

'I need to be here,' she said again. Paul could see from the look on her face she was determined.

He turned towards Selma. 'Can you give Doctor Marwood a lift to mine?'

The hotel room was off limits for her now, what with it being a crime scene. Plus Paul preferred the idea of Vanessa being close.

The young officer nodded. Vanessa grabbed her overnight bag, shoving some items wordlessly into it before pulling her coat on and following Selma out. Paul noticed her eyes lift to meet Damon's. He nodded, expression pained. Then Vanessa followed the officer down the stairs.

Paul walked over to Deano and Damon as the CSI team arrived, an exhausted-looking Gordon tending to Abe's body, his seventh in a matter of days.

'I've got Doctor Marwood's and Mr Oberlin's first accounts, Boss,' Deano said, gesturing to his notepad.

'Good job,' Paul said. He then steered Damon into a corner of the corridor. 'How about you tell me what you told my colleague? How did you discover the body?'

'Of course,' Damon said, seeming uncharacteristically serious. 'I was just leaving Vanessa's room, and I opened the door to the body lying right before me, on the floor, just as you see it now.' He shook his head as he looked at Abe. 'Insane.'

'Did you touch anything? Move anything?'

'Of course not. I was too shocked.'

Paul regarded his face. 'You don't seem that shocked. In fact, you seem awfully calm for someone who just found a dead body.'

Damon closed his eyes. 'Jesus, not *this* again. I did not kidnap Abe Abbott, kill him, then wrap him in silk, Detective Chief Inspector Truss.'

'Did I say you *did* do that?'

'Come on, you implied it.'

'We'll need to know your movements over the past few days. As much as you can remember.'

'Well, I can give you a list now,' Damon said. 'Monday, I found my brother's dead, stuffed body. Tuesday, I got arrested. Yesterday, I got punched. Today, I found another body.'

'This isn't a joke, Damon.'

'I didn't say it was.'

Paul stepped close to him, leaning down to whisper into his ear. 'I mean it. I'm going to keep an eye on you.'

Deano reappeared then, clearly noticing the tension between the two men. 'Sharon's waiting for you, Boss.'

'Great,' Paul said, still holding Damon's gaze. 'Mr Oberlin is going to provide us with a *detailed* list of his movements of the past few days. Can you make sure we get that?'

'Sure, Boss.'

Paul dragged his eyes away from Damon and jogged downstairs.

42

The rest of Friday, and the weekend that followed, cast an eerie stillness over the once tranquil village. The air was thick with a sense of disbelief and unease, as residents struggled to grapple with the reality that The Cobweb Killer was still out there. After all, Clive and Ricky were behind bars when Abe's body was placed on the stairwell. And Ricky simply wouldn't have done that to his son.

The atmosphere pressed down hard on Vanessa's shoulders as she stayed with Paul and Helen. There wasn't much she could do, other than checking in on Abe's beloved pets and making arrangements to have them taken to a local wildlife centre once she left. At least she felt like she was doing something for Abe, considering she couldn't help with the investigation. There wouldn't be any insect samples on Abe's body as the flies wouldn't have been able to get through the binding. She just knew she couldn't leave Greensands without knowing who was behind these murders. She found herself trapped in a numbing routine with Helen and the twins, the shock of the young teen's untimely demise weighing heavily on her mind.

It was a relief when Paul suggested she attend the expedited post-mortem with him on Monday. So when she should have been in New York, she found herself walking towards the changing rooms outside the post-mortem suite, the antiseptic scent filling her nostrils as she prepared herself for the sombre task ahead. She tried to force away the thoughts and fears pushing at the edge of her mind. Tried to push away the grief that threatened to overwhelm her, too. Sure, she hadn't known the kid for long, but it had been long enough to form a connection.

Just as she was about to head into the changing room, Paul walked over. 'Can I have a quick word?'

She nodded. 'What's up?'

'It's about your mum.'

Vanessa frowned. Well, *that* wasn't what she'd expected him to say.

'It's been too crazy to talk to you properly about it all,' Paul said, 'but during the interview with Clive, he revealed she was involved in illegal insect trading with him and Arthur.'

'What?'

'Apparently, she was present at meetings and helped get them clients in the art world.'

Vanessa went quiet, contemplating it. She used to think her mother was perfect, above reproach. But after she walked out on them, that had all changed. She had seemed like a completely different woman to Vanessa.

'I guess it doesn't surprise me,' she said.

'Were there hints of it then?'

'Not from what I recall. But the way she just walked out on us. It showed her true colours. Will there be repercussions for her, and Arthur?'

'Only if we can find evidence of their involvement. We're working with the National Wildlife Crime Unit to dig deeper into any illegal insect trading that's been going on in the village. They've already started seizing computers and looking at all the insect evidence we found. But Arthur has good solicitors. It will be a challenge.'

'Any findings so far?'

Paul shook his head. 'Not yet, I'm afraid. So far, the NWCU team haven't found any concrete links to any of the people named by Clive, apart from Benjamin. They've covered their tracks well.'

Vanessa peered towards the post-mortem suite room. 'Shall we get started?'

Paul nodded and ten minutes later, Vanessa was standing with Mio and the Home Office forensic pathologist, a robust, smiley woman in her fifties called Dr Hope Knowles. Paul watched from the viewing area, looking at Abe's body wordlessly. The teen lay like a macabre masterpiece of silk and flesh. His limbs, once animated with movement, were now ensnared in the silken webbing, frozen in a twisted ballet of final repose. The silk clung to his clothed form, highlighting the straight lines of his young body. It was awful to think only a few hours before Abe had been subjected to this, Vanessa had been with him.

'I thought this case couldn't get more surreal,' Hope said gravely, 'or more horrific.'

Vanessa nodded, unable to get many words out. Paul watched her, brow creased.

'So you think this is another form of mating ritual?' Mio asked.

'Yes,' Vanessa replied. 'Balloon flies present their mates with carcasses wrapped in silk as a gift.'

'What sort of silk do they usually use?' Mio asked. 'This stuff is pretty tough.'

'It's secreted from the fly's dermal glands, located in its forelegs,' Vanessa said. She smoothed her gloved finger over the tightly wound silk that was around Abe's neck. 'But I think this is spider silk. Maybe even the same as the silk used in the first three victims.'

'But there's loads of it,' Paul remarked through the open window between the two rooms. 'Not a few inches, like before. Wouldn't that take days to extract from a spider with that little spool? It must have taken *hours* to bind him, too . . . Unless it's from the batch Clive procured for Indra.'

Vanessa nodded.

'Poor thing,' Hope said. 'Let's get the silk off, shall we? I've already taken samples to be tested.'

With the utmost care and precision, Hope and Mio began the delicate process of removing the silk from Abe's body as Vanessa and Paul watched.

'May I?' Vanessa asked, gesturing to the silk they'd removed and placed in a large aluminium tray beside them. Hope nodded and Vanessa took a strand of the silk between her gloved fingertips, inspecting it beneath the light.

'What do you think?' Paul asked.

'It looks like silk from the golden silk orb-weaver.'

As more silk was removed, it left behind intricate patterns on Abe's pallid skin, a beautifully macabre sight. Eventually, his clothes came into view. Vanessa frowned. The green t-shirt he was wearing was way too small on him, exposing his thin torso. There was also something about the T-shirt and the large spider depicted on its front that felt familiar.

A cold shock of realisation ran through her. But she needed to be sure. So she tucked her gloved fingers beneath the T-shirt's collar and pulled the label out. There was a name on it, scrawled in her father's distinctive handwriting.

Vincent.

43

Paul watched from the viewing area as Vanessa leaned down, gulping in deep breaths.

'What's wrong?' he called out to her.

'The T-shirt Abe's wearing,' she managed in between breaths. 'It looks like the top Vincent was wearing when he disappeared.'

Mio frowned. 'Your brother?'

Vanessa nodded. 'Except . . . that's impossible. But Vincent's name is on the label!'

Paul took in a sharp breath. It *was* impossible. 'Mio, check the label.'

Mio carefully pulled away the back of the T-shirt, and nodded. 'It's there in black and white. *Vincent.*'

Paul's eyes travelled over the T-shirt. It was too small for Abe. And that spider motif on the front, it *was* the kind of thing Vanessa's brother used to wear. But how could it be?

'Can we get this T-shirt forensically checked?' he asked Mio. 'I want to know if there are any traces of DNA, fibres, or other potential evidence. Its age too, of course.'

'Yes, of course.'

Paul watched as Vanessa wrapped her arms around herself. 'It's unlikely it's connected to your brother. But we'll get it checked.'

Vanessa gave her old friend a look, her face pale. 'Paul, this is Vincent's T-shirt. I don't need to wait for DNA results to know that. Don't you think I'd recognise what he was wearing on the day he went missing? And even if it *wasn't* the actual T-shirt Vincent was wearing, which I know it is, it's too much of a coincidence. In fact,' she said, her stomach turning over as something occurred to her, 'it feels like a message to *me*. Like whoever's doing this is trying to say "Look, Vanessa. Look what you've been missing the past few days, you fool."'

Paul sighed. 'So what could we have been missing?'

'A connection to Vincent's *unsolved* case. What if whoever took Vincent away from us is behind all this horror?'

'But it's been over twenty years, Vanessa! Why do all this now?'

'Maybe whoever's responsible for Vincent's disappearance was in prison for something else all these years?'

'Oh come on. Your brother's name on one label leads you down this road?'

'On the label of a T-shirt worn by The Cobweb Killer's latest victim! Think about it, Paul – it's not too much of a stretch.'

Paul looked up at the ceiling, trying to wrap his head around this extra twist in this horrific tale: a twist he really didn't need.

'Can you get your hands on the old case files about Vincent?' Vanessa asked.

Paul hesitated.

'Come on, Paul,' Vanessa said. 'It wouldn't do any harm looking over them, see if we can find some kind of connection.'

'OK, fine,' Paul conceded.

For the next two hours, they all remained there, watching as each piece of silk was removed from Abe's body until that T-shirt could carefully be taken off and placed in an evidence bag for testing. They even stayed to watch Hope and Mio complete the post-mortem, determining the cause of death to be asphyxiation from the silk.

When it was over, Paul went back to his house with Vanessa. Until he could figure out what this T-shirt was all about, he didn't want her to be alone. If this sick fuck was trying to send a message to his friend, he didn't want her out of his or Helen's sight. When he was sure Vanessa was OK, he went back to the police station and into the incident room.

'So it seems the perpetrator is still out there, stalking Greensands' villagers,' Paul said as the room quietened down.

'Could be three of them doing it,' Selma suggested. 'Clive Craviso, Ricky Abbott and whoever killed Abe Abbott?'

'Maybe,' Paul said. 'In fact, I've already had it confirmed the blood we found on the rug in Clive's garage is Harvey Wheatley's.'

'That was quick bloodwork,' OS said.

'Well, yeah,' Paul said with a sigh, 'a potential serial killer on the loose kinda puts a rocket up people's arses. Anyway, that's why we still have Ricky and Clive in custody.' Paul flinched slightly as he recalled Ricky's feral scream when he broke the horrific news about his son. 'But it's a stretch to think Ricky Abbott would kill his son, I have to admit.' He sighed. 'Right, let's focus on figuring out Abe's final moments. His neighbour said he saw Abe leave the house on Thursday evening at about nine, not long after Vanessa Marwood saw him. The neighbour doesn't recall seeing Abe return. Where did he go? Who saw him? Get to work,' he said, clapping his hands. As the officers all got back to their work, Paul approached OS.

'I need your help with something,' he asked him in a low voice.

'Sure thing, Boss.'

'I need you to read over some old case notes with me.'

OS looked intrigued. 'What case notes?'

'A misper case from a few years back. Vincent Marwood.'

'Marwood?' OS said. 'Like Vanessa Marwood?'

Paul nodded. 'Her twelve-year-old brother went missing twenty-five years ago, from the grasslands behind the butterfly farm. And Abe Abbott was wearing a T-shirt Vanessa says looks like the very T-shirt her brother was wearing when he went missing. Plus Vincent's name was written on the label.'

'Shit.'

'Yep.'

'So what are we thinking? Whoever's responsible for this kid's disappearance is carrying all these murders out now?'

'I don't know. What I *do* know is it doesn't feel right to me. I'll email the case notes to you now.'

OS nodded and went to walk to his desk, but Paul stopped him.

'Keep this on the downlow,' Paul said. 'I don't want to make a big deal of it at the moment.'

'Will do.'

Paul walked into his office and closed the door behind him, sinking down into his seat as he spread the files out before him. They all had the same name signing it off: Detective Inspector Reg Truss, Paul's stepdad. He'd been a good man. The kind of man Paul's biological father hadn't been capable of being, wrapping Paul, his younger brothers and Paul's mum up in his powerful arms. Sadly, his mum and stepdad divorced a few years back. Paul still saw him every now and again, but the bond seemed to have broken. He sighed and looked at the first sheet, a transcript of the chat his stepdad had had with Vanessa's dad at 7.03 p.m., three hours after Vincent had disappeared.

The transcript ran over the events leading up to that moment. Before then, Vanessa's father had searched the grasslands for Vincent, a few of the other butterfly farm workers joining him. Paul remembered seeing the search take place from his bedroom window, Vincent's name being called out, over and over in the streets outside. When there was still no sign of Vincent, Tony had driven around the village with Vanessa, scouring the pathways and fields. More people joined the search until that phone call to the police, leading to the chat Paul's stepfather had with Vanessa's father. Really, there was nothing new in the transcript, or the other files, either.

He flicked through the rest of the pages then paused, recognising one name at the top of one of the sheets: *Derek Founder.*

Derek was Helen's dad.

His eyes moved across the lines, a knot tightening in his stomach. Seemed he was a suspect, after being accused the year before of being overly friendly with a young boy living next door. The words on the page revealed a tense exchange as Paul's stepdad alluded to various allegations made against Helen's father in the past. Incidents involving young boys, whispers of unsettling behaviour.

Did Helen know about this? If so, why the hell hadn't she told Paul?

In fact, now Paul thought about it, Derek's death from a heart attack wouldn't have been long after Vincent went missing. Paul remembered Helen telling him he'd died on the worst possible day: her fifteenth birthday.

He got his phone out to text Helen, then paused.

She was so sensitive about her dad. He needed to talk to her face to face about it.

He grabbed his bag and walked out of his small office.

'Just popping out for half an hour,' he said to the officers still working.

'You found something?' OS asked.

'No, just need to pop home quickly. I'll be back though.' He turned to the rest of the room. 'Anyone who was supposed to be back home hours ago though, go and get some shut-eye.'

Nobody budged. Paul could see the exhaustion and frustration etched on their faces. They'd been working all afternoon and into the evening. And yet still they wanted to remain. It made him feel a sense of pride, this collective determination to find the fucker who was stalking his village.

Paul walked down the corridor and descended the stairs before stepping out into the darkness a few minutes later, surprised to see it had been raining. The atmosphere felt cleansed and charged, as if nature itself had taken a deep breath and exhaled. He wished he felt the same. It took him a few minutes to walk to his car as the main car park had been full. As he opened his car door, a cool breeze sent shivers down his spine.

'Paul?' a voice said from behind him. He turned to see a dark figure watching him, holding a box. Suddenly, an explosion of wings swarmed out at Paul.

They were butterflies, their flimsy forms filling the surrounding air, their wings flapping against his face and body. Where the hell had they come from?

Paul flapped his arms about in response, panic overwhelming him as he tried to swat them away. But they seemed to stick to him, clinging to his clothes and hair. He stumbled backward, landing on his butt on the ground, his heart beating erratically in his chest.

As he tried to get back to his feet, a hand clamped over his face from behind, an acidic smell filling his nostrils. He tried to break free, but whoever was holding him was too strong. The world spun around him, and he felt himself losing consciousness.

Then everything went black.

44

Vanessa sat in Paul and Helen's spare room with her laptop on her knees, reading the files from Vincent's case that OS had emailed over. The clock displayed a time that wasn't conducive to reading. But how could she sleep? It was impossible. *This* was possible though, scouring over the notes about her brother's disappearance and trying to find a clue that would lead her to whoever was playing these spider-and-fly games with her.

It was difficult reading about that awful time again. It brought back the scent of her father's nervous sweat and the sound of Vincent's name being called out by their fellow villagers. But there was nothing she didn't already know in there. She got to the last page and frowned. It was a transcript of an interview between Paul's stepfather and a man called Derek Founder, alluding to previous accusations and disturbing whispers linked to Derek's conduct in relation to young boys.

Derek was Helen's dad.

Vanessa sat up, heart pumping. Did Helen know about her father's dark history? She always talked about him with such reverence. So maybe she didn't.

Or maybe she did . . . but didn't believe the accusations?

Something hovered at the edge of her periphery as Helen's name ran through her mind.

She clicked into her email, finding the initial toxicology results from the first three victims that Heena had sent to her. As she scanned through the reports once more, her eyes settled upon a minor detail: a tiny trace of *resin* had been detected in the lethal mixture that had claimed the lives of the three men. Helen used resin to make her jewellery.

A shiver coursed through Vanessa's spine. Could it be mere coincidence, or was there something more sinister at play? Maybe the heart attack that had claimed Derek Founder's life was triggered by the intense scrutiny surrounding Vincent's disappearance? A small voice whispered: could it be that Helen, consumed by grief and fuelled by an insidious resentment, held the village responsible for her father's death?

Vanessa's heart sank. No, not Helen. It just wasn't possible.

She pushed the tendrils of doubt aside, but they kept coming back, again and again. So she jumped up and opened the bedroom door . . . to find Helen on the other side, a frantic look on her face.

'I'm worried about Paul,' she said.

Vanessa's stomach dropped. 'Why? What's happened?'

'He texted me forty minutes ago to say he was on his way back. He should have been here by now. The journey from the police station only takes twenty minutes.'

'Maybe he stopped to grab some food to bring back?'

Helen shook her head. 'No, he would have told me. He knows I get worried about him driving since the diagnosis. I-I worry he'll have an incident, end up in a ditch somewhere.'

End up in a ditch somewhere.

'I'll go and look,' Vanessa said. 'You stay with the kids. But first, quickly: did you know your dad was questioned in connection with my brother going missing?'

Helen's eyes widened. She looked genuinely shocked. 'My father was questioned?'

'Yes, I read the transcript of the interview just now.' Vanessa hesitated, carefully choosing her words. 'And resin was found in some of the toxicology reports from the first three bodies?'

'Jesus, Vanessa, what are you trying to say? That *I'm* The Cobweb Killer? I didn't even know about my dad being questioned, and I haven't bloody worked with resin in months. I donated *all* the remaining items to the school.'

Their conversation was interrupted by the piercing ring of Helen's phone. She looked down at it, frowning. 'It's OS.' She quickly put the phone to her ear and Vanessa watched in concern as Helen's face clouded over.

'Shit,' she heard Helen say.

'What's happened?'

'Paul's car was discovered just now with the door open. And-and the CCTV footage showed him collapsing and—' Helen took in a sharp breath. 'And someone dragging him away.'

'Fuck. Can I talk to OS?'

Helen nodded, giving the phone to Vanessa.

'OS, it's Doctor Marwood. When did you last see Paul?'

'About half an hour ago. He said he needed to look into something.'

'Can you send me the CCTV footage?'

'Yes,' OS said. 'What's your email addy?'

She reeled it off to him.

'I better go,' OS said. 'It's all hands on deck. Look after Helen, yeah? That's what he'd want.'

What he'd want. It was something people said about dead people.

'I will.' Vanessa gave Helen's phone back to her.

'Should we go to the station?' Helen asked, biting at her lip.

'No. Stay by the phone.'

As she said that, her phone buzzed. The video from OS. Vanessa clicked on it and it started rolling. Her heart sank as she watched her friend walk to his car, shoulders sunk with exhaustion.

When he opened his car door, he paused, looking at something that was off camera. Then he put his hand up to his face, as though shocked, and stumbled away.

Vanessa paused the video, zooming in.

Butterflies. Scores of butterflies were flying towards Paul. He *hated* them.

She watched as he fell to the ground, frantically batting his arms about. Tears flooded Vanessa's eyes. 'Oh God, Paul.'

Then she noticed a figure walk over to Paul. Dark. Barely distinguishable. Whoever it was clamped their gloved hand over Paul's nose. Paul swayed before slumping over. Then the figure grabbed Paul's prone body under his armpits and dragged him out of shot. Vanessa frowned, rewinding the footage to when the person walked over to Paul. As she played the footage again, a chilling realisation washed over her. The figure had an unusual gait. Or, as some might say, a *waddle.*

It was the teacher, Andrew.

She looked out of the hallway window towards the school. Helen said she'd donated her resin to the school. Then her eye caught something in the distance, coming from the butterfly farm.

Something on fire.

Vanessa put her phone to her ear and started running down the stairs.

45

Paul's eyelids fluttered open, a heavy weight pressing down on his limbs. He tried to move, but his body refused to respond. As his vision cleared, he looked around him in the semi-darkness. At first, he couldn't get a sense of where he was. But then the outlines of signposts and trees came into a view, the moon filtering in through cracked glass above him.

He was in the butterfly atrium.

Why was he here? Questions filled his mind, but before he could voice them, he realised something was terribly wrong. He couldn't open his mouth to talk.

He was paralysed.

A figure emerged from the moonlit shadows, and relief washed over him as he recognised Andrew Kirk, the twins' teacher. Paul tried to communicate, ask for help, but his words were trapped in his throat. Andrew walked over with some kind of container in his hand. As he drew closer, Paul realised with horror that there was a dark brown spider inside it, its hairy legs spanning over six inches.

'Beautiful, isn't it?' Andrew said.

Oh no. Not him. Not the girls' teacher.

Paul strained against his paralysis, his heart pounding with a mixture of fear and desperation.

You fucking fuck, he wanted to shout out.

'It's a Brazilian wandering spider,' Andrew continued, crouching down next to Paul as he cradled the container. 'It used to be Abe Abbott's. I've been saving it for a special occasion.'

Paul saw Abe's lifeless eyes then. He saw how devastated Vanessa had looked. He imagined that same look on her face when she learned he was dead. On Helen's face . . . on the twins' faces.

Fuck. Fuck. Fuck.

'In fact, I've brought quite a few creatures along, just for you,' Andrew said, gesturing to a large plastic container behind him, shadows leaping and crawling inside. 'I liked the idea of them burning with you. The cruelty of it.'

Burning?

Andrew looked over his shoulder towards a flicker of orange in the distance. Something was on fire in the fields. Then he turned back, looking down at the enclosed spider. 'This spider's venom is a powerful neurotoxin,' he said. 'Do you know what a neurotoxin is?' He drew the letters out as though talking to one of his pupils. 'Of course, you can't talk because of the atracurium pumping through your veins. Let me explain: a neurotoxin is a substance that can make the nerves in one's body go to sleep and stop working, just like when we take a long nap and can't move our arms or legs. I thought about extracting the venom to use on you, Paul. But after how long it took to extract the silk from Abe Abbott's golden silk orb-weaving spider, I realised I wouldn't have the time.'

There, he was confessing it all.

Paul supposed, in that moment, that if he did indeed die tonight, at least he would die knowing who The Cobweb Killer was. The frustration at not being able to pummel his smug face in was unbearable though.

But what possible motive could this *teacher* have?

With a strange smile, Andrew carefully opened the container. Paul felt all his instincts to move away burn through him. But it was like he was a bodiless head. Now he knew how the other victims felt.

Michael.

Simon.

Tim.

Benjamin.

Harvey.

Natalie.

Abe.

Soon, him.

The spider extended its long, hairy front legs out of the top of the container. Then it raised its body, balancing on its hind legs, displaying a menacing stance and fangs that looked too big for a spider to possess.

Paul wanted to scream but nothing would come out.

'When it bites,' Andrew said, 'its neurotoxins target the nervous system, causing a cascade of effects. First, there's intense pain, a searing sensation that spreads through the body. It paralyses the muscles, leaving its victims immobile, unable to move or speak. But you won't notice all this as that's already happened, thanks to the atracurium,' he added with a wry smile. 'When it travels to the heart, it can make it go haywire, like a wild dance we can't control, leaving the victim in an abyss of suffering.' Andrew smiled. 'That won't be enough for me though. I want to see your face when all the other spiders join him. I know how much these creepy-crawlies terrify you, Paul. Imagine it, those last seconds of life, watching as they make a *playground* of your body.'

Paul's mind raced, his heart pounding in his chest. He wanted to scream, to fight back, but his body remained paralysed, a captive to the twisted game unfolding before him.

'Oh but that's not where my final masterpiece finishes,' Andrew continued. 'What I particularly like about this beautiful creature is the defensive stance it's adopting now. You know it's a mating stance too? Strange how it uses the same stances, but then there *is* a fine line between love and hate, as they say. Watch it closely.' He moved the container even closer to Paul, the lid still open. Terror and revulsion ripped through Paul. 'This will be how your body will be displayed, legs elevated, arms extended forward like a spider's defensive stance. Grotesque, surreal.' He paused, face darkening. 'People won't understand at first. But Doctor Marwood will know straight away. She'll see the art in it.'

Vanessa? Why was he talking about Vanessa?

As he said that, there was movement behind Andrew. Somebody had stepped into the atrium.

Vanessa.

Paul's eyes locked with hers, a silent terror passing between them.

46

Vanessa stood in the butterfly atrium, just as she had over a week ago. Moonlight streamed in through the shattered glass above, lighting up the cobwebs that clung to the wall beside her. It also lit up two figures in the darkness. Paul, slumped and motionless against the palm tree near where the first three men had died. And Andrew, crouched down beside him, holding something. Behind them both, through the open door at the back, something was on fire in the grasslands, the stench of acrid smoke drifting in towards her.

Paul's gaze fixed on Vanessa. She could see it in his eyes: as she too had suspected, Andrew Kirk was The Cobweb Killer.

She walked towards them – towards the very place where she'd seen those first three victims. The sound of her soles crunching over leaves caused Andrew to look over his shoulder at her. He seemed confused at first. Disappointed next. But then a quiet resolution appeared to settle over him. He placed whatever it was he was holding on the floor, between Paul's splayed legs, then stood up.

'Well, this has complicated things,' Andrew said.

Paul's terrified gaze caught on the object, and Vanessa realised why he looked so scared: a Brazilian wandering spider was in the open container between his thighs, testing the side of the container with the ends of its furry legs. It was Abe's stolen spider.

There was another container on the floor behind Andrew too. A large plastic box.

'Ah, yes,' Andrew said, following her gaze. 'I brought along more guests, even my class's beloved tarantula, Moana.'

Vanessa's eyes flitted to the spider between Paul's legs again. It was probably sensing the air above, and a chance for freedom. A chance too, maybe, to bite whatever got in its way when it tried to make that bid for freedom.

Vanessa's logical brain kicked in. Humans could survive a bite if they got help soon enough.

Not humans with a heart condition, though.

'Andrew,' she said carefully. 'Let me sit with Paul.'

'I'm afraid I can't allow that. Can't risk you getting bitten too.'

Sirens whined in the distance. 'The police are on their way,' Vanessa said. 'It's over. You won't have time to do anything with Paul.' She looked over at her helpless friend. 'No posing, no manoeuvring of limbs. Your last victim will be . . . pointless.'

'But it's Detective Chief Inspector Paul Truss.'

As Andrew said that, the spider suddenly crawled up the glass container, its eight legs carrying it over the rim and towards Paul's prone body. Paul's eyes betrayed his horror as the spider jumped onto his leg and traversed up it. Paul's hand, which lay pale against his thigh, twitched.

Shit.

The spider stopped in response, turning towards the movement and adopting its defensive stance.

It was about to attack.

Vanessa knew she had to act fast. She thought about simply picking the spider up. But that could be fatal to her. What use would she be to Paul if she was paralysed too?

She looked around the room, eyes landing on the large container where Andrew had gathered all the classroom pets. How cruel to shove them all in together. The tarantula had probably already killed a few of the school children's beloved beasts by now.

Killed.

The class tarantula, Moana. A formidable foe for a Brazilian wandering spider.

Without hesitation, Vanessa ran over to the container and yanked the lid off. Butterflies and moths flew out at her, but she didn't flinch. Instead, she carefully reached in for the large tarantula, which sat among other insects too, like ants and millipedes . . . and a golden orb-weaver.

'What *are* you doing?' Andrew asked, looking almost bemused.

She ignored him as she picked the tarantula up, jogging over to Paul and dropping it onto his leg as Paul looked at her in abject horror. Moana reacted immediately, sensing the other venomous spider's presence. The tarantula lifted its legs, revealing its massive body, and slowly moved towards the Brazilian wandering spider.

The two creatures faced off, each ready to attack. The Brazilian wandering spider lunged forward with its deadly fangs, but the tarantula quickly dodged out of the way, moving with lightning-fast reflexes across to Paul's stomach as Paul watched in horror. Andrew, however, observed the display with a small smile on his face.

'Nature's predators engaged in a dance of life and death, just like us,' Andrew said as he watched them. The tarantula made its move, lunging towards its enemy. 'It's a beautiful and brutal world, isn't it? Look how the tarantula, with its raw power and cunning, overpowers its venomous adversary.'

Vanessa's gaze flickered between the harrowing spectacle before her and Andrew's sinister presence.

'The struggle for dominance, the fight for survival,' Andrew continued. 'It's all part of the intricate web of existence.' Andrew's dark amusement grew as the Brazilian wandering spider convulsed under the lethal grip of the tarantula's venom. 'Ah, the irony. The hunter becomes the hunted.'

As the life force drained from the defeated spider, Andrew's eyes narrowed, revelling in the demise of the poor creature. 'A fitting end for a spider that wreaks havoc with its venomous bite, isn't it, Nessy?'

'Nessy?' Vanessa repeated. 'My brother used to call me Nessy.'

Andrew's eyes caught on hers. 'I did, didn't I. Still do, it seems.'

For a fleeting moment, his eyes softened, and the corners of his mouth curled in a gentle, sad smile – the very smile that their mother used to wear. It was a snapshot of a face from a past life, and it drove a splinter into her heart. A splinter that made Vanessa's entire being collapse.

Andrew Kirk was Vincent . . . her brother.

And her brother was The Cobweb Killer.

47

He looked different. Red hair instead of black. Blue eyes instead of brown. Nose not as straight. But that was all thanks to hair dye, contact lenses, a broken nose. He was so tall now, and broad-shouldered too, compared to the skinny boy she once knew. Clearly strong enough to carry his victims. Despite his size, now that she looked at him, *really* looked at him, she knew Andrew was Vincent, her missing brother.

A memory came to her then of the morning he disappeared. They'd been waiting in the grasslands for Damon. Vincent had the butterfly set their mother had sent him for his twelfth birthday and he'd just caught a beautiful peacock butterfly, its vibrant wings adorned with intricate patterns of rich reddish-brown, black, blue and yellow. As Damon approached, Vanessa had got up, shielding her eyes from the burning sun.

'Nessy, look,' Vincent had said. She didn't turn, too fixated on Damon. 'Nessy, look!'

She'd turned back to her brother just in time to see him carefully pulling the butterfly's wings off.

It wasn't the first time. She'd caught him doing things like that before, always completely absorbed in his task, his face a mask of concentration as he pulled insects apart to understand how they worked inside. Their father had often witnessed it too, much to his distress, repairing the wings of the insects his son sought to destroy.

Vincent had always been different, even before their mother left. But after she was gone, he became even more withdrawn and prone to odd, sometimes violent behaviour. Vanessa hadn't understood it at the time, but now she saw with an awful clarity that her brother had struggled even then with dark demons, those insects just the first of his casualties.

'Why?' she asked him.

'For you,' he answered.

'Me?'

'Yes. I just wanted you to notice me, Nessy.'

As he said that, the sirens sounded out from right outside the farm.

'They're here,' she said. 'It's over, Vincent.'

Vincent's eyes widened, then he suddenly darted out of the door at the back. Vanessa went to run out after him, but then she heard a small moan escaping Paul's mouth. She looked over to see the tarantula crawling on her friend's cheek so ran to him instead.

'Vincent's back,' she whispered, tears falling down her cheeks. 'He's back, Paul, and he's The Cobweb Killer.'

Paul couldn't answer her. But she could read the horror in his eyes.

She gently picked the spider up and placed it back in the container.

'They're all here now,' she said. 'I have to go after him. But you're safe.'

Then she ran outside after Vincent.

After *her brother*.

48

Vanessa's heart pounded in her chest as she followed her brother's fleeing form towards the grasslands and whatever it was that was burning out there. Of course, it would have to end where it all began.

She stepped out. The stench of smoke was stronger here. She felt grass brush against her fingers, just as it had all those years ago, when Vincent went missing.

'Vincent!' she called out.

There was no response. Vanessa took a deep breath and continued walking, using the light from her phone to cast an unsteady beam over the area. Suddenly, something rustled against her cheek. Vanessa jumped, heart racing. But it was only a moth, drawn to the light. Vanessa let out a shaky breath.

'Vincent, please,' she shouted. 'I want to see you.'

'Nessy.' It was a whisper. So close.

She spun around to see Vincent standing behind her. The darkness hung heavy around him, but she knew it was her brother. She saw it in the flat of his cheekbones and the way his fingers delicately fluttered up to his neck to scratch at his skin. His hair looked dark again too in the night gloom, just as it had once been.

It really was Vincent. Her Vincent.

'All these years. Where have you been?' Vanessa asked.

'I went to Brighton to look for Mum.'

'Did you find her?'

He shook his head. 'Brighton's huge, Vanessa. I was a kid. No smartphones then either to do internet searches. I went into arty-looking shops, asked around, got nowhere. Thought about coming back but I had no money.'

'You could have just called me. I would've found a way to come to you.'

He shook his head. 'You wouldn't have left Damon.'

'Of course I would have!'

'Don't lie. He changed everything.'

'Vincent, don't—'

'Just let me talk!' Vincent snapped. 'Don't you get it? I honestly thought you were the only one who cared for me. Mum left. Dad was always so busy. But you, you were always there. But then, that summer.' He sighed. 'It felt like you left too. I saw you spending more time with Damon, and it was like I was four again, watching Mum leave.'

'I never left you. *You're* the one who left me.'

The guilt almost brought her to her knees. She held her hand out to him then dropped it as she remembered what he'd done, all the dead bodies she'd seen over the past few days spinning silently through her mind. She glanced at the fire in the distance. 'What is that, Vincent?'

She went to walk past him but he grabbed her arm. 'Wait,' he said. 'Let's talk. I want you to know it worked out OK in the end.' She tried to push away from him to get to the fire. She needed to make sure no one else was in danger. But his grip tightened. 'I found a new family on the streets of Brighton,' he continued, lost in his memories. 'Other kids who'd been abandoned, let down. I learned some skills back then too,' he added with a small smile. 'Burglary, deception, the benefits of alcohol!' he added. His face grew sombre. 'Then drugs. That's where I got my hip injury, in a drug-addled fight when I was fourteen. And this too,' he added, gesturing to his wonky nose.

Fighting. Drinking. Taking drugs . . . at fourteen?

The guilt was back again, swirling inside her. Could she have stopped all this, paid more attention to him? And in the process, saved the people he'd killed? No, that was Vincent's fault. Plenty of kids had to endure their parents leaving them at a young age. They didn't do what Vincent did. Still, he was her brother. Her broken monster of a brother. But she still loved him. She always would.

'How long were you on the streets?' she asked.

'Years,' Vincent said. 'Years and years. Then ten years ago, I saw an article about you. I still remember the headline: "Forensics bug expert solves stranger rapes". My big sister, a big shot. And specialising in insects, too.' He sighed. 'It was bittersweet though. In the article, you mentioned Dad had died. I very nearly tracked you down.'

'Why *didn't* you?'

'A homeless druggie and burglar? No.' He looked up at the moon. 'After I saw that article about you, I got into a fight with another homeless man. Wasn't unusual, it happened a lot. But this time, the darkness took over. I killed him. That was my first.'

Vanessa wrapped her arms around herself. *My first.*

'I didn't mean to at the start. Hands just sort of automatically went round his neck.' He raised his hands even higher, mimicking a strangling motion, the look in his eyes as disturbing as the action. 'I found it fascinating. Remember how I used to watch bugs die? I could sit there and watch them all day. This was the same. His name was Andrew Kirk. He used to be a teacher but had fallen on hard times after a divorce.'

'You took his identity . . . his qualification as a teacher . . .'

Vincent nodded. 'I saw an opportunity to become someone worthy of your love and attention again. Two years later, I got a job working as a teacher in a primary school in Brighton. It wasn't easy, but people are forgiving when you tell them you've had a tough past. I kept telling myself, one more year and I'll reach out to Nessy. But as each year went by, I told myself I just needed another year to make myself even more worthy of you. Then last year, I saw a teaching job at Greensands Primary pop up. It was a sign. Before I knew it, I'd been offered the job.'

'Jesus,' Vanessa whispered.

He shot Vanessa a confused look. 'I hoped you'd come back for visits, but not once did I see you. So I made plans to *force* you to visit. Those plans were accelerated when I read about your new job in New York. I found that very interesting, by the way,' he added, 'seeing as our mother went to art school in New York. Was that why you chose the city as your new home, to be close to her somehow?'

Yes, the same thought *had* occurred to Vanessa. Maybe she had subconsciously decided to go to New York because of her mother's connection to the city. She didn't want to tell Vincent that though.

'Why were your plans accelerated?' she asked instead.

'I *had* to stop you from leaving.'

'You *killed* to bring me here . . . and to stop me from going to New York?'

Vincent shrugged. 'Partly. I knew you'd come running to help. I was right, of course. I also got to destroy my former tormentors in the process.'

'Tormentors?'

He nodded. 'It was just meant to be Benjamin at first. An Oberlin brother to really grab your attention. The worst of the tormentors, too. You know Benjamin even pretended to lace my drink with deadly nightshade on my twelfth birthday? Remember when I was acting all weird? I was still shaken up from it.'

She thought of the way the plant had been shoved down Benjamin's throat. A tool of revenge for Vincent.

'So that was my focus. Benjamin,' Vincent said. 'I had it all planned. I'd heard rumours of Molly Barnes' empty garage from the kids talking at school, so I broke in one night to take a look. When I saw roadworks were taking place, I even managed to knock a door through without being heard. A neat way to frame Clive. The original idea was to suggest the two men were having a gay affair . . . What better way than to show a link from Clive's garage to the site of Benjamin's murder?'

'How did you get Benjamin in there?'

'Oh, it was so easy to lure the drunk fool with promises I'd found something in Clive's garage that he simply needed to see. I mean, it wasn't a lie – I *did* discover Clive was involved in the village's little illegal insect enterprise after I broke into his garage one day. Difficult to break the burglary habit, you see. On the way to the garage, we then bumped into Michael, Simon and Tim so I thought, what the hell, they could join Benjamin for the ride.'

Vanessa shook her head. He was being so flippant about it.

'And they really did get a ride later,' Vincent continued. 'Honestly, the difference a good-quality wheelbarrow can make, though I nearly lost Benjamin going over the ridge that night when I wheeled him to his resting place. He half fell out of the wheelbarrow, truly pissing off some of those miner bees.'

That would have been when Benjamin's foot was stung.

'That was one trip. Then I had to do two for Michael, Simon and Tim. Michael was not the *smallest* of men.'

Vanessa's stomach churned.

'Don't look so sad,' Vincent snapped. 'He played his part in bullying me too, back in the day. Simon and Tim, too. Even more of a sign this was meant to be when I saw them walking home from the pub.'

Vanessa shook her head in disbelief. 'I don't understand. They all *bullied* you?'

'Yes, during the summer holidays while Dad worked,' Vincent replied, his face twisted. 'Even Emi, the old crow.'

'That was why you targeted her?'

Vincent nodded. 'I followed her home from one of her moon-worshipping sessions. Silly woman doing lives from her TikTok. Didn't realise you'd be walking past with Paul, did I? Nearly got caught. Of course, it *should* have made me stop my little crusade. But then the Wheatleys fell into my lap.'

'But why target the Wheatleys?' Vanessa whispered. 'They've always been so nice.'

He shook his head. 'No, they really weren't back then. And it was like fate when I saw them walking their dog in the forest just after I walked back from the incident with Emi. So easy to lure them over with a cry for help. So simple to make Harvey do what I wanted and follow me into the garage, where I grabbed his wife and held a knife to her throat.' A look of rage crossed his face. 'They didn't even remember bullying me! Maybe they were still reeling from the shock when I told them who I really was. But still, not a flicker of recollection. It *enraged* me. I can barely remember what happened when I got them both into the garage. I can barely remember mutilating Harvey after, too, I was so angry.'

Vanessa pursed her lips, turning away. How terrified they must have been. 'And then you planted the result of that mutilation in Ricky's bedroom? Why?'

He shrugged. 'Another person to frame, just in case.' He swallowed. 'I never wanted it to be like this,' he said, gesturing between them. 'I never wanted you to know what I did.'

'Abe Abbott wasn't a bully,' Vanessa said.

'I'll be honest,' Vincent mused, 'I didn't enjoy killing Abe. But I had no choice. He'd figured it all out.'

'How?'

'He was out walking on Thursday night, probably looking for his precious poisonous spider. When he went past the school he must have noticed a light on and come in to look for me. I'm often there late. He probably thought I'd understand because of Moana, that we had a *connection*.' Vincent laughed. 'Anyway, that's how he found me with his golden silk orb-weaver, the one I stole to extract the silk. I'd brought it in to show the kids. Stupid move getting his little pet out . . . But I just wanted to *look* at it, Nessy. You know how much I love observing these fascinating creatures, just like you do. It's in our *blood*.'

Vanessa swallowed down bile. She wanted to say they weren't alike. But she also needed to know what happened to Abe. So she said nothing.

'Well, of course he got very angry,' Vincent said. 'Stupid me left the side entrance open so he stormed in and started ranting and raving. He guessed I'd planted Harvey Wheatley's cock in his father's bedroom, too, to help frame his father. I had no choice but to kill him. It saddened me,' he continued, brow furrowing, 'though I suppose wrapping him up in the silk had a soothing effect. It would have been better if it was silk from his own spider, but that would have been too much of a ball-ache.' He shook his head. 'Honestly, Vanessa, have you ever extracted spider silk from an actual spider? It takes *ages*. I knew if I wanted to give you something made from spider silk one day, extracting it like I did for the first three men would take me days. I was actually pondering the very problem as I had a fry-up in the pub on Sunday morning to perk myself up after being awake all night.'

Awake all night murdering men, Vanessa thought.

'Indra was at the pub too,' he continued, 'and I heard her crowing about buying spider silk for a dress she was having made, and how strong it was. I had a look in her office that night, it wasn't hard to find. It was clearly ordered from some nefarious dark web company, there was no way she would ever report it missing. I wasn't even planning on using it, but it certainly came in handy in the end, for dear Abe.'

'Abe reminded me of you,' Vanessa said. 'Not now though. Not the Vincent I see before me.'

Vincent's face hardened. 'That Vincent died long ago, on the streets of Brighton. The ridiculous thing is, it was only supposed to be a few days. I was going to come back once I found Mum. Damon had given me enough money to—'

Vanessa looked at him in shock. 'Damon?'

Vincent nodded. 'Yes. He gave me money for the train fare and a hotel, too.'

'I-I don't understand. *Damon* gave you money to go to Brighton?' Vincent nodded as Vanessa's mind spun with disbelief. 'No.' She shook her head, desperate to dispel the tendrils of doubt creeping in. 'You were just a *kid*. He wouldn't have put you at risk like that.'

Vincent sighed. 'You're so clever, Nessy, and yet still so *stupid* when it comes to Damon. I bet you haven't even figured out the worst of it yet. You think what's happened the past few days is a one-person job?'

Vanessa went very still. 'You're telling me Damon has been helping you?'

He laughed. 'You think I could have done all this alone?'

Vanessa felt like she was drowning, the water closing over her head as she struggled to make sense of Vincent's words. Oh God. Only the night before, she'd been entangled in Damon's arms.

Paul had always suspected him. Parts of the village, too. Why had she closed her mind to the possibility?

A scream rang out in the distance.

Vincent smiled. 'That'll be him now, with his latest.'

Vanessa followed his gaze to whatever was on fire in the distance.

'Oh God, who does he have out there?' Vanessa asked, already running towards it.

'I don't know,' Vincent shouted out as he ran after her. 'He mentioned something about Sharon Regan hating him?'

'No. Not Sharon.'

She quickened her strides, the blades of the long grass brushing against her skin just as they had all those years ago when she'd desperately searched for her missing brother. As she drew closer to the fire, she was shocked to see it was her mum's abandoned art installation that was burning. It had always been imposing, but now it was a monster ablaze, hungry flames licking up the twisted iron and wood towards Sharon, who was somehow tied to the top, the flames snapping at her feet as her screams were muffled by the roar of the fire. She noticed Vanessa, and quickly shook her head, eyes desperate. Vanessa darted forward, despite the horrible heat. She had to save her friend.

But then arms were wrapping around her. 'Can't have you dying,' Vincent whispered in her ear.

Vanessa tried to struggle against her brother but it was no use; he was too strong. She let out a sob.

'Do you remember when Dad told us about fire chaser beetles and how they're attracted to the still-smouldering wood after a fire?' he whispered, looking up at the fire in amazement. 'That wood makes a perfect breeding ground, safe from predators who have fled the fire. They even have special sensors to help them locate fires from a distance. Damon *loved* that concept, didn't you, Damon?'

Vanessa followed his gaze towards someone who was sitting on one of the abandoned chairs in the field, watching the flames dance higher.

Damon.

So he really was Vincent's accomplice. She shuddered in horror.

'Damon!' she yelled, her voice drowned by the roar of the fire. 'Damon, what the hell have you done?!' But he didn't turn, just continued watching his masterpiece.

'Once again,' Vincent said, 'the three of us reunite here in the grasslands.'

Terror and disbelief churned within Vanessa. Her brother, Vincent, and Damon. How could she reconcile the boys she once knew with the gruesome acts they'd committed? The horror of it all roared through her like the flames before her, threatening to topple the fragile walls she'd built around her heart. She looked up at Sharon again, feeling hopeless.

'Turn away, Nessy,' Vincent hissed into her ear. 'We don't want that brilliant mind of yours tarnished by the sight of your friend burning to death.'

There was a sickening fondness in his voice that made her skin crawl. But she couldn't keep her eyes from her friend, *wouldn't*. So she kept looking ahead, watching as Sharon sobbed and tried to twist and turn to get out of whatever had her held tight to the sculpture. Vincent grabbed her chin with his fingers though, forcing her to turn away. She glared at him, his features lit by the fire's dance and painted by the ghostly glow of the moonlight, as familiar as they were alien. Then her gaze fell on his hand. In the lurid light, she noticed a fresh burn. Had *he* ignited the flame? But he said Damon had.

Unless . . . Damon hadn't.

Her eyes flickered towards Damon. He was still unmoving in that chair, and as she stared she saw his body was unnaturally rigid, a stillness that was uncharacteristic of the expressive, lively man she knew.

A puzzle piece fell into place in Vanessa's mind. Maybe Vincent was the sole puppeteer in this macabre play, after all? Her heart hammered in her chest as a potential plan took shape. She had to cause a diversion.

'Mum,' Vanessa breathed out, her gaze locking onto an imagined figure in the distance.

At her word, Vincent's grip loosened slightly as he turned to look. Seizing the moment, Vanessa aimed the solid sole of her DMs at his crotch. He grunted, doubling over in pain. Vanessa took the chance to sprint towards Sharon, the ground beneath her feet feeling uneven, unstable, her heart pounding a staccato rhythm against her ribs. When she passed Damon, she paused. His face was set in a silent plea, his body stiff.

Vincent had *paralysed* him, just as he had his other victims. He was innocent. Relief rushed through Vanessa as panic flashed in Damon's eyes, darting not to her, but to Sharon. The unspoken message was clear: *save Sharon*.

But how? The flames were engulfing the base of the installation. Vanessa's eyes followed the periphery of the flickering light, searching for a solution. That's when she spotted it – a large tarpaulin sheet, discarded and forgotten, lay nearby. She sprinted to it, her heart pounding in her ears.

She quickly dragged it to a large puddle of mud formed from a recent rainstorm, her arms aching with the effort. The moisture in the mud would help to cool the flames and block the fire's access to oxygen, she reasoned. She pushed the sheet into the puddle, coating it in the dark, waterlogged mud, making it heavy and sodden.

With a deep breath, she gathered her strength, and started dragging the mud-coated tarpaulin towards the pyre. As she did, she felt a tight grip on her arm. She turned to see it was Vincent.

'No you don't,' he said, trying to pull her back.

With every ounce of her being focused on saving Sharon, she tugged her arm away with a force that surprised even her, making Vincent stumble back.

'Get. Off. Me,' she growled.

Then she turned and pushed towards the fire, dragging the tarpaulin behind her. As she got closer, the heat intensified, hot air pushing against her. But Sharon's terrified cries spurred her on.

Vanessa heaved the heavy tarpaulin with the last ounce of strength she had left, and threw it onto the fire. It landed with a dull thud, sending up a cloud of steam and smoke. The flames hissed and crackled, flickering wildly for a moment before starting to die down, the fire smothered under the weight of the wet, muddy material.

A blur of movement and light lit up the dark grasslands. Vanessa turned to see several officers approaching, OS leading the way. Vanessa went to run to them, desperate for them to help her get Sharon down. But Vincent was on her again, pulling her close and wrapping his arms tight around her.

She struggled against him.

'Don't, Nessy. This might be our last ever hug.'

'Get off me. I'll *never* forgive you.'

'You'll also never *forget* me, will you?' he whispered in her ear. 'Did you know that praying mantis nymphs—'

'Shut up, Vincent. You don't really know anything about insects. Most of the heinous acts they carry out are for survival. But you? You did it all for the thrill.'

'What I was going to say is,' Vincent quickly continued as he watched the officers dart towards them, 'praying mantis nymphs are known to eat their siblings.' Then he sank his teeth into Vanessa's cheek. Searing pain sliced through her and she let out a scream. OS rushed forward, trying to pull Vincent away. But Vincent's teeth were still in her skin.

'Please,' she begged. 'Please, Vincent.'

He released her and was dragged away, Vanessa's blood dripping from his lips. 'You'll always remember me now,' he shouted to her as officers descended upon him. 'Whenever you look in the mirror, I'll always be there.'

49

Vanessa walked down the sterile corridors of the hospital. Everything felt clean and antiseptic around her, yet she could still smell the acrid ash in her hair from the flames the night before. For a moment, she paused, taking in a deep, shaky breath. It was over now.

Just then, one of Paul's twin girls darted past her in a flurry of giggles and pink tulle, Helen hot on her heels. Vanessa swooped down, catching the fleeing child. Surprise surprise, it was Summer.

'Trying to make an escape, Summer?' she said as she began to tickle her, evoking squeals of delight.

'She's *always* trying to make an escape,' Helen said with an eye-roll as she took the child from Vanessa.

'How's Paul?' Vanessa asked.

'Alive, thanks to you.' Helen squeezed Vanessa's hand as the twin squirmed against her other arm. 'How are you doing? It must have been such a shock to—'

'I'll be fine,' Vanessa quickly interrupted her, not wanting to hear her brother's name.

'Go and see Paul,' Helen said, jutting her chin towards a room in the distance. 'Molly's with him, but she's asleep. I'll take *this* one for some cake.'

Vanessa nodded then headed down the corridor, pushing open the door to Paul's room. He was lying in bed, propped up on an assortment of pillows, Molly curled up asleep in the crook of his arm. He looked *so* frail, a stark contrast to the robust detective she'd come to know. His skin was pallid, and dark circles framed his eyes – eyes that still held that familiar spark, but were shadowed by the weight of what had happened the night before. Vanessa felt her heart clench; even her eyes began to sting. Damn this man for making her so emotional.

He spotted her watching him. 'Ah, Doctor Marwood. You here to throw more tarantulas at me?'

She forced the tears away and smiled as she walked over, taking the chair next to him. 'Only if you need saving again.'

'Bugs to the rescue.'

Her eyes took in the heart monitor beside him. 'You should have told me about your . . . condition,' she whispered.

Paul sighed. 'Yeah, maybe.'

'Is your ticker OK?'

A soft smile from him. 'Still life in it yet.' His eyes flickered over the gauze on her cheek. 'You OK?'

'I will be.'

'I can't believe Vincent—'

'Don't,' Vanessa interjected, her eyes glistening. 'Don't say his name.'

Paul reached out and took her hand, gripping it firmly. 'I won't.'

Vanessa pursed her lips, trying to stop the tears coming as she kept her eyes on Paul's hand around hers. 'He said he did it to get my attention. All these dead people, people I know . . . because of *me*.'

Paul tightened his grip on her hand, as if willing her to absorb his next words fully. 'Listen to me. What he did, he did for himself. It wasn't about you.' She opened her mouth to protest. 'No, I don't want to hear it. Don't you *dare* carry that weight. Don't you fucking dare! You've spent the past twenty-odd years feeling guilty about his disappearance when it was all down to him. You're not going to spend the next twenty years feeling guilty about this. It was all on him, Vanessa. This was *not* because of you.'

The door swung open then, and Sharon hobbled in on crutches, her foot wrapped in bandages. Vanessa had learned in the past few hours that the night before, believing the killers had finally been caught, Sharon had gone to the butterfly farm to spend some quiet time in the place where her son had lived his last moments. The problem was, Vincent was there with Damon, too. He'd been so angry when he'd discovered Damon had been in that hotel room with Vanessa that he'd made a decision: he was going to kill Paul, the person Vanessa was closest to in Greensands, and pin it on Damon. He just needed to get the two men together. So he'd lured Damon to the butterfly farm, telling him Vanessa had been found hurt there. But just as Vincent was injecting Damon with a paralysing agent,

Sharon turned up for her vigil. So he'd drawn her into his plan too. Again, it had felt like fate to him. Now he had *two* villagers Vanessa loved that could be 'killed' by Damon. Obviously, in the process, Damon would die too – made to appear like he'd taken his own life after leaving behind a confession.

That was the idea anyway. But now they were all safe, thank God.

Vanessa rushed over to Sharon and helped her take a seat. 'Are you OK?'

'Just a little burn to the foot, and still feeling woozy from the crap that scumbag injected in me.' Sharon rubbed her hand. 'I'm so sorry. Little Vincent . . . all this time.'

Before Vanessa could respond, a loud, booming voice came from the doorway. 'All right, all right, make room for the cavalry!'

OS sauntered in then, holding two protein shakes. Paul rolled his eyes as OS handed one to him. 'Trust me, Boss, a few of these a day and you'll be right as rain.'

'I don't think so, mate,' Paul said, wrinkling his nose as he put the drink to the side.

OS sighed and turned to Vanessa. 'He always been this disobedient?'

'Always,' Vanessa replied.

'So when's the flight, Bug Lady?'

Vanessa looked at her watch. 'Four hours, which means I *really* have to go soon.'

'Well, New York's gain is our loss,' OS grumbled.

Sharon smiled. 'That's very true. You'll be missed. Goodbye, love. And thank you, you saved my life.' She leaned over and gave Vanessa a big hug.

'Well, this is it then,' Vanessa said as she stood up. 'I just wish we'd all seen each other under better circumstances. Take care, OK? All of you.'

Vanessa caught Paul's eye. He softly shook his head. He'd told her many years ago when she'd left to go to university he couldn't tolerate goodbyes. So she just held his eye a moment, and then left the room.

As Vanessa walked down the corridor, she noticed Damon being wheeled towards her by a young female hospital porter.

'How are you doing?' Vanessa asked as they came to a stop beside her.

'Oh, just a little wobbly on my feet, hence this thing,' Damon said, gesturing to the wheelchair. 'I'll be back to my perfect self by tomorrow, apparently.' He frowned, his handsome face suddenly very serious. He peered up at the porter. 'Give us a few moments, won't you?'

The porter nodded and walked away. 'What about you?' Damon asked when the porter was out of earshot. 'Will *you* be right as rain? I mean, at least your brother is alive. That's . . . something.' He grimaced. 'Though one has to ask, what's better? A dead brother, like mine, or a serial murderer brother, like yours?'

Vanessa flinched.

'What I mean is,' he quickly added, 'at least you have answers, after years of wondering what happened to him.'

Damon was right. She did have answers. *Some* answers, anyway. But other questions remained, especially about her mother, now that she knew she was involved with the illegal insect business. Not to mention Sharon's revelation about her being upset at the Oberlins' party not long before she finally left. All this new information was niggling at Vanessa, burrowing into her mind like mining bees in sand.

'Look at me, rambling on,' Damon said. 'I presume you finally have a flight to catch?'

She nodded. 'I do.'

'Can't say I blame you,' he said, 'getting away as fast as you can. Wish I could.'

'No reason why you can't.'

'And leave my old man to spend his money all by himself? Not a chance.'

'I presume you know about your father's possible involvement in the illegal insect trading ring here? Paul said his computers had been seized.'

Damon sighed. 'Indeed I do. My father is *most* put out. His solicitor has managed to stop a search of the cellar. Easily done when the only thing linking my father to the trade is the word of a horny gay novelist.'

Vanessa chewed at her lip. 'Clive mentioned my mother might be involved too.'

'Yes, I heard.'

'Did you notice anything, back in the day?'

Damon was quiet for a few moments. 'They did all have their little soirees in the cellar.'

'Soirees?'

'Oh you know, after-party parties, they'd all disappear down there. Hence the cult rumours,' he added with an eye-roll. 'I personally think it was just some innocent orgying.'

'That "innocent orgying" include my mum?'

'I don't know, do I? I was a child.'

'Who else was involved? Did my dad know?'

'Saint Tony Marwood? As if!' Damon shrugged. 'I really can't remember, Vanessa. I've asked my father and as always, he's tight-lipped about it. Maybe you should ask your mother?'

Vanessa smoothed her hand over her black hair. 'I don't know. I think I've had my fill of family secrets.'

'You *will* need to talk to her one day, you know. That's the only way to get your answers,' Damon said. 'I mean, who knows, maybe my father *did* run a cult? Wouldn't that be exciting? Either way, wouldn't you love to know?'

'One day, maybe.'

'Look, before you go,' Damon said in a low voice. 'I need you to know: no matter what Vincent may have said, I would *never* have helped him.'

'I believe you, Damon.'

He smiled. 'Good. I also need you to know . . .' He paused, taking in a deep breath as he raked his fingers through his dark hair. 'I need you to know I meant what I said, that I never stopped loving you.'

'Damon, I—'

He put his hand up, stopping her. 'I know. I *know*. It just wasn't ever meant to be, blah blah blah.' His face softened. 'I'm pleased we had one more night though.'

She nodded. 'Me too.'

He opened his arms. 'Aren't you going to come in for a goodbye hug?'

Vanessa smiled and leaned down, letting Damon wrap his arms around her. 'Take care of yourself, Vanessa,' he whispered into her ear. 'New York will be a better place with you in it.'

She breathed in his familiar scent one last time. Then she stepped away, heading for the hospital exit and her final moments in the village she'd once called home.

A Note from the Author

Hello,

It's so great to see you here, at the end of VENOM IN THE BLOOD! First off, a ginormous THANK YOU for joining me as I ventured into the dimly lit alleys of my writer's brain. This story was an exciting but eerie detour even for me, and the fact you chose to take time out to read it really warms my little author heart.

Don't want to leave Dr Vanessa Marwood behind? Sign up for my enewsletter at tracybuchananauthor.com/venombonus to get a FREE insight into the first three months of Vanessa's new life in New York and a fascinating case she works on.

Want to keep the conversation going? I'd love to hear what you thought, what freaked you out, or even what you had for breakfast (we authors are nosy creatures!). You can catch me on social media—just follow the breadcrumbs (or should I say, the maggot trails? Too much? Okay, I'll stop):

- www.facebook.com/TracyBuchananAuthor
- www.facebook.com/groups/thereadingsnug
- www.instagram.com/TracyBuchananAuthor
- www.tiktok.com/@tracybuchananauthor

Until the next Dr Vanessa Marwood installment, keep reading, keep questioning, and remember – the creepy crawlies are more afraid of you than you are of them. Probably.

Acknowledgements

Now to thank all the wonderful people – and creatures – who helped me make this creepy-crawly tale a reality. A massive shoutout to Professor Amoret Whitaker, who took time out of her busy schedule to make sure I didn't botch the forensic entomological bits. Seriously, I owe you a drink – or maybe an insect-themed cake?

Big love to author Imogen Clark, who gave me the kick in the pants I needed to dive into this story when I was teetering on the edge of 'Should I? Shouldn't I?'

Huge props, as ever, to my husband, Rob. Not just for his detective smarts, but for also not running for the hills when things around here got a bit . . . maggoty.

Speaking of which, Scarlett, my darling daughter, your epic 'Ewww, Mum, that's disgusting!' reactions were exactly the vibe check I needed when I was attempting to 'grow' maggots in my office. You're my official gauge for all things gross.

To my tribe at the Savvy Writers' Snug, which I'm honoured to lead, you all rock. Your passion and writerly camaraderie light up my life.

Caroline Hardman, my phenomenal agent—thanks for your endless enthusiasm and the patience of a saint. Embla Books, you've been a dream. Cara, my editor for this novel, your zeal for the manuscript made me feel like I'd hit the jackpot.

As always, my late mother deserves a special place on this list. Mum, you made me a reader, which made me a writer. I miss you every day but I know you'd be first in line to buy this book.

To all my family and friends, you're the ecosystem that keeps my freakish mind whirring.

And last but not least, a nod to the creepy-crawlies of the world.

You fascinate me, terrify me, and make my skin crawl in the best way possible. Keep doing your thing; you're the unsung heroes of this story.

About the Author

Tracy is a bestselling author whose books have been published around the world, including chart-toppers *Wall of Silence*, *My Sister's Secret* and *No Turning Back*. She lives in the UK with her husband, their daughter and a very spoilt Cavalier King Charles Spaniel called Bronte.

About Embla Books

Embla Books is a digital-first publisher of standout commercial adult fiction. Passionate about storytelling, the team at Embla publish books that will make you 'laugh, love, look over your shoulder and lose sleep'. Launched by Bonnier Books UK in 2021, the imprint is named after the first woman from the creation myth in Norse mythology, who was carved by the gods from a tree trunk found on the seashore – an image of the kind of creative work and crafting that writers do, and a symbol of how stories shape our lives.

Find out about some of our other books and stay in touch:

X, Facebook, Instagram: @emblabooks
Newsletter: https://bit.ly/emblanewsletter

Printed in Great Britain
by Amazon

44110129R00172